DEAD IRISH

DEAD IRISH

A NOVEL BY

John T. Lescroart

DONALD I. FINE, INC.

NEW YORK

Copyright © 1989 by John T. Lescroart
All rights reserved, including the right of reproduction in whole or in part in any
form. Published in the United States of America by Donald I. Fine, Inc. and in
Canada by General Publishing Company Limited.

Library of Congress Cataloging-in-Publication Data

Lescroart, John T.
Dead Irish : a novel / John T. Lescroart.
p.   cm.
ISBN 1-55611-159-2
I. Title.
PS3562.E78D43   1989
813'.54—dc20   89-45443
CIP

Manufactured in the United States of America

10 9 8 7 6 5 4 3 2 1

DESIGNED BY IRVING PERKINS ASSOCIATES

I would like to thank Bob and Barbara Sawyer, Elaine Jennings, and Holt Satterfield for help in preparing the manuscript; Drs. Gregory Gorman and Chris Landon; Dalila Corral; Don Matheson for a few bons mots, and Patti O'Brien for two big words.

Most especially, I would like to thank Al Giannini of the San Francisco District Attorney's office, a great friend as well as a resource for technical and procedural matters, without whom this book truly could not have been written.

Any technical errors are the author's.

"I have certainly known more men destroyed by the desire to have a wife and child and keep them in comfort than I have seen destroyed by drink."

—WILLIAM BUTLER YEATS

1 ✿

FROM HIS aisle seat, Dismas Hardy had a clear view of the stewardess as her feet lifted from the floor. She immediately let go of the tray—the one that held Hardy's Coke—although strangely it didn't drop, but hung there in the air, floating, the liquid coming out of the glass like a stain spreading in a blotter.

The man next to him grabbed Hardy's elbow and said, "We're dead."

Hardy, as though from a distance, noted the man's hand on his arm. He found it difficult to take his eyes from the floating stewardess. Then, as suddenly as she'd lifted, the stewardess crashed back to the floor with the tray and the drink.

Two or three people were screaming.

Hardy was the first one to get his seat belt off. In a second, he was kneeling over the stewardess, who appeared to be unhurt, though badly shaken, crying. She held him, muscles spasming in fear or relief, gasping for breaths between sobs.

It was the first time Hardy'd had a woman's arms around him in four and a half years. And that time had been just the once, with Frannie née McGuire now Cochran, after a New Year's Eve party.

The pilot was explaining they'd dropped three thousand feet, something about wind shears and backwashes of 747s. Hardy loosened the woman's hold on him. "You're all right," he said gently. "We're all okay." He looked around the plane, at the ashen faces, the grotesque smiles, the tears. His own reaction, he figured, would come a little later.

In fifteen minutes they were at the gate in San Francisco. Hardy cleared customs, speaking to no one, and went to the Tiki Bar, where he ordered a black and tan—ideally a mixture of Guinness Stout and Bass Ale. This one wasn't ideal.

Halfway through the first one, he felt his legs go, and he grinned at himself in the bar's mirror. Next his hands started shaking and he put them on his lap, waiting for the reaction to pass. Okay, it was safe. He was on the ground and could think about it now.

In a way, he thought, it was too bad the plane hadn't crashed. There would have been some symmetry in that—both of his parents had died in a plane crash when he'd been nineteen, a sophomore at Cal Tech.

A crash would also have been timely. Since Baja hadn't helped him to figure his life out, nor had two weeks on the wagon, maybe there was simply no solution. If the plane had gone down, he wouldn't have had to worry about it anymore.

He'd spent his days under water in the reefs where the Sea of Cortez meets the Pacific. He had held the shell of a sea tortoise and ridden it for perhaps two hundred yards. He'd gone over the side of the *panga* into a school, a city, a landscape of leaping dolphins while his guide tried to tell him they would kill him. Well, if that was the way he was going to go, he couldn't have thought of a better one.

The nights, he'd sit at the Finis Terra high above the water, drinking soda and lime. He'd come down to Baja alone on purpose, although both Pico and Moses had offered to go with him. But with them, he would have been the same Hardy he was in San Francisco—a fast and cynical mouth, an elbow customized for drinking. He hadn't felt like being that Hardy for a while. It hadn't been working very well, he thought, which was why he'd needed the vacation.

The problem was, on vacation nothing else seemed to work too well either. He just felt he'd lost track of who he was. He knew what he did —he was a damn good bartender, a thrower of darts, a medium worker of wood.

He was also divorced, an ex-marine, ex-cop, ex-attorney. He'd even, for a time, been a father. Thirty-eight and some months and he didn't know who he was.

He tipped up the glass. Yeah, he thought, that wouldn't have been so bad, the plane crashing. Not good, not something to shoot for, but really not the worst tragedy in the world.

He figured he'd already had that one.

A shroud of gray enveloped the westernmost twenty blocks of San Francisco and extended from the middle of the Golden Gate Bridge down to Daly City. The fog covered an area of perhaps no more than five square miles, but within it gusting winds of thirty miles per hour were not uncommon and the temperature was twenty degrees lower than in the rest of the city. Nowhere was visibility greater than half a block, and squalls of bone-chilling drizzle drifted like malevolent ghosts across the drear landscape.

In almost the precise center of this fog sat a squat one-story frame house set back nearly sixty feet from the sidewalk. Hardy had thought when he bought it that it looked like the kind of dollhouse a sailor might have made for a daughter he'd never seen while he traveled to warm and exotic ports. It was a house that seemed to remember summers fondly, with a small, white latticed porch up three brick steps, broad white planks surrounding a jutting bay window.

Dwarfed on the left and right by medium-rise apartment buildings, the house seemed especially quaint and vulnerable. Next to the porch, in front of the windows, a scrub juniper hugged the ground as though for warmth. The rest of the area just in front of the house, cleared for a garden that might have once been there, was barren. The lawn itself was green and slightly overgrown.

Hardy sat in his office in the back. The shades were pulled and a coal fire burned in the grate. It was a Monday in the first week of June.

Hardy picked up a dart and flung it at the board on the wall opposite him. He reached for his pipe, stopped himself, sat back. The wind slapped at the window, shaking it.

Hardy pushed himself back from his desk and went to retrieve his round of darts, stopping to poke at the blue-burning coal. He wore a dirty pair of corduroys, a blue pullover sweater and heavy gray socks. He rearranged some of the ships in bottles on his mantel and brushed the dust from one of his fossils.

It crossed his mind that the average temperature of the entire universe, including all suns, stars, planets, moons, comets, black holes, quasars, asteroids and living things, was less than one degree above absolute zero. He believed it. It had been three weeks since he'd returned from Cabo.

He heard the cover drop at his mail slot, the late Monday delivery. As usual, his mail was a joke. He would have almost welcomed a bill just to have something addressed to him personally. As it was, he got an invitation to join a travel club, a special offer on cleaning his rugs (only

$6.95 per room, with a three-room minimum—maybe not a bad deal if he had owned any rugs), a tube of some new toothpaste, a free advertising newspaper, two letters to the previous owner of his house, who had moved nearly six years before, and a "Have You Seen This Child?" postcard.

He opened a can of hash and spooned it into a heavy cast-iron skillet. When it had stuck well to the bottom of the pan, he pried under it and turned it nearly whole. Poking three holes into the mass, he dropped an egg in each, covered it, and went to the tank in his bedroom to feed the tropical fish.

He went back to the kitchen and opened a newspaper to the sports section. The Giants were at home. That ought to keep the ghosts at bay.

He ate the hash and eggs out of the skillet slowly, thinking. When the skillet was empty, he placed it back on the stove, covering the bottom with salt. He turned the gas under it up high. When the pan was smoking, he took the wire brush that hung from the back of the stove and ran it around under the salt, dumping what he'd worked loose into the garbage. In twenty seconds, the pan was spotless. He ran a paper towel over it, then left it on the stove.

He'd had that pan longer than almost anything else he owned. It was the only household article he'd taken when his marriage to Jane had ended. If he treated it right—no water, no soap—it would last a lifetime. It was one of the few things he was absolutely sure of, and he didn't mess with it.

In his bedroom, he put on a three-quarter-length green pea coat, boots, and a misshapen blue Greek sailor's cap. Grabbing a pipe from the rack on his desk, he risked a glance outside, but someone might just as well have erected a slate wall there.

With the pipe clamped between his teeth, he walked through the echoing house as though fighting a gale. As he flicked the light switch in the hallway, there was a pop and a flash, then a reversion to darkness.

While he'd been in Cabo the wood in the front door had swollen. Normally, Hardy took care of carpentry that needed to be done, but he hadn't gotten around to replaning the door.

He had to yank on it twice to get it open. Standing for a moment in the hallway, contemplating nature's perversity, he drew on the cold pipe. Then he stepped into the swirling mist.

On the way to Candlestick Park he considered stopping by the Steinhart Aquarium to see if Pico would like to accompany him. But he decided against it. Pico would talk about his great passion—getting a live great white shark into the aquarium. Long ago, Hardy had helped "walk" the traumatized sharks that fishing boats brought in, hoping to coax them into swimming on their own. None of them had ever made it, and Hardy didn't do it anymore.

He didn't do anything like that anymore. You could put your hope in anything you wanted, he figured, but to put it in hope itself was just pure foolishness.

And as Hardy often said, "I might be dumb, but I'm no fool."

THE MEXICAN guy in the upper-deck front row two sections from where Hardy sat was trouble. He probably weighed two hundred fifty pounds. Sitting with his shirt off, a red bandanna around his head, and a big meaty arm around a stout Latino woman, he was intimidation incarnate.

By Hardy's best count, since the vendor had stopped coming around in the bottom of the fourth inning, the guy had put away a dozen large beers. He brandished a near-empty pint brandy bottle in his free hand. The entire upper deck smelled like marijuana.

Hardy had gotten his ticket from Jimmy Deecks, a cop who was working the second deck casual, moonlighting. Mostly it was an easy gig, consisting of exchanging tickets with the scalpers—you took their game tickets and gave them citations. Once in a while you'd take a drunk to the holding tank. Occasionally, like tonight with Hardy show-ing up, you'd give an old buddy one of the scalped tickets. You'd see a lot of good baseball.

But sometimes, Hardy knew, you had to work. A guy would try to prove he was the world's greatest asshole; Hardy had a feeling about tonight and this guy. Jimmy was going to earn his bread.

Although the sun was barely down and the sky was still blue, the lights were on. The asshole was standing up, waving his arms, trying to get the attention of a beer vendor, screaming *"Cerveza"* as though someone were torturing him by putting him through beer withdrawal cold turkey. Like a foghorn. Players on the field looked up to see who was making the racket.

Hardy looked around, wondering when Deecks and his partner were going to come bust the guy. Suddenly the asshole took a swing at the fan sitting behind him. The fan swung back, missed, and took one aside the head that sent him sprawling. That got some other guys up. A couple of women screamed.

The crowd up there roared, of course. What a good time! A bonus during the ballgame! Hardy left his seat. Jimmy Deecks or not, this bullshit had to stop.

But then he saw Jimmy running down the steps loosening his nightstick, no partner in sight.

The Mexican woman was pulling at her man's arm, trying to get him to stop, but three or four other guys were joining in now, with the asshole just screaming and swinging at random. Jimmy blew on his whistle to no effect. Hardy tried to keep moving through the seats, but more and more people were closing in to see the fun.

"All right, enough, hold it, break it up." He heard Jimmy's words, the same ones always used, the ones that never worked. Things started to quiet when Jimmy laid a couple of taps on shoulders with the nightstick.

Hardy, trying now to step over some seats, saw that only the asshole was still standing. His woman was pulling on his arm, glaring at Jimmy Deecks.

"Come on, now. Let's go downstairs."

The sweet voice of reason. Hardy loved it. He caught Jimmy's eye briefly, then saw him fix on the woman, seeking an ally. "Get him downstairs and take him home, huh? How 'bout that?"

The asshole just kept glaring. The woman pulled at his arm again and he looked down, as though just being reminded she was there, and casually cuffed her face, backhand.

"Shut up!" Then something else in Spanish.

Hardy couldn't get through the crowd that had formed. Jimmy rolled his eyes toward him, as if for support, then unsnapped his holster. Though drawing down on fans wasn't a recommended procedure at the ballpark, it seemed to work for an instant; the asshole appeared to forget what was going on. He looked up behind Jimmy Deecks and started yelling for beer again.

It was all the distraction Jimmy needed. He stepped toward the guy and slapped him hard alongside the head just over the ear, and the guy went down sideways right now.

There was a hearty round of applause from the stands. The woman, her own nose bleeding, leaned over the asshole, seeing if he was all right.

Jimmy turned again to Hardy, a plea for help in his eyes.

Somebody yelled a warning and he turned as the asshole was about to slam into him. Drunk, stoned, and probably half concussed, the guy was formidable. Jimmy sidestepped the main force of the tackle but still fell backward across some seats. The asshole was up again, as fast as he was, and he charged back down the steps.

Hardy saw Jimmy duck away and swing hard with his nightstick as the guy passed, hitting him high on the back of his neck, probably aiming for and certainly hitting the lower edge of the bandanna. The guy's momentum carried him down to the railing, which he slammed into, leaned over, weaving, went over some more, and finally, almost in slow motion, disappeared off the second deck.

Abe Glitsky was figuring out his chances.

He was one of 1,780 policemen in San Francisco. The voters in their wisdom had just rejected a mayor's referendum calling for a city/county-wide increase of two hundred cops. The rejection, completely unexpected though maybe it shouldn't have been in the City That Once Knew How, had come after the department had already hired many of the new officers, which meant they would now be laid off.

Worse, from Abe's point of view, was that all the promotions that had been based on the hirings would be rescinded. As usual in the bureaucracy, they were using "last hired first fired," so the officers with least seniority would get knocked back, robbery inspectors would go back to desk sergeants, desk sergeants to the beat, homicide guys to vice or robbery. And all because the citizens of this clown town thought too many cops would make the city a police state.

Glitsky's desk was in a cubicle of baffled masonite. He had a window with a view of the Oakland-Bay Bridge and his own coffee machine—seventy square feet of the high life, the perks of his seniority.

He sipped some cold herb tea and thought maybe he should move to L.A. Pick up the wife and kids and go someplace where they believed in law enforcement. He'd heard that down there they were increasing the size of the force by a thousand. A thousand! He ran that number around in his brain. And no one in their right mind would say L.A. was overrun with cops. Everyone already knew that half the town was controlled by gangs; a thousand new cops probably wouldn't even make a dent. And here in San Francisco, a mere fifth of that made people think about Mussolini.

Abe didn't get it.

He really ought to go home, he thought. Get away from it. The atmosphere in homicide, outside this cubicle, was not good. Three new guys, all just promoted, knew they were going back down. And this was happening in every department, which made the entire Hall a pure joy to work in.

To make matters more complicated, Glitsky's lieutenant, Joe Frazelli, was retiring. (Of course, this assured that only two of the three new guys slated for demotion would actually go back to their old jobs. One would stay in homicide. Wonderful for cooperation among the rookies.)

Abe, along with Frank Batiste and Carl Griffin, was up for Frazelli's job, which was nine-tenths administrative and which took you off the street, which was not what any of the guys wanted. But there were other considerations, like power and, not unimportantly, money. Also, it was another rung up the ladder to Captain, maybe Chief, and like most cops Glitsky entertained thoughts of moving up.

But it wasn't easy being half black and half Jewish. Some days, when his paranoia ran high, he was amazed he'd come as far as he had, which was homicide inspector. Other times he'd think the sky was the limit— he was a good cop, he knew his way around, he could lead others.

But if he was honest, he had to admit there were some problems. First, he knew he could direct investigations, but he had a problem working with the other guys. Out of the fourteen homicide cops, only two worked solo, and he was one of them. He told himself that it was just the way it had happened, but in his heart he knew that he'd worked it around this way.

He'd come up four years before when an armed-robbery suspect—J. Robert Ronka, he'd never forget—had dovetailed into a wife killer. Frazelli had admired his handling of that case and put him on another hot one as soon as he'd come on board in homicide. There had been no free partners at the time, so Frazelli had asked him if he minded going solo again until somebody's vacation ended or somebody else quit or got promoted, leaving another solo spot to be teamed. Then he'd put Glitsky together with that guy.

Except Abe had never pushed it, and it hadn't happened. And now he sometimes thought that not being particularly close to anybody might hurt his career.

But that wasn't as serious as the other problem—the race thing. The San Francisco Police Department has two unions—one for white officers and one for nonwhite officers. And Abe would be good and goddamned if he was going to use any affirmative-action bullshit to get himself moved up. When he finally did make Captain or Chief he didn't want even the tiniest smell of that in his background, and so far he thought he'd avoided it.

The trouble was, some black cops resented him for rejecting the hard-fought-for rights that they'd earned. And a lot of white guys wouldn't believe that he didn't get special consideration because he was black, regardless of what he said or did about it. Hell, he was solo, wasn't he?

(The fact that the other solo guy, McFadden, was white wasn't a comparable situation because everybody knew McFadden was just a mean sorry son of a bitch who hated everybody and their dog Spot. He wouldn't work with his own mother, and his mother wouldn't want to work with him.)

A telephone rang somewhere out in the main room. Glitsky could see three of the maybe five guys who were at their desks doing paperwork. The secretaries had all disappeared. It was close to nine o'clock on a Monday night.

Frazelli had gone home. Abe and Griffin had rank in the shop. Wearily, Abe stood, stretched, and walked to the entrance to his cubicle. Griffin, three cubicles down, poked his head out the same way. They nodded at one another warily.

As Abe feared, it was the desk phone. One of the new guys went and picked it up, listened for a minute, then covered the mouthpiece.

"Anybody want to see a dead guy?" he asked.

Abe wanted to go home. He was working on four current homicides and one he'd been hounding for sixteen months. On the other hand, his plate had been fuller, and he was gunning for looie. He stepped out of his cubicle. "Want to flip for it?" he asked Griffin.

"Where is it?" Griffin asked the new guy.

"Candlestick."

"Naw. Baseball's boring," Griffin said.

"Okay, I'll take it," Abe said, not liking it. Griffin should have gone for it too. And there seemed to be a personal edge to what he'd said. Something was going on.

Abe didn't like it.

The Giants beat the Phillies, 4 to 3.

After the last out Hardy stayed in his seat, drinking beer and waiting for what crowd there was to thin out. They stopped selling beer after the eighth inning and he'd gone back and bought three to hold him over to the end of the game. He still had one, open but untouched, in the deep pocket of his coat.

They left the field lights on. Hardy squinted below to the place the man had fallen. They'd stopped the game back in the seventh right in the middle of what turned out to be the Giants' game-winning rally, when they had two men on, nobody out and Will Clark coming up.

Most of the spectators had gone. He figured by now it was just the cops, so he got up and meandered through the seats, sipping beer.

The area was cordoned off with yellow tape. Deecks was sitting slumped, his legs hanging over the seat in the row in front of him. The Cougar—Rafe Cougat, Deeck's partner—was talking to one of the techs. They were getting ready to move the body.

Hardy felt a hand on his shoulder and turned around. "Abraham, my man," he said. Then, the thought occurring to him, "This a murder?"

Abe Glitsky grinned, and the scar running through his lips lightened. Fifteen years before, he and Hardy had walked a beat together. They still wrote Christmas cards.

"You see it happen?" Abe asked.

"No. I was watching the game."

"Still fascinated by crime, huh?"

Against Hardy's will, the sarcasm rankled slightly. "I read the sports page, sometimes the food section. I get my current events across the bar."

Glitsky jerked his head. "These low railings," he said. "I mean, you see kids leaning over 'em all the time going for fouls. They ought to put up nets or something."

Three men lifted the body bag and were carrying it over the seats. Another group waited on the cement stairs. The gurney waited at the top of the ramp. "I'm kind of surprised you bothered to come over and check this out."

Hardy lifted his shoulders an inch. "Parades," he said, "can't get enough of 'em." A section of seats separated them from the rest of the group. Hardy asked why Abe was here himself if it wasn't a murder.

Glitsky pursed his lips, thinking for a minute. "Long story," he said finally. "Politics."

"You? I thought you didn't do that."

Glitsky made a face. "I used to think you got political to move ahead. Now you need it to stay even."

Hardy sipped at his next to last cup of beer. "Gets to that point, it's too much stress."

"That's how people live, Diz," Glitsky answered. "It's how you stay alive."

Hardy took a long, deliberate drink. "Is it?"

Glitsky's nose flared. They had come up to the concession area, still away from the others, the gurney. "Yeah, it is. I got a wife and three kids. What am I supposed to do?"

The vehemence took Hardy back a step. "You feel that locked in, Abe?"

"I don't know how I feel. I'm trying to do my job right and not lose what I got."

"Well, there's your problem," Hardy said, trying to make it lighter, "you've got stuff you care about."

The gurney went by. Deecks and the Cougar followed it, talking quietly. One of the techs came up and started saying something to Glitsky. He listened, nodded once, started walking. "But to answer your question," he said, "no, this wasn't a murder. The gentle victim got a little overenthusiastic near the railing. Deecks'll write it up. End of story."

"So why'd you come out?"

Glitsky sucked his teeth. "Because, like you Diz, I am enamored of all aspects of police work." He flicked a finger at Hardy's cup. "You spare a hit of that?"

Hardy took the backup beer out of his pocket. "Boy Scout training. Be prepared."

They walked out of the park and started down Cardiac Hill, both of them sipping beer. "The politics really that bad?" Hardy asked.

"I don't know. Maybe I'm just on the rag tonight. Tired. This call came in, I was thinking about going home."

"So go home now."

"Yeah."

They got to Glitsky's green Plymouth. Hardy tipped his cup back. "You notice beer never gets warm here? It's one of the great things about this ballpark."

Glitsky squinted through the fog out toward the Bay. "Nothing gets warm here." He stood without moving, maybe waiting for some signal. "I'm gonna check in," he said suddenly.

Hardy eased himself up onto the car's hood, waiting, wondering. What was Abe checking in again for after he should have been home with his wife and kids five hours ago? Hardy didn't believe anybody had to be that much of a red hot.

But when Glitsky came out of the car, he was smiling his tight, scar-stretching smile. "Serves the fucker right," he said.

"Who?"

"The guy who scammed this"—he motioned back to the stadium—"off on me. Two minutes after I left he got himself a righteous homicide. Ought to keep him up all night." The smile tightened further. "You know, Diz, I think I better see how he's doing."

"That smacks of cruelty, Abe."

"You know, I believe it does."

They sat in the front seat and waited while Glitsky got patched through. "Carl? Abe. What you got?"

"What do you want to know for?"

"I got done here. Thought you might want some help."

Hardy heard the voice change. "I don't need no help, Abe."

"I said want, Carl. Not need."

There was a pause. "Okay. Sorry. No, we got it under control."

"What is it?"

"White male, mid-twenties, tentative ID Cochran, Edward. Shot once in the head—"

"Find out where it is," Hardy said.

"What? Hold on," Abe said to the radio.

"Find out where it is," Hardy repeated. "I know an Ed Cochran. It better not be him."

The rookie, Giometti, was coming back from the fence that fronted the canal.

"You all right?" Griffin asked.

The kid tried to look brave, even smile, but it didn't work. What he looked, even in the phony bright lights that had been set up for the techs and photographers, was ashen. His lower lip hung loosely off his mouth, as though he'd been hit and it had swollen. His eyes still had that watery look some people get after they throw up.

"Sorry," he said.

Griffin turned back to look at the body. "Happens to everybody. You get used to it."

No, he thought, that wasn't true. You don't ever get used to it. What you do is get so you don't react the same way. Your stomach still wants to come up at you, you still get that dizzy, light-headed yawing feel that you're going to go out, but if you want to stay working as a homicide cop, what you do is move that feeling into another plane.

You observe small things better, maybe, which keeps you from seeing the big picture that will make you sick. Or you deny altogether and make light of the gore—something the TV cops do so well. Or you just look at it, say yeah, and concentrate on your job, then go drink it off later. Griffin knew all that. Still, he put his hand on his new partner's shoulder and repeated, "You get used to it."

The body lay on its side, covered now with the tarp. Giometti kneeled down next to it.

"You don't want to look again, though," Griffin said.

"I better, I think."

"He ain't changed. Come on, get up. Check the Polaroids you want to get used to it."

Giometti took a breath, thinking about it, then straightened up without lifting the tarp. "Why'd he want to do that?"

"What?" Griffin asked.

"Kill himself like that, out here. Nowhere."

They were in a good-sized parking lot between two office buildings in China Basin. In the middle of the lot a car registered to Edward Cochran, the presumed deceased, sat waiting for the tow truck to take it down to the city lot. Griffin and Giometti had looked it over, finding nothing unusual in or about it except for its distance from the body.

"Why do you think he killed himself?" Griffin wasn't senior here for nothing. The boy needed some lessons.

Giometti shrugged. "It's pretty obvious, don't you think? The note . . . ?"

"The note?" Griffin snorted. He didn't know what it was, but calling it a suicide note was really stretching. A torn piece of paper in the front seat of the car, saying "I'm sorry, I've got to . . ." That was it. But he wasn't in the mood to chew out his partner, the kid, so he spoke calmly, quietly. "Nothing's obvious, Vince. That's our job, okay? Take what looks obvious and find out the truth behind it. The best murders in the world look like something else. If they didn't, nobody'd need us."

Giometti sighed. He looked at his watch. "Carl, it's eleven-thirty. The guy's got a gun by his hand. There was a note. I think there's a few things we can assume here."

"Yeah, we can assume you want to go curl up with your wife and go goo at your new kid." A pair of headlights turned into the lot, then another one. Photographers probably. If that was the case, it was time to go, but he wanted to make his point first.

"Get the gun, Vince, would you?"

Giometti walked the few steps over to their car. Other car doors were opening and closing. Griffin looked over but couldn't see anything outside the perimeter of light.

He opened the Zip-lock bag and stuck a pencil into the gun's barrel, lifting it to his nose. "Okay. It's been fired," he said.

"We knew that."

"We didn't know it. We found it next to the stiff and we assumed it. And we won't know for sure 'til the lab gets it. But," Griffin sniffed it again, "it smells like it's been fired."

Giometti rolled his eyes. "Are we detecting now?" he asked, looking over at the sound of footsteps. "Hey, Abe."

Glitsky nodded to the boy. "That the weapon?" he asked Griffin.

"No, it's a fucking garter snake. What are you doing here?"

"I got a potential ID."

"Yeah, us too."

Glitsky turned. "Diz?" he said.

Another man stepped out of the shadows. He and Glitsky walked over to the tarp. They both went down to a knee and Abe pulled up a corner of it. The guy put his hand to his eyes. Something seemed to go out of his shoulders.

Glitsky said something, got a nod, patted the man's back as he stood up. He walked heavily back to Griffin and Giometti. "We got a positive," he said. "Mind if I look at the gun a minute?"

Griffin handed it over by the pencil.

"It's been fired," Giometti said.

Glitsky, missing the joke, glanced at him blankly, then sighted down the barrel, backward, into the chambers. "Yeah, twice," he said.

Hardy and Glitsky sat in the Plymouth in the parking lot. The heater made a lot of noise, but didn't do much for the temperature or the fog on the windows. The only thing left to be done in the lot was towing Ed Cochran's car, and the tow guy was here now seeing to it.

Glitsky rolled his window down and watched without much enthusiasm. It was better than looking at his friend. These guys had worked together, partied some, got along, but most of it was on the flip side. When part of the work got to somebody, it made Glitsky nervous.

He glanced across at his ex-partner. Hardy was leaning against his door, arm up along the window jamb, bent at the elbow, his hand rubbing at his temples. His eyes were closed.

The tow guy came over and asked Glitsky if there would be anything else.

They sat in the car, hearing the sound of the tow truck dissipate into the still night. Then there was only the heater, which wasn't doing any good anyway. Glitsky turned the engine off.

Hardy let out a long breath, opening his eyes. "Just can't hide, can you?" he asked. "It comes back and gets you."

Sometimes Hardy would say things like that. If you stuck with him, Glitsky knew, he'd get around to saying it in English. But this time Hardy said fuck it, it was nothing.

Glitsky rolled up his window.

"You want a lift home?"

Hardy motioned with his head. "I got my car, Abe."

"Yeah, I know. Maybe you want company."

Hardy stared into the fogged-up windshield. "After Michael . . ." He stopped. He rubbed a hand over an eye. Glitsky looked away again, giving him the space. Michael had been Hardy's son who'd died in his infancy. "Anyway, I told myself I wouldn't feel this shit anymore." He shook his head as though clearing it. "Who'd want to kill Eddie?" he asked.

Glitsky just nodded. That was always the question. And it was easier talking about cases than trying to find some reason for the deaths of people you cared about. So Glitsky followed that line. "You see him recently, this guy Eddie? He say anything?"

"Anything like what? I saw him a couple of weeks ago, up at his place. He said a lot of things."

"I mean, anything to indicate troubles? Somebody pissed off at him? Maybe depressed himself?"

Hardy looked away from the dashboard. "What are you talking about, depressed?"

Glitsky shrugged into his coat. "Guy's dead alone in a parking lot with a bullet in his head and a gun in his hand. Possible he did himself."

Hardy took it in, said, "No, it isn't."

"Okay, just a thought. It'll occur to Griffin."

"What? Is he two weeks on the force?" He rolled the window down and looked across the lot. "Nobody comes out a place like this to kill themselves. People take people here and kill them. Or meet here and kill them."

There was no moon. The fog hung still. A streetlight behind them caught the lot in its muted, garish, yellowing pool. Hardy was right, Glitsky thought. This was an execution spot.

"Besides," Hardy continued, "Eddie wouldn't kill himself. He wasn't, as they say, the type."

He rolled the window back up.

"All right," Glitsky said, "you knew him."

"Put it out of your mind, Abe. It flat didn't happen."

"I'm not arguing."

But Hardy was staring into the middle distance again, unhearing. He abruptly jerked open the car door. "I better get going." He turned to Abe. "I'll probably be in touch."

Hardy came up to the doors where he worked and pushed his way through. Moses, who hadn't been home, was at the bar. Six closers—four at the rail and two at one table—were passing the time until last call. Willie Nelson was singing "Stardust" on the jukebox. No one was throwing darts. Hardy stood a minute, taking it in. Home, as much as anything could be.

"Hey, Diz." Moses automatically started a Guinness for him.

"What are you doing here?"

"Sent Lynne home early. Felt like tending some bar."

Hardy pulled up a stool in front of the spigots. Reaching over, he stopped the flow of the stout. The glass had gotten about two-thirds full.

"What am I supposed to do with that now?" Moses asked, his weathered face creased with laugh lines that Hardy knew wouldn't get much use in the next weeks. "You losing weight again? You stop drinking Guinness, my business goes to hell."

Hardy couldn't think of a damn thing to say. He cleared his throat, took off his hat and put it on the bar. "You hear anything from Frannie tonight?"

Moses started to answer. "You know, it's funny, she called here maybe—" Stopping short. "What happened?"

Hardy held up a hand. "She's okay."

Moses let out a breath. Frannie was about ninety percent of everything he cared about. "What, then?"

Hardy met his eyes. Okay, just say it, he told himself. But Moses asked. "Eddie okay? She called to see if he was here."

"We gotta go up there, Mose. Eddie's dead."

Moses didn't move. He squinted for a beat. "What do you mean?" he asked. "Dead?"

Hardy turned on his stool. He slapped the bar. "Okay, guys, let's suck 'em up," he said. "We're closing early." He got up, went behind the bar and sat Moses down on the stool back there. He was hearing the beginnings of the usual drunks' stupid moanings about how they needed last call and it wasn't fair. He lifted the shillelagh, an end-knotted, two-foot length of dense Kentucky ash, from its hook under the counter and ducked back out front of the bar.

He tapped the bar a couple of times, hard. Making sure he had their attention. "Don't even suck 'em, then. We're closed and you're all outside. Now."

Everybody moved. Hardy had wielded the stick before, and most of them had seen it. He glanced at Moses. "Let's go, buddy," he said quietly. "Let's go tell Frannie."

*A*LL TWELVE trucks were parked in their spots behind the squat building that was the office of Army Distributing.

At a backboard against the building, a tall black man named Alphonse Page shot hoops. He was a rangy semi-youth, with a hair net wrapped around his head, his shirt off revealing a hairless and flat chest, and high-topped generic tennis shoes. His fatigue pants were doubled up at the cuffs, showing six or seven inches of shiny thoroughbred leg between his white socks and his knees.

The backboard was set flush against the building, making lay-ups all but impossible, although if you swished the basket just right you could get a reasonable bounce back into the key and follow up with maybe an inside hook.

A fading orange Datsun 510 pulled into the lot, around the trucks, then behind the building back by the wrapping shed. Alphonse stopped shooting and began dribbling, all his weight on his right foot, bouncing the ball slowly, about once a second, and waited for Linda Polk to appear from around the building, which she did in under a minute.

He fell in next to her, dribbling, as she crossed the court.

"Nobody much around," he said.

"Daddy's not in?" A note of desperation, of hope long since abandoned.

"Shi . . ."

"But where's Eddie?"

"No show. He ain't here by six, everybody went home."

She seemed to take in the information like someone who was almost certain they had a terminal disease finding out for sure. She stopped walking. The sun, atypically strong this early morning, was behind them, glaring off the building. "You mean nobody's here? Nobody at all?"

Alphonse, the basketball held easily against his hip with one hand, pointed his other hand in toward himself. "Hey, what am I?" he said.

"No offense."

Alphonse offered her his white teeth. Except for some acne, his long, smooth face was not unattractive. His skin was very black, his nose was thin. His lips were sensually thick. There was a light sheen of sweat from the workout, and his longish hair, which Linda thought his worst feature, was held in by the net.

"No offense," Alphonse repeated.

Linda sighed. "So what happened to the papers?"

Alphonse began dribbling again, walking next to her. The papers weren't his problem. "Ain't too many anyway."

They rounded the building. In front of the warehouse, Linda could see the morning newspapers, still wrapped from their publishers. Without *La Hora*, they made a pitifully poor pile in front of the corrugated iron door.

Linda drew up again and sighed. "So I guess that's really it," she said. She threw her head back, looking to the sky for help, and finding none, she moaned, "I wish Daddy'd come in."

"Yeah, that's what I'm waiting for."

"And Eddie didn't come in at all? Did he call?"

Alphonse smiled again. "I don't do the phones, sugar."

They had come to the glass front doors. Linda got out her keys and let them in. Alphonse followed her across the small entryway into her office, which was in front of her father's. She went behind the desk and sat down.

Alphonse dribbled on the linoleum floor. The sound of the ball bouncing, flat and harsh, was interrupted by the telephone ringing.

"Maybe that's Daddy." Linda said.

She answered with a hopeful "Army Distributing" and then said "Yes" a couple of times. When she hung up, the terminal illness had progressed.

"That was the police," she said, and Alphonse felt an emptiness suddenly appear in his stomach. "They want to come by here and ask some questions."

Alphonse plumped heavily, quickly, onto the arm of the leatherette sofa. "What about?"

"They said Eddie . . ." She stopped.

"What about Eddie?"

"They said he's, like, dead." She fumbled at the desk for a couple of seconds, then reached into her purse for a cigarette. "I'd better call Daddy," she said, mostly to herself.

The cigarette was misshapen and half burned down. Alphonse nodded knowingly to himself as she lit the end and inhaled deeply, holding it in. He got up, crossed to the desk, and held out his hand.

"Cops be comin', they better not smell that."

Linda still held her breath in, handing him the joint. She let out a long slow stream of smoke. "So we'll open the windows."

"You callin' your daddy?"

"I'd better," she said.

"Yeah, you better," Alphonse said. "I gotta talk to him, too."

The police had already arrived at Frannie's—one black-and-white and another supposedly unmarked Plymouth parked closely behind it. The light over the doorway was on. Hardy and Moses could see shadows moving in the corner window. Hardy had decided he wouldn't go in. He left Moses and drove on home.

He let himself into his house, pushing hard, swearing, against the stuck front door. The house had been cold. The only light came from the muted glow of the aquarium in his bedroom.

He must have stared at the fish awhile, sitting on his bed, his Greek sailor's hat pulled down and his coat collar up. He didn't remember.

All he knew was that now it was morning. Bright sunlight streaming through his bedroom window was falling across his face. The coat was bunched under and around him, the hat flattened under his neck.

Hardy rolled onto his back, staring at the ceiling. It came back to him in a flood—the vision of Eddie on his side three feet from some nondescript China Basin building, a black pool under him.

This wasn't supposed to happen. This wasn't Vietnam anymore. Eddie wasn't into anything heavy. He was a regular guy, a kid, and this kind of stuff didn't happen to regular guys.

Before, sure. Hardy had lived for a while in that life-and-death reality, where things happened all the time. Vietnam, partnering with Glit-

sky on their beat, even his short time with the D.A.'s office. But he'd
passed on all that. A long time ago.

Now his life didn't need any adrenaline kick start. You cared too
much and it came back and got you. Now you had your job—not your
yuppie "career" that ate up your time and your insides—but someplace
you went and did reasonable work and got paid and came home and
forgot about. You had a couple of buddies—Moses and Pico did just
fine. You drank a little and sometimes a little more, but it was mostly
top-shelf goods or stout and you kept it under control.

Everything else—ambition, love, commitment (whatever that
meant)—was kid stuff. Kids like Eddie, maybe, who essentially didn't
get it the way Hardy thought he now finally got it. Hardy had been
through it. The kid stuff elements weren't real. They were crutches,
blinders, to keep you from seeing. Hardy'd proved that by getting away
from all of them and surviving. He got along. Okay, maybe he skimmed
over the surface, but at least he avoided deep shoals, hidden reefs,
monsters lurking in the depths.

Sure, Diz, he thought, that's why you went to Cabo, 'cause everything was so peachy, 'cause fulfillment was the very essence of your
existence.

"Goddamn it." Hardy laid his arm up over his eyes, shielding the
sun. "Goddamn it, Eddie."

The problem was, why was he feeling now like he had to do something, anything at all, to make some sense out of this? He shouldn't
have let Eddie, or Eddie and Frannie, get inside of him. He hadn't seen
it coming, so hadn't been prepared for it. He'd thought he'd kept them
outside enough—acquaintances, not friends.

Eddie was gone, and nothing was going to change that.

Still, something nudged him, hurting, almost like a cramp, or a screw
turning in his heart.

He moaned and sat up in bed.

The beginning—

Four and a half years before. New Year's Eve. Frannie McGuire, still
a few months shy of the legal twenty-one but damned if Hardy was
going to card her.

With madness raging all around and only swelling as the night wore

on, Frannie nursed a few rum and Cokes at the bar. Hardy, in what he
called his fun mode, pounded down everything in sight—beer, scotch,
tequila, gin. Yahoo!

And nobody to drive that party animal Hardy home except the quiet
little redheaded very much younger sister of his boss Moses.

Sitting in front of his house, then, the party over—really over—and
enough juice in him to forget that all of his own kid stuff was in his
past, that he didn't care about any of that. Not coming on to her, but
spilling his guts—the whole thing—and finally passing out, he guessed,
without so much as kissing her or even trying, waking up a cold dawn,
his arms around her waist, his head cradled in her lap on the front seat
of his old Ford.

And before he dropped her off back at her dorm, she said, "I hope I
meet someone like you, Dismas, before life eats him up. I'd marry him
in a minute."

She did.

His name was Eddie Cochran, and after about three dates she appeared with him at the Shamrock. Took Hardy aside and whispered,
"Remember what I said," as though she'd only said one thing to him
before in her life.

But he'd known what she meant.

One Sunday afternoon, a barbecue at Moses's apartment, up on the
roof looking over the Haight-Ashbury.

"The what?" Hardy had asked. "Get out of here!"

"Big Brothers." Frannie telling Hardy.

It wouldn't have been like Eddie to mention it. He didn't preach—
he just did. "Hey, it's one day a week, Diz," Eddie had said in defense.
"Gimme a break. Maybe do some good. Couldn't hurt, anyway."

It sure could, Hardy thought. It could hurt you, you fool. Most likely
your "little brother" will wind up taking a chip out of your heart. But
he didn't try to argue with Eddie—there wasn't much arguing with
Eddie on anything.

But Hardy had said, "You think you can make a real difference, don't
you?"

The two-hundred-watt smile that wasn't a put-on. "I doubt it."

Except what got to Hardy was that, underneath it all, Eddie didn't doubt it. He thought everything he did mattered a lot, that he personally really could make a difference. It reminded Hardy of the way he thought he used to be himself. Like Eddie. Long time ago.

Rose stood at the top of the steps by the back door of the rectory. Father Dietrick was crossing the parking lot, head down, returning from bringing Father Cavanaugh the news.

Bless them both, but it was going to be a hard month. June was always a hard month in San Francisco. It felt like God had given His promise in the spring and then taken it back. This morning Rose had thought it would stay bright and sunny, but already the fog was on them again.

She wiped her hands on her apron. Her eyes came up to meet the young priest, questioning. He sighed. "Not too well," he said. "He took off."

Though he wasn't yet thirty, he mounted the stoop like an old man. Rose followed him inside.

"Just took off?"

He sat at the kitchen table, his hands folded in front of him. Rose brought over a cup of coffee, three sugars and a drop of cream.

"You know Father Cavanaugh," he said, sipping the coffee. "There wasn't an easy way to say it. He stood there getting out of his vestments and I thought I'd try to make him sit down, but as soon as I asked him to he knew something had happened. . . ."

"I'm sure you did what's best, Father."

Father Dietrick sighed. "For a minute it was as though I'd hit him. Then he looked down at his hands, at the vestments, and just ripped the surplice off."

Rose made a note to go pick up the surplice. She'd just sew it back up and no one would be the wiser. She pulled up a chair next to Father and ventured a pat on his hand. "You know how he is, Father. He gets upset and it's like the priest in him gives up for a minute. He has to let something go. It doesn't mean anything."

"I know. But maybe I should have gone with him."

Rose knew what Father Dietrick meant. Father Cavanaugh was a bit of a rogue priest. It was, she was sure, why he'd never made monsignor.

Not that he'd ever done anything seriously wrong. Shoplifting that one time. Occasionally a little too much whiskey, but sure that was the good man's weakness.

"He'll probably go scream at the ocean," she said. And Lord, why shouldn't he, losing someone close enough to be his own son? Father had a temper, but he was still a beautiful man, and a fine priest, all the more human for his faults, she thought. Let him scream at the ocean—he had a right. Jesus himself had a temper. Didn't He throw the money changers out of the temple?

But this—Eddie Cochran's death—would not have loosed his temper. It would have broken his heart.

"I know where he's gone," Rose said suddenly. "Over to see Erin." The priest acted like he didn't know who she was talking about. She sighed, exasperated. "Come now, Father, you've got to learn to see things. Erin Cochran, Eddie's mother. He'll need to be with her."

"You think so?"

Rose bit her tongue and said only, "I'd bet so, Father." She didn't say what she also knew, that he'd need to be with her because he loved her.

The water was a long way down, slate gray through the fog. Jim Cavanaugh, shivering, leaned out over the railing of the Golden Gate Bridge. His teeth were clenched to keep them from chattering, whether it was the cold or everything else. He should have grabbed a coat before rushing from the church, but he'd had to get out—get out now before he broke down in front of Dietrick.

So it had happened. Eddie was dead.

And Erin? What would become of Erin now?

He knew he ought to go see her, but would she want to see him? Would she ever forgive him?

Could he be a priest to the Cochran family ever again?

Last week he had tried to kiss her, to tell her . . . It had been a temporary weakness, that was all, but it had made a breach between them.

And now this, with Eddie.

The family would need him. He would have to be there now for them all. The kiss, her rejection and his flash of anger at her, now they could all be forgotten.

She would forgive him. He could live again.

He put his hands in his pockets and began walking back toward the tollbooths.

4 🍀

$\mathscr{H}$ARDY HAD loved his Suzuki Samurai when he'd bought it, but since learning that it tended to roll in strong winds or on weak grades, he had renamed it the Seppuku. Now he parked it at the corner of Tenth and Lincoln. The fleeting sun that had gotten him up had long since disappeared. The fog, the June freeze, insinuated itself into every corner out here, swirling, gusting. Hardy pulled his pea coat up around his neck.

Now he was staring at the sign over his place of employment, "The Little Shamrock, established in 1893." He found himself marveling at man's originality. The sign, cleverly, was shaped like a shamrock.

The sign itself had been established in its spot over the swinging double doors in 1953, and the green paint had chipped enough over the years that the sign at night now read "le rock." Maybe it was a good thing, Hardy reflected, the shape of the sign. If it had been shaped like Gibraltar, people would think the bar was named the rock, or some French word that meant rock. Le rock. Maybe they should paint the *l* to look like a capital letter. Maybe they should have the neon repaired altogether.

But no, he thought, it fit the Shamrock. The bar wasn't exactly run-down, but it didn't place too much emphasis on fixing itself up. It was a neighborhood bar, and Moses McGuire, Hardy's friend and boss, the owner of the place, didn't believe in attracting an unwanted element (tourists) with too many ferns, video games or flashy signs. The Shamrock was an Irish dart bar, as nonpolitical as any of them got. It poured an honest (sometimes more than honest) shot and did a respectable business with locals, both male and female. Hardy had worked days there, Tuesday through Saturday, two to eight, for over seven years.

Every night Hardy worked, Moses McGuire followed him from six

27

until closing at two, and then until he'd rung out and cleaned up, sometimes having an after-hours drink. Sundays and Mondays a thirty-ish raven-haired beauty named Lynne Leish with an eighteen-inch waist and more than twice that on either side worked double shifts and brought in a crowd of her own. But she was a good bartender, a pro at it. Moses McGuire would have no other kind.

It wasn't yet noon. Most days Hardy would arrive to open the bar and get it set up in ten or fifteen minutes. Today, between his thoughts and the memory that they'd closed without the usual cleanup last night, he thought he'd come down and kill some time.

So he wiped the bar, took the peels cleanly off the lemons with an ice pick, cut up the limes, checked the wells and stocked the back bar. He ran himself half a morning Guinness and whipped up the cream for the hated so-called Irish Coffee, for which he cursed Stan Delaplane, the Buena Vista bar and the Dublin airport.

There were some glasses and bottles out front, left from the hurried exit of the night before. Some of the tables hadn't been wiped down.

The cash register. It hadn't been rung out. He refilled his pint glass to the halfway again.

Somebody knocked while he was counting the money. Through the door he saw that it was a retired schoolteacher, a regular named Tommy, who ought to know better.

"Two o'clock," Hardy yelled, holding up two fingers. Tommy nodded and shuffled on by, past the front window.

Hardy went back to ringing out. He looked at his watch. 12:20.

"Slow down," he told himself.

But he didn't. In five more minutes he was ready to open.

He sat at the stool behind the bar, time weighing a ton and not getting lighter. He didn't want to have that time to think. About the unaccustomed restlessness inside him. About ambition, where love had gone. Especially, he didn't want to think about the ridiculous idealist Eddie Cochran and his wife Frannie. He didn't want to think that it might be important to help her in some way—maybe keep her from losing what he'd lost.

The inside pocket of his pea coat, hanging on its peg at the end of the rail, held his darts. The leather case, velvet-lined, worked on him like worry beads as he rubbed it gently, passed it from hand to hand. Finally he opened it on the bar.

The three 20 gram tungsten beauties sat in their slots, awaiting their
flights, the pale-blue, dart-embossed bits of plastic that Hardy had
made himself, and that in turn made those hunks of metal fly true.
Carefully, he emptied the case and fitted the flights to the darts.

Over at the board, he threw some rounds, not really aiming. Not
really shooting. Just throwing. Three darts. Walk to the board and
remove them. Walk back to the chalk line. Do it again. Sometimes stop
for a sip of Guinness. It didn't matter where they hit, although, even
without trying, Hardy put all the darts in the pie bounded by 1 and 5,
with 20 in the middle.

Hardy, in the bar by himself, throwing darts.

Hardy, behind the bar, looked at the lined face of his friend, the oft-
broken nose, the mountain man's beard. McGuire's eyes were shot with
red. Moses had gotten his Ph.D. in philosophy from Cal Berkeley when
his deferment had run out. He hadn't viewed being drafted as the
tragedy many others had—he was a philosopher and believed that one
of life's seminal experiences was war. As it turned out, the war tem-
pered both his philosophical bent and his intellectual appreciation of
men killing each other and anything else that moved.

He was two years older than Hardy and, back then, only two steps
slower, which, Hardy had told him six hundred times, explained his
getting hit in both legs at Chi Leng while Hardy made it to cover, only
to turn around and carry Moses back out, picking up some lead in his
own shoulder in the process.

So, tritely, Moses felt he owed Hardy his life. When Hardy had
changed careers, Moses had been there with the Shamrock and, owing
him his life, had made a place for Hardy in the rotation, something he
would have done for no one else with the possible exception of his sister
Frannie.

"So?" Hardy asked finally.

McGuire looked into his glass, found it empty, twirled it between his
thumb and forefinger. The bar still hadn't opened.

Hardy reached to the top shelf behind him and brought down a
bottle of The Macallan, the best scotch in the house, if not the world.
He refilled Moses's glass.

"This afternoon I gotta go see about getting the body taken care of.
Frannie's in no shape to do it. Especially after all the cops. They were

all over the place, wouldn't leave her alone. Why so many cops, you think?"

Hardy the ex-cop said, "Reports, bureaucracy, bullshit."

Someone came and pounded at the door to the bar, still locked. "Let's go where they can't see us," Hardy suggested.

They went back to the storeroom. Cases of bottled beer lined two of the walls. On a third, wooden shelves held assorted bottles of liquor, napkins, peanuts, dart flights, other bar paraphernalia. Against the back wall was the stainless-steel freezer for the perishables that more than once had held the fish Hardy would bring by after a successful trip. McGuire lifted himself onto it.

"The thing is, there doesn't seem to have been any reason for it. I mean specific. Here's a kid got the world on a string. What the hell? Why'd he want to kill himself?"

"Who said that? That Eddie'd killed himself?"

"Well, nobody exactly, but . . ."

"But what?"

"Shit, Diz, you know. They find him in a lot with a gun in his own hand. What do *you* think happened?"

Hardy leaned against the back wall. "I don't think anything. It's not my job."

"You're a warm human being, you know that, Diz?"

"Come on, Mose. You know, or maybe you don't, that the police really do a number on any death, especially violent death. They don't just call something a suicide out of the blue. They check into it— motives, opportunity, all that. They really do. I mean, even an old man they find who died in his sleep they check out."

"So what do you think happened? You think somebody killed Eddie? You think he killed himself? You knew Eddie."

Hardy kicked at some debris on the floor. "Yeah, I knew him. I'm sure not saying he killed himself. But the cops aren't either, are they?"

"Not yet."

"Believe me, they won't."

"Why won't they? It could be, it could have been, right?"

Hardy scratched at nothing on his leg. "Mose, I've been a cop, right? Takes more than a gun in somebody's hand."

"Maybe there was more."

Hardy felt a chill somewhere behind him. Was Moses hiding some-thing? "What do you know?"

"I don't know anything." But Moses was looking down.

"It's bad luck to lie to your friends," Hardy said. "What do you know?"

Moses fidgeted, his heels hitting against the freezer. "It's probably nothing."

"Probably, but what anyway?"

"Just that Eddie has been a little down. Been in the bar a little more than normal, that kind of thing." Hardy waited. "You know, they planned things, Frannie and Eddie. Not like you and me. They had this savings plan, all that, for when he went back to school." Moses was still struggling with it, sipping at some scotch for something to do. "Any-way, his job's been fucked up lately, maybe ending. It looked like they weren't going to have enough money, or what they planned on, anyway. I offered to loan him some, but you know Eddie."

"And you think Eddie might have killed himself over a little money? Come on, Mose, not the Eddie we knew."

"Yeah, I know, but the cops might think it. I mean, with that and the possible note . . ."

"Abe—Glitsky—told me the note was bullshit. Just some old trash in the car."

"I don't know. It might be. I'm just thinking that the note along with the other stuff . . ."

"Well, if they do, it doesn't really matter, does it? It isn't going to bring him back."

"Yeah, but it matters. It matters they don't call it a suicide."

Hardy suddenly felt very tired. "Why, Mose?" Thinking he knew what his friend was going to say next.

"Frannie, mostly, I guess." Moses slid off the freezer and spun his glass, empty again. "If they . . ." He ran his fingers hard across his forehead. "Shit, this is hard."

"If what?"

"If they come up with suicide. I mean, think about Frannie. Re-jected for good, know what I mean? And there's also some money involved."

Hardy cocked his head to one side.

"Insurance policy doesn't pay on a suicide, though there's double indemnity on violent or accidental death. The policy was for a hundred grand, Diz, and I don't want to see Frannie screwed. She's already been through enough."

"Well," Hardy said, "then let's hope he didn't kill himself."

"He didn't."

Hardy said nothing.

"I just want to . . . I don't know. Protect Frannie's interests, I guess. Feel like I'm doing something."

Hardy figured Moses had been reading his mail. "I don't know what you can do. Be there for her. What else?"

"I thought I'd ask you if you'd watch what the police do. Make it your job for a week or two. Take a few weeks off here and just check it out."

Hardy couldn't bring himself to look at his friend, who kept talking. "I mean, you used to be a cop and all. You know the procedures—"

"Mose, I was a street cop a couple years before law school. That's a long way from homicide."

"Still, you could find out some things. Make sure they're doing it right.

"I don't think so. I don't do that anymore." He looked down. "And I'm out of Guinness."

"Fuck the Guinness."

"And fuck you."

The two stared it down. "Well, I don't know, Mose. Maybe I'll ask around a little. That's all. No promises."

"Okay, but I want to pay you. And I'll pay you for the time off anyway."

"Don't pay me. That makes it like a job."

"That's what makes you tick, Hardy. Call something your job."

"How about I do it for Frannie?"

"And what'll you live on?"

"Spongecake, man, shrimp and Guinness. Same as now."

McGuire threw a round. "How about twenty-five percent of this place?"

"The Shamrock?"

McGuire looked around. "Yeah, that's this place."

Hardy sat down on that, drummed his fingers on a table. "Why don't we first wait and see what the cops come up with?"

"And what if that's suicide?"

Hardy threw a dart. "I don't know," he said. "I guess I could look into it."

5 ❧

C ARL GRIFFIN knew he had to get over it, but it wasn't easy. He'd gone up for his performance review on Monday, yesterday, knowing that his performance had been more than adequate, and knowing it might not matter at all. Glitsky and Batiste, a mulatto and a "Latin surname"—Christ, he loved that, Frank being as absolutely white as he was—were also up for promotion, and there was a formal mandate in the entire city and county bureaucracy to move minorities up. He thanked God there wasn't a gay guy in homicide. He'd be a shoo-in for the next lieutenant. On the other hand, maybe Griffin should announce that he was gay, was coming out of the closet and because of his new status should be acclaimed the next lieutenant.

So he'd entered the office for his review with a bit of a chip on his shoulder. What he actually said was: "Look, I got any chance for this or not? 'Cause if not, let's cut the bullshit and I'll go back to work."

And Frazelli had looked over at Rigby, the Chief, and they'd both gotten that uncomfortable expression that seemed to come with upper management, passing it along to Carl's union rep, Jamie Zacharias, who had said: "If Glitsky or Batiste fuck up at all, you're in."

So Carl, before he'd even sat down, found his interview over. What had they been planning to talk about? he wondered. He'd gotten the bottom line out of them in about a second. Waiting for Glitsky or Batiste to fuck up would be like waiting for one of them to die. Eventually they would, but you didn't want to set your watch by it.

Maybe he should have asked if Abe or Frank had done anything better than he did, were better cops. But he knew it wasn't that. They had to pick somebody, and in today's San Francisco if that somebody was a honky on any level, there had better be a compelling reason. This was a city where people like Ralph Nader and Cesar Chavez were

34

considered near-Fascists by some. Hell, Griffin had interviewed people who believed that Karl Marx himself had been right wing because he hadn't invented women's lib, while he was at it, along with communism.

So he'd stomped out, slamming the door, then sulked in his cubicle the rest of the day, leaving his interviews to Giometti, then letting Abe follow up the Candlestick stiff, which left him the only logical choice when, an hour later, the call from down in China Basin had come in.

Now Carl Griffin was sitting in his car outside his partner Vince Giometti's apartment on Noe Street. The fog almost completely obscured the streetlight at the intersection in front of him, forty yards away. The steam from the cup of Doggie Diner coffee clouded the windshield. The stuff seemed to stay hot about half a day. Maybe it was the acid they put in it.

His partner and he had been up until after two, breaking it to the wife. So today was starting late. He honked his horn again. C'mon, kid, put your pecker back in your pants and come to work.

Christ! he thought. They ought not to let homicide guys be married. So what if he was married—it wasn't anything to talk about. It had never kept him home and never would, that was for sure.

He kept thinking about instinct.

If there was one thing that separated the good cops from the very good, it was instinct. You didn't want to overdo it, Griffin knew, and ignore evidence, but every once in a while a situation came up that seemed to point in an obvious direction and your instinct made you stop and reevaluate.

Glitsky was up for lieutenant. He was up for lieutenant. Frank Batiste likewise. Okay. So at this moment one of those two was standing in the roadway, trying to direct traffic, point Griffin in the obvious direction.

Nine years a homicide cop, and not once before had Abe Glitsky showed up at a scene with his two cents' worth.

Why do you think that could be?

Maybe Glitsky knew something he didn't know. Okay, the Cochran kid could have done himself, maybe not. But why would it benefit Glitsky if he—Griffin—came down for a homicide, which was the direction Glitsky was pointing?

Did he know something? Who was that guy he brought to the scene?

Giometti, cleanly shaved, smiling, opened the door. He had a ther-
mos of what was probably fresh coffee with him, a paper bag full of
goodies.

"Want a bagel, Carl?" he said.

"Something tells me Cochran might have done himself," he replied.
He took the bagel.

"But the gun was fired twice."

"Yeah, I know. First time could've been three weeks ago, two
months, a year even."

"And the wife said—"

"Wives don't know how their husbands feel about squat."

Giometti, he could tell, was thinking about saying something and
decided against it. He chewed his bagel. "What changed your mind?"
he finally asked.

Damned if Griffin was going to tell him everything. People talked,
even partners. Word got around. It would be good for Glitsky's career if
he fucked up. And Glitsky was pushing him—okay, subtly, but it was
there—to decide it was a homicide. And Glitsky, he was sure, knew
something he didn't, something that led in another direction.

Put it together, Carl, he told himself. Make damn sure you're not
being set up.

"Instinct," Griffin said.

Charles Ging's nose was a map of capillaries, and his breath smelled like
gin. His son didn't often get close enough to smell him, but now,
leaning over the blond desk in his father's office, it was nearly overpowering.

He was leaning over in anger. His own face was smooth, as though he
hadn't started shaving yet. His eyes were pale blue, hair light brown. He
was impeccably dressed in an Italian suit.

What he was saying was, "It's beyond me. Absolutely. You think
you're doing the right thing, you're the nice guy, doing everybody a
favor. It's bullshit, man. What you're doing is gambling with my future.
And don't reach for the goddamn bottle, please."

Ging shrank back into his padded chair. "I don't like you to use that
tone of voice to me, Peter."

"The hell with my tone of voice! Listen to what I'm saying, will you?

We get blackballed by the Catholic Church and I am personally screwed. You understand that?"

"Of course, but we're not going to be."

Peter slammed the desk. "Yes, we are. Don't you see that? Times are changed. Not changing, changed. Past tense. You don't play straight, it ever comes out, you're dead. And it doesn't matter to you, you're already finished. Me? I gave up being a doctor to get this place, continue the clean business of covering people with dirt, and now you put the whole thing on the line for what? For a favor to some asshole owns a bar? Jesus, it kills me."

The telephone on the desk rang. The older man went to pick it up; his son put his hand on the receiver. "Let the machine get it, would you? It's after hours."

He looked down at the hand covering his father's. "Jesus, Pop."

The machine clicked. They heard the woman on the recorder, another voice struggling for control, calling for arrangements. It almost didn't register for Peter anymore. He thought for the hundredth time maybe he'd made a mistake deciding to take over the business. The endless parade of grief still got to his dad. And look what it did to the guy. When he finally died, he'd already be pickled. Either that, or if they went to cremate him he'd go up like an alcohol lamp.

Charles reached for the bottle again, and Peter let him—even grabbed a couple of ice cubes from the refrigerator. Dilute it a little; maybe it would help. Then he sat down.

After the first sip, his father sighed. "What do you want me to do, Pete? Tell the guy, who I happen to know, that there's nothing I can do? His brother-in-law apparently killed himself, and the Church says he can't be buried in holy ground. You call that charity?"

"Fuck charity. This is business." And Peter suddenly knew he couldn't deal with the business on this level much longer. He had to get his dad out of it; the man didn't see reality anymore.

"Look, Pop, you tell this guy— What's his name?"

"McGuire."

"Right, you tell McGuire there's a chance it's not a suicide, you think that's the end of it?"

"There is a chance it's not a suicide."

"You saw the powder burns, the wound, the whole thing. The guy shot himself."

"Still, there's a chance he didn't—"

"So you tell Cavanaugh there's reasonable doubt . . ."

"I didn't tell him that. Father Cavanaugh and I go back a long way. He told me he guaranteed it wasn't a suicide. The boy was like a son to him. And Jim Cavanaugh and I, we understand each other."

"And it's all good old boy, isn't it? You defraud the Church, Cavanaugh goes along with it, nobody loses, right?"

"I know you don't agree, but right."

The son looked at the father, shook his head.

The father lifted his glass and drained it.

Hardy, his shift over, back at home in early dusk, was looking at a picture of himself and Abe Glitsky in uniform. Glitsky's broad unlined forehead, he decided, was the only part of his face that couldn't terrify. The rest of it could keep small children awake with nightmares— hatchet nose, overlarge, sunken cheeks, eyes whose whites were perenially red, thin lips with a scar through them upper to lower, the result of a teenage parallel bars accident, although Glitsky told his fellow cops it was an old knife wound.

Abe chewed ice on the telephone. Sometimes he was easier to talk to when you weren't looking at him. Hardy heard the ice crunching like rocks. Glitsky chewed some more, and Hardy pictured him tipping up a Styrofoam cup and hitting the bottom to loosen the last of the ice. He kept chewing.

Hardy blew again on a cup of espresso at his kitchen table. He waited, thinking Glitsky could make an ice cube last as long as a stick of Juicy Fruit.

"I'd just like to see the pm, check the file, see if I'm missing something," Hardy said.

Glitsky must have flicked at the near-empty cup. "Yeah, I know what you want."

"Come on, Abe. I'm not getting paid for this. It all comes down to insurance for the widow. I'd rather have you guys find it a homicide, and that's what Moses wants me to check into. I have no interest beyond that."

"You don't think we're competent to do that, to find that out? 'Cause that's what it sounds like you're saying, and that kind of pisses me off."

Hardy sighed. "Are we a little defensive here in our declining years, or what?"

Abe chewed on some more ice. "You don't understand what it's like here lately."

"Yeah, but I'm not asking for much, either."

"You're asking to get in somebody's face around their investigation. That's pretty much."

"Well, then you do it for me."

Glitsky laughed. "Yeah, that'd work." Hardy knew that the humor he heard wouldn't ever get to his eyes. "Do you even know what we've got? Why don't you wait a day or two? If it's a homicide, we'll likely decide it's a homicide."

"I know that."

"And don't brownnose me."

Hardy had forgotten that he'd never been much good at getting things by Glitsky. He was beginning to remember. "Look, Abe," he said, "it's not like I'm a private investigator wanting to go around you guys. I'd just like a little information, that's all."

"That's the line, huh?"

"It's the line, but it's also the goddam truth."

Glitsky flicked at his Styrofoam—rat-tat-tat, rat-tat-tat. "Griffin and I aren't exactly sleeping together," he said. "You'll have to play it very straight."

"I just want to meet the guy," Hardy said. "I'll dazzle him with my Irish charm."

6 ❧

*T*HE SUN had come out. The morning was beginning to get warm. Hardy took off his sweater before he got to his car. He felt slightly nauseous. He had felt it was his duty to look at the body again.

He'd seen quite a lot of blood in Vietnam before he himself had been hit in the shoulder. As a cop, he'd run across his share. But he was far from hardened to the effects of metal passing through flesh at high speed.

They hadn't yet dressed it. Hardy had started at the toes and worked up. Eddie had been five-ten, about 160 pounds. He had an old, healed moon-shaped scar about three inches long on his upper right thigh, calluses on the tips of the fingers of his left hand, a fairly new bruise on his left forearm, and a small scratch near his left ear, just under the hole the bullet had made going in.

He drove up Mission Street with the windows open. The radio in his Suzuki wasn't working, but still Hardy tried to turn it on three times in the thirty blocks between Ging's Mortuary and his destination. The damage done by the tiny piece of lead kept jumping up behind his eyes, short-circuiting other connections.

The parking lot was between a local office of the Pacific Telephone Company and the Cruz Publishing Company.

The lot was now filled with cars. Hardy had a hard time, for a moment, remembering what it had looked like empty. This was industrial wasteland, without a house around. Railroad tracks, train yards, glass, stone and cement. He parked along the curb, letting the site work itself into his consciousness. The sun was hot now and glared off the side of the Cruz Building.

❧

Arturo Cruz stopped dictating and dismissed his secretary, then gave all his attention to the two men six floors below him in the parking lot. Immediately he knew it had been a mistake to send Jeffrey to get rid of the cop—it must be another cop. Jeffrey was too young, inexperienced. Loyal as a dog, a body to die for, but not by any stretch a jack-of-all-trades.

Jeffrey was having a conversation with the man, showing him around the long, narrow lot that was now filled with the cars of Cruz's employees.

His publication was a newspaper called *La Hora*, which catered to the large Latino population of San Francisco. It was an intensely competitive market, and to make it you had to do things that maybe when you started out would have bothered you.

Now, the point was, you'd done them, and it wasn't good luck to have too many policemen making themselves at home in your parking lot. The other night, then yesterday, had been bad enough.

Cruz turned from the window and decided to go down himself to see what was what.

The back of the lot was bounded by a cyclone fence eight feet high, but entrance by the front was wide open. The canal, now at medium tide, ran parallel to the back fence perhaps thirty feet from the buildings. Between the fence and the canal was a no-man's-land of shrubbery and debris.

Hardy leaned against the fence, at the end of the ten-foot-wide corridor between the last row of cars and the building, squinting. He had brought his old badge—illegal but helpful—and was making what he thought was a little progress with a boy named Jeffrey.

Jeffrey had already admitted that he'd known Ed Cochran "just to talk to." He had no doubt—and Hardy briefly wondered why—Eddie had killed himself. What stumped Jeffrey was why he had gotten out of his car with a loaded gun and walked forty or fifty feet to almost lean against the building and shoot himself. It was a point Hardy hadn't considered. Hardy looked around, thinking for a fact it couldn't have been for the view.

"Everything under control, Jeffrey?"

Hardy looked into the glare where the voice had come from. "You must be Mr. Cruz," he said. "Sorry to keep having to inconvenience you, but there's always this kind of thing in a violent death." He kept talking. "Jeffrey was just showing me where the body was found. Pretty bad, was it?"

Cruz cocked his head, hesitating. He wasn't older than thirty-five, and he radiated both authority and good health. Black, perfectly styled hair capped a face with a slightly Arabic cast. But his eyes, or perhaps his contact lenses, were light hazel and his skin, though tan, was fair. His mouth turned in disgust. "It was pretty bad," he said.

Hardy smiled. "They probably covered this yesterday, but you know bureaucracies."

Cruz, understanding, nodded to Hardy. He dismissed Jeffrey with a look. "Anything to help," he said, though Hardy thought he appeared nervous.

"Jeffrey said it was near here, the body. But there's no sign of it now at all."

"It was right here," he said. "They had it cleaned up by the time we got to work the next morning."

"Was anyone still in the building?" Cruz was scrutinizing Hardy, his expression still wary, but he answered quickly enough. "No, I don't believe so. We don't encourage overtime. I know the lot was empty, except for my car, when I went home."

"And when was that?"

"I don't know for sure. I told the other inspector yesterday—maybe eight or eight-thirty. It was still light out." At Hardy's questioning glance, he volunteered: "I was the last one to leave. I always am. Bosses' hours."

Hardy grabbed at another straw. "Any chance that someone who didn't drive to work was in the building?"

Cruz waited, as though he expected Hardy to say more. "Slim, I would say. Gossip being what it is, I imagine it would have gotten around by now. Still, if it will help, I'll be glad to circulate a memo."

Hardy had noticed that the corner of the cyclone mesh fence had a gaping hole in it. "Is this new?"

Again there was that pause. "No, we've been meaning to fix it for months. I assume some kids did it to get to the canal. Saves going the long way."

Hardy dutifully noted on his pad, thinking, What kids?

The gravel and asphalt had been recently and carefully raked, obliterating any possible sign of struggle. Hardy walked to the edge of the building and peered along its mirrored surface. He squatted for a different angle, then walked along the length of the building, running his palm along the glass, to the side door. He turned to Cruz. "Well, we'll try not to bother you again."

Cruz's first smile revealed a perfect set of teeth, too perfect to be real. He held out his hand. "If I can be of any more help . . ."

Hardy asked, "Did you, by any chance, know Ed?"

The pause, when it ended, was clipped. "Who?"

"Ed Cochran, the guy who died."

"No," Cruz said now without missing a beat. "No, I'm afraid not. Should I have?"

At his car, Hardy looked back and saw that Cruz had returned to the hole in the fence and was standing, hands in his pocket, shaking his head from side to side.

Hardy hadn't gone to the Cruz building for any other reason than to see the site in daylight, and within a couple of minutes had found himself talking to the president of the company. No wonder his questions, he thought, had been so random.

At Blanche's, a rickety canal-side café and art gallery, the Campari umbrella offered shade from the sun but couldn't do much about the glare coming up off the canal. Hardy sipped at a club soda, not bothering to turn away from the canal's glare, and thought about this guy Cruz's obsessive concern over his parking lot and his obvious lie about not knowing Ed Cochran.

Hardy wiped the sweat and squinted into the city's early-afternoon haze. A small breeze carried on it the smell of roasting coffee and burning engine oil, and Hardy wondered what the fuck he was doing.

Carl Griffin stood by the one window that afforded a view of the building across the way and, four flights down, of the alley that ran between the parking lot and Bryant. Yesterday, he and Giometti had dealt some more with the wife and the kid's family, then Cruz, then driven down to Army Distributing, which looked like it was close to going out of business.

They didn't have a locked-up reason for Cochran to have killed himself, but neither did anything much indicate a homicide. There had

been two empty chambers in the gun, but he'd encountered that before
—one shot where you jerk the gun away just as you fire before you get
up the guts to go through with it the next time.

It was a drag—a young guy acing himself—especially dealing with
the relatives. But it happened a lot. More often younger guys than
anybody else.

He pushed some papers off to one side of his desk. Where the hell
was Giometti now? He was hungry. He tried, but wasn't having much
luck getting himself motivated to think about this guy Cochran. What
difference did it make? He could solve the Murder of the Century and
all he'd get for it would be a "Good job, Carl. Want to do another
one?"

He decided to fuck waiting on Giometti and go downstairs and have
a hero sandwich. He grabbed for his windbreaker, which he wouldn't
need, out of habit, just as his phone rang. He picked it up.

"Carl," Joe Frazelli said, "I got a friend of Glitsky's here, got some
questions about the Cochran thing. You got a minute for him?"

That's what he needed, he thought. He needed to help out a friend
of Glitsky's on one of his cases. "I was just going down to get a sandwich."

"Thanks, I'll send him over," Frazelli said, hanging up.

Swear to God, Griffin thought, if I'm ever looie I'm not going to do
shit like that. He threw his windbreaker on its peg and turned back to
the window. It looked like a nice day out there, even a hot one. He
pushed at the windowsill, trying to open it an inch or two for some sea
breeze, but it was painted shut.

"Inspector Griffin?"

He turned. It was the guy from the other night. They shook hands,
the guy introducing himself, and Carl offered him a seat, asking what
he could do for him.

"I'm kind of a representative of the family," the man began.

"The family?"

"Ed Cochran's. His wife's, actually."

"You private?"

The man shook his head, smiling, almost rehearsed, resting his
elbows on his knees, very relaxed. "I'm a bartender."

"You're a bartender," Griffin repeated.

"The Little Shamrock, out on Lincoln."

"Okay," Griffin said.

"Anyway, Ed Cochran's brother-in-law owns the place and I work for him. That's the connection."

"Good, we got a connection. What are you representing them for?"

Hardy sat back, crossing one leg over the other, pulling a cuff down. "They'd just like to make some official request that this be investigated as a possible homicide."

"It is being investigated as a homicide. This is the homicide department. I'm a homicide inspector."

"I realize that," Hardy said, "but I know it looks like a suicide, like it was a suicide—"

"Initially," Griffin said.

"But maybe it wasn't."

Griffin moved a few more papers, trying to cover his impatience. "Maybe it wasn't. You're right. That's my job, finding out if it was or wasn't. You got anything to make me think it wasn't?"

"Nothing specific."

"Specific's what we like," Griffin said. "How about general?"

"You had to know the guy, I guess." That called for no response, and Griffin waited it out. "His wife . . . I mean, he wasn't the kind of person who kills himself."

"He wasn't?" It was hard to keep the sarcasm out. Griffin had seen suicides from derelicts to socialites, from healthy beautiful teenage girls to terminally ill wheelchair patients. "I'll note that in the file," he said.

Hardy uncrossed his legs. "It's not as ridiculous as it sounds," he said, not defensive, as though he at least understood how it sounded. "Some people get depressed, you know. Life gets 'em down. There's some warning. I thought it might help to know that Ed—on the outside— was a positive guy."

"Look, Mr. . . ."

"Hardy."

"Mr. Hardy. We go on the assumption—"

"I know the routine, inspector. I used to be a cop. I was hoping you might go a little beyond the routine in this case."

Griffin felt his face getting red. Go beyond the routine for a friend of Abe Glitsky's who's implying I'm not doing my job well enough? Go beyond the routine when no matter how good I am I won't get promoted over any black or Latino or woman or fucking police dog if they had any constituency in the city? And was Glitsky somehow tied in to this, siccing a cop on him?

"I don't really like the implication there," Griffin said.

"I'm not implying anything, or don't mean to be."

"Seems to me you're saying my routine won't get the job done right."

"I'm saying that knowing what kind of guy Ed was might put things in a different light, that's all."

"Yeah, it might. I'll keep it in mind." Griffin stood up. So did Hardy. "So how's Glitsky involved?"

Hardy shrugged it off. "I just know him. I started with him."

"Yeah, well, this is my case. So you can tell Abe if he wants it he can go through channels."

Hardy held his hands out. "Look. Abe's got nothing to do with this. I'm a citizen. I'm here with a reasonable request. That's it."

Griffin studied the guy's face. No sign he was lying, which might mean he was a great liar. "Okay, but you got no evidence."

"I know."

"So unless we get something more that points to murder, it's gonna go down as suicide."

"That's why I was hoping maybe we could go over what you've got."

"Just go fishing, huh? Afraid I'll miss something?" Griffin couldn't stop himself. The anger just kept resurfacing.

Surprisingly, the guy didn't rise to it. Instead, he took it in for a beat, then offered a smile and stuck out his hand. "Nope. I'm sure if something's there, you'll find it. Thanks for your time."

Griffin leaned his butt back against his desk, watching Hardy walk across the office. Fucking watchdog, he thought. He didn't know what Glitsky wanted out of this, but if he wanted to find something so bad, let him find it himself. And on his own time.

So official cooperation wasn't likely to be forthcoming, Hardy thought as he drove out to the Mission District. And also, which he didn't understand at all, it seemed to be getting to be a better bet that they'd come up with a suicide, which would be a further disaster for Frannie. The fact that there was no apparent motive obviously wasn't making Griffin, at least, lose any sleep. In the city with the Golden Gate Bridge, suicide must not seem like all that much of an aberration.

7 ✖

*F*RANNIE AND Ed's place was a large corner flat with a rounded window jutting out from the living room over the steep street.

Hardy knocked at the door, straight in from the sidewalk without a stoop of any kind. It was four P.M., already a long day, and by far the hottest one of the year.

He barely heard the "Who is it?"

Frannie hugged him for a long time in the doorway. She was barefoot, wearing a white nightgown. She'd obviously been taking a nap. Her long red hair was a wreck, the skin around her eyes nearly black, her lips puffed like a wound.

She led the way to the living room and left Hardy there. The first thing he did was open two windows to let in some air. It didn't make much difference.

He heard Frannie somewhere behind him.

The room was a friendly mixture of Goodwill and teak. A stereo and some small but, Hardy knew, excellent Blaupunkt speakers, two mismatched, upholstered chairs, a couch, and two bentwoods, on one of which Hardy sat.

Hardwood floors reflected the late-afternoon sun onto clean painted walls. There were three framed works of art on the walls: one of Hockney's "Pools," a view of San Francisco from the Marin side of the Bay, and one of Goines's Chez Panisse posters. A coffee table was pushed into another corner, and on it was a small television set. Homemade bookshelves held an impressive collection of books and some records.

He sensed more than heard her approach. Still barefoot, barely five feet tall and ninety pounds tops, Frannie had tried to comb her hair and put some red in her cheeks, but she needn't have bothered.

47

Dressed now in jeans and a T-shirt, what she really wore most notice-ably was the loss.

He stood. She stopped in the doorway, not moving. "Sorry for the . . ." she whispered. "I'm just . . ." She tried again. "Would you like something? Beer? Coffee?"

To give her something to do, Hardy said a beer would be good.

She came back a minute later with two cans of Bud and a chilled mug. "Ed always liked me to keep a mug in the freezer." She poured expertly. "But you know that."

"You ought to work for Moses."

She tried to smile, but it didn't work.

Hardy took a drink. "You feel like you can talk? I know the police have probably gone over—"

"And over and over . . . I'm okay."

"Did Moses tell you why I . . . ?"

She nodded, and he decided to plunge right in. "Ed left the house when, roughly?"

"About seven-thirty. We finished dinner and talked for a while."

"And he just decided to go out for a drive?"

She hesitated, perhaps remembering, perhaps hiding. "No, not ex-actly." She looked at her lap, biting her lip. "Not exactly."

"Frannie, look at me."

The green eyes were wet.

"What did you talk about?"

"Nothing, just household stuff, you know."

"Did you fight?"

She didn't answer.

"Frannie?"

"No, not really." All strength seemed to leave her. Her hands went slack and the can of beer fell to the floor. Hardy jumped up and grabbed it, righting it and letting the foam overflow.

"I'll get a sponge," Frannie said.

Hardy put a hand on the tiny, bony shoulder to keep her from rising. "Forget the beer, Frannie. Did you have a fight or not?"

She slumped back, staring at Hardy as though she wanted to ask him a question. She looked about fifteen years old. Then she started crying, just tear after tear rolling silently down her made-up cheeks. Hardy, his hand still on her shoulder, felt the suppressed sobs.

"What about?" he finally asked.

The voice, now husky and nearly inaudible, came. "I'm pregnant. I told him I was pregnant."

Her eyes held on the floor between her feet. She whispered. "Ed always just said to go ahead when I was ready. That was the way he was. He said we'd deal with it when it came up, and if we waited 'til he was ready in advance, he might never be."

"And you'd just found out?"

"That day. I thought he'd be happy."

She looked up at Hardy, the tears still flowing. "But it really wasn't a fight or anything. I just wanted him to stay. I was all emotional, you know."

"But he went out?"

She shook her head, slowly, back and forth. "He went out."

"Do you know where?"

"That's the thing," she said. "That's the thing I hate."

"What?"

"Just seeing him go off, not even talking, and then . . ."—she swallowed—"now he's gone."

The thing Hardy hated, he told himself, was being in this position, the inquisitor. After a minute he told her as much.

"That's okay," she said. "At least you believe me."

"Who didn't believe you?"

"I don't know for sure, but I got the impression the police had a hard time with it. I mean, me not knowing why Eddie had gone out, or where."

"Maybe he just wanted . . . ," Hardy began, then rephrased it. "Maybe he needed to think about being a father."

"Maybe," she said, unconvinced.

"Except what?"

"Except he'd been going out a few times lately. I think it had to do with his business."

Uh-oh, Hardy thought. But he said, "Didn't you talk, you and Ed?"

"We talked all the time, about everything. You know that!"

"But not this?"

She shook her head, then punched her little fist into her other palm. "It made me so mad, I could've killed him." The hand went up to her mouth. "Oh, I mean, I didn't mean that. But we always shared everything, and this was like he was protecting me or something, like I couldn't handle what he was doing."

Okay, that was possible, Hardy thought. "So this night, Monday, after you told him about being pregnant, did you have a fight?"

"Not a real fight. More a disagreement. I wanted to snuggle, have him tell me it was all right, that he wanted to have it." She sighed. "But he said he had to go out." Again, Frannie shook her head back and forth. Her knuckles were white, clamped on her lap.

Hardy watched the beer she'd spilled spread slowly over the hardwood.

"See?" she continued. "His job was almost over anyway. I thought it was stupid."

"His job?"

She bit her lip, thinking. "I mean his concern with trying to save the business. I think he got tired of arguing with me about it, and just went ahead on his own, not wanting to bother me or fight anymore about it."

Hardy drank some beer. "I'm afraid you're losing me."

"I'd better get a towel."

She brought another beer back for both of them. "God, it's hot," she said. "Eddie always loved hot days, all two a year."

She sat this time in the deep chair in front of the window. More composed now, getting used to it, she started talking on her own.

"You know we were going down . . . He'd gotten into the MBA program at Stanford and we were going down there in September. His job was so . . . arbitrary. It wasn't a career. He just wanted to actually work a couple years so grad school wouldn't all be book learning, you know? So he got this job after college with Mr. Polk over at Army, because he wanted to get into distribution eventually." She looked out the window. "This seems so stupid now. Why am I talking about this?"

"Talk about anything," Hardy said.

"Then last Thanksgiving or sometime there, Mr. Polk got married and at the same time they heard they might lose the *La Hora* account."

"*La Hora?* That's Cruz Publishing."

Frannie nodded again. "I know, that's where he . . ." She tightened her lips and continued. "Anyway, the police said they'd check that. If there was a connection."

"If? There's gotta be."

"It sounded crazy to me, but one of the policemen said it could have been like a protest, Eddie maybe killing himself in the parking lot as a protest against Polk, like a Buddhist burning himself or something. I don't know if he was serious."

Hardy swore at that, shook his head.

"I know," she said, "but at least it does put him there—"

"So would a meeting with someone who wanted to kill him."

She didn't answer. Hardy felt a wisp of a breeze, and Frannie sat back in the deep chair. She turned her head to the window, away from him. He saw her wipe her face with the back of her hand, as a small child would.

"Oh, damn," she said.

"Frannie," he began, and she twisted to face him.

"I didn't want him to go," she said. "I didn't even know he owned a gun."

Now she sobbed, and Hardy got up, walking to the window, his back to her. The street fell away sharply outside. In the distance, the air shimmered over the rooftops.

"Did you tell the police about being pregnant?" he asked finally, turning around.

"No." She sniffed, rubbed a hand over her eyes. "I didn't see what difference it would make. I don't want anybody to know until I know what I'm going to do. You won't tell Moses, will you?"

"Not if you don't want."

"Because he wouldn't understand. I mean, I might not have it now. I might . . ."

"Frannie . . ."

"But Eddie would *not* have killed himself over that." She pounded a small fist against her leg. "He wouldn't have. He would have been happy as soon as he got used to the idea. He was happy. He was!"

In the next fifteen minutes, Hardy found out that the scar on Ed's leg was from trying to hop a train when he was a kid. His guitar playing, Hardy should have remembered, explained the finger calluses, and also made him right-handed, which Frannie verified. Sometimes at work he got little bruises from moving and lifting things, but Frannie noticed no new ones the last few days. He'd never had a fight she knew of, and he drank, she said, "way, way less than Moses, just a beer or two when he got home."

Finally Hardy lost his heart for going into details. He looked at her for a long minute. "You really, deep down, can't think of any reason for it? I know it's a hard question, Frannie, but could there have been anything?"

Frannie walked over to the open window. She stood there for what seemed a very long time, occasionally brushing the hair away from her face. When she turned around, she shrugged. "He just didn't. What can I tell you? He didn't do it. The rest I don't understand, I don't . . ."

She hung her head and turned around to face the window again.

Hardy stood up. "I won't tell Moses," he said to her back. "But if I were you, I wouldn't do anything too soon, about the pregnancy, about anything, okay? Let things settle a little."

She turned around. "I think I know now how you got the way you are."

At the door, she managed a last half-smile. Hardy thought of something. Awkwardly, he pulled his wallet from his back pocket and looked through it. "I know this might seem a little weird, but . . ."

Good. He still had a couple of cards he'd had made up for his dart playing—he thought they gave him a little psychological advantage when he passed them out at tournaments. Like, Wo! This guy's serious.

He gave one of them to Frannie. They were pale blue embossed with a gold dart. "If you need anything at all, even just to talk, call me, okay? And if you remember anything else, the smallest thing . . ."

"Okay."

He wanted to hug her again, somehow ease things, but it would be useless. Nothing was going to ease things for Frannie for a very long time.

He left her standing on the sidewalk, the sun behind her, staring down at the shimmering city.

Down the block, some kids were playing on the street. It seemed odd to Hardy that anybody could be laughing in the whole world, but they were. Laughing and laughing. Life was a ball.

Well, there were a lot of motives, he thought. Enough to keep him thinking for a couple of days. Eddie wouldn't have been the first man to be driven to despair by the thought of fatherhood, especially as he was preparing for three years of poverty and intellectual struggle. The business he ran was going bust—maybe he took that pretty seriously, too. It

was possible, though Hardy hated to admit it, that he was having a love affair that had gone bad. Hardy guessed the police would be checking into that, as well as Frannie's whereabouts that night.

He remembered Cruz's lie about not having known Ed. But the relationship there was so obvious—the parking lot and all—that the cops would be all over Cruz. How far they pushed things, he figured, would be a function of Griffin's gut feelings. If he smelled a murder, he'd dig in. If not, everything to do with Cruz and Frannie and Army would be essentially irrelevant.

Well, what Griffin did was out of Hardy's hands.

He came over Twin Peaks, down Stanyan, then through the Park out to 22nd. There was no sign of afternoon fog, and it gave his neighborhood an entirely different feel. People were outside playing Frisbee on the grass in the park, couples walked the streets hand in hand. The heat had let up somewhat, but it was still balmy.

He parked on the street in front of his house. He had to force the front door open again with his shoulder. This time, though, he walked directly down the hall to the kitchen, through it to the tool room, and pulled one of his planes off the wall.

In five minutes, he had taken the door off its hinges and was sitting on the front porch, planing. A stray cat came and sunned itself at his feet. Occasionally it would swat at one of the shavings.

When the door was rehung, Hardy changed the light in the hall, then went back to his study. He owned three guns—a 9-millimeter automatic, a .22 target pistol, and a regulation .38 Special that he'd used when he'd started in the police department. They were all in the lower drawer of the filing cabinet he'd made himself using no nails.

Eddie had been shot with a .38 revolver, so Hardy grabbed that. Double-checking to make sure it was unloaded, he clicked off a few rounds to make triple sure, then went into the living room and sat in his chair by the window.

The evening sun striped the room through the open blinds. Hardy put the gun on the reading table at his side, picked up a pipe and lit it. After a few puffs, he lifted the gun and aimed it at a few targets around the room. He passed the gun back from hand to hand, feeling the heft of it, checking its action.

He then aimed it point-blank at his head from several angles, using both hands. Finally, holding the gun in his right hand against his right temple, he closed his eyes, held his breath and squeezed the trigger, breathing out after the empty click.

He leaned back in the chair, still holding the gun in his right hand. Hardy was left-handed. Eddie was right-handed. The bullet had entered the left side of his head. So unless he picked it up wrong-handed, or somehow . . . No, it was ludicrous. "No way," he said, "absolutely no way."

8 ❧

*T*HE TOWN of Colma is tucked into a pocket behind Daly City and Brisbane, its corpses far outnumbering its citizens. It was normally shrouded in fog, which seemed appropriate, but this day, for Eddie's funeral, it basked in sunlight, bright and warm.

The Mass had been scheduled for ten, so Hardy timed his arrival at the cemetery for quarter to eleven, but no one else had made it yet.

Another group of mourners were gathered in a knot out over across the sloping lawn. A brace of eucalyptus at the front gate provided a feeble shade and a distinctive scent. Not at all deathlike. The sky was purplish blue. A warm breeze ruffled the high leaves.

Another hearse and its party appeared down the road, and Hardy, sitting on the fender of his Suzuki, watched the line approach. He put his hands in his pockets and walked out to the street. McGuire's pickup was visible midway down the line of cars.

It was a substantial group, which he had expected. Eddie Cochran, of course, had been well liked.

Hardy got into his car, waited, then pulled in behind McGuire. They went quite a ways back. Here the eucalyptus grew a bit thicker. Under the trees it was cool and pleasant. Picnic weather.

Father James Cavanaugh leaned down and glanced casually at his reflection in the car window. With his hair, still all black, flopping Kennedy-like over an unlined forehead and piercing gray-blue eyes, he was uncomfortably aware that he could be a walking advertisement for the glory of the priesthood. His body was trim, his movements graceful. The cleft in his chin was a constant temptation to vanity.

It was a glance, that's all. He didn't study himself, make any corrections to the look. He was, he knew, unworthy—of his gifts as well as his role, especially here, today.

And now here came Erin, Eddie's mother. And again, the temptations, the haunting realization of his sinfulness. What a beauty she was.

And so strong. In spite of losing her eldest son, she seemed not to need his support, though as she stepped into his arms and he held her, he felt for a moment the pent-up grief as she sighed once deeply into the shoulder of his cassock.

Her hand lifted to his face. "Are you all right, James?"

He nodded. "How's Big Ed?"

"He didn't sleep much last night. I can't say any of us did."

Unbidden again, the thought came. What if we had married? What if, when they'd both been eighteen, he'd pushed just a little harder? He had never met anyone else with her joy in life, her sense of balance, her wisdom, her brain. And, as if that weren't enough, even now, after four children, her body was rich, the perfect combination of curve and plane, of softness and tone. Her face was still smooth as a girl's, the skin cream white. A touch of light coral lipstick highlighted the bow-shaped, sensuous mouth.

"You're all right, though?" he asked gently.

She stared up at him, her eyes going dull. "I don't think I'll ever be all right again."

She turned, planning to go join her husband.

But she couldn't go to the grave just yet. She knew she should walk with Big Ed, be there for him, but the strength simply wasn't there. Her husband was walking with Jodie, trying to comfort her. God, this was impossibly hard.

And Frannie, poor Frannie, so small in black, stumbling over roots, held up by her brother Moses. She looked over to see her own two sons, Mick and Steven, pallbearers, waiting patiently by the hearse. They were good boys. Of course, they weren't Eddie. There wasn't any more Eddie.

She looked up at the blue sky, struggling for control—biting her tongue inside her mouth, digging fingernails into her palms. She stared up at the sky, took a deep breath. A strong hand gripped her right arm just above the elbow.

"Ma'am?"

She was nearly as tall as the man. He hadn't been at the funeral Mass. Perhaps he was, had been, a friend of Ed's, though he was older. His face looked lived in—loaded with laugh lines. He wasn't laughing now, though.

"Are you all right?" he said.

The hand on her arm didn't bother her. She reached over and put her own hand over it. "Just tired," she said, "very tired."

Then she gently shook him off and started walking toward the gravesite, slowly. The man walked alongside.

"Did you know Eddie?" she asked.

"Pretty well. Both him and Frannie." Then, "I'm very sorry."

She nodded.

"I'm here because of Frannie, mostly. Her brother."

She stopped now and looked at him again, their eyes on a level. "Were you at the wedding? Should I know you?"

He shook his head. "Weddings aren't my thing. I, uh, got called out of town, couldn't make it."

"But now you're . . . ?" Letting it hang. Her eyes wouldn't let him go.

"Moses doesn't believe . . ." He paused, started again. "I guess I don't either, that it was a suicide."

She looked toward the gravesite. The bearers hadn't yet moved the coffin from the hearse. She found herself gripping Hardy by the arm, talking through clenched teeth. "There is no way in the world that my Eddie killed himself. None at all."

Suddenly it was essential to tell someone what she knew in her heart. "Here's Eddie . . . he'd bring in a stray cat or a bird that had fallen out of its nest in a storm. He was almost . . . I don't know how to say it . . . but almost feminine in being sensitive that way. He hated football. Hated ice hockey. They were too brutal. His father and Mick used to tease him about it, but he was just a soft man. If you knew him at all, you know that."

Hardy thought a moment, did not meet her eyes.

"It's inconceivable he even owned a gun," she said. "What use would he have for it?"

"The gun is definitely one of my questions."

She stopped. She didn't want to press, didn't know why it was so important to make this point to this man. Eddie was gone. What difference could it make?

"I'm sorry," she said, walking again toward the grave. "I'm afraid I'm not being myself, but he didn't own the gun. I know that."

"Do you know where it came from? Where he might have gotten it?"

"No."

She stopped again and touched his arm, not knowing exactly what she wanted to say. But they had begun moving the coffin to the gravesite—the coffin that held Eddie's body—and her emotion choked her so she couldn't speak.

Steven didn't realize the coffin would be so heavy. His brother hadn't been that big a guy, but with the wood and the handles and all it was a lot of weight, and his arms started hurting as soon as they got it out of the car.

He wasn't going to show it, though, give anybody the satisfaction. It was only about a hundred feet, he guessed, over to the gravesite. Beside him at the back of the coffin was his brother Mick, two-letter jock, to whom the weight of the coffin would be nothing. But to him, little wimpy brother Steve, just standing here holding the thing was a challenge.

"Who's talking to Mom?" Mick whispered. Mick was a junior at USF, there on an ROTC scholarship. As far as Steven was concerned, they lived on different planets.

Steven just shrugged. He'd seen the guy with his mother and was sure he'd met him somewhere, maybe over at Eddie's one time, but it didn't matter, he didn't know who he was. No big deal, it wasn't his business. He wasn't going to waste breath speculating to Mick about it.

Father Jim motioned from the gravesite, and they started moving. The priest was okay when he wasn't acting holy, when he was just being a regular guy, having a drink at the house, or joyriding out along Highway One at the beach.

Yeah, the priest could be okay, he guessed. At least everybody else liked him. Grown-ups were a bunch of sheep that way anyway, herding up and following along. You want to be honest, the guy could be a little much, flipping between holy and funny, or getting that look at Mom, or when he was alone with him, trying to act like a kid, swearing and goofing. Who needed that shit? Be yourself, Steven wanted to tell him. If they don't like you, fuck 'em.

Like now, there he was being official holy, standing next to Frannie, talking quietly to her. It wasn't that he didn't like Father Cavanaugh— Eddie had loved him and that was almost enough for Steven right there —but it was like the man wasn't being himself. People should be themselves. . . . Yeah, but even Eddie had been like that lately. That's the way adults got—always smiling and playing games. But Eddie, he saw things. He was hurting, bummed about his work, what he was going to do with his life. Why else do they think he'd come around to the house so much the last couple of weeks?

His mom now was going over to the hole in the ground, the dug-up earth covered with green tarp. What, did they think they could take your mind off the dirt, off Ed being buried under it, if they camouflaged it?

Finally his arms got to relax as they put the coffin on the stand that would lower it. The last half of the walk had been real tough. Maybe he should work out once in a while, he thought, except he didn't want to wind up in ROTC like Mick.

His mom was standing now next to his dad. The other guy she'd been talking to was a little behind her, almost like a bodyguard. He'd seemed to be watching everything at once, but not being obvious about it.

Steven checked around. Eddie had taken him down to his work a couple of times—making sure Steven was included in his life—and introduced him to some of the people there. He was surprised to see Ed's boss, Mr. Polk, big ears bookending the saddest face in the crowd, standing behind Frannie with a young woman who was so pretty Steven couldn't look at her for long. Thick brown hair, olive skin, serious tits. He saw the guy who'd talked to his mother look at her, saw her look back at him with half a smile, which caused him to study his shoes. What was Ed's boss doing with a killer like that? He'd never understand adults. Who wanted to, anyway?

Overhead, birds kept chirping in the trees. He focused on that, rather than on Father Jim's words, which were bullshit. If Eddie had really killed himself, which Father Jim seemed to have reason to believe, then he was in hell.

Steven didn't think Ed was in hell. He thought he was nowhere, the same place everybody was going—in fact, many of the living were already there. He looked up, trying not to think about where Ed might be. Eddie and he had been friends, even with the age thing, in spite of being brothers.

Then, all of a sudden, the guy behind his mother was pushing at the crowd, nearly jumping over the coffin. He got to Frannie just as she lost it and started to go down.

Frannie seemed to weigh nothing, less than nothing. Her mass of red hair, the green of the lawn under her, only threw into greater contrast the stark pallor of her face.

Moses was at Hardy's side. He touched Frannie's face, rubbing it gently, trying to bring some color around the mouth. "She breathing?"

Hardy nodded. "Just fainted."

The priest came and knelt between them. He felt for a pulse in her neck, seemed satisfied, stood up. "She'll be all right," he announced to the mourners.

The color in Frannie's face was returning. Her eyes opened, then closed, then opened and stayed open. Moses said something to her, got her up on his arm and followed Hardy through the crowd back to where the cars were parked.

Hardy heard a muffled sob into Moses's shoulder, suddenly couldn't deal with it anymore, put his hands in his pockets and moved out of vision, out of earshot, down the drive back toward the entrance gate. Finally, he stopped and cleared a space under a eucalyptus tree, then sat down, trying to face away from any tombstones, which in Colma is not an easy thing to do.

9 ❧

HE COCHRANS' house was in a familiar neighborhood, near Hardy's own, on 28th Avenue between Taraval and Ulloa. They shared the same fog most days, but Hardy lived north of the park—south of it was about as close to suburban as San Francisco got.

Big Ed greeted him at the door and introduced himself. He was dressed in a shiny black suit that looked as though it hadn't seen much wear in the past ten years. The lapels were too thin, the black tie was too thin. The white shirt was brand new.

Hardy had the feeling that he'd caught him out of uniform, like running into a cop dressed as a clown at a parish festival. Ed Cochran looked slightly uncomfortable, but not in the least diminished either by grief or attire.

The eyes, though puffed, were clear and piercing. The solid man's face was startlingly controlled. His strong chin and flat fighter's nose conveyed an impression of suppressed power, reinforced by the handshake, which made no effort to crush or intimidate. The meaty vice gripped, shook, let go, but the strength was there.

His hand gently touched Hardy's back as he ushered him into the foyer. His wife Erin had used her hand the same way—to guide—at the cemetery. A family mannerism, perhaps. Ed's touch was as light as Erin's.

And here was the priest again, by the bar near the sliding doors that led out to the redwood deck. Good-looking man, another powerhouse, but in a more subtle way than Ed Cochran. Drink in hand, he turned just as Hardy and Ed arrived.

"Good, so you've come. I was hoping to meet you."

"Dismas, this is Jim Cavanaugh," Ed said. Cavanaugh's grip was firm and dry.

"Dismas? The good thief?"

Hardy smiled. "So I'm told."

"And you're Catholic, then?"

"Was."

The priest shrugged as though accustomed to the answer. "Was, is. It's all a matter of tense, and there's no time in heaven. Like the good thief, will you rejoin the fold at your final hour?"

Hardy scratched his chin. "Well, I'm not much like the original Dismas. I've never stolen so much as a candy bar. But you never can tell. Was he much good at darts?"

"Darts?"

"Darts. I'm a pretty fair hand at the chalk line."

Cavanaugh grinned broadly, displaying perfect teeth. "I'm afraid the New Testament is a little vague on that point. Get you a drink? Let me guess, Irish whiskey?"

Hardy had been thinking of a beer, but the Irish was okay. Cavanaugh had a knack, he guessed, for making his ideas feel like the best ones. He took the drink, they clicked their glasses, then moved out onto the deck, into the sunshine.

"That was a good move at the grave, Dismas Hardy," the priest said. "You saved Frannie from a nasty fall."

Hardy shrugged. "Marine training, mixed in with a little Boy Scouts. You're the famous Father Cavanaugh?"

Cavanaugh's eyes clouded briefly. "I don't know about famous."

"Anybody who knew Eddie's heard about you. You were like one of the family."

The quick flush of pleasure, as quickly controlled. "I am family, Dismas. All but." He sipped his drink. "I've known Erin and Big Ed since high school. Introduced them, in fact, baptized all the children, then married Ed and Frannie, and now with this . . ."

He stopped, sighed, looked out into nothing over Hardy's shoulder. "I'm sorry."

"The Lord giveth and taketh away, I suppose. That's my counsel to the grieving, isn't it?" He smiled crookedly. "But He levies some burdens I don't understand, never will."

"I don't know if the Lord did this one," Hardy said.

"What do you mean?"

"Well, if Ed killed himself . . ."

Cavanaugh fixed him with a hard gaze. "Eddie didn't kill himself."

Hardy waited.

"I just buried him in consecrated ground, Dismas. If I had any belief at all that he killed himself, I couldn't have done that. Do you understand?"

"Do you understand what that means, Father? What you're saying?"

The priest squinted in the sun.

"It means somebody killed him."

Cavanaugh's hand went up to his eyes. He didn't seem to want to believe that either. "Well . . ." He knocked back the last of his drink. "I just . . . he couldn't have killed himself. He didn't do it. I am as certain of that as I am of you standing here."

"Why? Do you have any—?"

"Call it a moral conviction, but there's no doubt."

"Your glass is empty." It was Erin Cochran. Hardy noticed that she had put her arm through Cavanaugh's. "And I am dry myself."

Cavanaugh went to get her a refill.

"He seems like the perfect priest," Hardy said.

Erin paused, as though savoring some secret, looking after him. "Jim?" she said. "Oh, he is. He is the perfect priest."

Frannie sat up, covered with a comforter, and looked around the wall of the den. Moses had just gone to get Dismas—for some reason she had asked to see him, to thank him for catching her, she supposed. She couldn't exactly remember. Her mind kept flitting from thing to thing. It was weird.

It was probably good that Moses and Mom—she called Erin "Mom" —had decided to lay her down in here. She still felt weak, light-headed. Maybe that was why she kept forgetting things, changing her mind. She felt her forehead, which was still clammy.

Leaning her head back against the pillow, she let her eyes rest on the wall opposite her. There were the family pictures, the whole history of the Cochrans from Dad and Mom's wedding through her own to Eddie's. She remembered the pride she'd felt, the sense of belonging to a real family for the first time in her life, when the picture of their engagement—the one that had been in the *Chronicle*—had found its place on that wall.

It had been the perfect Cochran way. No fanfare. Just one time she came by and was watching TV with Eddie, sneaking in a little petting when they were left alone, and the picture was suddenly there. She looked at herself, next to Ed, smiling so hard her cheeks must have hurt, though she didn't remember that now. And then, next to it, the wedding picture. How could that be in the same life as this?

Then she thought of the baby picture that she'd envisioned as the next one. The baby. She crossed her hands over her stomach. "Oh, God," she whispered.

There was a knock on the door. Before she could answer, it opened and Eddie's sister Jodie looked in.

"Hi," she said. "You okay?"

Hardy saw the women hugging, crying together, and thought he would wait a little longer before going in to see Frannie. A door farther down the hallway stood open, and he walked into that other room to wait.

It was a strange place, out of context with the rest of the house. Rock posters on the lower end of the taste spectrum covered most available wall space. Shades were pulled down over the two windows, and Hardy had the sense that they were left down most of the time. In one corner a television set was on, the volume turned all the way down, the picture snowy and untuned as though it hadn't been touched for months.

It bothered him, and he walked over to turn it off.

"What are you doing here?"

It was the younger son, Steven, hands on the doorsill. "This is my room. What are you doing?"

"I was waiting for Frannie and your sister to finish crying, and I saw this TV on. I thought I'd turn it off."

"I want it on."

"Great, I'll leave it on. Good show?"

Steven ignored that, seemed to be studying him. "I know you, don't I?" Grudgingly, still hostile.

"Yeah, we met. Up at Frannie and Eddie's one time."

"That's it."

Steven seemed to file it away without interest. Hardy was categorized and put on a shelf in a certain place. After that, it seemed, he didn't exist.

Steven went and plopped himself on his bed, feet crossed at the ankles, and ran his hand through his spiky hair a couple of times. "You want to get out of the way?"

Hardy pulled a chair from under the writing desk and sat on it backward. "I'm trying to find who killed your brother."

No response. Steven just looked over at the droning white noise of the television. Hardy stood, strode over and slammed it off.

"Hey!"

"Hey, yourself. I don't care if you want to rot here in your room, but I'm trying to do a little good for Frannie at least, and if you know something that can help me I'm damn well gonna find out. Is watching your blank TV supposed to impress me with how tough you are? You don't feel anything about Eddie? About anything, right?"

Hardy watched the kid's bluff fade. He wasn't really angry, had just let his voice get louder. Now he sat down again, pulled closer to the bed. "You know, the option is you can help me if you want."

"I just don't believe Eddie's gone."

Hardy folded his hands, exhaled, looked down. "Yeah," he said, "that's the tough part."

"What do you mean you're trying to find who killed Eddie? I thought he killed himself."

"Why do you think that?"

The kid rolled his eyes up. Hardy reached down, grabbed Steven's ankle and started squeezing. Hardy had a good grip. Steven tried to pull away but couldn't do it.

Hardy forced a tight grip and spoke in a whisper. "Listen, you little shit, I do not need to take any high-school tough-guy attitude crap from you. Do you understand me?"

Hardy's left forearm was burning from the pressure. Steven's jaw was set. "Let go of my leg."

"Do you understand me?"

Steven took another five or six seconds to save a little face, then nodded and mumbled, "Yeah."

Hardy figured that was good enough. He let go. "Now, if you remember, I asked you why you thought Eddie killed himself. Did the police or somebody tell you that?"

Steven rubbed his ankle, but Hardy had gotten his attention. "I mean, he had a gun in his hand, didn't he? There was a note."

"It's easy to put a gun in the hand of somebody who's already dead.

And the note could have been anything. What I want to know is why you think it—that he killed himself?"

" 'Cause he was smart, and who's smart wants to live?"

It wasn't mock macho. The kid meant it. It rocked Hardy a little. He hung his head a minute, took a breath. "Hey, is it that bad, Steven?"

The boy just shrugged, his thin arms crossed on his chest.

"Was he depressed? Eddie, I mean."

"Yeah, I guess so."

Hardy looked up at him. "Why do you think I'm doing this? You think I want to be here, going over all this with anybody who'll talk to me? Would that be your idea of a good time?"

"I don't have any idea of a good time," the boy mumbled.

Hardy swallowed that. "Okay."

Steven reached into the top drawer of the dresser next to his bed and pulled out a switchblade knife that he began to snap open and closed methodically. Modern American worry beads, Hardy thought. Hiding his surprise, he asked where it had come from.

"Uncle Jim brought it back from Mexico."

"Uncle Jim?"

"Sure. You know. Father Cavanaugh. But don't tell Mom, would you? She'd probably be nervous."

After a minute Hardy was used to it—the skinny little kid moping on the bed, opening and closing a switchblade for solace.

"So you want to help?"

Steven closed the knife. Not exactly trust yet in the eyes, but at least a lack of active distrust. Probably the kid couldn't help Hardy at all, but it wouldn't hurt him—the way he felt about himself—if he felt he was doing something about his brother's death.

"What could I do?" he asked.

"Keep yourself alert. Think about things over the past month or two, anything Ed or anybody who knew him might have said or done, what he might have been up to, anything." He pulled out his wallet. "Here's a card. Why don't you keep it to yourself, same for me and the knife, right?"

Secrets together. As good a bond as many. "This is a neat card," Steven said.

Hardy got up. "Be careful with that switchblade," he said. Then, at

the door, he turned. "Think hard, Steven. Something's out there."
Maybe the wrong thing to say to a kid, but he wasn't editing just now.

Jodie and Frannie, holding hands, were standing in front of the wall of
the den now, looking at the pictures.

Hardy didn't knock. "Your family keeps Kodak in business," he said.

They turned, and Frannie introduced Jodie. Eighteen or so, she was
just passing through gangly. Her freckled face was still blotched from
the crying. Some baby fat rounded, but only slightly, the corners of her
cheekbones. Her wide blue eyes, also reddened, had irises flecked with
gold. Her nose wasn't perfect, but Hardy liked it, a little too flat at the
bridge and sticking out at the bottom like a baby's thumb.

She was obviously Erin's kid, but as with Steven and Ed, and even
Mick for that matter, there wasn't much sign of Big Ed's genes.

"You wanted to see me?"

Frannie, confused momentarily, stared back at the wall of pictures,
then again at Hardy. "I think . . ." She turned to Jodie and smiled.
"My mind . . ."

"It's okay," Hardy said. "It can wait."

"No, I know I asked Moses if I could see you, but I . . . this other
stuff . . ."

"Sure."

Jodie spoke up, her voice the echo of her mother's, cultured, not so
deep as to be husky, but adult. "I thought you were wonderful catching
Frannie. Thank you."

She turned to her sister-in-law. "You really went out. I don't know
how Mr. Hardy did it, but he was over to you—"

"That's it," Frannie said. "That reminds me."

"What?"

"Why I wanted to see you. I just remembered."

She let go of Jodie's hand and sat on an ottoman. "I've never fainted
before, so I didn't know it was even coming. It's just the last thing I
remember was I saw Mr. Polk there. He's . . . he was Ed's boss, I
mean the owner. He wasn't really a boss, I don't think. Ed was the real
manager, but he made policy, you know."

Hardy put up with the rambling. She had obviously thought of something, and would be getting to it.

"So when I saw him, I remembered again that you said I should tell you anything that might matter."

"And Mr. Polk's being there might matter?"

She shook out her red hair, then closed her eyes as though the thought had eluded her again. Jodie sat on the edge of the ottoman and put an arm over her shoulder. "It's okay, Frannie."

"It's just so hard to think." She pouted, biting her lip.

"Mr. Polk," Hardy said quietly.

"Oh, Mr. Polk, that's right."

"Why would it matter him being at the funeral, Frannie? It seems perfectly natural to me. Had they been fighting or something?"

"Oh no, nothing like that. It wasn't him being at the funeral." She still couldn't seem to find it. Hardy put his hands in his pockets and wandered over to the wall of pictures. Surrounding what looked like a college graduation picture of Eddie were plaques, diplomas, honors. He turned back to the young women. "Phi Beta Kappa?" he asked.

"Eddie was really smart," Jodie said. "He just didn't like showing off, but he was the smartest of us, except for maybe Steven, if he'd work at it."

"I just met Steven again. We had a nice talk."

"He's okay," Jodie said. "He just plays tough."

Hardy shrugged. "We got along . . ."

"I remember."

Hardy sat down on the end of the couch.

"It was Mr. Polk. I was just surprised to see him. Eddie said he hadn't been at work all last week until Friday, and then he'd been all distracted."

Hardy waited for her to continue.

"That's all," she said at last. "I'm sorry. I guess it's nothing, but you said . . ."

"No, Frannie," he said, "anything might be important." He didn't push her. He could find out more about that when he interviewed at Army.

"It's probably nothing," Frannie repeated.

"You thought it was worth telling me about. It's like when you took tests in school and your teacher always told you to go with your first answer. It can't hurt to say it."

Frannie looked over again at the photo wall. Jodie, next to her, stood up and spoke with a strained brightness. "Maybe we should go outside for a while, you think?"

"In a minute, okay."

The girl was gone, closing the door behind her. Hardy slid over on the couch, closer to Frannie. "You know," he said, "the fainting might have had something to do with being pregnant."

A nod. "I thought of that just before Jodie came in. You haven't told anybody, have you?"

"I said I wouldn't."

"I know, but . . ."

"No buts. No is no."

She smiled. "All right. Thank you."

Her head started to turn to look at the pictures again. Hardy spoke up. "You feel up to going out yet? It does get close in here."

She glanced toward the wall. "You're right. I'm sorry."

Hardy crossed over to her and lifted her gently by the shoulder. She leaned into him. "Let's go," she said, forcing a smile, "I can handle it."

"I don't get it."

"In your state, that is small wonder."

Moses McGuire turned his baleful gaze onto Hardy, who was negotiating traffic on Lincoln Boulevard. He had rolled the canvas top back on his car. "You took my keys, didn't you?"

Hardy's eyes shifted. "I've often warned you of the perils of leaving things in your coat pockets. Myself, I keep my valuables in my pants."

"I keep my valuables in my pants," McGuire echoed. "I try to get my valuable out of my pants as often as possible."

Hardy dug into his pocket, produced McGuire's key ring, and tossed it onto his lap. "Friends don't let friends drive drunk."

McGuire tried to whistle, but it came out wrong—his mouth wasn't at a hundred percent. "That's good. You just make that up? And I'm not drunk."

"You want to run that whistle by me again?"

" 'Cause I miss a whistle doesn't mean I'm drunk."

"Say 'miss a whistle' three times."

McGuire tried it once, then, "What are you, my mother?" He settled back in the seat. "Miss—a—fucking—whistle," he said.

Hardy pulled the car up at a light and turned toward his friend. "So what don't you get?"

McGuire took a minute to answer. Hardy reminded him. "You said you don't get it. What?"

"True love," he said finally.

"You mean Frannie and Ed?"

"Nope." McGuire faded out for a minute, then came back. "I mean Ed's parents. Tell me you didn't notice her, Erin?"

"I noticed her, Mose."

McGuire tried a whistle that came out better. "I don't care how old she is, she's the sexiest woman I've ever seen."

Hardy nodded. Even burying her son, Erin Cochran was something far beyond reasonably attractive.

"And with Big Ed for going on thirty years. How do you figure that, if not true love?"

"I didn't really meet the guy. He was just at the door. Nice enough, broken up, trying to keep it under control."

"But Erin and him?"

"Why not?"

"Hardy, the guy's been a gardener at the Park for his whole life. Okay, he works for the city, probably a good gig, but where's the romance? I mean, the guy's gotta live in horse manure."

"Who needs romance?"

"Wouldn't you think Erin would?"

Hardy shrugged. "Interesting question. I don't know."

"Gotta be true love, and I don't get it."

Hardy pulled the car up a block before the Shamrock. The day was hot and still. McGuire had put his head back against the seat. He looked beat, breathing heavily, regularly. "You sleeping, McGuire?"

His friend grunted.

"You sure you want to open the bar?"

McGuire lifted his head. "That priest . . . he's the kind of guy she ought to go for. Don't laugh, it happens." His eyes were bleary and red, the muscles in his face slack.

"You can't buy true love, huh?"

"It's a beautiful thing for a night or two." McGuire leaned his head back again, sighed. He spoke with his eyes closed, slumped down, his head resting on the back of the car seat. "You think Frannie's okay? She seem okay to you?"

"She'll make it, Mose. She's a tough one. You going to open or not?"

McGuire covered his eyes, noting where the car had stopped. "I don't think I'm up to the fast-lane glamor of the bar business today, you know?"

Hardy nodded, turned the key, started his car up again. As he pulled into traffic heading toward McGuire's apartment in the Haight-Ashbury, Moses said, "How do they do it, Diz?"

"What's that?"

"Hold together. All that family stuff."

"You and Frannie do it."

"We had to do it."

Hardy looked over at his friend, head back, mouth open, eyes shut. He looked strange in dark pants, a tan dress shirt, his tie loose. Normally Moses was a jeans-and-workshirt guy. Hardy noticed for the first time that his black hair was beginning to be shot with gray.

"Maybe they have to do it, too," Hardy said, "for some reason."

"Not like me and Frannie did."

Hardy knew he was right. Moses had raised his younger sister from the time he was sixteen and she was four. When he'd gone to Vietnam, which was where Moses and Hardy had met, she had just been starting high school and Moses was paying to have her board at Dominican up in Marin County.

"And 'sides," Moses slurred, "I'm talking sex. Not brothers and sisters. Ed and Erin. How do you keep that going thirty years?"

Hardy found a place to park in front of Moses's building. He pulled into it. "Practice, I guess."

10 ❧

L INDA POLK got up from her desk and walked the twenty feet down the hallway to the women's room. At Army Distributing, the women's room was Linda's exclusive domain—she was the only female employee, and guests were few and far between, especially lately. Alphonse coming in, hassling her about where her daddy was, had been the only person who'd been in the whole day. And he'd gone long before noon.

She flicked the light switch and walked in front of the mirror to look at herself. Not too bad. Rings under the eyes were covered pretty well. The blondish bleach job was holding up okay. She liked the purplish tint to the eyeshadow. Maybe a touch-up on the mascara, not that it really mattered here.

No, she'd pass on that. She didn't come in here to fix herself up. She smiled. Yes, she did, she thought, only not that kind of fix.

She'd rolled the stuff at home, hidden it in the package of Virginia Slims, and taking it out, smiled again in anticipation. She'd really come a long way, baby.

It was the very best of the third world—C & C. Colombian and crack, although just a tiny bit of the latter. She lit the joint and inhaled deeply, holding it. Before she'd even let out the breath, the first jolt of the crack kicked in. She allowed herself one more. It was a good mix. The crack pumped you up to the sky, but the marijuana made coming down very nice.

Putting half the joint back into the cigarette box, she checked herself out one last time in the mirror and smiled prettily at herself. "Linda means pretty," she said aloud, and giggled.

The mood was nearly wrecked immediately as she came out to the hallway. First, the heel on her shoe slipped on the tile and broke off. She would have fallen but for the wall.

"Fuck."

Holding the wall with one hand, she was balancing herself to take off her shoes when an unknown face looked out from her office. "Can I help you?"

A man, and not bad-looking. Not too well dressed, but not a slob, either. She smiled crookedly, suddenly feeling dizzy with the rush of drugs. Damn, here she'd been alone all day and—it was just her luck—the minute she decided to let go just a little, someone shows up.

"I'm sorry," she said to the man, standing there in the hallway with her shoes in her hand. Next she'd probably run her nylons.

The man shrugged. "No problem. I was hoping to find Mr. Polk? Is he in?"

She walked toward him, then brushed against him as she went around to her desk. She'd be better if she was sitting down. The man looked at the nameplate on her desk. "Are you his wife?"

She laughed at that, shallowly. "No, his daughter."

Suddenly she stood up again, extended her hand. "Linda Polk, daughter of Samuel Polk and descendant of U.S. President James K. He was just after Lincoln, I think."

The man had a firm, dry, no-nonsense shake. "I think maybe a little earlier," he said.

"Whatever." The glow was coming up roses. She could feel herself expanding, becoming nicer, easier to talk to, to like.

"Is your father in today?"

"No. He had a funeral this morning, then he and Nika—" She stopped. Nika. She didn't want to get concentrating on Nika.

The man smiled. He had a wonderfully inviting smile. "I came from the funeral myself. I'm a friend of Ed Cochran's. Or was."

He extended a card that seemed to hover a long way away in his hand until she reached out and grabbed it. "My name's Dismas Hardy, Linda. Do you expect your father back today?"

"I never expect him back."

Whoops. She hadn't meant to say that. "I mean, back the way he was."

"Was when?"

"Back before Nika."

"When was that, Linda?"

She liked the way he kept saying her name. He really was a nice-

looking man, maybe a little old. Thirty-five? Good tan for a city guy.
Maybe he did a lot of work outside.

"Pardon?" she said.

"When was before Nika?"

She waved a hand abstractedly. "Nika, that's right. I guess late last
summer, then they got married before Christmas, and that's when
everything seemed to start going wrong."

"You mean with the business?"

"No, no, no. Not the business. That wasn't 'til later. I mean with me
and Daddy."

Oh damn, she was going to cry again. That was the only bad thing
about the pot—it got all the emotions stirred up. The trick was to quick
get onto something else. "The business," she said, "wasn't 'til the
whole thing with *La Hora*, like in February."

But the man, surprisingly, didn't pick up on that. "What happened
with you and your daddy?"

He acted like he really cared. He was sitting back comfortably in his
chair, hands folded across his chest, more relaxed than she was. In fact,
just looking at him made her feel better. "I'm sorry," she said, "I get all
emotional sometimes."

He nodded.

"Because before Nika . . . Well, you know my mom died when I
was ten—that's ten years ago, can you believe it?—and Daddy and I
were always, after that, like best friends. I mean, I came to work here
when he was building up the business and we did everything together,
and it was like we were a team. And it wasn't like he didn't have
girlfriends. That was cool. I mean, I wasn't, we weren't weird, you
know. But Nika was different."

He leaned forward. "Different how?"

"Just so, I don't know, overpowering. And I don't get it. Have you
ever seen her or my dad?"

"I guess they were at the funeral but I didn't know who they were."

"Well, come look at this."

She led the way back into her father's office, with its big desk. And
there was the picture, bigger than it needed to be in its silver frame.
"Here, there's my dad with Nika. I don't think she's that pretty."

For as long as she could stand it, she glared at her new step-mother,
probably only five years older than she was, though of course Nika

would never say. It was, she admitted, a good picture but not a good likeness. It made her look more beautiful. And she wasn't beautiful, not in real life.

She could tell the man only saw the outside, couldn't tell from the picture how ugly she was underneath. He said: "I wouldn't call her pretty at all."

He was standing very close, right beside her. He smelled like a clean man—some hints of after-shave, maybe a pipe. But no sweat or gasoline like most of the guys she saw.

"They don't really belong together," she said. She realized she was still without shoes. Turning, facing the man, she raised her chin for a minute, then hitched herself onto her father's desk. "What's your name again?"

"Dismas. Diz for short."

"I'm a little diz for dizzy," she said, giggling.

"Probably better to be sitting down, then." Unexpectedly, he reached out and touched her face, a light touch that tingled all over her. "Are you all right? Would you like some water?"

Without waiting for an answer he was gone, back quickly with her coffee cup filled with water from the fountain. It was like he knew his way around already.

She was ready for him to put his arms around her and do anything he liked at all, but instead he went to the couch and sat on the end of it. She sipped at the cup.

"So when Nika and your dad got married, things changed?"

She looked down. "He was like a different person. Just didn't have time for me or anybody, or even the business, anymore. All he wanted to do was spend time"—a shot at Nika's face—"with her."

"And you think that's been the problem with the business? I thought Ed was trying to get it back on track?"

"Oh, Eddie. Eddie was great. I didn't mean to say he wasn't good. At the job, I mean. Fair, and, you know, a really nice guy. No hassles, you know?" She sipped again at the water. "I can't believe what they say, that he killed himself."

Hardy let that go for now. "But there have been problems with the business, and they happened when Ed was managing, right?"

"Well, yes but no. It would've happened with anybody. It was all stuff about *La Hora* and *El Dia.*"

"You said that before. What does that mean?"

"You know *El Dia*, don't you?"

He shook his head.

"Well, it's another paper, you know, like *La Hora*, that wanted us to distribute it. *La Hora* was our biggest client but then they dropped us, took it all back in-house." She looked around her father's office. "And by then it was too late to get *El Dia*. They'd set themselves up with other distributors. Old Cruz really screwed us." She shook her head, swinging her legs in frustration.

"Is that why it's so deserted around here?"

Now was her chance. "That, just the slow business, and Ed's funeral being today. There's nobody here at all except us. Nobody's been in at all." Flirty eye move, shrug the breasts out. "And it's late. I don't expect anybody to come the rest of the day. I could even lock up now and it wouldn't matter."

He stood up, and she slid off the desk with a little bounce. "Well, you've been very helpful, Linda. Thanks."

Another handshake. Again cool, dry, firm. She held it an extra couple of seconds, looked into his gray eyes. "We could get a drink maybe. There's a lot we can talk about. Or just stay here," she repeated.

A little peck on the cheek. "Thanks. I'd like that," he said, "but I'm working now and I've got another appointment. Maybe a rain check, okay?"

"Sure, that's cool."

Out now to her desk. "Wait just a second," she said.

She jotted her name and number on her notepad and tore off the sheet. "In case you remember something you wanted to ask."

Then he was gone. She watched him walk across the empty lot through waves of late-afternoon heat. When he got in his car he turned back to look at the door and she waved a hand at him, but he probably couldn't see her through the reflection.

Anyway, he didn't wave back.

She turned the knob, locking the door, padded back to her desk and, sitting down, reached into her purse for the pack of Virginia Slims.

Linda was right, Hardy was thinking. I wouldn't call Nika pretty. It would be like calling the Grand Canyon pretty, or Michelangelo's David. Of course, he remembered her from the funeral, the way she kept staring at him. At least now he had a name to go with it—Nika Polk.

Where had she come from, he wondered, and what was it about sad-looking, basset-eared Sam Polk that had snagged her?

He closed his eyes, trying to visualize her again. She was tall, taller than her husband, perhaps five-eight, jet black hair over a classically hard Mediterranean face. A stunning face. Half-parted lips that she kept licking.

The only reason Hardy had caught Frannie when she'd started to faint was that Nika had been standing just behind her, and he had kept tearing his eyes away, forcing himself to look elsewhere. Frannie had been in his line of vision. It had been luck.

She had worn a simple woolen black cotton suit, severely cut, that nevertheless hadn't diminished the thrust of her breasts above a waist Hardy thought he could encircle with both hands.

He shook his head. No, Linda, he thought, Nika ain't that pretty at all.

He started the engine up. He wanted to go back and talk to Cruz, and besides, it would be cooler moving.

So Sam Polk had married Nika about six months ago. He looked to be around fifty-five. She was mid-twenties, maybe a little more. Got to be money, Hardy thought, at least to some extent. And after they'd gotten married, Polk had started having troubles with his business. It wasn't that far a leap to assume that those troubles had led to problems at home.

But what was he thinking? There had been no hint of any trouble between Sam and Nika. What had made him think that?

And then he remembered her eyes fixing on him at the cemetery. He'd seen eyes like that before—the flirting hadn't been playful, it was dead serious. The eyes of Nika Polk weren't those of a happily married woman.

Had she ever looked at Eddie Cochran that way?

*J*OHN STROUT made his personal policy very clear in the first month of his tenure as San Francisco's coroner. The responsibility of that position, according to U.S. Government Code 27491, is to determine the "cause, circumstances and manner of death" of individuals dying within a particular jurisdiction. And under "manner of death," there are only four possibilities: natural causes, accident, suicide, or death at the hands of another.

In the course of doing that job, however, other elements, many of them political, have an opportunity to come into play. Strout, a tall, soft-spoken gentleman originally from Atlanta, wasn't about to let anybody or anything affect his judgment on causes of death, and so he decided early on to send a message to those who would prefer a quick and sloppy verdict over a slow and correct one.

The victim in the case had been the cousin of the mayor and—not the greatest coincidence in the world, given the size of the city— brother-in-law to one of the supervisors. Strout came in to work that morning and found the morgue overrun with media people as well as with members of both the mayor's and supervisor's staffs.

Strout glanced at the body before going to his office, where he was hounded to issue some statement. He figured it was as good a time as any to get the word out.

A reporter for the *Chronicle* finally asked him point-blank, and rather insultingly, if he planned to make any decision at all in the foreseeable future. Strout had stood up to his full height behind his desk. "Seeing as this victim was stabbed twice and shot five times"—he said in his most syrupy drawl—"I'm very close, and you can print this, very close . . ."—he paused and smiled at the assemblage—"very close indeed to rulin' out suicide."

Strout wasn't about to hurry and be wrong. After eleven years as coroner, it was gospel that once Strout gave a verdict, you could take it to the bank.

Now Carl Griffin and Vince Giometti sat in the air-conditioned visitors' room at the San Francisco morgue. It was not a decorator's paradise. The long yellow couch was too low, the commercial prints on the walls were ugly and hung too high. The only living plant by the one window to the right of the couch was no greener or prettier than the three plastic floral arrangements that graced, respectively, the center table (too short for the couch), the blue plastic end table, and the pitted mahogany sideboard.

Griffin and Giometti sat on either end of the couch. Between them, in an almost-new cardboard briefcase, was the file on the Cochran case. Giometti, a new father, had just finished saying something that made Griffin explode.

"Do I gotta hear this right after lunch? You think this is interesting? You believe anybody cares what your baby's bowel movements look like, whether it's hard or soft or runny or whether the goddamn corn gets digested on its way through?" Griffin jumped up, unable to sit still. "Christ!"

"If you had a kid, you'd know how important it was."

"Why do you think I never had a kid? You think that was just dumb luck? You may not believe this, but I thought about it at one time, and you know what decided it for me?" He went down on one knee in front of his rookie partner. "I asked myself this question: I said, 'Think about the reality of babyhood, and what's the first thing that comes to your mind?'"

Giometti started to answer, but Griffin put up a hand.

"No, let me finish. The first thing that came to my mind was shit. Rivers of it every day for like a couple of years. Then I asked myself another question: Is there anything I like about shit? I mean, its smell, texture, various colors? Do I look at it the way Eskimos look at snow, with nuances and a hundred different names? No, shit is shit. And I am not interested in any of it—your kid's, my own, any of it, okay?" He stood up. "So from today on can we do without the daily bm moment, please?"

He turned away and walked over to the window, breathing hard. He rubbed a leaf of the plant between thumb and forefinger.

"It's a natural function, Carl," Giometti said. "You shouldn't be so uptight about it."

Griffin thought he'd leave a thumbprint on the leaf, he squeezed it so hard.

He heard the door open. Strout was shaking Vince's hand, coming over to him. It wasn't exactly how he'd wanted it. He would have preferred to be calm and dispassionate, and now, if he knew Strout at all and he did, his mood might affect Strout's decision. Well, if he played it right, maybe it could work to his advantage.

"So, boys," Strout said after he'd sat in a straight-back chair he'd pulled up to the too-short table, "what have you got here?"

Giometti opened the briefcase and took out the file. Griffin thought it would be wiser, also good experience for the kid, to let his partner talk until he'd calmed down, and he loitered again over by the window, hands in pockets.

"Well, sir, the deceased was having troubles at work. In fact, the job was about to come to an end."

"Any medical corroboration of depression?"

"No, sir, not formal."

"Informal?"

"The family, not his wife, but his family family."

Griffin saw Strout's face stretch slowly. "You mean the one he grew up with? We call that the nuclear family, officer."

It went right by Giometti. "Yeah, well," he said, "the nuclear family said he'd been on edge the last couple of weeks."

Strout turned to Griffin. "Serious?"

"Couple of arguments with his father. Like that."

"Did they say over what?"

Giometti took it again. "Something, he thought, about his work."

Griffin: "We checked it out. The place is going bust. He was the manager."

Strout was inclined to be skeptical. "He cared enough about it to kill himself?"

Griffin finally sat down. "It's possible, sir. Guy was an overachiever his whole life, was planning on going to business school down at Stanford this fall. Could've ruined his image of himself, running a company going down the tubes."

Strout nodded, silent. "All right," he said, "marital?"

"Okay, even good," Giometti said.

Griffin added, "The wife spent the night of his death talking to his mother. Two-hour conversation. Phone records verify it."

"Worried about him?"

"This and that, but generally that's my conclusion," Griffin said.

"Any mental history at all?"

Giometti shook his head. Griffin said, "How 'bout you, sir? You find something?"

Strout leaned forward, putting his weight on his elbows, his elbows on his knees. Griffin noticed that the man's eyebrows were so bushy they tangled in his lashes when he opened his eyes wide.

"I find a healthy young man," Strout began, "with a good marriage. Good family. No history of mental illness. He's got powder burns on his left hand and a hole in the half of his head that's left."

Giometti spoke up. "Oh, the gun was fired twice, you know."

"The gun was fired twice. So what? Only one slug went in." Strout's lashes kissed his brows, looking at Griffin.

"Happens a lot," Griffin said. "And while we're at it, the gun was unregistered."

Strout nodded. "Of course."

Giometti butted in. "While we're at things, nobody seems to want to talk about the note."

"The fuckin' note . . . ," Griffin said.

"It was a note," Giometti insisted.

"It was a piece of crumpled paper," Griffin answered, not wanting to get drawn into anything in front of Strout.

But it was too late. "Are you telling me we have a suicide note, officer?" Strout rolled his eyes up, up, out of his head. "Are we wasting our time here?"

"It's not exactly the Rosetta Stone of suicide notes," Griffin said.

"It's a note next to a body lying by a gun, though. . . ."

"Not even that." Griffin told him about finding it in the car, what it said, or, more particularly, didn't say.

Strout chewed on it a moment, then nodded, deciding, going on to something else. "Might he have been gay?"

That was always a question in the city, Griffin knew. "No sign of it," he said, glad to put the note behind them.

"No, there wasn't," Strout agreed. "Anyway, that's what I find. Let's be frank, gentlemen. Have you found anything points to a homicide here?"

Griffin and Giometti exchanged glances. "What we found," Giometti said, "doesn't point either way. We got a dead kid alone in a shitty place at night. A couple of random weirdnesses, like two shots," he glanced at his partner, "maybe, *maybe* a note. Maybe he just got depressed, I don't know. Maybe we need more time."

"Everybody needs more time," Strout said.

"On the other hand," Griffin said, "it wasn't a random parking lot—Cochran did deliver there. People knew who he was, but we've checked into that and there's nothing evident."

Strout cracked his knuckles. "But we do have a note, don't we?" He sighed. "In the absence of any hard evidence to the contrary, I'm inclined to lean toward a suicide, then. But I'm a little reluctant. It's not very tight, is it?"

Giometti spoke up. "You know if we go with suicide, the widow gets no insurance."

"Insurance isn't my problem," Strout snapped. "Carl, you got something, give it to me, would you?"

Griffin thought about the chances of himself becoming lieutenant. He knew he could continue to conduct the best investigation in the history of the department and it wouldn't mean beans. On the other hand, if Glitsky fucked up . . .

Face facts, he told himself. Strout was right. There was no hard evidence that the boy had been murdered. If there was, *and* if they busted tail for a week or a month, chances are that he and Vince would find something. *If* it was there. But the two of them so far had been thorough, if not inspired. Maybe somebody wanted him especially, Carl Griffin, to hump his ass for a month and come up empty. Okay, then, he thought. They want inspiration, they can hold the carrot out.

"I don't know," he said, "I'm a little worried about the lack of motive. Nobody we talked to had a bad word to say, much less wanted to kill him."

Strout rose to it. "All right, then, let's go with suicide/equivocal, see if something turns up."

Back in their car, Giometti seemed sullen.

"What's eating you?" Griffin asked, knowing full well what it was.

"This guy didn't kill himself."

"He didn't, huh?"

"You know he didn't."

Griffin slammed the dashboard. "Don't tell me what I know, Vince. I been at this a long time." He was feeling Giometti's look on him. He took a breath. Giometti hit the ignition. "Turn off the car," he said, leaning his head back against the seat, closing his eyes. "I'll tell you something, Vince. I honestly don't know. I'm an evidence cop. You give me something to go on, and I'm on it like white on rice. But what do we got here? We've interviewed the wife—suspect number one if you go by the stats. She was home all night talking to the guy's mother. Who else? Cruz, the guy who owns the lot and building? He's with his boyfriend. Okay, maybe not, but we couldn't break him—either of them—could we?"

Giometti nodded grudgingly.

"Polk? His foxy wife? No way. This guy Cochran was their star. It was all on him to make the business work, or keep working. Losing fight, and he took it hard. It may not be a good motive, but right now it's our only motive. He drove out there, depressed. He started to write a note, saw the futility of that and stopped in the middle. He'd gotten this piece from somewhere and shot it once to make sure he knew how it worked. It's sad as hell, but I can see it happening. I've *seen* it happen. A lot of times."

Griffin was winding down. "Look," he said, "we got five righteous homicides besides maybe this one. Maybe, probably, another gets reported this afternoon or tonight. How much time you want to waste on this one?"

"It's not wasted if somebody killed him."

"True. But we got nothing pointing anywhere. We get something, anything, we go back on it. It's not like it's closed—it's equivocal. We haven't given up, technically. We're just putting it on hold in lieu of evidence. Vince, look, we're in the collar game. You want to make it in homicide, bring in your collars. These other ones, put 'em on your desk. Check 'em every few months. Keep an open mind. But if nothing sticks out after three, four days of looking—and I mean nothing . . ." He shrugged.

"Cruz wouldn't see you today?"

"Too busy today, he said."

"Does he think you're a cop?"

"Abe, I'd never impersonate a police officer. That's a felony, I'm pretty sure."

"But he might, at your first interview, have reached the conclusion that you were of the city's finest?" Glitsky tolerantly scratched at the scar that ran between his lips.

"It's always surprising what the mind can sometimes come up with," Hardy said. "I guess it's possible he thought that if he let his imagination run wild."

Glitsky's telephone rang. It was five o'clock, and Hardy settled back, relaxed. It had been a long day, but not without its rewards. Even Cruz refusing to see him had been instructive.

Into the phone, Abe was saying something about angles of knife wounds, heights of suspects. Hardy listened with one ear. It was real, that kind of stuff, like his problem with Eddie Cochran having been right-handed.

Glitsky hung up. As though there'd been no interruption, he continued. "So what about when Cruz realizes that you're not a cop?"

"Why would he do that?"

Glitsky tried to sound patient. "Because, Hardy, cops get interviews. They don't say, 'Sorry, I'll come back tomorrow.' They flash their buzzer and say, 'Look, I'm busy too.' "

"I never used to do that."

"Which is not to say it's not the proper procedure." The inspector got up abruptly. "Want some coffee?"

Hardy shook his head. "If you got a beer?"

Glitsky reached into the drawer under the Mr. Coffee and tossed Hardy a warm sixteen-ounce can of Schlitz. "Alcohol is forbidden anywhere in this building." He didn't go around again behind his desk but sat against the edge of the steel file cabinet sipping at his black coffee, waiting.

Hardy pulled the tab on the can, sipped, and grimaced. "It ain't Bass Ale."

"Fresh, though. It's probably only been in there about two years."

After the first taste, though, it didn't bother Hardy. He took another. "So what's suicide/equivocal?"

"Suicide/equivocal means Strout—the M.E.—wants to straddle the fence."

"Why?"

" 'Cause he's got a rep for not being wrong."

"But I've got to have it come down one way or the other."

Glitsky stared out the window, sipping his coffee.

"Yo, Abe," Hardy said.

"Griffin came by and said it was a bullshit verdict, should have been a righteous suicide. He said he'd recommended that to Strout."

"So he's not inclined to do anything else?"

Glitsky motioned to his desk. "There's the file. He gave it to me, said I should tell my friend—that's you, Diz—to call him if you found anything. So no, I'd say Griffin's not gonna do much."

"But the case is still open?"

Glitsky shrugged. "Some cases stay open. It's a technicality."

"It sucks." Hardy drank half the can of beer as Glitsky continued memorizing the skyline until he finally said, "If you got anything, I'll listen."

"I got *nada*," Hardy admitted. "Cruz told me a flat-out lie. I directly asked him if he'd known Eddie Cochran and he paused, thought about it, and said no. I wonder why. That kind of thing."

"And he wouldn't see you."

"Yeah, that."

They were silent. Outside Glitsky's office, there were sounds of people going home. Hardy could see the traffic backing up on the Oakland Bridge. He drank some warm beer, then reached over and grabbed the file off Glitsky's desk, began leafing through the few pages.

After a minute, Hardy tapped the file. "Like here. Look at this."

Glitsky came to stand over his shoulder.

"Yeah, that's weak," he said.

" 'I'm sorry. I've got to . . . ,' " Hardy read. "What's that supposed to mean?"

"Maybe he had to go to the bathroom."

"Maybe anything. Griffin calls this a suicide note?"

"He doesn't say not."

Hardy closed the file. "Abe, this isn't exactly what you'd call compelling. Where'd they find it?"

"In the car." Glitsky pointed down on the page. "See, there. In the car."

"Not on his person even? He might've written this a year ago."

"I know." Glitsky crossed to the window, leaned out over to see the street down below. "Maybe something else is going on."

"Yeah, and maybe that something is screwing Frannie out of her insurance."

Glitsky, without turning around, nodded. "Maybe."

Hardy went back to reading, tipping the beer back. "And this? Griffin couldn't tell me this?"

"What?"

"The gun was fired twice. What? Ed wanted to take a few rounds of target practice so he'd be sure he didn't miss?"

Glitsky said nothing. Hardy turned more pages, paused at the photographs, closed the file and drank more beer. "Sucks, this really sucks."

Glitsky went back to the file drawer and leaned against it. "I tell you what, Diz. You find me some evidence for feeling like that."

Hardy nodded. This was a first-time, maybe one-time offer. A good sign. It undoubtedly nagged at Glitsky too. Hardy forced himself to look back at the pictures of Ed, the gun maybe a foot from his right hand. Under his head, a large pool had formed, looking black under the camera's lights. He stared at the picture a long time, the body lifeless, lying on its side, perhaps two feet from the building.

"You also wonder, if he killed himself, that he wasn't sitting back against the building when he pulled the trigger," Hardy said.

Glitsky finished his coffee and dropped the Styrofoam cup into the wastebasket. "Yeah, you do," he said. "It's a marvel how much there is to wonder about."

12 ❦

*A*RTURO CRUZ had the top down on his Jaguar XK-E, enjoying the rare warm evening as he drove up out of China Basin on his way home.

Last night, he'd been furious with Jeffrey. For one of the first times since they'd been together, they hadn't made love. Jeffrey had gotten huffy and stormed out before dinner and hadn't come back until this morning.

So when he walked into the office, all Cruz could think of was his relief that he was back, and he hugged him, his anger forgotten, the reason for the fight, everything. If he was back, then everything was okay.

And everything had been all right again. A good day, a good issue on the streets, another good one put to bed. The May figures of *La Hora* had come in and ad linage was up six percent over last May. Revenues up over fourteen percent!

And the revenue increase was all because of their circulation, on which they based their ad rates. And now, with distribution going in-house, the bottom-line figure would skyrocket next year. If they could keep *El Dia* away from their market share. But they would do that. *La Hora* was the better paper. *El Dia* was still a rag, maybe five years away from quality.

Still, the threat, though distant, caused him to frown. He had to keep his eye on the ad linage. If that dipped, even a little, it might mark a trend. He'd better have some projection graphs made tomorrow.

He dictated a memo on that, then put the handheld tape recorder into its holder on the dashboard. That was enough business. And it *had* been a good day.

Until that fellow Hardy had come back. And thinking of that, he almost got mad again. Why had Jeffrey told Hardy he had known Ed

87

Cochran? And how had he, Cruz, then been so stupid as to deny it? The day before, he'd told the other inspector, Giometti, that they'd been business acquaintances. Well, that's probably what Hardy had come back for, about that inconsistency.

Cruz would just say—now that he'd examined it—that he thought Hardy had been talking about a personal relationship between him and Cochran. That would take care of it. But in any event, he had to clear up the misunderstanding with Jeffrey.

He turned his car left onto Market, lowered the visor against the setting sun. He should have taken care of it today, but with Jeffrey coming back, he'd been so happy, it had just slipped his mind. That wouldn't do, he thought. That kind of carelessness.

He would have to watch it. And, uncomfortable though it might be, he would have to talk to Jeffrey about it again. But this time it would be when he was relaxed. And he wouldn't be angry—he'd simply explain it all very clearly so that all the nuances would be understood. Then, if Hardy or Giometti came around again, they'd be ready for him, and the questions could stop.

That was all he wanted, really. That the questions stop.

Hardy opened the door to Schroeder's, an old-fashioned German restaurant downtown, and was nearly overwhelmed with a sense of déjà vu. It had been a favorite haunt back in his post-cop days as an assistant D.A., before the divorce with Jane.

He realized he hadn't been in the place since that time, maybe eight years before. He wasn't at all surprised to find it hadn't changed a bit. What was atypical, he knew, was how he felt—he actually wouldn't mind casually running into someone. Almost anybody. And Schroeder's had been that kind of place back then—off-duty cops, other D.A.s, reporters, attorneys who weren't corporate and didn't want to be. People hanging out, mingling, schmoozing over a few beers.

Tonight, if it worked out, he might get back in touch with the city he lived in. Or not. He thought it sort of interesting that he considered it.

Afterward, he wasn't sure about the order of the two jolts. He had just gotten his Dortmunder and was looking around, enjoying the feel of things, when his ex-wife Jane stood up not forty feet from him across the room. That was the first one. Then came the sharp first tremor of the earthquake.

Hardy stood up and made his way through tables, away from Jane, until he got to the hallway leading back to the rest rooms.

It was a good shaker, perhaps a five or six, and it continued rolling as he walked. The restaurant became quiet as everyone held their breath. The chandeliers swung heavily and several glasses fell from the back of the bar. Hardy stood, in theory secure under a beam, and waited.

The tremor stopped, and after a round of nervous laughter, the room went back to being itself. Hardy watched Jane walk directly toward him.

She looked, after eight years, impossibly the same. Now thirty-four, she could have passed for twenty-five. Her face was still as unlined, unmarked by the passage of years, as a baby's. That made sense, Hardy thought. It's what lack of a sense of guilt could do for you.

She was still unaware of him, and he couldn't help taking her in. Tall, slim, radiant dark hair casting highlights even in the dim room. Looking down slightly as she walked—graceful, serene. The face again, he kept coming back to the face, with its slightly Oriental cast, though no one knew where that had come from. It was really only a heaviness in the eyelids, but with the wide cheekbones, the rosebud lips, there was a geisha air. She was elegantly dressed, as always. Gold earrings. A blouse in pink silk, pleated dark blue skirt, low heels.

Now ten feet away, she finally looked up, and there it was, that million-dollar slow smile that had completely changed his life. She stopped, looked, let the smile build just slowly enough to work on him. And it did. He found himself smiling back.

"Small world," he said, his first words to her since he'd left their house.

Of course she would kiss him, hug him. But not gushing. Slow and savoring. An old, old and very dear friend. "You look wonderful," she said. "How have you been? How are you? What are you doing now?"

He had to laugh. "I'm good, Jane. I've been fine."

She touched his arm, smiled into his eyes. "I can't believe I'm seeing you."

She stopped, impulsively hugged him again.

Some sense-memory made him remember why it had been so hard to consider someone, anyone else. His whole being just responded to her. It wasn't a social thing. He just looked at her and smiled, his life full and complete, like a moonstruck teenager.

But a half-dozen-plus years don't, after all, go away without a trace. Whole new synapses had been created, and the warning janglings that he felt had become a part of his makeup were sounding like crazy.

"Who are you here with?"

She still held his arms, just above his elbows. "Just Daddy and some friends."

Daddy. Judge Andy Fowler. The doyen of the San Francisco bench —who'd gotten Dismas his first interview for D.A., who'd been, during the troubles, a surprising confidant.

Then that sly look. "Why do you want to know?"

He told himself to stop smiling, dammit, but standing here so close to her, looking into her amused eyes, even now catching a whiff of the perfume . . .

"I thought maybe a drink would be nice."

She nodded. "I'd like that." Then, "If you want."

He laughed, shrugged. "I don't know if I want, to tell you the truth."

She kissed him again, quickly. "Let me go pee and dump Daddy."

"No one?" she asked. "Didn't you wish you could love anybody?"

She drank Absolut now, rocks. She had given up smoking. He told himself she couldn't possibly care about his nonexistent love life.

"I don't know anymore if love's a feeling or an attitude."

She laughed, throat extended, looking up. "Dismas," she said when the laugh was all finished. She sipped her drink. "That is such a Dismas thing to say."

Why didn't that annoy him?

"Well, the point is, I never felt enough, you know, to make any decisions."

"Decisions?"

"Not decisions, really. I guess commitments." He swallowed the rest of his scotch and signaled the bartender for another round./

Jane covered his hand with her own. "I'm sorry. I wasn't laughing at you."

"I know."

She squeezed the hand gently, not coming on. Not consciously coming on.

"Anyway,"—leaving his hand on the bar covered with hers—"there hasn't been anyone. Where there was anything going on, I mean." He didn't like the way that made it sound—as though he'd been pining away for Jane. "But it's been no big deal," he said, "one way or the other." There, that put it in perspective. "How about you?" he asked.

To his surprise, she'd been married and divorced again.

"It wasn't very serious," she said. "It was more a rebound thing."

"Being married wasn't serious?"

She sighed. "It seemed serious for a while. I guess I was just lonely, confused, you know. It wasn't long after"—she hesitated, perhaps wondering what it would sound like—"us."

The new round came, and she moved her hand. Hardy watched it tap the bar once, then settle into her lap. He reached over and held it.

Holding her hand in her lap.

"I don't care," he said, not sure what he was referring to.

"Dismas," she began, squeezing his hand.

He interrupted her. "Let's go outside."

The night was still warm. The building felt almost hot as he pressed her up against it.

No nonsense. None at all. Out the side door to the alley and around the back, near the employee entrance, between some parked cars, empty cardboard boxes scattered here and there. A building or two down there was a light, up high.

Holding hands all the way out, then stopping when they had turned the corner. The kiss openmouthed, hungry. Backing away a step, pulling up the skirt, stepping out of the shoes. A quick look around, then the hose down and off and thrown somewhere, maybe into one of the boxes.

And then the warm building, Hardy's pants not even down, pressing it to her, into her, wet and ready, legs hitched up high on his hips, the kissing wonderful wordless pumping of it.

"Oh, God, Daddy's still here."

Hardy had her arm. They, neither of them, were about to invite the other back to their respective houses, and so they decided on a nightcap back inside.

"What if he'd come out . . ."

"Knowing Andy, he would've come back in here and had a drink and he'd never let on he saw us."

"What if he notices my stockings?"

Hardy squeezed the arm. "You're not wearing any."

A look that said "That's what I mean," when suddenly there was no avoiding him, getting up from his table as they came in.

Hardy was still weak in the knees, wanting to talk to Jane about what it might mean, but knowing he'd have to put that off. Andy saw him, flashed a look at his daughter, then closed the space between them.

"You said an old friend," to Jane, with some hint of reproof, "not old family."

The eyes took Hardy in. "You look fine, son. Life treating you okay?"

They got through the small talk, meeting his dinner companions, who were going home anyway, getting to the bar. If Hardy looked fine, Andy looked incredible. Still skinny as a stick, face unlined, hair thick and the color of stout. Dressed now in a camel's-hair sport coat and tie.

Andy wasn't famed for a beat-around-the-bush approach. "So what's with you two together?" was the first thing he asked at the bar.

"Pure accident," Jane answered.

"Anybody believes in pure accidents in this life isn't paying close enough attention." He sipped a cognac. "Maybe meeting here was an accident, but sitting here with me two hours later has the ring of volition."

Hardy laughed. Andy had the same style from the bench. He took it right to Hardy. "So what are you doing with yourself? I keep expecting to see you in court one of these days. Get back to the trade."

Jane sat between them, included by position. Hardy talked a little, occasionally touching Jane's back with the flat of his hand. She leaned back or over—into it.

Hardy, ex-assistant D.A., shook his head. "I'm just not that cerebral. I think if I did anything I'd go back to being a cop."

Andy raised his eyebrows. "Doesn't rule out cerebral."

"Maybe we don't know the same cops."

"If we're talking cerebral, maybe we don't know the same attorneys."

"Anyway," Hardy continued, "I think my friend Glitsky might try to help me get back on the force, but I'm not really inclined to it. I don't like having a boss."

"Me neither. Oh, for a spot on the federal bench!"

But this was an old lament, and not too sincere. Federal judges were appointed for life and, barring outrageous impeachable conduct—a likelihood never ever to occur with Andy Fowler—the job was one of those on earth most resembling God's. But Andy had been at Superior Court for twenty-five years, and Hardy knew he was happy there. Not that he wouldn't take the job with no boss, but he wasn't lobbying for it.

After Hardy had gotten into what he was doing now, Andy stopped smiling.

"I know a little about Arturo Cruz," he offered. "He's a dirty son of a bitch, isn't he?"

This was news to Hardy, who knew only that Cruz was a liar. "If I get the case, I'll have to disqualify myself. Damn shame."

Hardy looked blank, and Andy explained. One of his foursome out at the Olympic Club represented some people in litigation against Cruz. A bait-and-switch case. Seems Cruz had suckered a group of his distributors into laying out big bucks to buy into his newspaper's growth—trucks and coin machines and so on—and then when the paper got into the black, he cut them off, went in-house with the distribution.

"And, of course, being good third-world brothers and sisters for the most part, it was all oral."

Jane touched her father's arm. "Daddy."

"I'm not worked up," he said, "and that wasn't a racist remark. And if it was, even here in the bosom of my family, I retract it."

That's why he might lie, Hardy was thinking, about knowing one of his distributor's employees. "Could I meet this guy, your friend?" Missing the father-daughter exchange altogether.

Andy nodded, finishing his drink. "Sure, got a pen?"

He gave Hardy the number on a card, then kissed his daughter. "Well, we working stiffs have to get up in the morning." He stood up, extended his hand again. "Dismas, I mean it, I've missed you. Come around sometime. Get arrested if you need an excuse."

He took them both in. "Damn shame," he repeated, as though to himself, about as subtle as a dart in the eye.

They watched him weave through the tables. Jane put her hand on Hardy's thigh, let it rest there. "Now what?" She half turned to him on the barstool.

His thoughts had suddenly turned to Cruz, back to Ed and Frannie. "I guess I'm going to call your dad's friend."

"No, Dismas." The eyes flickered briefly with amusement. "About us."

It was a flat question—no coy girl stuff. "Us?"

"You and me. Us."

"It seems funny, doesn't it?"

"It didn't seem funny a half hour ago."

She'd gotten him there, he had to admit. "No, it didn't." Then, "Do I have to answer right now?" He reached out his hand along the bar, and there was hers again, holding his. "Shit, Jane, we're divorced."

Jane lifted his hand and kissed it. "Out there . . ."

Hardy nodded. "But that was never the problem anyway."

"No, I remember."

No smile. Just stating a fact.

"Maybe that was rare, huh?"

"Maybe."

They both went to their glasses. Jane's hand rested on his, unfamiliar and frightening. He noticed the coral nail polish flawlessly applied, the cool trace of blue vein under the olive-tan skin. Jane's hand right there. He put his glass down and reached over with his other hand, covering it.

"How about, maybe next week or so, we go on a date?"

That had been something between them when they'd been married. They'd gone on dates.

"A real date?" she asked.

"Yeah, you know—dinner, a movie, like that."

She thought a minute. "What night?"

*A*T THE rectory Jim Cavanaugh sat in his library, a book face down on his lap. It was ten in the morning, and the unseasonable warm spell was continuing. That day he'd gotten up at five and walked the streets around St. Elizabeth's for a half hour reading his breviary. After the six-thirty Mass, attended by twenty-three elderly women and his two altar boys, he had returned to the rectory and gone directly to the library. That had been nearly three hours ago.

Rose peeked in to see him staring at the window. "Father?"

He looked at her, grief all over his face. "Are you all right?"

The question seemed to throw him. "I'm fine, Rose, thank you."

The old woman paused, not wanting to push him, but concerned. "Will you be having breakfast, then? I could just reheat the eggs. The micro works good on those. Or even make up some new ones."

Cavanaugh smiled at the housekeeper. "I forgot breakfast, didn't I? My rhythms seem all off."

She supposed he meant to laugh at himself—that was how he was, secure enough to enjoy his own foibles. But he didn't laugh. Maybe, as he'd said, his rhythms were off. Instead, he sighed and went back to staring at the window.

She didn't like to see him taking the death so hard. Not that Eddie hadn't been a wonderful boy.

No. She guessed he was—he'd been—a man, though sometimes it was hard to realize it when they grew up right in front of you like that.

But that was the way life was, she thought. A vale of tears, as the prayer said. Eddie's death was a tragedy, no doubt of that, but you didn't let yourself sit and stare out windows. At least not for too long.

She learned that when Dan had been killed in the War. That was life. It wasn't fair. It was a tragedy, all right. But it was God's will, not for her to understand. And she never would, not ever. She would just have faith and believe that she would see Dan again in heaven. And if she hadn't pulled herself up by her bootstraps and forced herself back to life, she might not have ever recovered. That all seemed so long ago now. Strange to remember that she really thought she wouldn't survive. Not that there wasn't some pain, but it was a different kind now, certainly nothing to die over.

So she could understand Father's reaction. In many ways, Eddie was the son he could never have. And his death was another bond to Erin, lost, too. She wondered if that hurt him as much as anything.

No, she thought. He was, after all, a priest. He probably didn't let himself think like that, though a blind person could see the love he had for that woman. Well, she couldn't blame him for that. Erin was a saint, and beautiful to boot.

She sighed. "Father?"

The priest faced her but didn't even seem to see her. His eyes had that hollow look they sometimes got. It was her privilege to see him like that, when he wasn't "on." He was lost inside himself.

She'd try to bring him back, but slowly, in the proper time. No sense bothering him anymore this morning.

Quietly, she closed the door and walked back to the kitchen. For lunch, she thought, I'll go out to the store and buy some corned beef and a fresh loaf of rye. He'll be hungry come lunchtime. He'll never turn down a corned beef on rye.

Erin was thinking that it must be easier for everyone else, with their daily activities: Big Ed was back at work, Steven and Jodie were in finals week, Mick had gone off to ROTC drill camp, Jim Cavanaugh had his duties at church. Everyone had something to take the mind off it.

She sat at the table in the breakfast nook, a cold cup of coffee at her elbow, her calendar open in front of her—the calendar by which she ordered her time, being there for everyone who asked, always finding the energy. Now she looked down at it. Slowly she turned the page back to the past week.

All those appointments unkept. Look at them. Dinner plans with Ed for Wednesday, Friday and Saturday nights. His Knights of Columbus picnic (and her note "Make pasta salad") on Sunday. Volunteer work at St. Mary's Hospital. Take Mrs. Ryan to physical therapy. The S.I.

women's committee had their annual housecleaning—getting the classrooms at St. Ignatius prepped for the painters before summer school started. Baby-sit Lottie's kids while she and Hal went to Monterey.

And that was just the "public" list. There was also the general housecleaning for her perfect house. The screens had to go up. She had wanted to plant the impatiens for summer. The wallpapering . . .

She and Jim Cavanaugh had had their usual Thursday lunch, although after last week . . .

Well, he'd apologized for that, had called her that afternoon, broken up but managing to sound very much like his old self. What had gotten into him, wanting to kiss her? Naturally, she had known Jim felt something for her, but it was probably like the seven-year itch in marriage. The priesthood must have its own cycles. It had been her fault, really—listening to him so sympathetically over lunch. She had been stupid to ignore the signs. She knew them well enough with other men. Jim was a man, and all men, even priests, had their egos. She hadn't meant to hurt him, of course, but . . .

But really, that whole thing—God! less than a week ago—had happened in the far distant past. What did it matter now?

She glanced down at the calendar. What did any of it matter now?

She sighed. What if she had seen, one week ago, the real calendar? Monday, Eddie is killed.

What would happen this week?

She touched her face, her hand shaking. No, don't start thinking like that. But she looked down anyway. The week held far fewer appointments, none of which she felt she had the strength to keep. She wondered who had taken Hal and Lottie's children, if they'd gone on their vacation to Monterey after all. They hadn't been at the funeral.

"Stop it," she said aloud. But her mind kept humming. She saw Eddie's casket at Ging's, heard Big Ed's one sob as he knelt before it, saw Frannie almost go down at the gravesite.

She shook her head again. Yes, the others had it easier now. It had been bearable, getting breakfast made because Big Ed had been there, next to her, touching as they passed one another. But now, with nothing to do but think and remember, she didn't know if she could stand it.

Maybe she should go and wake up Frannie?

But Frannie, nowhere near as strong as she was, needed her rest. She was sure of that.

"Hi."

There she was, in the doorway. Erin hadn't even heard her. "Are you okay?" Frannie asked.

"Sure. I'm just"—she motioned to the calendar—"the week . . . just seems kind of long."

Frannie came over next to her. She was barefoot, wearing one of Jodie's robes, and ran her hand across Erin's shoulders, leaving her arm draped there.

Erin shook her head again, unable now to see the calendar. Why is that? she thought. And what is this rushing sensation? She turned into her daughter-in-law, hiding her face in the front of the robe. Frannie hugged her close, and suddenly Erin couldn't hold back anymore.

"It's all right," Frannie said, "it's all right."

Over and over, as the tears wouldn't stop.

Bunch of dorks, Steven thought as the class filed out around him. Everybody talking about how tough the test was. What was hard was having to sit there after you were finished for twenty minutes while the rest of the class labored over this bullshit.

Okay, so if that got to him, he'd just stay longer, until everybody'd gone.

"You finished, Steven?"

Mr. Andre, a major-league nerd, though he knew his math, stood up by the desk, waiting. Normally, he called Steven Mr. Cochran. All the kids here at S.I. were Mister. So maybe Andre felt sorry for him because of Eddie.

Well, fuck that. "I was done a half hour ago."

"Too easy?"

Steven shrugged.

Andre was stacking the other tests, cutting him all the slack in the world. "You want to bring it up?"

He gathered his books, head hung down. Andre was standing right over his desk. "I'll take it. I'm very sorry about your brother."

Thanks, that helps a lot, Steven thought as he squeezed out by him. "Yeah," he said.

Big Ed didn't tell Erin that he called in sick. He figured not telling her didn't break their rule about being truthful to each other, even when it would hurt. She didn't have to know he'd come here. She'd only worry about him, and she had enough on her mind.

The gravesite seemed different. They had put the stone up, was one thing. "Edward John Cochran, Jr.—1962–1988."

He wished he could somehow wipe off the last numbers, make them not have happened. Go back with his wife and kids to two weeks ago and just stop everything right there for all time.

Kneeling on the wet morning ground, he thought about the last time he'd seen Eddie alive, the disagreement they'd had. He wished it hadn't happened, the same way he wished every tiny event of the last week hadn't ever been, as though any small change might have prevented what was.

Anyway, the argument hadn't been important. And it wasn't as if father and son hadn't gotten along in general. Sometimes Eddie got a little carried away with his brains, was all, maybe thought his dad was a little too salt-of-the-earth.

Ed didn't know. Maybe he was a little simple. Things seemed to work for him, though. What was so tough, you had to get all worked up over them? He didn't get it. You just did your job, you were faithful to your wife, you stuck by your friends. That was it.

Not, he knew, that there weren't hard questions. Like Eddie's problem with his boss. Sure, that wasn't easy to figure out. Maybe the man was in trouble, and getting deeper. But Big Ed really believed it wasn't Eddie's problem. If it got too serious, Eddie could just go get another job for a couple of months before starting graduate school. There were tons of options.

All of 'em gone.

He moved back into the shade and pulled himself up to sit on a horizontal cypress branch.

He guessed he'd come up here to say a few prayers, but for some reason, they weren't coming out very well. His mind kept jumping.

Or rather, remembering . . .

"What if," Eddie had said, "what if you'd been alive in Germany in the thirties and had seen what was going on with Hitler? Would that have been your business?"

"Well, sure."

"So where do you draw the line?"

And Ed had sat there in the trophy room surrounded by the memorabilia of his family's life and said: "It's a commonsense thing. You figure where it's going to hit you."

"So what if you weren't Jewish and you had a good government job in the Third Reich? It wouldn't have hit you at all?"

"Yeah, but there you're talking evil."

"God versus the devil, huh?"

Big Ed realized how dumb that sounded. "I guess you also have to figure out if it's a big enough issue. If it is, you get in it."

"How about if getting in it early might keep an issue from getting big in the first place?"

He couldn't help smiling as he thought back on it. How'd he raised this white knight?

He had changed tacks. "What's the matter, are you bored at home? Not enough to do?" Meaning it to be funny.

But Eddie didn't have much of a sense of humor about his notion of right and wrong. He hadn't actually spoken harshly to his dad, but Big Ed could tell he'd said the wrong thing. "Sometimes," Eddie said, "there are just things you've got to do, even if everything in your life is rosy, or it's inconvenient."

"I agree with you," he'd said, placating. "All I'm saying is you've got to pick your shots. You waste your ammo taking target practice, and when real shooting time comes you're out of luck."

That's really what he'd said, and suddenly it brought him up short. He had really talked about guns and ammo. And then, less than a week later . . .

If there was a connection, he thought, between that talk and his son's death . . .

His brain jumped again. What had Eddie said about his boss—Polk at Army Distributing? Something about him and his wife and the business. Was it just that they were in some kind of trouble, or was that only what Big Ed remembered?

Across the cemetery, through the trees, a black limo was pulling slowly up the hill, leading another group of cars to another hole in the ground.

No, he was sure Eddie hadn't said what it was. Big Ed kicked at the ground, then stood up. Goddamn, he thought. I should have listened to him, not argued with him. Maybe I'd have some idea now about the why of it all.

They'd laid the sod over Eddie's grave. It was a good job, he noticed, all but seamless. As he'd done countless other times working at the Park, he walked the sod's edge, pressing it into its bed. He wanted the grass over this grave to grow.

Nobody home.

No surprise there.

He put his books on the table adjacent to the front door and walked back to his bedroom.

Probably out do-gooding somewhere. Making Frannie feel better by taking her to lunch or a museum or a park. Never mind it's my last day of finals, never mind how I might feel about Eddie being gone. Never mind anything about ol' Steven.

And Eddie was gone. He was dead. Eddie dead. Say it say it say it.

She hadn't made the bed again. Well, that experiment had certainly worked. Sure, Mom told him it was his job, but funny, it hadn't been Eddie's, or Mick's. Or if it had been, they hadn't done it and Mom had covered. But she didn't cover for him. Not one time. And every day he left the bed unmade, hoping she'd come in, as he'd seen her do every day with his brothers in their room. She'd cluck disapprovingly—but then make the beds.

He turned on the television. Game shows. Give me a break. He couldn't believe all the smiling and crapola for a couple of questions that he'd known every answer to since he was about six.

He and Eddie, testing each other on dumb things, but loving it:

What island is Tokyo on?

Name the Pharaoh who believed in one god. What was that god's name?

Who was Alben Barkley?

What kind of books did Yogi Berra read on the road?

Yeah. Well, that was over.

He punched the remote and killed the sound. Watch a game show without sound someday if you want to see what they're really all about.

So, he thought, summer vacation!

He pulled the window blinds up and looked out onto his backyard,

with its orderly flowers and its fence that he and his dad would patch
for the hundredth time in the next few weeks.

Back to the bed, into the drawer there next to it. Snap the switchblade—open and shut. And there was that guy's card. What does the
dart mean?

He closed the switchblade and laid it on his stomach, then crossed
hands behind his head on the pillow. You think that guy Hardy was
really doing something about Eddie? What could he do? Eddie was in
the ground, so what could it matter?

He blinked hard, wiping a hand over a leaking eye. Standing up
abruptly, switchblade in pocket, card in pocket, he went to the window
again and stared at the fence. Pop was going to have to fix it himself.
That wasn't his summer.

He looked back at the unmade bed and nodded. That told him
everything he needed to know. What a joke hanging around waiting for
something to change. It was all right here to see if you opened your
eyes.

It might be hot now, but he wouldn't be tonight, so he grabbed a
jacket and carried it outside over his shoulder. Uncle Jim crossed his
mind—maybe he ought to go and talk to him? Sometimes he said a few
things that made sense. Not always, but once in a while.

But he'd already walked two blocks down to 19th, which was the
opposite direction anyway, and it would be just too much trouble—one
last little fling at trying to salvage what he knew couldn't be.

Time to grow up, Stevie.

He stood at the corner of Taraval and 19th, watching the traffic line
up, waiting for the light, southbound. He stuck out his thumb.

14 ☘

*A*NOTHER BEAUTIFUL day. This was getting weird, Hardy thought as he opened the window in his bedroom to let in the fragrant air.

Eddie Cochran and Jane Fowler were playing tag around in his mind.

If someone had told him he would make love to his ex-wife ever again in his lifetime, he would have bet the ranch against it.

So here he is last night, wandering this house from office at the back to living room up front, wondering how it could have happened. And at how he felt now.

That, he supposed, was the thing. How can someone who he'd been with so intimately seem like an entirely different person? Had she changed that much? Had he? Or had they both just forgotten?

They'd met at a party her father had thrown for her graduation from Columbia, to celebrate her return to San Francisco. Hardy had been hired for the night as a rent-a-cop, moonlighting, finishing out his last few months on the force before starting law school.

There had been some good years, he admitted. Diz in law school, thinking he was coasting after Vietnam and police work, married to the beautiful daughter of a judge.

Yes, he remembered, thank you. The memories had kept him up until dawn, which was why, when he'd finally slept, it had been until noon.

Now sitting at the kitchen table, sipping espresso, when the telephone on the kitchen wall rang, he bolted up, knocking over his coffee cup. He hoped it was Jane, forgetting that his number was unlisted and he had, intentionally, not given it to her.

"I don't know," Glitsky was saying. "The more I think about it, the more it bothers me."

"It bothered me the first time."

"That's 'cause you're a genius, Diz. Me, I'm just a street cop."

"So you are looking into it?" The pause was a little too long. "Hey, Abe. Yo!"

"Yeah, I'm here." Glitsky let out a long breath. "I had a talk with Griffin this morning."

"A rare pleasure."

"All too."

"And what did the talk encompass?"

Hardy could imagine Glitsky's face, angles sharpened by intensity. "I don't know, Diz. The more I think about it, the harder time I have with it. It's like I'm being set up."

"For what?"

"Remember the politics we talked about?"

"Is Griffin part of that?"

"We're both up for lieutenant." As though that might mean something to Hardy.

"So?"

"So it's Griffin's case, no matter how I feel about it."

"But he's wrong."

"He's not necessarily wrong. You don't get to homicide being wrong a lot."

Hardy waited.

"Maybe he wants me to make a wave, then wipe out on it."

Hardy's kitchen window faced across the Avenues in the direction of downtown. The top of the Pyramid and a couple of other skyscrapers floated over Pacific Heights like mirages, shimmering silver against the deep-blue sky. "So why are you calling me?" he finally asked.

"You got something at stake here. I don't."

"I got zip," Hardy said. "This is mostly a favor I'm doing for Moses." Even as he said it, it didn't ring very true.

"Okay, but I'll be damned if I'm going to get officially involved, be wrong, and look like a horse's ass."

Hardy played reasonable. "Abe, don't you think the whole might of the force would have a better chance of finding something than me by myself?"

Glitsky snorted. "I'm a professional investigator. I'll be around to bounce things off."

"Okay." Hardy took a breath. "How 'bout this—I found out why Cruz might have lied."

He ran it down, though it, too, seemed somehow flimsier in the daylight. Glitsky evidently shared that feeling. "People lie, especially to cops. You know that. Doesn't mean they kill."

"I never said it did."

Glitsky sighed again, loudly into Hardy's ear. "You know Griffin's report wasn't completely worthless, don't you?"

Hardy waited.

"I mean, we ran paraffin and Cochran did fire the gun. There weren't anybody else's latents on the weapon. No witnesses saw anybody else leave the area."

"Yeah, he aced himself. I guess I'll quit—"

"Hardy . . ."

"Motive, Glitz. I've got this old-fashioned idea that people don't just yawn after dinner, get up and blow their brains out without some reason."

"But in a week you haven't found one?"

"Four days."

"Okay."

"Okay yourself."

After he hung up he stared for another minute out the window. His job was simple. He didn't have to find who'd killed Ed. He only had to come up with enough evidence to have the coroner conclude that there'd been a homicide—by person or persons unknown would be fine for his purposes.

He reached into his pocket, took a piece of yellow paper from his wallet and dialed again. No answer at Frannie's. What he was lacking was a sense of the sequence of events. He wondered what time Ed and Frannie had finished dinner.

Glitsky's call wasn't any kind of help, but it made him feel better, as though he wasn't in so much of a vacuum. Through Abe, he could (maybe) get his hands on lots of information if he could come up with the right questions. Just now, though, he didn't have them.

His date with Jane was tomorrow night. He supposed that after most of a decade he ought to be able to wait another day to see her. So he went back to his office, sat at his desk, and started trying to figure out some areas where Glitsky might be able to help him. He then called the friend of Jane's father—Matthew R. Brody, III, it turned out—and was told he could have an appointment on Monday morning.

He tried Arturo Cruz at his office and learned that the publisher had taken an early, and what was expected to be extended, lunch.

He listened to twelve rings at Army Distributing before deciding that Linda Polk probably wasn't at her desk, and if she was, she was staring at the ringing thing there, either thinking it was really groovy or wondering what would make it stop.

Well, he thought, that killed fifteen minutes.

It was one-thirty. The Shamrock opened in a half hour. Maybe Moses and he could while away another few hours, so long as he was careful to omit any mention of Jane. The Mose had spent many hours reconciling Hardy to having put Jane out of his life. He might have a hard time accepting putting her back in.

"Well, wait, he's here right now."

Moses handed him the telephone and returned to preparing the bar for Friday night. He pulled the backup bottles from the cardboard boxes on the floor, humming off-key as he picked up the near-empties, dusted the shelf, and put the full new bottles behind him.

Hardy was the only customer and wasn't yet halfway through his first Guinness in what seemed like a month. Although nobody knew for a fact that he was here, anyone who knew him at all knew they had a decent chance of finding him at the bar. He took the phone, spoke for a couple of minutes, and hung up.

Moses glanced over at him. "Getting born again doesn't really make you younger, I don't care what they say."

"Just 'cause he's a priest doesn't mean he's not a human being," Hardy answered.

Cavanaugh drank Irish whiskey, but by the time he'd finished his first one, the bar had gotten crowded. Hardy suggested a walk, maybe through the park across the street.

"While we're talking about reversing roles," Hardy said, "you ought to be playing detective. How'd you locate me at the Shamrock?"

"I called Erin and she asked Frannie, who gave me your number at home, and then when you weren't there she said to try calling her brother, that he might know where you'd gone. It was just luck you were there right then."

"If you believe in luck."

"Luck, faith, all those intangibles. They're my stock in trade, Dismas."

But something else struck Hardy. "How'd Erin get in touch with Frannie?"

"She just asked. Frannie's at her house. She didn't go home after the funeral yesterday."

Hardy should have remembered that somewhere. He wasn't thinking very well.

"Why do you want to know?" Cavanaugh asked.

Hardy shrugged. "Just something I wanted to remember to ask her."

They had come up by a lake with lots of couples in paddleboats. It was a slow midafternoon, still and warm. They walked along a red cinder path, covered over closely with pines, dotted sporadically with horse dung. On the lake, swans floated among the paddleboats while, nearer the dock, a dozen ducks quacked for a young girl's bread.

"Innocence," the priest said. "What a beautiful thing."

Hardy looked sideways at the priest, alert for a touch of the blarney, but Cavanaugh seemed genuinely moved. His eyes roved around, to the trees, the sky overhead. He seemed almost to be memorizing this moment, as though its innocence—if he wanted to call it that—were something he'd later need to draw on in a different life.

"I just couldn't get going this morning," Cavanaugh said enigmatically. Their steps crunched in the cinders. Hardy, hands in pockets, nodded. "I really appreciate this," the priest repeated, apologizing for the third or fourth time.

Reversing roles. That's what he'd said. There'd been a bond, he felt, with Hardy. Instant. Two guys, Catholic backgrounds. A lot in common there.

He needed to confess. No, more, he needed absolution. And not from another priest. He didn't just need the form of forgiveness, but its substance—the understanding of one of his fellow men.

So, sure, Hardy had said. Why not? He felt oddly drawn to the man himself—victimized perhaps by the charisma, but most of Hardy's friendships had started like that. Some spark, something a little unusual, as long as there was that confident presence. And Jim Cavanaugh had presence to burn.

But this apologizing was getting a little old. "Hey, Father. You talk, I'll listen. Then maybe you buy me a beer. If I get bored, I'll let you know."

"How about you call me Jim?"

"Okay, Jim, what's the problem?"

Jim waited until a couple on horseback had passed. "I feel like . . ." He stopped, and Hardy had the sense he was going to apologize again, but he didn't. "Nope. That's not it," he muttered to himself. Then he took a deep breath. "I am fairly certain that I sent Eddie to his death."

The crunching sound of their footsteps suddenly sounded more loudly in Hardy's ears.

"He came by last week. I'm kind of, I guess you'd say, the other father figure in that family." He chuckled without any mirth. "I've always prided myself on my . . . how can I put this? My moral courage. It's what people talk to priests for, I guess. What they want to hear.

"The rest of the world says to compromise and just get by, but I've always viewed our role—my role, the priest's role, that is—as counseling that the hard choices, the right choices, get made."

"And Eddie had some hard choice?"

"I'm sure it's why he came to me. He wouldn't have bothered if he didn't want to hear it."

"You're sure of that? Maybe he just wanted to talk."

Jim Cavanaugh shook his head. "No. He'd had a fight—more a disagreement really—with Big Ed . . . his dad. If he didn't want to hear somebody else come up with his answer, he just would have driven home and forgotten about it.

"You can tell, Dismas. Our Jewish brethren have a saying, 'If you've got to ask, it's not kosher.' This is a little the same thing. Ed felt he had to ask me." He laughed again at himself. "He wanted to hear that the right thing to do was what he planned to do anyway. More, he wanted to see if he could get away with not doing it. And, moral authority that I am, I told him he couldn't. Although his father had said he could."

Suddenly the priest stopped up short. He kicked at the wooden border to the riding trail so violently that it broke. "Fuck!" he said. The wooden slat had splintered at the vicious kick. Cavanaugh stood shaking his head, the outburst over. He went down to a knee and tried to pat the border back in place. Then, still genuflecting, he made the sign of the cross. A few seconds later he stood and faced Hardy, shamefaced.

"I'm sorry." That self-effacing chuckle. "Some priest I am, huh?"

Hardy shrugged. "Shit happens," he said.

Cavanaugh hadn't heard that one before. He laughed, looser now. "Well," he said, "now you know why I didn't want to go to regular confession."

"So what was it Eddie had to know about?" They were walking again, turning down now through lengthening shadows onto the paved road again.

"You know about the troubles at Ed's work?"

"The distribution thing? A little."

"Well, that's not all. I mean, it was bad for the company, all right, but Eddie thought they could just tighten belts and build up again within a year or so. He was talking to this new company—some other newspaper. . . ."

"*El Dia?*"

"Yeah, *El Dia,* I think. Anyway, he was also trying to get back in touch with the guy who'd cut them off." Cruz, Hardy thought.

The priest continued. "To make a long story short, it was just a matter of time before they were rolling again. At least that was Eddie's opinion."

"So what's the moral dilemma there?"

"That's not it. That's background. The problem was that Eddie's boss—Polk, I think his name is—he was having a hard time dealing with the long-term approach."

"He didn't want to rebuild the business?"

"Essentially, that's right. He'd recently married a younger woman— very much younger, evidently very beautiful."

"She is."

"You've seen her?"

Hardy nodded. "So have you. They were at the funeral."

That stopped Cavanaugh. "Son of a bitch," he said. Hardy was again surprised at the man's flair for Anglo-Saxon.

"What?"

"I think if I'd known that, I might have . . . I don't think I could've done the service."

"Why's that?"

"I think we're going on the assumption that somebody killed Eddie, isn't that right?"

"I don't think he killed himself."

"Well, if somebody did kill him, I'd just about bet my breviary that Polk was involved."

"Don't tell me Ed was sleeping with Polk's wife."

Dusk was catching up with them. They came out of the park halfway down to the ocean and turned back up toward the Shamrock.

Clearly the thought had never occurred to the priest. "I was Eddie's confessor, Dismas, and I'm not abusing the secrecy of the confessional when I tell you that he was faithful to Frannie. Completely. He was madly in love with her."

Hardy thought he knew that, but it was still nice to hear it. "Okay," he said, "so what about Polk's wife?" Cavanaugh was grappling with something. "All this, you understand, is just trying to get at the truth," he said. "I don't want to be saying things that may be scandalous if they're irrelevant to what you're doing."

Jesus, Hardy thought, suddenly remembering all too clearly why he had left the Church. If you took it all seriously, as Jim Cavanaugh certainly did, the rules could bind you up 'til you couldn't even think, much less take any action.

"Why don't you let me decide? This is confession, remember. It ain't going anywhere else."

The priest considered a moment, then nodded. "Eddie thinks— thought—that Polk's wife was in it for the money. And after the drop in business, when the company started losing money, suddenly maybe Mr. Polk wasn't so attractive anymore."

"Did he know this, or was it just a feeling?"

"He found out . . ." Again that hesitation, that slow decision to continue. "He found out something."

Hardy couldn't help himself. He stopped walking and laid a hand on the priest's shoulder. "I said I'd tell you if you're boring me."

Cavanaugh grinned back, self-conscious. "It's like I can't just keep talking. Every single further step seems like a separate decision."

"In high school," Hardy said, "I'd make out with somebody and wonder if the kissing and petting were all separate sins. Finally I decided no. If it was a sin, it was just one of 'em. Same thing here. You've made the commitment, so let's get it out."

Cavanaugh grinned his movie-star grin. "Maybe you would have made a good priest, after all."

"I think my past was a little too checkered."

The priest got a kick out of that. "You'd be surprised. Quite a lot of priests have, as you put it, checkered pasts. I didn't find my vocation 'til after high school myself."

That was interesting, Hardy thought, but it didn't get any closer to Nika Polk.

"So Mrs. Polk . . . what did Eddie find out?"

"Polk was in a hurry for money. He laid off a lot of guys Eddie would have kept, and kept a couple Eddie would've let go. The staff was down to a few marginal workers. Anyway, one of those guys figured Eddie was in on it, too, and let it out that Polk was planning some drug deal."

They'd arrived back at the Shamrock. Behind them an orange and pink dusk was settling onto the Pacific. The Friday-night traffic here on Lincoln was kicking into gear. The bar was hopping, juke-box blaring, Moses working the bar like the artist he was. He had Hardy's Guinness and Cavanaugh's Bushmills in front of them so fast he might have seen them coming up the street four blocks away.

The couch against the back wall was flanked by entrances to the bathrooms. Over it, a dirty stained-glass window let in a bit of the day's last light. Patrons kept up a steady stream going by. In all, it was as private as any confessional Hardy could remember.

Cavanaugh had removed his collar. He sat hunched forward, shirt open, startlingly handsome, sipping slowly at the Irish. His reticence was gone. It had to come out.

"So here I am listening to a boy I could easily feel—hell, I do feel!—is my son, and he's just burning, I tell you Dismas, burning to do the right thing. He wants to confront Polk, somehow convince him that it can all work out with his wife, then go back to the publisher, take 'em all on one at a time and win them over just by the force of the argument. He really saw it so clearly. If everybody involved was fair and upstanding, it would all work out. The company would be saved, Polk could keep his wife happy, the whole magilla."

Hardy sipped his Guinness. "That's Eddie. Sure as shit, excuse me."

Although apologizing for swearing in front of this man was, upon reflection, unnecessary. "He really thought that way, didn't he?"

"Yeah, he did."

"And you tried to point out a little, uh, reality?"

Cavanaugh sat back now, the broad shoulders sagging. "There's my sin, Dismas. That's what I've been getting at." The eyes lowered, matching the voice. "We talked a long time, Eddie and me. He was the most wonderful speaker, even one on one. Passionate, elegant, really convincing. He was the kind of kid could flatter you that he wanted your opinion." He drained his drink. "So here I am, Father Cavanaugh, and I send this fine man off to slay the dragon. Do I think about the reality of it, about his pregnant wife, his real duties, whether he's the man for the job? No way. Not me. The good holy Father Cavanaugh thinks about how right he is, what a wonderful notion it is, how everyone will be so proud."

His eyes came up. "Pride, Dismas. My pride killed Eddie Cochran."

15 ✿

SAM POLK stood in the upstairs bathroom, combing his hair. Out the window in the warm night he heard the bubble of the hot tub's jets, the soft music his wife was listening to.

It was nice having a beautiful naked woman in your hot tub. Hell, it's nice having a hot tub.

He took the tiny pair of scissors—he could barely get his thick fingers through the holes—and carefully snipped at the hair that persistently grew out of the top of his ears. His stomach tightened up on him again. Not now, he thought. Just think about Nika downstairs. Not the other stuff.

The hot tub was new. The whole house—after a lifetime in a flat in the Mission—was new. His life was good. Think about that. Don't let the stomach betray you.

He opened the cabinet and popped two antacids.

"Sammy!"

He opened the window. The tub glowed in the surrounding darkness. Looking down from this height, he saw her body through the water— the patches of shadow, the curve of flesh.

"Be right down," he yelled out the window.

He didn't care what it took, he wasn't giving this up. It was bad luck the way the business had gone just after the marriage, and sure, he should have thought more for the future during the good years, but he would be damned if he'd let anything interfere with this.

He'd worked his whole life, starting as a shoe-shine boy downtown before he was ten, then selling peanuts at Seals games, finally getting a job with the old *Call-Bulletin* as a newspaper boy. And where the other kids his age had seen it as a part-time gig for spending money, he figured he could turn some decent bread by covering the same route, and then all the adjacent ones, for all four of the local papers. Those jobs had bought his first truck.

And now it was fifty years later, near what should have been his retirement, six months after buying his estate in Hillsborough, eight months into his marriage to the woman who'd made him remember what it was to be a man. Nosiree, he wasn't going to get beaten at this stage.

But he was getting nervous.

The money had been in his safe at work all week. That had made everything suddenly seem very real. Before that, while not exactly a lark, it had had the quality of make-believe. He hadn't yet done anything illegal. Or at least anything he could be caught for.

But then the call that the boat had arrived put everything into a new light. It was out in the Bay, waiting for the drop. Did he have the money? Where and when could he take delivery?

So Friday had been a scramble day, and though he'd prepared for it, he found there was no way to lessen the fear of carrying around over one hundred thousand dollars in cash.

He'd gone to different branches of his bank in the course of cleaning out his savings in the hopes that no one would review the account activity. And by the end of the week, he'd told himself, he'd been sure he'd have it all back reinvested and no one would be the wiser. And now it was the end of the week.

The problem with this drug thing was that nobody had ever written a book on how to do it. It was all seat-of-the-pants, and the cash aspect was a major problem. If they only took American Express.

And then there was the whole situation with the middlemen. His business acquaintance, his supplier, was one thing. They were exchanging product for money. But Alphonse Page, who worked for him at the shop, was another matter entirely. Young, black, street smart, neither intelligent nor creative, he was nevertheless the person Sam found himself depending on the most to pull the whole deal together. He had the connection to get rid of this stuff in town. He was important. He eliminated a whole layer of distribution. The problem was, after his years doing business, he didn't like the fact that someone like Alphonse had become important. It made his stomach hurt.

He smiled at himself in the mirror, and his stomach answered him with a growling cramp.

He grabbed his robe from the bathroom door and padded out to the landing, down the stairs through the alcove by the front door, and into the living room.

"How are you doing, Sam?"

He nodded and swallowed. "Alphonse," he said, and seeing his daughter now behind him, "Linda." He tried to smile. "What's going on?"

"I was kind of wondering the same thing."

"What do you mean?"

Alphonse was taller—far taller—than Sam, but he had an economy of movement, a swift jagged way of acting that made him all the more of a force. He was absently cleaning his fingernails with a pocket file, and Sam saw the quick flick outward before he checked himself.

"Today's payday, man."

Linda popped in. "Remember? You were gonna come in to sign the checks. I mean, Alphonse really needed the money. . . ."

Alphonse smiled all around. "I don't do charity, man, 'cept my own."

Sam, feeling the sweat start to run down under his arms, tried to sound calm. "Right. No problem there."

"See, Daddy," Linda was saying, "so I figured it would be cool if we just came by. I mean, I knew where you were, so—"

Sam held up a hand. Sure, Linda, he thought. Take the man I most want to avoid and walk him inside my face. His daughter, he thought, was hopeless.

"No, it's a good idea. Why don't you go make yourself a drink while Alphonse and I go in the office?"

She seemed to look to Alphonse for permission. He definitely gave her some message before she started moving back to the bar off the kitchen.

"Linda?"

She turned.

"Would you mind telling Nika I'll be out in a minute? She's in the hot tub."

"Nice place," Alphonse said as he entered the office. Then, as the door closed, "What the fuck's going on, Sammy?"

Sam, his stomach now a jumbled mass of razor blades and ice picks, leaned against his desk. "I think we'd better leave it Mr. Polk, Alphonse. Okay?"

Reestablish that old authority, he thought. Alphonse took the knife, and before Sam had seen it move, his arm was bleeding through the slash in the white robe.

"We do business and it's Mr. Polk," Alphonse said most reasonably as Sam felt the blood draining out of his face. "You fuck with me and it's whatever I want."

Sam looked down at his arm, registering the blood as interesting. He felt no pain, except in his stomach.

"I'm not fucking with you."

"You didn't come to work today. Fact, you didn't come to work this week."

"I didn't know Ed Cochran was going to get killed Monday night."

"You didn't?" Alphonse had turned around and was running his hand over the leather on the back of one of the chairs.

"No, of course not. Why would I?"

Sam considered getting to the desk drawer and pulling the gun on Alphonse, who was getting way ahead of himself, Sam thought, probably thinking about his future riches. But then he remembered that until the deal was done, he needed him.

Suddenly his arm throbbed, and he looked down to see the blood. He lifted a thigh over the corner of the desk and slumped against it.

"I feel bad about Ed," Alphonse said. "I really do. I liked the guy." He turned back to his boss. "But, like you and me, we had business. Hey, you all right?"

Sam was feeling himself going over. Alphonse snapped the knife closed and crossed to the front of the desk. He held Sam upright, pulled the arm of the robe up roughly. "Come on, man, get a grip. You ain't hurt."

"Let me get in my chair. Go ask Linda to get me a drink."

Force of habit, Sam thought. Alphonse still obeyed orders when they were given like orders. That's the way to keep control—never show your own weakness. He was in his chair, the terry cloth now pressed tightly against the wound.

"Nothing. We're just talking," he heard Alphonse say to Linda.

Then he had the drink, a water glass filled with bourbon. He drank off half of it. "All right," he said.

"All right what?" Alphonse swung his legs, heels tapping the front of the cherry desk.

"What did you want me to do? The place was crawling with cops. Didn't you tell that to your people?"

Alphonse sucked at his front teeth. "My friends, the time thing is, like . . . it's like critical with them."

"I understand that." The booze was working. He took another drink. "What's the matter, Alphonse? This got you nervous?"

The boy had evidently worked his way up and past his earlier bravado. Now the rush was wearing off. "I'm not nervous. My friends got contracts they gotta fill."

Sam forced a cold smile at his employee. "Don't give me any of this pseudobusiness bullshit, Alphonse. They got a buncha junkies they gotta keep high—squeeze all the money they can out of them before they die."

"That money's your money."

"A very small percentage, Alphonse. Very small."

"But a nice package."

Yeah, Sam thought. Four hundred twenty-five thousand dollars cash. A nice profit for his one-twenty investment. But only if it worked. If it didn't, he was basically tapped out. He couldn't think much about it if it didn't work. Tapped out could be the least of it.

His stomach was arguing with the bourbon, but it felt so good everywhere else he ignored it. "My guys wouldn't deliver. Not there, and not on that particular Tuesday. That's all there was to it."

"So where and when?"

Sam put his head back against the firm leather. This wasn't going to fly very well, and he knew it. "They're gonna let me know."

"Shi—"

"What can I tell you? They said this weekend, tomorrow maybe. They want to find a better place."

Alphonse pushed himself off the desk, walked nearly to the door, turned around. "So what do I do meanwhile?"

"What I'm doin', Alphonse. You wait."

He came right up under Sam's nose, and Sam thought he could smell the fear. "I can't wait, man, they're on my ass. They been holdin' their money a week now."

Well, Sam thought, I know what a good time that is. "Couple more days. Tell 'em by Monday night."

"I'm wrong again, they'll cut my nuts off."

Sam finished the bourbon. "Every business has its risks, Alphonse. Point is, you gotta trust me. 'Cause if I'm scamming you, you're meat anyway. You're the one sold me to them, remember?"

He'd been in distribution his whole life. Buy something from one source, move the merchandise, and sell it to another for profit. That was the American way.

The only hitch was, in this cocaine business, you had people who were not entirely trustworthy. That was fine, Sam knew, as far as it went. People cheated wherever they could, at solitaire even. But it would be especially stupid to forget it here.

And he had done that with Cruz—forgotten that cardinal rule. After playing straight for all those years, the bastard had just walked away from the deal. Keep Cruz in mind, Polk told himself, if ever again you're tempted to trust somebody in business.

The arm had stopped bleeding. Alphonse had been right—it wasn't a bad cut, maybe four inches down the front of his arm.

Since he wasn't about to trust anybody on this deal, he thought he'd set it up smart. He still thought so. The connection had been from years before. An importer, a businessman. Never touched drugs himself. They'd talked at a party—it must have been the early seventies, when cocaine was just starting to catch on.

But at the time, Sam was doing fine with newspapers—who wouldn't in San Francisco with the *Free Press, Rolling Stone* and the other hippie rags, to say nothing of the majors? He hadn't needed to risk anything back then.

"Hey, any time. I mean it. Seed money's always in demand," the connection had said.

So now the newspaper business had gone belly-up, and Cruz had hung him out to dry, cut off using him for distribution, just when he couldn't afford to go broke. Nika wasn't the kind of woman to go betting on the come. He'd promised it up front, had delivered up to now. That was their deal. If he broke it, he wouldn't even blame her for walking.

Who could? A woman who looked like her, who could do what she did, she could have it all, and right now. She could demand it anywhere and get it, and he knew it. More importantly, she knew it.

So he'd made the call to the old connection. One hundred twenty would bring him between three fifty and five, or, if he wanted to step on it himself and peddle the street, maybe a million or two.

No, he didn't want that. He wanted in and out. What he wanted was to put up the money to make delivery worthwhile. Then unload the stuff. Deal with buyers and sellers individually—to groups of guys who didn't know each other, who wouldn't be likely to get to each other and set him up. Everybody makes a profit and everybody needs the middleman, so he's safe.

That was the theory.

The only problem was he had to take delivery himself. He needed Alphonse for when it was time to pass the trash and deliver him his money, but he didn't want anybody else involved with the actual delivery. For that, the canal behind Cruz's had been ideal. He'd gone down last weekend, cut the fence, set it all up perfectly. By all rights it should have been over already.

Goddamn Cochran, he thought. God damn Ed all to hell.

"Jesus, Sammy, no robe even?"

"I don't notice much on you. Move over."

Nika looked at her husband with approval. He didn't have a great body, but he was hung like a peeing horse. And for an old guy, he sure wanted to use it a lot. Well, as long as he didn't try to pull any more of that holding out her allowance he'd tried last week. Two could play the holding-out game. As she'd taught him.

She reached over and touched the cut on his arm. "What happened?"

She ran her finger along the cut.

"A lamp got broken. Linda tripped on a cord."

"What was she doing here, anyway?" Nika asked.

Sam shrugged. "I forgot to sign some checks, that's all. She's gone."

"Does it hurt?" She moved next to him, thigh to thigh. He felt a hand come to rest above his knee.

"It's nothing," he said. "Can't even feel it."

16 🍀

*H*ARDY HAD never heard of the town of Gonzalez. His first inclination after he got the call was to think that for some reason Cruz had wanted him out of Dodge and had asked one of his workers to call him.

But that would have made no sense coming from Cruz. After he hung up, Hardy went to his map and found the place—south of Salinas on 101. It was a real place.

On the way down, he thought he should have made some calls before getting in his car. He almost pulled over in Redwood City, but then thought it would be better not to worry anybody needlessly. What if it wasn't what he thought it was?

Also, he was reasonably certain that someone—possibly Cavanaugh, especially after their heart-to-heart yesterday—would have tried to reach him earlier.

He hadn't been down the Peninsula in nearly a year, and it hadn't changed. What was left to change? The whole thing had been developed so the only possibility of something new was a face-lift on a business park, a Tastee Freeze turning into a Burger King, Astro-turfing a gas station.

Around Palo Alto, the Bay and the flats struggled for the natural look for a few miles along the freeway before widening out into Moffett Field, with its airplane hangars so big that it rained inside them, and then the other Santa Clara fun parks—the mini-golf courses, batting cages, go-kart tracks.

Hardy kept his eyes on the road. His head hurt just slightly from too much beer. Really from getting up too early, he had told himself. Really from too much beer. The old not-enough-sleep routine as the reason for his hangovers was wearing thin, even to himself.

South of San Jose the countryside began to open up, the foothills still green from the spring rains, the scrub oaks starting to bud. Man, he thought, when California doesn't screw with itself, it is some kind of beautiful place.

He was speeding and knew it, but didn't care. The road was all but empty, and he had always had a knack for spotting the Highway Patrol. Besides, he would say he was on a summons from Sheriff Munoz of Gonzalez and probably get off with a warning anyway.

But for some reason—maybe the thickness in his head—he found he couldn't concentrate for long on the reason for the trip. It made his headache worse.

Getting into Steinbeck country, he rolled down the car window to Gilroy and the smell of garlic. The sun was higher now, though there were still wisps of mist over the occasional patch of water. It was getting on toward ten o'clock.

A sign at the town limits told Hardy that Gonzalez was the home of the Tigers. "They sure kept the move from Detroit a secret," he thought as he passed the one-story high school with its faded billboard.

His destination was a square concrete emergency clinic painted an institutional yellow, set two streets back behind what passed for downtown.

Sheriff Munoz greeted him at the door. With a head of balding gray hair and a deep soft-spoken voice, he had all the authority of the small-town cop with, apparently, none of the arrogance. Maybe he'd been in the job a long time. His uniform was lived in, his body solid and big but with no flab. The face was square, clean-shaven and worried. "Is this your card?"

Hardy nodded.

"It's the only thing we had tying him to anything."

"No wallet?"

Munoz just looked at Hardy—not glared, looked—but his eyes were saying that they'd already covered that.

"Is he still alive?"

"Physically. He hasn't come up yet. He'll come around. Now he's sedated."

There were only two rooms behind the open reception area. Steven Cochran was in the second one.

Hardy swallowed hard, remembering the vision of the brother, Eddie, less than a week ago, on a similar gurney. Jesus, they look alike, he thought. He hadn't noticed it before—Steven had initially struck him as much thinner. He forced himself to look. Maybe because the damage appeared so similar. The right side of Steven's face was covered with bandage, his right arm in a sling with a bandaged hand sticking out of it.

"What happened?"

"Do you recognize him?"

First things first. Munoz was right. "We gotta call his folks," Hardy said.

"If you don't mind, sir, what's your connection to this boy?"

They were in the other empty examination room, drinking 7-Eleven coffee brought in by the nurse receptionist. Hardy's headache was gone. He explained how Steven had come to get his card.

"Funny that's all he had." It was a statement, not meant to be accusatory.

"Where was it?"

"Front pocket."

"Maybe he lost his wallet."

The sheriff nodded. "Maybe."

"Listen," Hardy said, "I'm not any kind of official, but you mind if we talk about it? I've got a reference you might . . ."

Munoz struck Hardy as a thorough cop, so it didn't surprise him much when he got up to make the call to Glitsky's home number. When the sheriff returned, he seemed satisfied. "Okay," he said, "you think this is related to what you're working on?"

Hardy drank some coffee and asked him what exactly had happened.

Munoz had his elbows on his knees, hands out in front of him holding the nearly full Styrofoam cup. His black sunken eyes focused unblinking on the wall over Hardy's head. Hardy thought they were about the saddest eyes he'd ever seen.

The sheriff said, "Lady named Hafner grows 'chokes maybe six miles south. She and the family were on their way up to the farmer's market in Salinas. They usually leave before dawn and try to get a good place, you know. So they're turning onto 101 and one of the kids sees what he thinks might be a deer by the road. Anyway, that's food, you know, so Momma stops and it's . . . Steven's the name, huh?"

"Steven."

"So she got here and the doc called me." There was a long pause, as though Munoz was trying to fathom how things like this could happen. "I figure—and the doc says it makes sense—he was thrown from the vehicle already unconscious. That's probably why he lived, he was so loose. Just pretty much peeled the right side of his body, broke his arm, collarbone, couple of foot bones."

"Could he have just fallen? Bounced out of the back of an open pickup maybe?"

"Yeah, he could've. He didn't, though."

Hardy waited.

"He was," Munoz paused, "sexually molested. Maybe the rest of the injuries—that look a hell of a lot like a beating—maybe they could have come from the impact hitting the ground at sixty, but the one . . ."

"Got it," Hardy said.

"Just once I'd like to catch up with somebody does something like this. Not after a trial or anything, but catch 'em red-handed."

"It would be a great joy," Hardy agreed.

"Your friend Glitsky in the city, he gonna call missing persons, you think? Let 'em know?"

Hardy thought that he probably would—Glitsky believed in following through, but Hardy didn't feel right making the commitment for him. After all, Glitsky dealt in homicides. Lost and found children were not his problem, and if somebody in San Francisco had the bad grace to get killed on this fine Saturday morning, it's possible he might forget.

"It wouldn't hurt if we called," he said, though he let Munoz do it officially.

Warm and drowsy. Smell of fresh linen. Had Mom finally made his bed?

Steven tried to open his eyes. They didn't seem to work. The eyelids were too heavy, his whole body too weak.

Well, just a few more hours' sleep. Can't hurt. It's the summer, after all.

But that jarred some memory. Leaving the house, striking out on his own, riding in the truck with those two guys heading for L.A., but in no real hurry. Mostly, they'd said, into partying, into cruising. That sounded okay.

It began to come flooding back, and involuntarily he groaned. They'd accepted him right away, including him when they stopped for a few road beers before they'd left the city. The beers didn't taste very good, but Steven wasn't about to let on. This was part of being an adult, and he was tired of being treated like a kid, or, worse, a nothing. So he'd act like an adult, go along, be cool.

He got a little more worried when the joints came out, but knew he was just being uptight. Lots of guys in school smoked dope all the time. It just hadn't been his thing. But it wasn't as though it was any big deal, or really wrong. It did make him cough, though, and the guys had laughed at him a little, but he could tell it was all in fun. They coughed, too, only not so much.

After that, in this blurry haze, they'd stopped for something to eat— maybe in Gilroy?—some really fantastic burgers that they took to this "special spot" for a picnic. And then things got scary kind of, with the two guys starting to tickle him and other stuff. Then really rough.

If he hadn't been so dizzy and messed up, he probably could have outrun them, but when he pulled loose and tried that, his coordination was gone. And after they caught him, he thought he remembered other things, but the drowsiness was still there, and it was too hard to think about.

And where was Mom, then, if the bed was made? Just in the other room probably. God, it'd be great to see Mom. He called out for her.

That was a sound. Hardy, waiting for Munoz to return from his phone call, ran around the corner to Steven's room.

The boy lay, still unmoving. This was the hostility kid, he remembered—switchblade, fuzzed-out television and all. He shook his head. Talk about a bad week for the Cochrans.

Had Ed's death somehow precipitated this, driven him over the edge of his own despair? Or was there some more immediate link? Like, might Steven have known something he shouldn't have?

Hell, he'd find out when Steven came to if he had known his assailants. Or, more particularly, if Hardy knew them.

Big Ed looked anything but big.

Staring down at his bandaged youngest son, he was a shell of the man in the old but elegant suit Hardy had met at the funeral reception. Now a very worn green USF sweatshirt hung loosely over work pants and boots. Everything hung too loose. One bootlace wasn't tied.

He stared as long as he could, then squeezed his thumb and forefinger into his eyes.

Munoz stood next to him. "Are you all right, sir?"

Big Ed nodded. "Long night," he said. "We thought, we thought . . ."

"Sure. But he's not. Not even close."

"He's not close," he repeated. And suddenly a shudder went through him and he was crying.

Hardy went out to the reception area, where a small boy with the beginnings of a shiner and a large red knot on his forehead sat stoically as his mother explained to the receptionist how he'd stepped on the tines of a rake and the handle had popped up and hit him in the face.

Hardy walked outside into the bright sun. He was hungry. The place on Gonzalez's main street sold burritos the size of a suitcase for $2.49, and Hardy bought three, chewing on one while he carried the other two, wrapped, back to the clinic.

Munoz and Ed, talking by the sheriff's car, took the food. Big Ed seemed a little better.

"Sorry I didn't recognize you in there," he said to Hardy.

"How's the boy?"

"Still sleeping. You have any idea who did this?"

"I wish," Hardy said. "You reported him missing. Did he run away, or what?"

"What's the other option?" Munoz asked.

Hardy shrugged. "It's unlikely, but he might have been kidnapped."

"That's crazy," Ed said. "We don't have any money."

"It might have been to keep him quiet. Maybe he knew something." The two men chewed their burritos. "About Ed, I mean."

That stopped Big Ed. "What do you mean? They say Eddie killed himself." He swallowed hard.

"I doubt it. I doubt it very much."

"Well, then, what . . ."

Hardy could see it was almost too much for the man. His hand went up to his eyes again. He shook his head as though trying to clear it.

The receptionist came to the door. "The boy's awake," she said.

At least he wants to be home, Big Ed was thinking. That's something. Being back home. He'd said it. Daddy, take me home. Daddy. Nobody'd called him that in ten years. It was always either Dad, Pop or Ed. Well, if Steven wanted Daddy now, Daddy was taking him home. There he and Erin might be able to figure out if and where they'd screwed up so he wouldn't want to run away again.

He looked around to the back seat where Steven lay, sleeping again, strapped down by the seat belts.

"He okay?" Hardy asked.

Ed nodded.

Munoz and Hardy had thought it'd be better if Ed didn't have to drive back alone with his son, so they arranged that the sheriff's one deputy would drive Hardy's car back to the city later.

Ed again glanced into the back seat. He couldn't look enough at his son, couldn't really believe yet—after the fears of last night sitting up with Erin, his daughter Jodie and Frannie—that Steven, along with Eddie, wasn't dead and gone forever. Whatever had happened, whatever he'd been through, at least he was still with them, breathing. He must've sighed with relief, because Hardy looked over at him.

This guy Hardy was driving well—slow and careful. No bumps on the kid. And it was a good thing he was driving—Ed was pretty sure he couldn't have kept his mind on the road.

They were up to San Mateo. The sun was behind the mountains already. Where had the hours gone to? In another half hour they'd be home.

Maybe sometime today Erin had gotten some sleep. He hoped so. She hadn't slept now in almost a week.

Erin. His thoughts, as always, were never far from his wife. He didn't know how they were ever going to get over this time, though something told him they would. Well, almost. They'd never be the same, of course. The wound—losing Eddie—was too deep to ever heal completely, but there would be something—some new challenge that would get things into a new perspective. At least, he hoped so.

Why had his boy run away?

"You have any proof somebody killed Eddie?" he asked suddenly.

"Nope." But then Hardy told him what Cavanaugh had said about Sam Polk—the drug thing.

"That's something," Ed said. "I knew something was going on with Polk. Eddie and I kind of argued about it."

"That's what Cavanaugh said—that Eddie wanted another opinion."

"When did you talk to Jim?"

"Yesterday. Last night. He thought he might have something of a lead. I was going to check around a little today, but then this morning . . ." He ticked his head toward the back seat.

"I don't know why you're doing this, but thanks."

Hardy kept his eyes on the road. "I knew Ed and Frannie pretty well. Her brother's my best friend."

Turning west up the 380 now as dusk deepened, passing the huge cemetery with its thousands of white squares, gridding the grassy fields, marking the graves of military dead.

Ed reached behind the seat and rested a hand on his son's leg, feeling the warmth of it through the blanket. Steven stirred and moaned softly, but didn't open his eyes.

"Almost there," Hardy said.

He'd made a dumb turn coming up this way, even though it was the most direct route. The cemetery was closing Ed up, and Hardy swore at himself—he should have remembered it. Maybe he could distract him a little, get his mind off it. "Your friend Father Cavanaugh is some kind of character."

"Jim? Yeah. He's a great guy."

"Only thing I can't figure is why he's not a cardinal or something—at least a bishop."

Ed smiled. "I know. He's got that flair, don't he?" He paused. "But if he were a bishop, he'd have to leave Erin, and I don't think he'd like to do that."

That remark surprised Hardy. He must have shown it. "It's no secret he's in love with my wife," Ed said, but then held up a hand. "No, no, not like that. He's one of us. Erin's his best friend. He's hers. Except maybe for me." He smiled again. "Except sometimes I'm not sure of that either."

"I think that'd make me nervous," Hardy said.

"Well, after thirty years, I figure Erin's my gal. We've talked about it, but she says the physical thing just never was there with Jim." He shook his head. "How do you figure that? She prefers a galumpf like me, she says. I figure it's her one flaw, but believe me, I'll take it."

Hardy glanced over at him. He said it in such a self-effacing way, you almost missed the serene confidence. This man knew, without a trace of doubt, that he knocked his wife out.

"It's good to know they don't always go for the movie stars, not being one myself," Hardy said, relieved they had finally gotten by the cemeteries, into Daly City and all the little boxes on the hillsides.

"I don't think they'd let Jim be a bishop anyway."

"Why not?"

Ed shrugged. "He's not political enough. Done a few unusual things. For a priest."

Such as coming to me for his confession, Hardy thought, but asked, "Like what?"

"Oh, nothing serious. Just stuff."

Okay, they weren't going to talk about it. But then . . . "It took him about twice as long as anyone to get out of the seminary. They kicked him out twice."

"Kicked him out?"

Ed shrugged. "Well, it was the fifties, early sixties. The Church thought it had a lock on these guys. Any little thing, they'd say you didn't have a true vocation and boot you. Not like now, where if you've got a history as a gun runner to Nicaragua you still got a pretty good chance, they need priests so bad."

"So what did he do?"

"Jim?" Ed laughed, remembering. "I should know. I went with him. He got about two weekends off a year, and so this one time we got plastered and took in some strip shows—Erin was at school so the two of us were ripe for some hijinks. But the problem was, the next day he showed up back at the seminary hung over and confessed everything. Bad scene. They put him out for a semester to rethink his vocation."

"What was the other time?"

"That was different. I don't know I ever got the story right. Erin and I were on our honeymoon. It was maybe a month before his ordination. We'd already received the invitation. Anyway, Jim had decided he wasn't worthy, or something like that. He wanted to be a priest, but didn't feel he was holy enough. Can you imagine that? If Jim wasn't holy enough, there was no hope for anybody else. I mean, where it counted."

Hardy looked across the front seat. By now it was nearly dark. The streetlights in the lower Avenues had come on.

"See, they tried to tell him everybody had those doubts. Priests weren't supposed to be saints—they were humans like the rest of us. They weren't about to let him drop out. He was the president of his class, was going to be the speaker at the ordination. They'd invested too much in him."

"So? What happened?"

"So he stole the dean's car, crashed out through the front gate and disappeared for three days."

"Cavanaugh did that?"

"And then showed up looking like a bum, and without the car. He never talks about those three days, except to say it was his time in the desert. Whatever that meant. Anyway, he pissed everybody off pretty good. Now those same guys, his classmates, are becoming the bishops, and they all like Jim, probably, but think he's a flake. Or at least a little bit of a flake. For sure too unstable to move up in the hierarchy."

"But he did finally get ordained?"

"Yeah, two years later, he'd done his penance. But he wasn't valedictorian."

They turned onto Taraval. In the back seat, Steven moaned gently.

"Almost home, son," Ed said. "Almost home."

Frannie looked much better, Erin much worse. Hardy sat drinking his second scotch, waiting for the opportune moment to make an exit. Everybody here was tired—hell, exhausted. Jodie was already asleep, her gangly frame draped over the love seat. Erin and Ed, sitting together like statues, holding hands, kept looking at each other as if wondering what was going to happen next. But there was a toughness Hardy noticed in Ed.

Here was a man who'd lost a son only a week before. Just that morning, Hardy had seen him break down into tears. But here, now, sitting next to his wife, he was hanging in there for her, in spite of his own hurt. Hardy thought he might be the bravest man he'd ever met.

"Thanks for the drink," he said. "I think it's time I called a cab."

Frannie walked with him outside. "How are you making out?" he asked her. "Can I ask you one more question?"

"Sure." Her red hair gleamed in the porch light. She looked like she'd finally eaten something. Her eyes were clear.

"You said Eddie left right after dinner?"

She nodded.

"Do you have any idea what time that was?"

He hated to ask, to see her eyes cloud over again, but he had to know.

"It was still light out. Pretty early, I guess, sevenish. Why?"

The cab pulled up. "Because it shouldn't take two and a half hours to drive from your place out to China Basin."

"No, it's only like fifteen minutes."

"Yeah, I know."

He admired the way when her shoulders started to sag she tightened up her jaw. He leaned down and pecked her on the cheek. "I'm checking this stuff out, Frannie. You keep hanging in there."

She put her arms up around him and held tight for a moment. The cabbie honked. She let go.

When the cab got to the corner, Hardy looked back. Frannie was still standing out by the curb. Hanging in there, Hardy thought.

"Nope."

"Abe, come on."

"You said yourself he'd never seen the guys before. How can there be a connection?"

"It's too big a coincidence, don't you think?"

"No, I don't think."

"But that plus the drug thing with Ed's boss?"

"*Possible* drug thing. What's the matter with you, Hardy, you taking drugs yourself?"

After another minute, Hardy hung up. What more did Glitsky need? Where there's smoke, there's fire, right? And there was enough smoke here to cure meat.

It was ten o'clock Saturday night. The deputy hadn't yet arrived back from Gonzalez with his car.

Not for the first time, Hardy wished he didn't have a rule about keeping hard liquor in his house. He went into his bedroom, fed the fish, walked back to his office. He picked the six darts from the board by the fireplace and stood by his desk, just at the tape line he'd put down there, and threw methodically, trying to let his mind clear.

Frannie was positive that Ed had left the house around seven. Cruz said that he had left work around eight-thirty and nobody had been either in the building or the lot at that time. It was about a fifteen-minute drive from Ed's to Cruz's.

Hell of a lot of time to kill, and that was the minimum. He might not've gotten to Cruz's until ten. Nobody knew.

Damn Glitsky. There was something here, Hardy was sure of it. A little manpower and they could at least get a fix on the whereabouts of all the principals. Where, for example, had Cruz gone at eight-thirty? Maybe he'd just sat in the lot, waiting for a meeting. And Polk—what had Polk been doing Monday night? Maybe Ed's meddling in his private business was going to cut into Nika's lifestyle, and he couldn't allow that.

All right. He had the background. It was beginning to look as if he'd have to do some old-fashioned police work, and he didn't relish the thought. That's why they have police departments, he thought. Because the legwork is awesome. It's why they have rookies, and he hadn't been a rookie in nearly twenty years. But if Abe wouldn't help . . .

He reached again for the phone, intending to give it one more try, even if it was a Saturday night and Glitsky was at home relaxing with his wife. He turned off the answering machine in the office and plugged the phone into the jack.

The doorbell.

Oh, my God! Jane!

He dropped the darts on his desk and sprinted around the corner, through his bedroom and kitchen, and down the hall. It wasn't Jane.

"Mr. Hardy?"

Hardy nodded.

"Your keys, sir, and the sheriff says thanks again."

Hardy remembered his manners. "You want a cup of coffee? How you getting back down?"

He had stood up Jane. There was no way she was still waiting for him.

"Highway Patrol will pick me up if I could borrow your phone? The sheriff—he got it okayed."

Hardy made a pot and the two men talked baseball for most of an hour while they waited for the Highway Patrol.

After the deputy had gone, Hardy stood outside on his front lawn. The fog had come in, though it wasn't heavy. It presaged a return to normal weather. Without a coat on, he walked up to the corner and saw the restaurant where he was to have met Jane. The lights were still on.

He stood outside its front window looking in. Jane wasn't there. Cold now, he jogged back to his house. Coming up the steps, he heard the telephone ringing, but it stopped when he was inside, running back to the office. Maybe if it was Jane he could meet her for a nightcap, explain what had happened. Maybe she'd even believe him.

But there was no message on the answering machine, because he had unplugged it.

Somebody's trying to tell me something, he thought, picking up his darts again. He hit every number from twenty down to the bull's-eye in thirty-four throws.

*H*E AND Jeffrey had to get it straight.

It had eaten at Cruz all day, from the early-morning jog along the Marina to brunch at Green's. It had kept him from his Saturday nap, had even driven him from his house to the office in the middle of the afternoon. Now, after the late dinner and two bottles of wine, in the afterglow he saw no way to avoid it any longer.

Jeffrey lay flat on his back half covered with a pink sheet. He appeared to be asleep, but Cruz didn't think he was. He was very much like the cats he loved so much. He just relaxed completely, with his pilot on slow burn. At the gentle touch, Cruz running a finger from armpit to nipple, he opened his fantastic eyes, visible as blue even in the half-light.

"Hi," Jeffrey whispered. "I'm right here."

This was the boy's element. The trick, to Cruz, was to be happy with him here and to quit trying to turn him into something he wasn't. He'd thought about it all day. Jeffrey wasn't made for intrigue or business—he was made for pleasure, for relaxation.

"You are here, aren't you?"

"Always."

Cruz sighed. God, he loved him. "Can we talk a little?" Funny how he wasn't really the boss here at home, and it didn't bother him at all.

"Sure." He sat up, pulling the blanket around his waist.

"I think we have to get clear between us that Ed Cochran never came here."

Jeffrey cocked his head. "But he did, Arturo."

"I know, I know he did. But our story, yours and mine, should be the same if anyone else asks about it."

Jeffrey opened his eyes all the way. "But why shouldn't we tell the truth? We talked to him. What's wrong with that?"

"In itself, nothing. But there are people who might try to make it something."

"But why?"

"Because, Jeffrey, he was killed in my parking lot."

"But he wasn't killed. He killed himself. You said he did."

"Of course," Cruz said, speaking slowly now. "I know that. That's what I meant. But his death is connected to me by that very fact. And I think it would be smarter not to draw any further attention to it."

Jeffrey reached out a long hand and drew his fingernail across Cruz's jaw. "'Turo, you didn't kill him, did you?"

Cruz folded his hands in his lap and forced himself not to lose his temper. Jeffrey tended to keep missing the essential point. "No, Jeffrey. I didn't kill him."

"But you did see him? That night, no? When you came home so late."

"We agreed I came home before nine o'clock, didn't we? We've already told the police that."

"Arturo." Jeffrey shook his head from side to side. "Yes. And I love you. For the world, you came home when? Around nine, right? But between us . . ." He let it hang.

"The police think it was a suicide."

"You called the police?"

"I just happened to notice it at the office this afternoon. The daily police reports for the paper, you know."

"That's why you went to the office."

Cruz hated that bitchy, petulant tone. But then the real hurt showed. "You could have let me know," Jeffrey said, reaching out and touching his face. "You don't tell me enough. We are together," he said, "we share."

"We do share," Cruz said. "I want to share."

Jeffrey got up and walked naked over to the window. "And you want me to say we never met Ed here?"

"Probably no one will ask. I just want to make sure."

Jeffrey turned back toward him. "I think being honest is the best thing, Arturo. If you start telling lies, they tie you all up. You can even forget what the real truth is."

"Jeffrey, I agree with you. I'm finding that out now. The only thing is, I already told the police I didn't know Ed. If we just—on this one thing—agree, we won't lie about anything else."

Jeffrey sat again on the bed. "You promise?"

"Promise."

How could he expect Jeffrey to understand? He sat on the brocaded couch downstairs, facing the fireplace. The vodka, which had once been iced, was nearly untouched and had now gone warm. Through the gossamer drapes, light from the street filtered into the living room, enough to make out the familiar outlines—the chandelier over the twelve-foot marble table, the twin sculpted marble pillars that bracketed the fireplace, the polar bear rug at his feet, the trio of original Gormans on the far wall bought long before his tiles had become available in every boutique in the West.

In the quiet house, Cruz took stock of what he'd acquired. It still felt like it was worth it. In fact, it wasn't complete yet. The room was beginning to feel a little small, the house just slightly worn. He was ready to move up again.

Keep that in mind, he said. Comfort is stagnation. Keep wanting more, that was the key. Keep that sharp edge. If you weren't expanding you would contract.

A car labored up the steep hill, and a minute later Cruz heard the soft plop as the Sunday paper hit his driveway. Morning already, the darkest hour before dawn, before the black began turning to gray.

No, it would be impossible for Jeffrey to understand. Jeffrey hadn't come up the way he had. Cruz didn't even have to try to remember: it was always with him. When he'd been Jeffrey's age . . .

He was starting to think like an old man, sound like his father had sounded when he talked about the *bracero* life. "I used to be up by three, 'Turo, to work the fields before the sun got too hot." Well, Cruz had done his own laboring, only in different fields.

No, Jeffrey could never understand what it was like to be Mexican, poor and gay. And Cruz was never going back to poor.

Even now, in San Francisco where the heteros joked about their minority status, in the Latino community to be gay was to be a leper. Macho still ruled—Cruz knew it would never change during his lifetime.

Every week or two he would come across a story about one of the Mission gangs or another beating, mutilating or killing some poor *maricon*. Long ago he had decided not to run those stories. People didn't want to read them; they weren't news—what happened to those *pervertidos* was not important, at least not among *la gente*, not among his advertisers and readers.

Cruz had learned well. No one could ever know about him. His parents had died never suspecting. At least his mother never stopped pushing girls at him, especially after *La Hora* had started to become successful.

So he'd simply done without sex, except for the vacations that had brought him back home disgusted with himself. He had done without —until he'd met Jeffrey.

And even with Jeffrey, even with love for him pumping so hard through his veins that he didn't feel he could control himself, he had been cautious. First hiring him, getting to know him at the office—a joy just to watch him move. Then a late meeting or two, until the declaration.

And after that—bliss.

But still the need for secrecy, which Jeffrey didn't really understand but respected. Gayness to Jeffrey had never had to be that big an issue; he was the type of boy who'd always known what he was and who was happiest in a relationship. They lived quietly, at home, a publisher and his employee, private lives discreetly handled.

The house creaked somewhere upstairs. Was he up? Cruz listened, but the place reverted to silence.

Even Ed Cochran's visit—the most surprising thing that Cruz could remember in his business life—hadn't started out badly. If both Jeffrey and Cochran hadn't been so naive, so idealistic, it might've been okay.

He slugged at the tepid vodka, his face contorting into a grimace, remembering that Thursday night. It hadn't yet gotten dark. They were finishing an early dinner when the doorbell rang, and Jeffrey had jumped up to answer it. Seeing the nice-looking kid in a coat and tie, with a briefcase, Jeffrey had said, sure, they had a couple of minutes.

Cruz had wanted to scream, "No, Jeffrey, we don't! Not here!" But Ed Cochran was already inside the house, shaking hands, and there was nothing to do but be polite and bluff it.

And they'd sat right here, in this room, as Cochran had explained that he hadn't been sent by his boss or anything. He'd just done some figuring on his own and had devised a way to keep Army—Sam Polk's company—in the distribution chain for another year, after which time they could be phased out and Cruz could have his in-house operation at no loss of profit.

See, he'd explained, it was more or less a loan situation that would enable Army to keep drawing income and stay in business while Polk set up some other networks to cover for the loss of *La Hora*. Cochran had had all the details right there on paper. He was sure that Cruz didn't mean to wipe out all the families who worked at Army—especially when there was an alternative. And it was just a matter of a slight compromise on his part.

Cruz couldn't believe it. Here was some dumb kid asking him to forgo his entire reorganization to accommodate some businessman who'd gotten caught in the squeeze.

"But it won't have any negative effect on your business," he'd said after Cruz had said no.

"It will affect cash flow for a year, minimum."

Why had he even argued with him? It was strictly a business decision, having nothing to do with the personal fortunes of another company's employees.

"But you could survive that, couldn't you? Wouldn't it be worth a little sacrifice for the grief you'd save other people?"

Was this kid for real? No one, not even Cruz, could predict what his business would need to survive. What might *El Dia* do if he gave them a hole to crawl through?

Cruz had been about to toss Ed, but then Jeffrey had butted in: "He might be right, Arturo. It could perhaps be done."

"It can't!" It had been an outburst—atypical behavior for him. Normally, it would have rolled off him. But, he recalled, he had felt Jeffrey might be coming on to Cochran.

Well, in any case, he should have kept his cool, not started bickering with Jeffrey—and in front of Cochran, where, if the boy wasn't blind, he would see that they were arguing not like employer and employee, but like lovers.

Even if it could be done he wasn't going to do it. He had no investment in Army Distributing or any of the others. What happened to them was their own problem, and if they hadn't planned contingencies for the loss of *La Hora*'s business, it just showed poor management and validated his decision to stop dealing with them in the first place.

Thank God he had realized what was happening in time. He'd smiled, pulled back into himself, and asked Jeffrey to go get a bottle of wine. When he was gone, he'd turned to Ed Cochran.

"I will meet with you after hours at my offices. I do not discuss business at home. And Jeffrey, though welcome to his opinions, does not help me make policy. Is that very clear?"

Cochran had nodded. "I appreciate it."

"There will most probably be nothing to appreciate."

Cochran gave him a warm smile. "Well, at least I'll have tried."

"Yes, you'll have done that."

And, before Jeffrey had come back, they'd agreed on Monday night at nine-thirty. Just the two of them. To talk.

18 ❧

*T*HE MORE Alphonse thought about it, the more it didn't hold up. He sat having early ribs and greens at Maxie's on Buchanan, trying to figure how to keep himself alive until this deal went down.

James, his man, was losing faith in him. This being his—Alphonse's—first pass at middleman, his credibility was low. It had taken all of his jive to persuade James to keep the buy happening. And even at that, he wasn't certain any longer that it would come off.

If he couldn't get the deal closed right now, it would be over. Everybody else would just walk from it. It would maybe take him some time, but Polk would find other buyers, and James would just write him off as a loser and go on to a better source, if he didn't just off him. Meanwhile, Alphonse got no bread for all the hassle and wound up where he'd always been, on the goddamn street, unconnected and going nowhere fast.

He thought about it. The smart bloods made things happen themselves, didn't wait around while everybody else figured how they were going to get their piece. And the more he thought, the more it felt all wrong.

I mean, Cochran for instance.

Nicest guy in the world, no two ways about it. But why had he been at the delivery spot? Straight Eddie must have been part of this thing. And that meant Polk was somehow trying to cross him.

He chewed on some gristle, trying to figure out these money guys. Outside, it drizzled through light fog, still as death. A dog peed on the building across the street, sniffed at one of the paper bags in the curb.

Everybody had gotten nervous when the money hit the table. That was the problem. Until last week, everybody'd been very cool, just putting together some times when the transfer could get made. And down at Army, with most of the crew laid off, with Cochran out trying to drum up new business and Sam gone half the time, there hadn't been any work, so he and Linda had just hung out around the office getting high.

But then suddenly it wasn't just talk, and everybody seemed to want to move very fast. And there had been nowhere to move to. Polk didn't have the stuff. Sure, there was an excuse, about Eddie being killed there, but that smelled bad. That smelled really bad the more he thought.

Maxie was pouring some more chicory coffee into the cracked white mug. She was a good mama, black and fat as they come, but just hanging back, cooking her ribs, keeping cool.

"Hey, Maxie," Alphonse said, "I ask you a question? I need a second opinion."

Maxie stopped pouring, looked down at him. "Yep, you ugly." She laughed and laughed. Alphonse smiled himself, waiting 'til she stopped. "Okay, honey, what?"

But suddenly, before he could even ask her, he saw it. It was so obvious he couldn't believe he hadn't seen it. He put his full mug down hard, spilling it out over his hand.

"Watch out, child, what you doin'?"

He smiled up at Maxie. "Thank you, Mama."

He had to get away from it a little, maybe just far enough to laugh for a minute—to see it all clearly. Everybody was playing the same game. James had protection for his money—major-league protection—and still he was nervous. And Polk had the same case of nerves, which meant he had the same basic situation—his money was sitting waiting to move. It was on the table, out, but in Polk's case it probably wasn't protected.

The question was, where was the table?

Alphonse was surprising himself, and liking it. The thing with Linda on Friday had started it, when he'd been so uptight about James that he just couldn't deal with any excuses about how her dad was having a tough time and couldn't Alphonse wait 'til Monday for his check. He couldn't have cared less about the goddamn check—what he wanted was to talk to fucking Sam Polk, who was stringing him out.

So he'd slapped Linda. Hard. The first time he'd slapped anybody.

He didn't think much of guys who slapped their women around before. And of course, Linda wasn't his woman. But slapping her had gotten her attention.

Of course, she had known where her dad was. She just hadn't wanted to tell Alphonse. But then, suddenly, they were allies of a kind. It was as though she looked at him now not as a jive-ass employee of her father, younger than she was, but a man worthy of respect—somebody who could get things done.

It was a good lesson.

He got off the bus and transferred to the cable car near Union Square. It took him up by the Fairmont and back down toward the Wharf. He jumped off without paying. The tourists, oohing and aahing, freezing their asses off, they paid.

He'd never been to Linda's apartment before. Standing in the gusty alcove, he had a moment of doubt before he rang the bell. What if she wasn't home, wouldn't let him in, wasn't alone? Maybe he should have called to make sure.

But then he remembered the slap, the power he was starting to tap into. He was on a roll. He had to go with the feeling. And Linda might know where her father was keeping the money. She might not even know that she knew. But Alphonse now had no doubts that he could convince her to talk, and if something was worth finding out, it would come out. He could make it happen whenever he wanted now that he knew how to go about it.

Damn. She should have fixed herself up. You just never knew what was going to happen.

Now here it is before noon on a Sunday and somebody's at the door, and if it's Daddy he's going to see me in my robe and hair still uncombed and the place a mess and he's going to think I'm a slob. When really I'm just alone and it's hard to do all these things for yourself with nobody to care about it.

Pushing the voice button: "Who is it?" Pressing the door buzzer at the same time.

"Hey, it's Alphonse."

She had to stop doing that, letting people in before she knew who it was. But then, he was probably inside the door downstairs and there wasn't anything she could do about it now. Besides, thinking about it, what a nice thing. She'd thought about Alphonse a couple of times this weekend, just spaced out watching the tube yesterday.

Sure, he was, like, pretty young and black and all that, but he did have kind of a cute face and a nice hard body, and it was a neat rush just to fantasize.

And driving home from Daddy's, with Alphonse sitting so quiet next to her, she really had gotten the feeling that he was nervous, like he was thinking about them being together in the car at night. He hadn't done anything, though. It was like other things were on his mind.

Over Saturday, maybe he'd been fantasizing a little, too. Maybe he really liked her a little. She'd studied him on Friday, after he'd hit her —it wasn't any big thing, she knew. Guys just got riled up sometimes and had to make a point—Daddy would still do it, cuff her from time to time. But with Alphonse, it had kind of made her look at him different. Like he was showing her this private part of him, opening up. Flattering, in a way.

She was four floors up and it wouldn't take him long, so she ran into her bedroom, dropped her robe on the floor and pulled on a pair of jeans and a T-shirt. No time for underwear. Then a quick brush through the hair—barefoot was okay. In the bathroom the water was cold but felt good on her face. No makeup, but at least she'd be clean. A last look. Not bad.

The place wasn't exactly a mess. Certainly it had been much worse. A couple of pillows out of place, some dishes on the drain. On the way to the door she dropped the pizza delivery box into the garbage, then kicked the coffee mug and the box of Ritz and the empty Coke cans under the couch.

"Hey," Alphonse said, sauntering in past her. "What's happenin'?" He wore a red tank top under unbuttoned Army fatigues. His face seemed to shine in the room's light.

"How'd you know where I lived?"

He smiled, looking his real age for a minute. "I looked it up, man."

He bopped over to the window and looked out. His body became very still, hands at his side. He stared without a word at the Bay and Alcatraz beyond, as though something was on his mind. Well, she could give him time.

She didn't know him very well yet. This was kind of how he'd been on Friday, though at work he had always seemed more energetic, jumpy almost. Especially that last week when they'd done the toot—then he'd really been fun, laughing and cutting up. He could do Eddie Murphy better than anybody.

He turned around, motioned with his head. "Righteous," he said, "the view."

He seemed to notice her for the first time. His eyes rested for a second on her breasts, traveled down her body.

"I'm glad you came by. I wasn't doing anything." She made what she thought was a cute shrugging gesture. "You want a beer or something, help yourself in the fridge. I'm not done making up yet."

She went back into the bathroom, heard the refrigerator door open. A second later he was leaning against the doorway, looking at her in the mirror as she brushed on some powder.

"Hey,"—she made it sound light—"I'll be out in a minute, okay?"

He just stayed there, sipping at his beer. "Come on, Alphonse, you're making me nervous."

He shrugged. "Nothing to be nervous about. It's just me." He put the beer down on the back of the toilet, just reaching over casually. She felt his hand on her waist, then move down across her backside. "What are you doing?"

Moving a step sideways, away from his hand, but turning around toward him, giggling. "Come on, give me a minute."

"I don't got a minute," he said. His eyes weren't laughing. She caught a look at them in the mirror, then turned completely to face him. "What's the . . . ? *Hey,*" she said.

"Tha's right."

He still wasn't smiling. His penis was jutting out from the front of his fatigues, his eyes locked onto her face.

"Alphonse."

He held it in his right hand and pulled her toward him with the other. "You want some of this."

It wasn't a question. He took her hand and put it on him.

It was going pretty fast. Now his other hand went behind her neck, and she was kissing him, still gripping him hard as though holding for her life on a thick piece of wood. It felt hard as wood.

She pushed him back. He wasn't fighting her anymore—they were in it together. She let go of him for a minute and undid her jeans, pulling them half down, getting herself up on the countertop.

"God, Alphonse." Throwing her arms around his neck.

"Yeah," he said. "Yeah."

"I got this situation."

They sat at the glass-topped kitchen table, each drinking some Mickey's Big Mouth from the six-pack that Alphonse had gone down and bought on the corner about a half hour earlier. He was finally getting around to what he'd come for. Or getting around to something else he'd come for.

They weren't exactly doing lines as a thing, where they'd just keep going through the day and into the night, but they'd had a few toots from the small pile of blow on the tabletop. Alphonse was wearing his red tank top and his camouflage pants. Linda had some hip-cut bikini briefs that, with the T-shirt hanging a little low, made it look like she was wearing nothing when you looked from the side.

Say what you want about the face, Alphonse thought, the girl has got legs that go all the way up. But that part was over for the time being, and he had some business to conduct.

She looked at him with a cocked head, loose now and feeling pretty good. "Talk to me."

"It's like this," he began, and ran down to her the scam he'd developed on the way over, borrowing heavily from his experiences in the past two weeks. He had this situation—he liked that word, the mysterious authority behind it—where he knew two guys. One of them had formed the impression that he, Alphonse, was a dealer. Another dude he knew was, in fact, a dealer. Anyway, the first guy had a couple of grand to lay out for some good blow, but his source had dried up, where the second guy had a good stash and was always looking for buyers.

"So, I figger, put 'em together and what's for Alphonse?" He sucked on his index finger and picked up some powder, running it around his gums. Then a little wash with Mickey's. "Get me?"

Linda nodded solemnly.

"But"—Alphonse smiled a big smile—"I lay my hands on some green, I buy the stash, cut it, sell it, keep a pile for you and me to party a bit, and"—he held up his still-damp index finger—"and have some pocket money left over, maybe do the whole thing again."

"It's hard to get money," Linda said.

"Getting started, that's always the thing." He sipped at the beer again, taking his time, then reached a hand across the table and patted her face. "You a bad woman," he said gently. He ran his finger over the table again, pressing into the pile of coke to get a lot on it, and put it at Linda's lips. She opened her mouth and he put the finger down under her tongue and left it there a second.

"Umm," she said.

"Bad."

She held his hand there, his finger in her mouth, with both of her hands. They stared at each other. When all the cocaine was surely long off the finger, she took it out, and giggled. "Wow," she said. She looked down at the last of the pile. "Getting low."

"Thing is," Alphonse said, "if we could just score a loan."

"They don't loan for that."

"But think. Maybe two hours the whole thing takes. That's all we need is some bread for two hours." Alphonse sipped beer again, then brought the bottle down in mid-drink. "Hey!" As though he'd just thought of it. "Your old man."

Linda shook her head. "He's not into stuff like that." With the rush and all, feeling pretty good, it was hard for Alphonse not to laugh. "Maybe he wouldn't have to know. He could front it and never know it."

"Like think it was something else?"

"Maybe you ask him for a down on a car, like that?"

"Six months ago, maybe. Not now."

Alphonse looked down, disappointed. Now play this one cool, man, here is the punch line. "You think he got anything at the office?"

"The office?"

"Yeah, you know, petty cash, like that." Linda shook her head. "No, I don't think so. Sometimes, but . . ."

"Worth lookin'?"

"I don't know. It's . . ."

"Hey, it's gone two hours, if it's there. Who'll know?"

"Like where, though?"

"He got a safe or something, or what?"

"Yeah, sure, in the back behind his desk."

"We check it out, what do we lose?"

"What if he's there?"

Alphonse looked at her. "He been there all week?" He reached over and touched her face again, like a reminder. He tapped her cheek. "We look, huh? Nothing there, no big deal."

"We'd have it back . . ."

"Hey, like tonight even. He'd never even know."

Linda, still unsure. "He just wouldn't have that much in the safe."

"Hey, but if he does . . ."

"Why would he, the way the business is going?"

"Shit, girl, I don't know. Maybe he's saving to buy his cute piece o' honey something—don't want her to find out."

Linda stopped arguing, looked down at the table, ran her own finger through the last of the pile and rubbed it in against her gums. "You're right," she said, her voice suddenly gone husky, "it can't hurt to check, can it?"

"You know the combination?"

"I know it's under the blotter on the desk."

But it wasn't.

So they spent about forty minutes looking for it, until Alphonse got on the floor and pulled out the elbow rest or writing pad or whatever it was that was stuck in the desk with a little groove on the bottom that you could put your finger in and then pull out.

"He always kept it under the blotter."

"Hey baby, it's cool. The main thing is we got it now." He whistled. Five numbers, up to eighty. "You ever open the thing?"

She nodded, sliding off the desk where she'd been sitting, sulking, coming down very hard. "You got any more blow?" she asked.

Alphonse had a few lines, as always, and he hadn't poured them out back at Linda's on the general rule that you don't tap out. But, he figured, now was tap city or bust.

This be the table, jacks. He felt it, and as he'd earlier proved, he was on a roll. "Maybe a line, two." He smiled his bright smile. "And the man be dealin'."

He was careful, pouring the cocaine onto the wooden desk, cutting it cleanly into four lines with his pocket knife, the one he'd used on Sam. It was a sharp knife.

They made a game out of it. "Right two," Alphonse said, and Linda, on her knees with her ass sticking out—was she doing that on purpose?

—and her tits—and Alphonse loved tits—big and firm-looking held up under the T-shirt, just turned that little dial. "Left, eighteen."

"Daddy's gonna shit we don't get this back."

"We'll get it back. Right seventy-seven."

"Sunset strip."

"You wanna?"

She giggled.

"Right nine," he said.

"Okay."

"Left—don't go past it—sixty-three." He expected they'd go at it nine, eleven, forty times, but goddamn if the thing didn't open just like a refrigerator.

Linda, wordless, reached in and pulled out one of the packets of hundred-dollar bills, tied with a banker's ribbon on which was written, in red felt-tip pen, "$10,000."

Alphonse eased his ass off the desk and made himself go slow the fifteen feet across to her. She just held it out, like, "What is this?"

He took it, riffled it, realizing deep in his heart that it was the real thing, that this was the number-one end of the line roll to end all rolls.

He crossed back to the desk. The packet of money fit easily into the front pocket of the camouflage pants. "Goddamn," he said, surprised at the high end to his voice. He turned to look at Linda, still kneeling by the safe. "God-damn! You hear me? God . . . god-damn."

He felt like he had to go to the bathroom. "How much is there?" Linda asked, her voice small now behind the cavernous roaring rush in Alphonse's ears.

He didn't even hear her. Over at the desk now he saw the knife and maybe a quarter line of powder and, knowing he'd just busted the house, he leaned down and scraped it into a small pile, licked his finger, ran it over the wood and then popped it into his mouth.

"How much is there? Enough for your deal?"

He turned around. What was she talking about? She was still kneeling by the open safe, which seemed to be filled with packets like the one in his pocket. And she was crying.

"Is that enough?" she repeated.

It was like he couldn't understand what she was saying. He crossed over to her, took her face in both his hands.

"Hey." Going to kiss her, but she turned away. Again, "Hey."

Her eyes came up to him. "It's all for her, isn't it?" she asked. "He saved all this for Nika."

What?

"What are we gonna do, then?" she asked. Alphonse didn't know what she was talking about, but he understood the literal question. "We gonna walk outta here," he said, pointing inside at the stack of money, "with that shit."

"No," she said.

"What do you mean, no?"

"I mean no. It's not ours. Just to borrow." She went to close the safe door. He remembered the lesson then, the slap that had made her somebody he could control, and he slashed out.

What he forgot, just for that second, was that he still held the knife, razor sharp, open in his right hand. And the next thing he knew there was blood all over him, the floor, everywhere.

Linda just opened her eyes wider, as if wondering what was going on. She opened her mouth, but no words came out, just more of that blood.

Alphonse looked down at the knife in his hand, remembering. He dropped it, grabbed at his shirt, couldn't rip it, and so pressed Linda's shirt up against her neck as she collapsed into him.

"Hey, girl, it's all right. It's all right now," he said. He patted her head on his lap, but the blood was getting out everywhere, spreading in a stain across the floor. He backed himself out from under her, cradling her head in his hands, then laying it gently in the pool that had formed under it.

He leaned back on his heels. "Shi . . ."

But the blood was spreading over to where he kneeled, and he thought he already had enough on him, so he slid back, then forced himself up. "What'd you go do that for?" he said. He didn't know, though, who he'd asked.

The pockets in the pants were big, but they wouldn't hold twelve of the packets of money, and that's how many there were all together— eleven more. He took them out of the safe and stacked them on the desk.

Outside Sam's office, past Linda's secretary spot, and down the hall, across the parking lot back to the warehouse, he walked to where they wrapped newspapers when it was wet, which was most days. The machine there spit out wrapping plastic and had a bar that heated it and cut it off clean. He flipped the switch on.

It took him only two trips, trying not to look at Linda. He could hold three of the packs in each hand—three and two the second trip. He put two of the packets of three end to end, then next to them put the last packet of three and the one of two. The ten grand in his bloodstained pocket never entered his mind. What he'd put together wasn't exactly symmetrical like a newspaper, but the machine worked perfectly, sealing the whole thing together so it would seem like one long package—a loaf of a bread maybe.

Alphonse, breathing hard now and not high in the least, found one of the brown paper bags they used for Sunday papers and slipped the plastic-wrapped bundle of money into it.

Out in the parking lot Linda's car sat alone in the overcast and windy midafternoon. Alphonse walked by it, carrying the bag, on his way to the street.

He had the money. He didn't need to drive. If he walked tall and fast, he'd be home by dark. He never even thought about the knife, lying on the floor in a thickening pool of blood, about midway between the open safe and Linda Polk's head.

Nika always slept after they made love, and normally so did Sam, but he couldn't get his mind off the money. He could get down to Army, check it out, and be back within an hour, and after that he'd get some rest tonight. It had been a long weekend, and it still wasn't even Sunday night.

He got the call that morning. Same time, same station, okay? No, it wasn't, he'd said. The Cruz parking lot was just too stupid. Why run up flags? How about the Coyote Point marina, the old cement dock nobody used anymore? Monday at eight-thirty?

So that was settled, but the money still kept his stomach churning. He'd just check the office safe and make sure it was okay, then tomorrow would be the delivery and it would be all over.

He'd tried to reach Alphonse, but nobody was home. That was all right. Alphonse would be in at work in the morning. They'd lay out the details of the transfer then—but after Friday's display, Sam would bring his gun. Couldn't be too careful, he thought.

Nika slept soundly, breathing heavily, uncovered above her waist, one leg out wrapped over the blanket, on her side. Sam ran a hand along her flank as he took a last look at her before heading up to the city, perhaps checking if she was worth all this. He decided she was.

He made it from Hillsborough to the Army Street exit in twelve minutes, then in another three he was at his lot. And there was Linda's car.

Overtime? It was possible, though he knew that they had been having their troubles lately. With her there, he knew the money would be safe. He almost turned to drive back home, not wanting to deal with her, to hassle her jealousy.

But he softened. Look at her, she's okay, working in here on a Sunday, trying to keep it alive.

Maybe with the new money I'll take another run at it, he thought. Patch up things with the kid.

He pulled into the lot.

19 ✿

*H*ARDY WAS walking a shark.

Wearing one of the wet suits that hung on the back of the door behind Pico's office, he trudged around and around in the circular pool in the basement of the Steinhart Aquarium, his gloved hands trying to hold on to the great white shark that some fisherman had delivered in the hope that it would be the one that somehow would survive the trauma and become the centerpiece of Pico's shark tank.

But Hardy wasn't walking for fame, for the feather it would be in the cap of Pico Morales, who happened to be the Steinhart's curator. Hardy wasn't walking the shark to make Pico's career. He walked it to save its life. When Pico had called him this morning, suddenly it had occurred to him that though this shark madness had always been futile, that didn't necessarily make it any less worthwhile. He'd surprised himself this time by saying he'd do it.

Pico had first gotten the bug maybe two years before, and he'd explained it to Hardy: "To breathe, sharks need to move through water, Diz. Time they get here they've usually been badly mangled, sometimes just kept on deck while the boat limits out, then rolls in from the Farallones. So they're wasted when they get here. I figure if we can keep one moving long enough . . ." He shrugged. "So I need volunteers to walk around with 'em, and you, a true aficionado of things nautical, to say nothing of the underdog, or undershark in this case, seem to be the perfect candidate."

Hardy couldn't say why, after the long hiatus, suddenly the endeavor was bearable once again—more, it was appealing. Pico had never given up on him, kept calling every two or three weeks, whenever they got one. And Hardy'd kept saying no thanks until this morning.

It was now three o'clock, though if any place were timeless, it was this enclosed green room within the bowels of the Aquarium, sur-rounded by its vague bubblings and hums, its shiny wet windowless walls.

Hardy was on his third one-hour walk. The other volunteers were as unlikely as he was—a retired car salesman named Waverly and a Japa-nese kid named Nao who worked mostly as a porter at the Miyako Hotel, and of course Pico. There were other eccentrics in Pico's stable, but today it was Waverly and Nao. Hardy had gotten in at seven A.M.

He hadn't been planning on doing anything about Cochran today anyway, and he'd just as soon avoid thinking about Jane.

Pico arrived to spell him. In his clothes, Pico appeared to be moder-ately overweight. In his wet suit, Hardy thought he most resembled a sea lion heavy with calf.

He stood at the side of the tank, smoking. His mustache drooped to his jawline, his thick black hair was uncombed. Under his arm he held a newspaper.

"How's Orville?"

He'd taken to naming his sharks. Helped them with the will to live, he said, although the theory hadn't proved itself out. At least not yet.

Hardy didn't stop walking. "Orville"—he goosed the shark under its belly—"is lethargic."

Pico walked into his office and reappeared a second later without either the cigarette or the newspaper. Vaulting the side of the tank with an agility that belied his size, he fell in next to Hardy. He put a hand on the huge dorsal fin and, walking sideways, tested for reflexes in the tail.

"Lethargic? You call this lethargic? He's in the pink. Orville"—he petted the shark's head—"forgive him. That was just some poorly timed sarcasm." He gave Hardy the bad eye. "Try to be a little sensi-tive, would you?"

Hardy let Pico take over, hoisted himself out of the tank and went into the office to change. When he came out in a couple of minutes, Pico's newspaper was in his hand. Pico was coming around with the shark, and Hardy started walking outside the pool along with him.

"You read this?" Hardy asked. *"La Hora?"*

"Sí. Keeps me up on my ethnic heritage."

"You know anything about the publisher?"

"About as much as you know about William Randolph Hearst."

Hardy opened the paper, scanning the front page as he kept walking. The water slushed behind Pico and the shark.

"I talked to the guy. He lied to me."

"Who?"

"Who are we talking about, Pico?"

"William Randolph Hearst. What, did Patty get kidnapped again?"

Hardy pressed on. "Cruz." He tapped the paper. "The publisher."

"He lied about what?"

That question stopped Hardy. It was one he hadn't asked himself, and should have. Cruz had lied about knowing Eddie—at least Hardy had felt pretty sure about that—but maybe that hadn't been all. Pico had gotten to the other side of the pool.

"What'd he lie about?"

But Hardy was already at the door, headed out. "Thanks, Peek."

Pico tightened his grip on the shark. "Don't let it get you down, Orville. He's just like that. Sometimes he forgets to say good-bye."

Hardy hit the twenty on the first throw, then the nineteen, eighteen, seventeen. The sixteen took him two. Fifteen through twelve he nailed, but eleven, his "in and out" number in 301, hung him up for four throws. That was really abysmal. He prided himself on never using up an entire round of three darts on one number—and especially on eleven, hanging out there at nine o'clock—for a lefty, the easiest angle on the board.

He shook his head in disgust.

The Shamrock hummed slowly in the late afternoon. Bruce Hornsby was on the jukebox, allowing as "that's just the way it is, some things they never change." Lynne was behind the bar.

Hardy had the dartboard to himself, a fine time for emptying the brain, just letting things happen. A Guinness, his first of the day, was half finished on the table next to him.

He began the next round, shooting for the ten, and when two out of three of the darts missed, what he felt wasn't disgust anymore. Something had worked its way up, ruining his concentration.

He picked his darts from the board. In the back, by the bathrooms where he'd had his talk with Cavanaugh under the stained glass, he made himself sit still in one of the deep chairs. He put the Guinness on the low table in front of him, then leaned forward and removed the flights from his darts—light blue with an embossed gold dart, just like his business card—folding them up carefully and putting them in their slot in his case. He laid his tungsten darts, one at a time, into the worn velvet grooves. The case went into his jacket pocket.

Okay.

He sipped the stout and leaned back in the chair. If he wasn't going to be getting any official help, he was going to have to start paying more attention to details. He resolved to start a written report when he got home that night. For now, something was bothering him. What else had Cruz said?

Almost nothing. It had been the most superficial of meetings—if he hadn't lied about Eddie, Hardy would never have thought of him again.

He went over everything they'd said. First, the kid who'd freely admitted he knew Eddie. But then Cruz had gotten rid of him pronto. Then there was the vandalism with the fence, which had apparently caught Cruz by surprise. Hardy remembered him standing at the fence after he'd gone to his car, just staring at it, hands on hips, shaking his head. Kids must have done it, he'd said, but again Hardy came up with a question: What kids?

And what about the car Eddie had driven to the lot? Had the department checked it out for prints? Hairs? Fabrics? Had Griffin? Maybe it was still in the city garage.

He got up and went to the bar. Lynne gave him a pen and some paper and he scribbled a few notes while he waited for the next Guiness to settle out.

He looked at his watch. It was nearly six o'clock. He'd put it off long enough, getting out of the house early to walk Orville. Maybe that's why he'd said yes to Pico this time, without even thinking about it too much.

He asked Lynne to hand him the phone over the bar, dialed information, got the number and called it. She answered on the first ring.

"Please don't hang up," he said.

A long silence, then: "Why not?" she asked.

He struggled through an explanation.

"I don't know why," she said when he'd finished, "but that upset me more than I can remember." He sat biting his lip, not knowing what to say, hoping she'd stay on the line. "I thought you were just getting back into character, running away," she said.

"I'm not doing that anymore." He'd let her get her jabs in—he owed her at least that much. "I called now, didn't I? We're talking."

"Please, Dismas, don't do this if you just can't. I don't think I could take it."

He thought about it long enough that she repeated his name.

"Okay," he said.

"Okay what?"

"How about we try again tonight. I swear to God I'll show up."

"Why don't you give me your phone number? That way if you don't, I can do something about it."

"You got a pencil?"

They went to a place on upper Fillmore that specialized in Cajun food. They sat in a booth, next to one another on a bench as though they expected another couple. A maroon cloth was pulled across the front of the booth between visits from the waiter. Jane sat closest to the wall, Hardy on the outside.

They had oysters with Cajun martinis while Hardy talked in a little more detail about the events of the day before. For entrées, Jane ordered catfish cut into strips and tossed with peppers, onions and baby shrimp. Hardy had a blackened filet, extra rare, with a tamale. They shared a bottle of white wine and found out a little more about each other.

When she and Hardy had been together, Jane had worked in the advertising department at I. Magnin, but after a couple of years had become more fascinated, she said, with the fashions than with the actual selling of them. She had become a buyer, starting over from the bottom, and liked it now very much, traveling to New York, Los Angeles, Chicago, even to Europe and twice to Hong Kong.

Hardy regaled her with tales of bartending, Moses, Pico and his sharks, a little about Eddie Cochran. Their desserts arrived—a couple of crème bruleés and some espresso. The talk wore down. Hardy looked at his watch. Jane half-turned on the bench to face him. She reached out and covered his near hand with hers. "Do you think," she asked, "it's time we talk about Michael?"

Hardy looked straight ahead, across the booth, at the knotholes in the redwood-stained plywood. He lifted his espresso cup, then put it down without drinking. He moved his hand out from under hers.

"Don't," she said.

"I'm not doing anything."

"You're pulling away from me again."

Hardy, trapped in the booth, said, "Maybe I am."

Jane again reached for his hand, putting it, as she had the other night, in her lap. She kneaded it slowly with both of hers. "Because what's the point now? Is all this just social talking, catching up on each other?"

"All what?"

"Dinner. Clever repartee."

"Come on, Jane."

"You come on," but gently. "Knowing what somebody's doing isn't knowing them."

"Maybe it's enough."

"Well, then I wish you hadn't called me." She let go of Hardy's hand with one of hers and quickly, with her index finger, wiped a tear from each eye, one after the other. "It wasn't your fault, you know."

Hardy was a block of carved wood, unyielding, inert.

"Have you ever talked about it?" She held his hand in hers again. A couple of tears had overflowed onto her cheeks, but she wasn't sobbing. "Do you ever think about it even?"

"I never *don't* think about it." But then, as quickly as it had come, it was gone. "It doesn't matter," he said, "I'm sorry I yelled at you."

"It doesn't matter?" she asked quietly. "You think yelling at me is the problem? I'd rather have you yell at me any day than just disappear."

He barely trusted himself to breathe. "It won't bring him back." Hardy finally looked at her. Seeing the tears, he brushed Jane's cheeks, turning on the bench to face her. "You didn't kill him, Jane. I did."

"You didn't. He'd never stood up before. How could you have known?"

"I should have known."

Michael, the seven-month-old son, had stood up for the very first time in his crib. Dismas had put him down for the night with the sides lowered. The baby got to his feet, leaned over, and fell to the floor, head first. He had died by noon of the next day.

"I should have known," he repeated.

"Dismas," she said, "you didn't know. That's over. It's long over.

How long are you going to suffer for it? It was an accident. Accidents happen. It just wasn't anybody's fault."

He picked up his coffee cup, staring across the enclosed space, and put it to his mouth, tasting nothing.

"Every time I looked at you I blamed myself again. What I put you through. Me and you."

"You didn't put me through it. You didn't cause it. Look at me now," she said.

She was beautiful to him. Her cheeks glistened with her tears. "I'm telling you I never thought it was you. It might as easily have been me. I should have known, too. All the books said he was getting ready to stand up, and I never thought of it." She brought his hand to her lips and kissed it. "The worst was losing you both."

"I couldn't face you."

"I know."

"And everything else just seemed, still seems"—he shook his head—"I don't know . . . it stopped meaning anything."

"Me, too?"

He closed his eyes, perhaps visualizing something, perhaps remembering. "No, you meant something. You've always meant something." He hesitated. "All the other stuff . . . I couldn't work up any interest."

They sat facing each other, turned together on the bench in the Cajun restaurant. They held each other's hands, both of them, between themselves.

"When you called me from in the bar, on the phone," Jane began, "you said you weren't running anymore."

He nodded.

"You want to think about that?"

He nodded again.

There wasn't anything else to say. He let go of her hands and pushed the button at the side of the booth, signaling the waiter to come and give them the check.

Glitsky's voice had said to call no matter what time Hardy got home.

After leaving Jane, his mind a jumble, he had driven back down to China Basin to view the Cruz parking lot another time. He walked to the hole in the fence, now inexpertly patched with baling wire. The cyclone fence hadn't been pulled away by kids. It had been cleanly cut top to bottom.

He'd called Pico from a pay phone to see how Orville was doing. The machine answered from Pico's office. Hardy tried his friend at home and learned that the shark hadn't made it.

"I should have warned you about my luck lately," Hardy had said, and told him about the baseball game. But then he had remembered that Steven Cochran hadn't died yesterday. Maybe his luck was changing.

Pico sounded depressed, and Hardy had asked if he wanted some company. Pico had said okay, and they'd sat up around the kitchen table, playing Pictionary with Angela and the two older kids for a couple of hours.

So it was late when Hardy got home. He called Glitsky immediately. The sergeant wasn't in high spirits, just asked Hardy if he could come see him first thing in the morning about the Cochran investigation.

"Sure," Hardy said. "Something happen?"

"Yeah. Somebody else died, and it definitely wasn't a suicide."

Glitsky hung up.

20 ❧

$\mathcal{E}$MPTY. EMPTY empty.

The word kept replaying like a looping tape in Sam Polk's head ever since he'd pulled his car into the driveway. Empty. The house, Nika gone now, completely empty.

He had called her to tell her after the cops had been at the shop for a couple of hours. She'd expressed sympathy over Linda's death, but by her voice, he could tell she wouldn't be there when he got back home.

Oddly, her absence was all right, preferable in some way. The note on the table in the hallway had read: "Sammy, I'm sorry, but I just can't handle two funerals in one week. All this is getting so heavy, I thought you wouldn't mind if I went to Janey's (you know, in Cupertino) for a couple of days and try to get my head straight about all this. You can call if you want (the number's in our book). Sorry about Linda."

Sorry about Linda. That was all. Sorry about Linda. The empty house seemed to echo more in the darkness. No point in turning on any more lights—the one in the kitchen above the stove was enough. All he had to see was the bottle.

So this is where it all—all the work, all the planning and sweating and saving and effort—this was where it had gotten him. To a kitchen table at an empty hour in an empty house, drinking alone at midnight.

He wondered why it was he really didn't drink so often—now it was the only thing he wanted to do. First it had hurt his stomach, but after a while that had stopped. He poured another splash into the glass, got up, stumbled a little, and grabbed a handful of ice from the automatic ice maker.

Back at the table, he flipped the picture album open again, the one he hadn't been able to find for nearly a half hour. Nika had put it in one of the drawers underneath the bookshelves, not even out in plain sight.

There was Linda. He forced himself to look. She hadn't been beautiful, but there was something about her, a willingness to please. People liked her. He hadn't thought enough lately about how much he had liked her. Not that they'd talked all that much the last few years, but some people didn't communicate that way. Especially since she'd grown up and started doing some of her own things—the drugs, guys and so on.

But what could he have done about that? It wasn't his business, really, after she got out of high school. He told himself she had been an adult.

He poured again, clinking the bottle loudly. Why did Linda think he had become interested in his love life again anyway, gone looking for someone else to put in his life? Linda had made it clear that she had her own life. Okay, then, he'd go and have his. God knew, he'd earned it, raising a daughter alone and running a business by himself. She had had no right to begrudge him what he found with Nika.

The telephone rang in the empty house and he felt his stomach tightening, cramping again. Even if it was Nika, he didn't want to talk. He let it ring eleven times, then it stopped. He went upstairs to his bedroom, carrying the glass with him, his heart pumping now with fear. He realized who had been on the phone, probably, and it wasn't Nika.

But that was stupid. How could anybody know yet? Tomorrow, maybe—no, definitely—they would know, but not yet. He sat on the bed. He'd forgotten all about that. Or not forgotten, but put aside. He couldn't afford to keep doing that, not for long.

He was in trouble. How could it have gotten this complicated so fast? Just two weeks ago he'd had a simple problem with money, and a simple solution, and now he had nothing going on less.

Naked, he walked downstairs again, his glass empty. He had to hold the banister, and even then the steps seemed to fall unevenly.

Well, so what. He was alone and could do as he damned pleased, and if he was tired and drunk because his little girl had been killed, then he was, and fuck anybody who didn't like it.

But then another thing intruded. God, there was so much it didn't seem possible it all fit together. But this was important. This was more important, even, than Linda—*no*, he didn't think that.

But it *was* crucial. He'd told the police there wasn't any money. But what if they found Alphonse and he had the money? That meant it wasn't his—Sam's—money. And of course Alphonse would have the money.

But, on the other hand, once he said it was his money . . .

Shit, there ain't no one on earth forgets a hundred and twenty thousand dollars, even if his daughter just died. At least it would be there in the back of your mind.

So what could he tell the cops? They'd seen it, all of it, the excuses and the bullshit, and they would smell this one all the way to Sacramento.

If he'd told them right away about the money, then it might've been all right, because, goddamn, seeing Linda lying there had gotten to him, and they would have asked him some questions and anything would have worked.

. . . a lopsided smile and admitting that he played stakes poker.

. . . a slush fund for the good workers, tax-free, until the troubles with Cruz had been resolved.

Goddamn. Something.

But now he had trouble seeing it. They wouldn't buy it, and Sam couldn't blame them. He wouldn't buy it himself.

"You mean, Mr. Polk, that you had one hundred twenty thousand dollars in that safe this morning and you *forgot it* for how long . . . six hours? Mr. Polk, how old you think I am?"

The bottle of Jack Daniel's was empty. Empty. Like the safe, like himself. He went to the cabinet and grabbed another bottle, this time some French brandy that Nika liked.

Okay, so he was in trouble but the thing was not to lose the money. Once he had that back he could think of something. It didn't matter what the police might think of him. He hadn't done anything illegal yet, and if he could just remember that he'd be okay.

He walked outside. Up in the city it had been cool, but the weather still held here only a dozen miles south. He smelled the first gardenias, maybe a touch of jasmine. He breathed in again. Small white lights led out through the manicured garden to the hot tub. He looked at them in a kind of awe. He owned this. This was where he'd arrived at. It wasn't just a crummy kitchen drinking alone, it was a goddamn Hillsborough estate with grounds and landscaping and a hot tub, thank you.

He tripped on the first flagstone step, but didn't go down. Out at the hot tub he lifted the thermometer and saw it was 104 degrees.

If he just got loose and thought, he'd come up with something.

The water stung, but only for a second. He sat on the first step, looking down at his balls, and thought it was still a little too cold, and he could also use the jets.

There, now, that was better. A bottle of some French shit at my elbow, a glass in my hand, and some jets blasting away all the tension and worries. People had worked hard their whole lives and gotten to worse places.

He closed his eyes and leaned his head back against the bricks lining the tub. And had another sip of brandy.

Maybe I don't think enough, she said to herself. Maybe I've been on automatic too long.

There was only the one light on in the trophy room, as they called it, down the hall from Steven's. The one with all the pictures. She'd been gravitating to it a lot lately.

Big Ed's snoring was audible from time to time in the next room, but it didn't bother her. Really—it was funny—not much of what Ed did bothered her. Cigars, maybe, once in a while, but she had her vices that he tolerated, too—not being home enough, for example, running around helping everybody who asked, being unable to say no.

She looked at the wall with its pictures. She and Ed had talked about taking down the ones of Eddie, but then she realized that there would be no reason for it. It wouldn't lessen the pain. It was just another of the idiotic ideas she'd entertained in the last week.

Now she ran a finger across the bottom of the frame of the one where he was down at the merry-go-round at the old Playland at the Beach. He'd been seven or so when the picture was taken.

The little boy—mounted on the horse, mane splayed out in the wind —smiled out at her like his face would break. Erin remembered the day too perfectly. She saw the smear of mustard still on his cheek from what had been his first corn dog. Somebody's hand was just visible at the bottom of the picture. That had been Mick, reaching up to ride double.

She let her eyes go around the other pictures. It was true, there weren't many of Steven, and none in the past two years. There was

Mick, playing ball, graduating, diving from the pier at the place they'd rented the past few summers at Bass Lake. Jodie was accepting her debating award last year, biting her tongue in the front of her mouth in concentration over her cooking at the Girl Scout camp, in her first formal dress for the frosh hop at Mercy.

Stepping back, she tried to find the most recent picture of Steven. There was one of him with Eddie at the wedding two years ago, before he'd done that ridiculous thing with his hair that Big Ed had wanted to scalp him for. Another one, the year before that, was really just a snapshot of him and his dad and Eddie when they had come home with their limits of salmon.

That was it for the latest ones of Steven. The most recent after those was Steven at about eight, with Jim, Steven forcing a smile from the front seat of that Corvette Jim had loved so much. Before that was his First Communion, with the white pants and jacket.

How could she and Big Ed have missed what this wall proclaimed so clearly? There wasn't one shot of Steven all alone, by himself, the star of the show, for at least the past six years.

Last night, after everyone else had gone to sleep, she and Ed had sat in this room, wondering if they could have done things differently. And even then, with all these pictures staring down at them, they hadn't seen it. It was the same as always, she thought. They just took for granted that Steven was up there on the wall with his brothers and sister, a good well-adjusted kid like the others. They'd raised them all the same—same environment, same values. Of course they'd all turn out okay.

After agonizing over every parental decision with Eddie, then Mick, then of course Jodie because she was the first girl and there were lots of things that hadn't come up with Eddie or Mick, by the time Steven had come along they'd done it all before, right? So raising Steven would be the same as it had been with Eddie or Mick.

And finally she had been able to start taking the time she'd craved for herself, to somewhat offset the nagging guilt that she wasn't accomplishing much in her life except raising kids. Not that that wasn't important, but she had more to offer.

And Big Ed, too. He'd finally found the time for the fishing trips he couldn't ever take when the kids had been little. And for the poker once a month. And, mostly, just for the solitude—reading in the room out behind the garage, or walking down to the beach.

Neither of them had meant to be neglectful of Steven. Maybe, she reflected again, maybe it had just gotten too hard to think about. Forget what the evidence of their own eyes was telling them—that Steven was getting away from them, that he was nothing like the other kids. No, that didn't fit in with the leisure they thought they'd earned, so ignore it. It would probably work out.

And now the boy lay broken and bandaged down the hall, and Erin had no inclination to blame anybody but herself.

"Thank you, God, he's still alive," she whispered, a real prayer, just talking to God. She hadn't done that since she'd gotten the news about Eddie, and she didn't really think about it now. Just thank God Steven wasn't gone, too.

She walked down the hallway. The house felt empty. Because Frannie had gone back home today? No, probably just a reflection of how she felt—empty.

Ed snored once again. She heard him turn over in bed. Steven lay on his back, breathing evenly. She leaned over and held her face above his, taking in the sweet-smelling air he exhaled. It was still not adult's breath, but that wonderful stuff that came out of kids' mouths. The air in heaven, she thought, must smell like a baby's breath.

She touched the good side of his face, but so lightly he didn't move. Moving up a chair next to the bed, she sat and forced herself to keep thinking about the things she was going to change in her life. She really had stopped thinking enough the past few years. You could be endlessly busy and still not be doing enough of the right things. Maybe she and Ed had gotten lazy that way, morally lazy, selfish.

She put her head down on the blanket, up against his hip. She didn't know how long she'd been dozing when he moved, moaning. She reached up and caressed the side of his face.

"Mom?" he asked.

"I'm here, Steven," she said, "I'm right here."

21 ❧

"ALPHONSE PAGE?" Hardy said, somewhat surprised to hear a name he had never come across.

Glitsky, out in the Avenues on another homicide, stopped by Hardy's as promised. It made three days in a row that Hardy had been awakened before seven A.M.

"Alphonse Page. Of this there is little doubt."

They were in Hardy's kitchen. The fog outside was thin and still, the kind that had a chance to burn off.

"You think he killed Cochran?"

Abe shook his head. "I am fairly certain he killed Linda Polk, that's all. Different MO than Cochran anyway. Cut her throat."

"Money? What else."

"Well, it gets a little funny there." Hardy waited. "Her father called it in—the same guy you told me about, huh?"

"Short, sad, dumpy?"

"That's him."

"What was he doing at work on a Sunday?"

"He said he was feeling guilty he hadn't been in all week. Wanted to get a fresh start, jump on Monday, like that."

"Oh, certainly."

"I know."

The two men nodded at each other. "So," Glitsky continued, "there was no money around, although there was a safe in the room, closed up tight, and the victim, Linda, was lying in a pool of blood right by it."

"So he emptied the safe."

"In any event, it was empty when Polk opened it up for a look. I guess it was either him or Alphonse, maybe."

"What do you mean, maybe? Why else would she have been aced?"

"Diz. The lab tells me she was filled with sperm. They also found three or four hairs in her crotch. Appear to be from a black man."

"Jesus, she was raped?"

"I don't know, but that waters down the money as the only possible motive. She'd certainly had sex just before she died, like, within an hour or two."

"But why did she go to the office, where the safe was? It had to have something to do with money."

Glitsky shrugged. "No, it didn't. It probably in fact did, but it didn't have to."

Hardy got up and paced. "Well, shit, Abe, so who's Alphonse Page?"

Glitsky took out a photograph he'd gotten, reluctantly, from Page's mother when they'd gone to his house the previous night with a warrant. Hardy's forehead creased, studying the picture, as Glitsky went on. "Polk identified his knife at the scene. Prints with blood on 'em all over the place—some even in the back at a wrapping machine."

Hardy threw the picture onto his table. "And there wasn't any money?"

"Good point," Glitsky said, and noted something down on his pad. "Anyway, lab's doing a run on the car, but I'm sure enough I got the warrant, put out the APB. Alphonse came home early last evening, dumped some bloody clothes in the hamper, packed a sports bag and split. So far he hasn't come back, and I'm not expecting him. He did it."

"Could he have done Eddie?"

"I don't know. We don't know where he was that night, but we'll find out. After I talked to you last night I got out the file on Cochran. Read it cover to cover. 'Specially read about the car, Cochran's. You'll never guess."

"Black man's hairs."

Glitsky smiled. "In the front seat. You're a genius, Hardy. Lab's not done with the comparison, but you want to bet they're not Alphonse's?"

Hardy sat down. "You know what I think?"

"What do you think?"

"I think we've got a drug deal gone bad here."

Glitsky rubbed the scar that ran through his lips. "Well, damn, what an incredible idea!"

Glitsky then told him about the trace of cocaine found on Polk's desk.

"So did you bring him in? Polk?"

"He was pretty incoherent after it hit him. I mean, his daughter had just been killed. He's coming downtown this afternoon. Wanna be there?"

"I wouldn't miss it. Cavanaugh seems to think Polk did it, you know. I mean did Eddie."

"I didn't think he raped his daughter."

"Maybe she wasn't raped."

"And who's Cavanaugh?"

Since it was now part of his active investigation, Glitsky wanted to get it firsthand. He and Hardy drove separately over to St. Elizabeth's and both of them parked in the empty lot behind the rectory. Rose greeted them at the door.

"Father's rehearsing the graduation over to the church," she said. "You can wait here or go on over."

They walked through the lifting fog. Sixty boys and girls in uniforms —gray corduroy pants and white shirts, maroon plaid dresses and white blouses—were lined up at the door of the church. Two nuns fluttered around trying to keep order.

"They still do this? Uniforms, even?" Glitsky seemed genuinely surprised, parochial elementary schools not being his everyday turf.

"Hey, if it works don't fix it." Hardy held his hands out. "Look what it did for me."

Glitsky, his eyes still on the line of kids started moving again. When the last child had gone inside Glitsky and Hardy followed and sat in the sixth row in the first empty pew.

"What are they graduating from?" Glitsky whispered, but before Hardy could say anything a bell rang by the side of the altar and Father Cavanaugh, in cassock, surplice and stole, flanked by two acolytes, appeared through a side door. He came up to the altar rail, surveying the crowd, nodding to Hardy. He brought his hands together, palms up, and at his signal the children all stood. Hardy nudged Glitsky, and they got up too. The sergeant appeared puzzled.

"Let us pray," Cavanaugh intoned with a deep resonance.

"I know that guy," Glitsky said.

🍀

" 'Course I was younger then, still in uniform, even before Hardy and I were teamed," the policeman was saying.

Rose was used to policemen not wearing the blue. Except for *CHIPs* and a few of those older shows, no one on TV wore a uniform anymore. This man, officer Glitsky, had very nice manners, even if he talked a little loud, but he looked scary with that scar running through his lips— nowhere near as good-looking or friendly as her favorite black police- man, Tibbs.

"No, I think I do remember," Father replied. Rose was pouring coffee from silver into fine china. The policeman used a lot of sugar. The other man, the one who looked a little like Renko, drank his coffee black. Father, of course, had a lump and half & half. He'd had cream until last year, when the doctor had told him to cut down on his cholesterol. Margarine instead of butter, half & half instead of cream. But he still had his eggs most mornings. "We talked about the riots at Berkeley, the police role there, if I recall."

Inspector Sergeant Glitsky sucked rather loudly on the coffee. Maybe it was too hot to drink yet. "You know, Father, I think we did. How do you remember that?"

Bless the father, he had a memory.

"It made a great impression on me at the time, Sergeant. You were the first officer I had talked to who didn't just spout the official police line."

"What was that?" the other man asked. Rose wasn't exactly eaves- dropping. She had been planning on dusting this room today anyway. And she felt she should be around to pour more coffee if any of the men got low.

Father answered. "Once the students threw or broke something, it was open season for the police. They had the right then to use whatever force was necessary to keep things under control."

"It was just a pissing contest," the sergeant said. "Stupid. They should've just got some guys who didn't think all those students were revolutionaries, that's all."

"So who'd they get?" the other man asked.

"Bunch of rednecks they recruited from Alabama or someplace. Deputized for the riots. You know, bust some heads and see the Berkeley chicks running around without bras on. Weren't you around for that, Diz?"

Dismas, that was his name. Dismas smiled halfway and said his major concern at the time had been stopping those dominoes from falling, whatever that meant, although Father and the sergeant both seemed to get it.

"Well, your friend here, Dismas, is too modest. He was quite a force for moderation back then. It took some courage for a policeman, and a black one, to take that kind of stand."

The sergeant seemed a little embarrassed and sipped at his coffee, but not so loudly. "Mostly self-preservation, I'm afraid," he said. "The trend of importing southern gentlemen for the police force wasn't going to do my career any good."

"So what were you two guys doing together?" Dismas asked.

Father smiled, remembering. "The activist days . . . sometimes I long for them again."

He had never really been a radical, of course. An activist, yes, but within the system. The kind of man he still was—working for the homeless now, or getting some of the businessmen in the parish to hire boys from the projects.

"A few of us were volunteered to assist Father, that's all. He had an idea—who knows, it might have worked—that there should be a gun drive where every unregistered piece could be turned in and the citizen would get an immediate amnesty, no questions asked."

Father shrugged at Dismas. "I'm afraid we were all a little naive back then."

The sergeant came to Father's defense. "It didn't do all that bad. I was surprised we got the response we did." He turned to his friend. "Got about a hundred and fifty weapons city-wide."

"One hundred and sixty-three."

Father and his memory. Rose was proud of it. She walked over to the pitcher and picked it up. The sergeant held out his cup for more.

Father believed, he was saying in his humble way, that it was better to try things and fail than not try at all. They didn't know it wouldn't work until they tried it.

"I know," Sergeant Glitsky replied, "back then anything seemed possible. The times they were a-changin'."

Father sat back in his heavy chair, sighing. "Ah, yes, those changin' times. Back then Reagan was governor, now . . ."

All the men laughed.

"Thanks, Rose, a little more, please. Now what brings you gentlemen to the church's door this fine morning?"

Darn! It was more about the Cochran boy's death. And Father had seemed to be getting over that the last day or two. At least his appetite had returned. Perhaps the accident with Steven had forced him to turn his mind to more immediate problems, but that's how life was, wasn't it? One thing after another.

She put the pitcher down and went back to her dusting. There was some talk about Dismas hearing Father's confession, but that didn't make any sense, then Father was talking about Eddie coming by with that problem.

"When was that, Father?" the policeman asked. "Do you remember?"

"Actually, he came by twice. Once, I believe it was the Wednesday before . . . before he died. As I mentioned to Dismas the other day, one of his co-workers had said something about not having to work for very long, that he and Mr. Polk wouldn't need much money pretty soon. That he, Eddie, didn't need to worry about building up the business again."

Father came forward now in his chair. "Eddie was a very smart kid. He put a few things together and came up with the idea that Polk was going to do something illegal—he didn't know what. So he came by here and wanted my take on some options he'd worked out. But at that time he really didn't know much, so he left pretty unresolved. Anyway, when I saw him the next time—"

"And when was that?"

Father looked out the window, trying to remember. "If I'm not mistaken, that was Sunday."

Rose frowned, trying to remember something. Lord! It was hard always remaining a silent fly on the wall. But then she saw Father look at her and smile. She lit up with contentment. With his memory, he was undoubtedly right, and that was the end of it.

"In any event"—he turned back to the others—"he had kept on kind of pushing Alphonse to say specifically—"

"Alphonse? The employee was Alphonse . . ." That seemed to excite the sergeant. Rose was forgetting to dust.

"Yes, I think that was the name. Anyway, evidently Alphonse wasn't too bright and said something about drugs."

"Well, excuse me, Father, but it's not clear to me where you come in."

She knew this was a hard question for Father. She knew where he came in—for Eddie, for two dozen or more other people, really for anyone who asked. But how does he tell the sergeant without sounding like he's bragging?

"Oh, I think Eddie just wanted someone to talk to about it."

"About what?"

She was getting a little annoyed at the sergeant. He didn't have to push—Father would tell him.

"What he should do, I guess."

"This is what he was telling me," Dismas said to his friend, "at the Shamrock."

Father nodded sadly. "You had to know Eddie. He was—" he paused, then went on a little more quickly—"he was kind of like all of us were back in the sixties. Thought it was his business to be involved. That if he just stuck his head in and pointed in the right direction, people would see it. He would go and talk to Mr. Cruz—you know him?" Both men nodded. "And see if there might be some way to get back his business for a period of time while Army—Eddie's company—rebuilt. Then in the meanwhile, if that happened, he thought he had a chance of talking Polk out of it"—he paused—"out of doing something wrong, something that might hurt him."

Now Father hung his head. "So he asked me about it, and I"—his eyes turned back to the room, pained now—"I, wizard counselor that I am, said he might as well go ahead, that he didn't have anything to lose."

Silence. He didn't need to add—nothing except his life.

"One more thing," Hardy was saying as he got into his car. "Last night I remembered another thing Cruz had lied to me about."

"Cruz? Oh yeah, Cruz." Glitsky was late for another appointment, not at his most attentive.

"I asked him about the scene—his parking lot—what shape it had been in. He told me it was pretty bad."

"And it wasn't?"

"No, Abe, wrong point. How could he have seen it? His boy, secretary, whatever, told me it was cleaned up by the morning."

Glitsky thought a moment. "Maybe he saw it on the late news, ran down to check it out."

"Who called it in?"

Abe rolled his eyes to the still-clearing sky, reached into his car and handed something over the roof to Hardy. "You coming down for the Polk interview? One-thirty?"

Hardy nodded.

"So study the report between now and then and bring it back with you."

Hardy took the folder.

"But as you're going through it, checking out Mr. Cruz, say two words to yourself every couple minutes, would you?"

"What're those, Abe?"

"Alphonse Page."

22 ❧

$\mathcal{M}$ATTHEW R. Brody, III, was the managing partner of Brody, Finkel, Wayne & Dodd. The firm had twenty-eight associates and the entire fourteenth floor of Embarcadero I.

Brody, forty-one, stood six feet four and had lately begun using Grecian Formula on his thick head of (now) black hair. He wore a charcoal pin-striped three-piece suit, the coat of which now hung on the gilt rack inside the door to his office.

His face still looked as young as he wished his hair did, with a wide but shallow forehead, a patrician nose, a strong chin. The only moderately distinctive thing about his looks, and it wasn't much, was his upper lip, which was too long by a centimeter. He would have worn a mustache—did, in fact, while he was in school—but his wife had told him it made him look foreign, so he'd cut it.

(It was one thing to shoot hoops with blacks and have a beaner roommate, she'd told him after he'd passed the bar, when she'd decided to marry him, but another altogether to look like a successful attorney.)

Brody didn't build the firm to its present status by taking on poorer Latino clients such as those litigating against *La Hora* for distribution hassles. But neither did he do it by being unfriendly or turning down clients.

In the *La Hora* matter, he had gone to bat for Jaime Rodriguez because he was the cousin of his college roommate Julio Suarez, who, in turn, just happened to run the most successful construction company in Alameda, which was currently developing a three-and-a-half-acre waterfront mall about two miles from the naval station. Coincidentally, Brody was handling the paper on that development.

Rodriguez had been distributing *La Hora* in Lafayette and part of

Richmond. After meeting with Brody, he had talked all of his fellow distributors, except the main guy in San Francisco, into the co-op lawsuit.

After he'd studied the facts of the case, Brody got into it a little. It wasn't often he ran across a real human issue. This wasn't wills or codicils or a contract featuring an endless series of "WHEREAS" followed by a "NOW THEREFORE."

Of course, there wasn't much money in it, but it wasn't strictly *pro bono* either. Hell, someone had to represent these folks. He felt good about it.

From his desk in his corner office he could see the clock on the Ferry Building. It was eleven-thirty. He was prepared for the meeting. He was always prepared, he knew, but when Judge Andy Fowler sent someone his way it was doubly important to have done his homework.

Donna buzzed him and told him Mr. Hardy was here. He had, of course, checked back with Andy about Hardy. Used to be the son-in-law. Brody tried to recall if he'd ever met Jane's first husband, but that had been before he was successful enough to have joined Olympic and gotten to know the judge. Still, he was ready to recognize him if he looked at all familiar.

He didn't. The man was a little too casually dressed for Brody's taste. Andy had said Hardy was an attorney, and there were rules of dress within the fraternity. But then, Hardy didn't practice law anymore, so maybe something else was going on.

He declined coffee, tea, anything, which was good. Brody had said he'd give him an hour, but hoped it wouldn't take that long. Interesting cases were one thing, but let's not forget time was money. Hardy did thank him immediately for his time. Maybe he was still in the club.

Brody shrugged and smiled. "When His Honor beckons . . . How can I help you?"

"I'd like to find out, if I may, if this man Cruz might have had a motive to murder one of Sam Polk's employees."

Brody sat up straight, then fished for a cigar in the humidor on the desk. He didn't like being surprised when he ought to know what was happening. Lighting the cigar gave him a moment. He took a stab in the dark.

"Polk, the San Francisco distributor?"

"That's him."

Brody inhaled the cigar. He probably hadn't heard the name in six months, but he hadn't taken memory training for nothing.

"There's been a murder in this case?"

Hardy shook his head. "We don't know for sure. There's two dead people as of now, with an angle to Polk. There may be some connection to Cruz."

"Two?"

Hardy explained.

"You know, Mr. Hardy, Polk is not one of my clients."

Hardy obviously didn't know it. "I thought you were handling it."

"For everybody but Polk. He was the only one isn't Mex . . . Latino, among the distributors, but he was also the first and the biggest. He wasn't interested in the suit."

"Why not?"

"I don't know. He wouldn't even meet with me to discuss it, although my other clients tried to bring some, uh, leverage to bear."

"How was that?"

Brody held up a hand. "Nothing illegal, I don't mean that. No threats or anything. Just some business incentives."

But Hardy pressed a little. "And when he didn't come on, did it really hurt your case? What I'm wondering is, could someone have tried to scare Polk by hurting his people? Then maybe there was an accident?"

Brody acted legitimately shocked. "Oh God, no. No chance. All this went down months ago. At that time I would have given a very qualified maybe to that theory—very; now, it's not even possible. You must be out of litigation awhile. Anything in recent history couldn't be relevant." Hardy said okay, and Brody continued. "I don't understand it really. It, the lawsuit I mean, was to Polk's advantage."

"Maybe he didn't want to pay the legal fees."

Brody shook his head. "Minimal. In my opinion, I think he just stopped caring about his business. He's an older fellow, probably rolling in money, maybe just figured it was as good a time as any to hang 'em up. His daughter was *killed*, you say?"

"Yesterday."

"And the other one, his manager?"

"We don't know he was killed. In some ways it looked like a suicide, maybe was made to look like a suicide. The police leaned that way until

Linda was killed. But now they've got a suspect for Linda and they're willing to consider they're related."

"Just too much coincidence to buy, right?"

Hardy thought that was it.

"And you think Mr. Cruz might have had a motive . . . ?"

Hardy walked over to the globe and gave it a spin. He appeared to be thinking hard. "All I know, or think I know, is that Cruz lied to me twice while I was interrogating him. I'd like to think he did that for a reason."

"Why did he let you talk to him? He's stonewalling us."

"Eddie's body was found on his lot. We had a lying contest—I told him I was a cop."

"I hope you didn't tell Andy that."

"No, I don't think the judge would approve. Anyway, I got to see him and he lied to me about having known Eddie. I also think he was there at or near the time Eddie was killed."

Brody whistled, sitting in one of the comfortable chairs in front of his desk. "If you can prove that, you've got something."

Hardy took the other chair, saying, "I know. But if my uncle had tits he'd be my aunt."

Brody drew on his cigar, shaking his head. "The case really pisses me off, you want to know the truth," he said. "Here's this guy, Cruz, needs more money like a toad needs warts, and ruins his relationships with people he's worked with for years. Friends, even."

"Socially?"

"Not really. He's got no personal social life, though he's big in, as they say, the community."

"Well, that's a contradiction, isn't it?"

"Not really. The community is his ad base."

"So why'd he do it? Cut these guys off, I mean. Wouldn't that hurt him the same way?"

"I don't think so. It's nine guys spread out all over the Bay area. And it's not the kind of news the TV or the *Chronicle*'s likely to jump on."

"What is?" Hardy asked.

"Well, if *El Dia* prints it, it's publicity bullshit and sure as hell *La Hora* isn't going to run the story."

"So what are you building your case on?"

Brody crossed a long leg. "Oral contract. Past performance." He rolled his cigar slowly in his right hand. "Actually, we're almost to the point of going for a settlement and calling it a moral victory, though don't quote me on that."

"Who's 'we,' your clients?"

"We is the firm."

Hardy followed that. The case was nearly lost. Brody had said almost, and Hardy had known lawyers like Brody who didn't use the language carelessly. He mentioned it to him.

"We got a private eye looking for dirt on Cruz, but I'm skeptical of finding anything."

"Why would that even matter?"

Brody shrugged. "As I say, I think it's a waste of effort, but my clients felt if we got to the last resort, and we're there now, we might try some form of *legal* blackmail."

"Like?"

"I don't know. It's what we're looking for. Something to harm his image with the community, make him lose the ad support if it comes out. Then my clients remain discreet in return for a return to their original distribution contract." Brody stood up, looked at his watch. "Long-shot city," he said.

Hardy got up too. The interview was over. "You have any leads on that? He beat up his dog, or what?"

"No. We're dealing with the macho thing. There's some rumor he might be gay."

Hardy had to laugh. "I can't believe it. Here in San Francisco?"

"I know. But it's no joke among the Latinos, let me tell you. It's another bit of news that doesn't make the papers, but any Saturday you want you go down to Mission Park on Dolores and you can check out the Mexican gangs beating the shit out of anybody who swishes even a little."

"So if Cruz is gay?"

Brody made a face. "It might be some leverage, that's all. It's probably nothing."

Hardy thought of something. "What if Cochran had found out Cruz was gay, say, and tried to use it himself? Get back Cruz's *La Hora* distribution business for Polk that way? Or, maybe, keep the cash for himself?"

"That's a lot of ifs, but given all of them, I'd say you might have a motive there."

Hardy thanked him, they shook hands, and again Brody was alone in his office. The clock on the Ferry Building said it was just past noon. The fog had completely burned off, and the flags along the Embarcadero were flying in what looked to be a light breeze. He loosened his tie, sighed, and returned to his desk, punching impatiently at his intercom.

Here was Hardy, thinking Eddie Cochran had been the nicest guy in the world. One of the bona fide good ones. He'd known him pretty well, and had bought his act completely—but it couldn't have been an act, this is Eddie we're talking about. Hell, he was married to Frannie, and she was the sister of Hardy's own best friend. Didn't he *have* to be a wonderful person?

And besides, Hardy thought as he picked at his dim sum (waiting for one-thirty, when Polk would talk to Glitsky), they weren't even suspecting Cruz. Alphonse Page was the suspect.

Okay, say Eddie had known Cruz was gay, and had known all about Polk and his drug deal. Now, how about he puts the squeeze on Cruz, or wants a cut from Polk, or both?

No. That wasn't Eddie.

Was it?

23 ❧

*G*LITSKY PRIDED himself not on being smart, but thorough. Though he didn't even remotely think that Sam Polk had killed his own daughter, he had gone ahead and run a little background on the man—you never knew what might turn up.

Hardy's tip or hunch or whatever it was about a drug connection looked like a winner—the cocaine on the desk hadn't been blown there on a passing wind—so he had ordered a guy to check out his recent banking activity. There, aside from an amateurish run to different bank branches, he had found enough to warrant calling up the DEA. He didn't really care about the drug deal—what he wanted was leverage on Polk during the interview.

He had seemed legitimately strung out yesterday at finding his daughter's throat cut, and Glitsky didn't think it would be too difficult to get him to start talking about some possible connection between Linda's death and Ed Cochran's especially if he thought he—Polk— would be named some sort of accessory to his own daughter's murder.

What would be ideal, and what Glitsky fervently hoped for, was that Cochran's death would turn out a clear homicide and get in his own backyard. Glitsky's thing was homicides. He was getting a lot closer to certainty that somebody had killed Ed, and with Alphonse looking like a lock for Linda's murder, he seemed a reasonable suspect for having done Ed . . . well, at the least a good guy to start with. Of course, a few hairs in a car seat, by themselves, weren't going to convince any jury, but Alphonse had proved himself well beyond careless with Linda. Glitsky figured that if he'd killed Ed he'd left some indication of it. And if that were true, Glitsky would find it.

It was a nice stroke of luck—hitting on Polk's account. That money was somewhere out there, and that always shook things up, which was good.

He popped the last bite of his bagel and followed it with a mouthful of cold coffee. Dick Willis, the DEA guy, would be up in another minute, and Hardy any old time. He wiped at the desk with a paper napkin, caught some crumbs in the palm of his hand and dumped them in the wastebasket by his right knee.

This was the part he really liked. The case should break within the hour. It was all but broken now. With the new leverage, Polk should crack in about five minutes. Tell him the DA might cut him a deal on the Cochran thing, then sit back and let the tape recorder get it all.

He allowed a smile.

It was almost too easy, but he'd take it.

Hardy was whittling a Popsicle stick into a totem pole. He'd already done the eagle at the top, then a kind of half-assed bear's head (which could as easily have been a wolf—he should have done it in profile), and was about to start on a duck as a goof when Glitsky came back to his cubicle.

Hardy looked up. He didn't have to ask, but he did. "Not there, huh?"

It was two-fifteen. They'd waited until nearly two o'clock, at which time Glitsky had called down to Burlingame to ask if they'd send a squad car to Polk's house and see if something was wrong.

Willis from the Drug Enforcement Agency had gone, saying he'd be available whenever Polk did show up, but he wasn't about to waste any more of an afternoon for a lousy one-yard deal.

Glitsky figured Polk might have been detained at the morgue, or making arrangements to get Linda's body to a funeral home, and he'd gone out to make a few calls, then check to see if he'd just gotten directed to the wrong room or something at the Hall.

Hardy stayed in Abe's cubicle, whittling. His new doubts about Eddie's character were still eating at him. It was great that Glitsky had established a link to drug money and to Alphonse, although that didn't necessarily mean Alphonse had killed Eddie.

"You think he ran? Polk?" Glitsky suddenly asked.

"I'm out of practice," Hardy said. "That never occurred to me. Why would he run?"

"As in take the money and . . ."

Hardy shook his head and closed his knife. The totem pole got flicked into the wastebasket without a glance. "I don't think he took the money. Alphonse took the money."

"Yeah, I know. That's what I've been thinking, but where is the guy?"

"Traffic, Abe. Shopping. In the bathroom."

Glitsky straightened the line of something on his desk. "Okay. But I hate getting this close and not nailing it. He might have run, anyway."

Hardy decided to let him spew. He might have done anything. But how could he know the police had discovered the money thing? Improbable. No, he would try to bluff things out when they started asking about money. But he'd show. If he didn't, he'd be running up a flag.

When Abe had wound down, Hardy said: "The report says the call on Cochran came in at eleven-fourteen P.M. You tape it?"

"Of course. It was a nine-eleven."

"You mind if I give it a listen?"

"No. Help yourself. You gonna recognize the voice?"

Hardy hadn't thought of that before, and wouldn't that be a nice surprise? "The call came from a booth at the corner of Arguello and Geary," he said.

"If you say so," Glitsky said, "but what difference does it make? Polk gets here and starts talking, ten minutes later we know everything we need to know."

"About Linda, maybe."

"Also, maybe, about Ed."

"It's the maybes that get to me. Maybe we get lucky, and Polk finks on Alphonse, who maybe killed Eddie in a wild drug-induced spree of passion and mayhem. Then maybe we got a homicide, where the insurance pays on Eddie."

"You want to make book," Glitsky said, "Ed's a homicide."

"Make it official, my job's done and I'll go home and be out of your hair."

At Glitsky's baleful stare, Hardy smiled. "I figure until it's official," he said, "I can play with it."

Hardy walked to what passed for a map of the City and County of San Francisco on the wall of Glitsky's cubicle. The map had been stabbed to death by pins long ago, but the occasional street name wasn't completely obliterated. "Arguello and Geary is here," Hardy said, pointing roughly to the middle of the map.

"Goddamn. When did they move it?" Glitsky said.

Hardy punched his finger into the lower right quadrant of the map. "Here's Cruz's building."

"Yep, just about there."

"Can't exactly throw a hat over 'em, can you?"

"So?"

Hardy looked out the window. "Just something else to think about."

The phone rang and Glitsky snatched it up before the ringing stopped. He said "Yeah" a few times. Hardy turned around and started hoping this wasn't about Polk, because if it was it was bad news.

The scar through Glitsky's lips turned white with the pressure he was putting on it. He mentioned a few things about jurisdiction, if he could send some men down, like that. Then he hung up, a study in frustration.

"Say it ain't Polk," Hardy said.

Glitsky sat at his desk, picked up a pencil and broke it. After he put the two halves in his hands and broke them again, he frowned up at Hardy. "They just found him dead in his fucking hot tub."

Glitsky, almost to himself, clucked grimly. "Timing. I gotta work on my timing," he said. Then, "I was thinking about putting a tail on him overnight. I'm slowing down, Diz."

Hardy sat. "Well, at least if we can put Alphonse there . . ."

Glitsky shook his head. "Uh-uh."

"Sure, it makes sense. Look. Alphonse knows Polk can identify him—"

Glitsky held up a hand. "Spare me, Diz. I know the facts and you don't."

"Which are?"

"No sign of struggle. Polk wasn't offed."

Hardy just cocked his head.

"We get one of these every few months. You drink too much and sit in a hot tub, you get poached."

"Get out of here!"

Glitsky looked at the bits of pencil in his hand. He sighed wearily. "You get out of here, Diz, I got work to do."

❧

He hadn't even gotten to talk about the Cruz angle, if it was an angle. He almost stopped on his way out of the office, but then figured Abe would only cut him off, and Abe was probably right. It wouldn't do to forget that Abe had a bona fide murder and suspect in this affair, and anything else Hardy might find might be interesting and all that but wouldn't have shit-all to do with Glitsky's investigation.

So the afternoon gaped open before him. He stopped by the audio lab with the requisition slip Glitsky had signed and got the lady there to give him a copy of the 911 tape. He'd listen to it at home.

While waiting for it to be copied he glanced through the *Chronicle.* There was a story about Linda's murder (no mention of any connection to Eddie), along with the picture of Alphonse. Hardy read it over and learned nothing new.

Tape in pocket, he stopped at the concession stand for a candy bar, then walked across the tiles in front of the wall with the names of policemen killed in the line of duty. Sixteen this year so far.

Andy Fowler was presiding in Courtroom B. When Hardy entered, the judge had his glasses on and appeared to be reading something at the bench. The prosecuting attorney, whom Hardy didn't know, was whispering to someone by his side. The defense attorney was on her feet, pointing out something that the judge should note on whatever he was reading. Hardy walked up and sat in the second row on the aisle.

The judge finished reading, raised his eyes to the gallery, looked from one attorney to another and called a recess. He spoke to the bailiff on his way to chambers, and the man walked across to Hardy and said His Honor would see him.

When he got into the book-lined chambers, Hardy closed the door behind him. "That's what I call service," he said.

Andy shrugged out of his robes and motioned to the wing chairs in front of his desk, a little tray table between them. "So you seeing Jane again?" he asked.

"I hate it the way you fiddle-faddle around." Hardy let Andy pour some coffee. "We're trying, to see each other I mean."

"You got plans?"

"Well, if it works out I'll probably try to see her again."

"About that far, huh?"

"That's a hell of a lot farther than it's been."

Andy put a hand on Hardy's knee. "No push from here, I mean it. I'm just interested." He sat back.

"What I came by for," Hardy said, "I met your friend Brody this morning. I just wanted to say thanks."

"Was he any help?"

Hardy outlined it for him. Cruz, Ed, Linda, Alphonse, and now the latest with Polk. Andy sat back, interested, listening, sipping occasionally at his coffee.

"But you have a thread through this Polk structure."

Hardy nodded. "Oh yeah, everybody—all the dead people anyway— they're all connected to Polk one way or the other."

"So what's your problem? You got a suspect, you got motive, you got opportunity."

"True, but I've got one apparent suicide by gunshot, one murder by knife, and one accidental death. I'm not sure I see the same guiding hand over it all."

"This guy Alphonse, isn't he pretty likely?"

"He's pretty likely, I guess, given everything. I mean, a lot seems to have gone on in his neighborhood." Hardy leaned forward, elbows on knees. "I guess what bothers me is Cruz. If he's no part of this at all. You know, there's a whole other scenario here between Eddie and Cruz, and I mean it leaves Polk out entirely, and the damn thing is, it works."

"You want it all tied up neat, huh?" The judge chuckled. "You're in the wrong business, Diz."

"Okay, I acknowledge that."

The two men laughed. It was an old joke from when Jane had been thinking about going to EST. Hardy and Andy had acknowledged her into submission and she'd eventually given up the idea.

"You really think Ed was blackmailing Cruz?"

"That's what doesn't work. No way was he that kind of guy."

"Then why do you think it?"

" 'Cause he could've been, I guess. It would have given Cruz a reason to lie to me."

The judge stood up. "You gotta cut the deadwood, Diz." He held up a hand. "I'm not saying it couldn't have happened. Do you know where Cruz was that night? Didn't you tell me the report says he was home by nine? That should finish it right there. Look, you just told me that if it comes out he's gay, it's bad news for him. So suppose he had a date. He'd cover that, wouldn't he? He'd lie to cover it, sure he would, and that's got nothing to do with Ed."

Hardy hung on that for a beat. "You're right, I guess."

"Damn straight. You want my opinion, see where Alphonse leads. At least you've got a good idea he's murdered someone. That makes him a killer. Whether it's a knife or a gun might not matter. Some of these guys get creative. Anyway, I'd check him out first. All this other stuff" —he shrugged—"more than likely it's deadwood, and if it is you gotta cut it."

"Well, I guess that's why I came to talk to you. I just couldn't see it."

"You ever work on a case didn't have half a dozen plausible wrong turns?"

Hardy stood up.

"Goes against the grain just to follow the little arrows, doesn't it?"

"A little. That's probably it."

The judge looked at his watch, seemed to decide something. "You know, I'm not saying just drop it to make your life easy. If it's bothering you, find out what he was doing. But it's probably a wild hair."

Hardy smiled. "Probably," he admitted.

*E*DDIE COCHRAN's car was still at the police lot—when Frannie had called that morning from her first day back at work, they had told her it was being held now as part of another investigation.

She was stunned to hear that Linda Polk had been killed, but what did Eddie—what did their car—have to do with that? She asked if they were saying that Eddie had been murdered. No, they were not saying that. Not yet.

Still very weary of everything to do with Eddie's being gone, shaking off some morning sickness, she hadn't pursued it with them. She did take out Dismas Hardy's card and left a message for him to call her when he got home.

Then she worked most of a whole day without taking a break or lunch or even thinking about it. The paperwork, after a week off, had piled up, which had taken most of the morning, what with everybody coming by and wanting to know if she was okay.

Well, no, she wasn't okay. But it wouldn't do to say it. She still hadn't put it anyplace where she could accept it. She still expected to get home and then be making dinner and hear the door slam and Eddie's cheerful voice doing the "Honey, I'm home" Ricky Ricardo impression he'd picked up the last month or so.

But she just nodded, trying to be polite with all the questions, saying she was fine.

It was odd. Until the seed had been planted today that Eddie might have been murdered, Frannie had slowly been letting herself get convinced that her husband had in fact killed himself. And each time that supposed reality struck home, it cut deeper. If Eddie killed himself, it meant he hadn't loved her the way he'd said he did, the way she felt he had.

But you couldn't argue with facts. If he probably had killed himself, and the police had investigated and said he had, then whatever she had thought they had together hadn't been true. And what did that make the baby she was carrying?

She worked it around and around, coming back to it like a tongue to a hole in a tooth, forcing herself to feel the pain so that maybe she could get used to it. Eddie had rejected her. Eddie hadn't loved her like she'd thought.

But then, this morning, as soon as she'd heard some official doubt, it was like a fresh wind clearing the rooms of her mind. If the police weren't even sure, then she wasn't a fool to believe it wasn't true. She never should have stopped listening to her heart.

She remembered the time making love when she'd conceived. She knew it had been that Saturday morning when she had come back to the bedroom after her shower, to Eddie sleeping in. There was no faking his response to her. And afterward, lying there, touching her everywhere, nibbling. "I love your eyelids," he said. "I love your elbow." And laughing. "I love this little spot, what you call this?" right at the top of her leg in the back.

She had to believe he loved her. He did love her. And if he loved her, he didn't kill himself.

That's why the anger surprised her. Before, up until today, since Eddie had died, all she'd felt was this numb, horrible loss. Almost sleepwalking, trading consolation with Erin, not letting herself think too much.

But now, at ten to five, cleaning off the desk for another day tomorrow, she had to put her head down, the wave of anger came so strongly. "Oh, Eddie!" She almost said it out loud.

Because now the next reality hit. Before, while she was thinking he had committed suicide, it hadn't mattered. But now, if somebody had killed him, she had a pretty good idea of why they had done it.

All of his pushing, all of his idealism, his visits to Cruz and Polk, trying to convince them to be something they weren't, to be little perfect Eddies, play fair, do the right thing.

Oh, Eddie, she thought, shaking now, why couldn't you just leave them alone and be like everybody else? I told you a hundred times it wouldn't do any good. If you'd have listened to me you'd be alive now.

The shaking passed. Somebody walked by and asked if she was all right. Again.

She thought about the insurance money on the bus going home. It was the first time it had occurred to her, and like her anger earlier, it made her feel guilty.

Maybe this was the process, she thought. Little things moving in to take the place of the pain. She told herself this was probably natural, the beginning of the healing, but it didn't help with the guilt.

She didn't really care about the money. Then, for a sickening moment, she did. Well, not really, it was just if she did decide to have the baby, then she'd be able to stay at home with it for a while instead of having to keep working.

Something else was happening, and she tried to keep it out of the forefront of her thoughts. Like so many other things lately, though, it seemed out of her control.

It might be romantic nonsense, but that first day she'd found out she was pregnant, all she could think was that it was her and Eddie's love, the mixture, that had made the baby. It was as though their love had become a separate thing outside of themselves, proving it, existing alone.

But then the last week, becoming more and more sure that Eddie hadn't wanted the baby, hadn't loved her like she'd thought, she'd come to doubt whether she wanted it at all.

She sat by the window in the bus, not caring, not even aware, that her face was streaked with tears.

She *did* want the baby. It was Eddie's, all she had left of Eddie. She crossed her hands over her stomach.

Hardy had his elbows on Frannie's kitchen table. He hadn't been home yet. Frannie had called Lynne at the Shamrock while Hardy had been having one. She wanted to know about the other investigation, and Hardy didn't want to get into it on the phone at the bar.

Frannie's hair was shining again, and pulled back into a severe bun, it made her face look older, more in control. She wore a plain white blouse, a black wraparound skirt. The face was still pallid, without makeup, but a string of green malachite pearls set off her eyes.

Hardy was explaining. "I really didn't want to say anything, get anybody's hopes up, until we had something a little more definite."

"But don't you have something definite?"

"Well, yeah, but still maybe not definite enough. Did Eddie ever mention a guy named Alphonse Page?"

"Sure. He was one of the last ones they were keeping on at Army."

"Why him?"

"I don't know. It kind of bothered Eddie. Some kind of relationship with Mr. Polk, I think. You have to understand, Dismas, this situation at his work got funny about six months ago. I guess the company was just going under and Polk didn't care anymore."

"So why did it mean so much to Eddie?"

She sighed. "It was just a project, I think, at least at first. He hated to see the other men laid off when it might have been avoided. He didn't like it that one customer kept the whole company alive, that kind of thing. So he tried to keep things happening, but Polk just didn't want to put in the time anymore, and wouldn't give Eddie any real authority."

"Why didn't he just quit?"

"I don't know, really. Half was the challenge, I guess, but also he was starting school in the fall and figured he only had a few months so why start with somebody else?"

"So he thought he might as well do something worthwhile until he left?"

"Something like that, I think." She paused. "We didn't exactly agree on everything, you know. But then he realized something else was going on—with Polk I mean—and that's when he got this idea to save everybody."

Frannie got up and walked back into the kitchen. "Dammit," she said, just loud enough for Hardy to hear. She opened the refrigerator, then closed it.

Hardy followed her in. "Do you know? Did he actually go and see Cruz?"

"Uh-huh. Then he was planning on meeting him again. . . ." She stopped and turned, her eyes wide now. "God, I think it was that night. How could I not have remembered that?"

"Monday, the night he was killed?"

She leaned back against the counter. "Well, no. I mean, it couldn't be. He didn't . . ." She was shaking, the white fabric of her blouse shimmering over her shoulders and breasts.

"He didn't what?"

"He didn't leave here to do that. I'm sure of that. He said he wanted to think about . . . about the baby, that he'd be right back."

"Maybe he remembered his meeting with Cruz while he was out."

She didn't answer.

"But he'd seen him before? You know that for a fact?"

She nodded absently.

"Frannie, it's important."

She walked back to the table and sat again. "At least once, the week before, I think it was. He went to his house."

There had been no point in trying to talk to Frannie about Eddie maybe blackmailing Cruz. But driving home, it began to make more and more sense. If he was starting school in the fall, what was he planning to live on? And with a baby on the way, there'd be that much more pressure. Frannie wouldn't be able to work, at least for a few months. Extra money might come in very handy.

Maybe he only got the idea that night. He had the meeting planned anyway, and it just came to him. Then it backfired.

It was possible, if only Eddie had been the kind of guy to try that, and all indications still were that he hadn't been.

But turning onto his street from Geary, he remembered Abe's advice and repeated the name Alphonse Page to himself several times out loud.

He let himself into his dark house. Frannie's earlier message was on his machine. So was a call from Jane . . . "Just to hear your voice."

He went to his desk and took the 911 tape from his pocket. It was an educated male voice, made nasal either by some effort at concealment or from the recording. It said, "There is a body in the parking lot of the Cruz Publishing Company. Thank you."

Very formal, and little else. The "Thank you" jarred slightly. Hardy listened to the clip five times, hoping to recognize something about the voice. It was not female. It was not accented.

It was early—not yet nine-thirty of a long and nonproductive day. Tomorrow he would get to see Cruz if he had to kidnap him, just to get to the bottom of his lies. He also wanted to check up on Steven, see how he was getting along. Maybe Glitsky would even collar Alphonse.

He was pretty sick of it. All he needed was Eddie's death declared a homicide, and he thought Glitsky had enough evidence to do it now. But really, there was no new evidence directly relating to Eddie. There were just possible motives and random weirdnesses, like the phone call from the goddamn middle of the city.

Hardy picked up the telephone, dialed a number and listened for three rings. When Jane answered, he said he had to see her.

25 ❧

ODIS DE la Fontaine was more impressed with what the papers had called rape than with the murder, but he was most impressed with the money. And Alphonse—his own older first cousin Alphonse—did he ever have money!

Odis had never seen so much money in one place before. And Alphonse hadn't even unpacked the sports bag yet. What Odis saw was the one loose pack of hundreds that Alphonse was now carrying flat in the front pocket of his black baggy pants.

Odis checked it out again as Alphonse got up to go to the toilet. There wasn't a sign of bulge in the pocket. Alphonse had stopped on the way to the airport and bought a pair of sandals and a Hawaiian shirt that he wore hanging out over his pants.

He took the sports bag with him to the bathroom, but Odis would have done the same thing. That was just smart.

Alphonse wasn't worried. Why should he be? He looked different enough, Odis thought, with the new threads and the short hair. The picture in the paper had his Afro and the beginnings of that goatee he'd started a year before, then shaved off. So it wasn't likely anybody was going to recognize him in the dark airport bar.

That morning, after his mother had gone out to work, Odis had cut Alphonse's hair, then gone shopping for both of them. "And don't get us no Montgomery Ward shit either," Alphonse had said, peeling off five of the hundreds. "Get us some real clothes."

Odis, nineteen, had gone into Macy's up at the Skyline Mall and picked himself up a warmup jacket, a new pair of Adidas, a bunch of T-shirts. For Alphonse, he got some of the baggy pants, more T-shirts and a dress coat that cost nearly a bill. On the way out of the mall he passed a hat store and bought Bogart hats for the both of them. They hadn't decided on Hawaii at the time.

He still had two unbroken C's and maybe thirty more. Alphonse hadn't even asked him about the change.

They'd left the house before Odis's two sisters had come home from school, and definitely before Odis's mother got back from work. She hadn't been happy about Alphonse appearing on the run at their doorstep, but he was her sister's only kid and she wasn't about to turn him away. But she'd made it clear it was a one-night stopover, no more.

Taking Odis's car, they'd shot some pool in San Bruno 'til six o'clock, during which time they decided on Hawaii to chill out until things got more mellow around here. They got some steaks at a Sizzler, couple of glasses of wine, and then they'd stopped while Alphonse bought his shirt. They had parked the car in the long-term lot.

Now Odis, thinking about white pussy, waited for Alphonse to return. He hadn't heard nearly enough about it. Alphonse had said it was just like any other pussy. He didn't seem that much into talking about it.

He told Odis he hadn't raped the girl—she was a friend of his—and when she died it had just been an accident, which sounded right the way he told it. Alphonse sometimes hung out with some bad brothers, but he wasn't ever going to kill anybody on purpose. He was too nice a guy.

He looked out at the planes taxiing out in the night, wondering if the plane he'd be on in a couple of hours was one of them.

"Another round?"

Alphonse had ordered up some drink with an umbrella in it from the bar when they'd come in. Odis turned his head and looked at the waitress—mesh stockings right up to her ass over great legs, blond hair surrounding a model's face, tits pushed out the front of the scoop-neck blouse.

He nodded.

"What're you having?"

Odis cleared his throat. " 'Nother one of these. No, two of 'em." He smiled at her. "Going to Hawaii."

She smiled back. "That's nice. I wish I was. What is that, a mai tai?"

Odis didn't know, but he nodded. "Yeah. Two of 'em." That was nice, the girl talking to him like that. He watched her walk back to the bar. Nice wiggle. A small little ass like some white girls had, but a pretty, pretty face. She looked back at him from the bar, catching him looking at her. He smiled. She smiled back.

Wonder what she meant saying she wished she was going to Hawaii too? Maybe she was coming on to him a little. The thing that was on his mind kept getting bigger, and he turned his head to look at the runways again. Hey, what if he just asked her when she came back?

There she was, looking at him again, saying something to the bartender. And now coming back, definitely showing him something.

"I'm sorry," she said, "but I'm going to have to ask you if I can see your I.D."

Odis just looked at her, thinking, What's this? "Hey," he said, grinning, "I've already had one, right?"

She shrugged. "The bartender doesn't remember serving you. He doesn't think you look twenty-one."

"Tell him thanks, would you?"

"I will. But I need you to prove it."

There was something going on between them. He was sure of it. Odis leaned back in his chair and tucked in his shirt, pulling it tight across his chest. Then he looked her up and down. She liked that—he could tell.

Okay, then. He reached into his pocket. "Look," he said, "I don't got no I.D. right now." He took out his roll of bills. "But I got a lot of this, and my cousin, he got more."

She nodded and smiled, getting it, looking right into his eyes. "Okay," she said, walking back to the bar.

Damn, this is easy!

And here comes Alphonse, sitting down, smiling. "The plane's on time," he said. " 'Bout an hour and a half."

Odis looked back over at the bar, the girl now just waiting while the bartender was busy for a minute talking on the phone. She looked over to him and smiled, so everything was cool. Odis smiled back.

Alphonse noticed. "What you doin'?"

"Nothin' yet. But you got me thinking about it."

"What's that?"

Odis jerked his head toward the bar. "What she got."

"Well, you think when we get over there. We got no time for that here. I tole you it ain't no different."

Alphonse picked up his umbrella drink and sucked at the straw. He stared into the empty glass. "I could get used to these, you know? Maybe that's all I'll do over there is suck up piña coladas."

"Piña coladas?"

Alphonse shook his head, patient. "That's what we're drinking here, Odis. Piña coladas."

Odis was just about to tell him that he'd ordered some mai tais for the second round when this guy looked like the Refrigerator came up and hovered over their table.

"Excuse me," he said, all business, a giant standing light on his feet, hands folded in front of him. "Can I ask you gentlemen to show some identification?"

That's when Alphonse bolted.

Expecting him was one thing. Actually seeing him at the door was another.

It had been *her* door for so long she'd forgotten that it had once been both of theirs. Dismas coming home from work every day those—how many?—years. Up the stoop, then hearing the key in the deadbolt. In those days, even before the baby, Jane getting home before him, making some hors d'oeuvres or blender drinks before he got home, sometimes bringing her friends with her, sometimes Dismas getting home with his. Once in a while twenty people descending on the Hardy fun house.

But most nights, just Dismas, home from work, loving her.

And now here he was, again, on the stoop, with no keys of his own, ringing the doorbell. The door's top half was a frosted window, and through it the silhouette was Dismas, her Dismas, who'd once wanted it all and then none of it.

She opened the door.

"Hi." She was, for some reason, embarrassed, unable to say more. She wore dolphin shorts and a tank top and was barefoot, this buyer for Magnin's. She backed up a step.

He walked in all right, then the weight of the place slowed him down. Through the living room he seemed to feel it more. Without talking, she headed for the bedroom. She was forgetting what he'd have to pass.

He got to the door that entered the hallway. By that time she'd come to the entrance to the bedroom. Dismas stopped in front of her little used sewing room. He stood there a long time. The door to it was closed.

"Remember how we wouldn't close the door the first few weeks?" he said.

"How we wanted to hear every sound?"

He leaned back against the wall. She walked a few steps toward him. She heard the long breath.

"Maybe I should have come over to your place," she said.

"You think I was wrong?" he asked, letting himself down to the floor. "Now, here, it seems so . . . immediate."

She came a little closer. The only light in the hallway came from the kitchen, around an L-turn to the left by her bedroom. "I guess I got used to it," she said. "The house, I mean. The room." It didn't sound right, but she had to say something. "I had to go on."

"I couldn't."

"I know."

Jane came and knelt next to him. She touched his hair. "If it's any help, I understood. Even then."

"Things just stopped mattering."

"I know they did."

"I mean, why do anything anyway? I thought everything made a difference. I'd make a better world."

She pulled his face into her breast. "Shhh," she whispered.

"I was just like Ed Cochran. And see where that gets us."

She stroked him—his face, his hair—letting him get it out. At least he was with her, not running, his arms around her.

"I didn't—" He stopped, pulling back slightly. "Leaving you," he said, "that was wrong."

"It wasn't a lot of fun," she agreed, "but I lived."

"I never explained it, did I? Just upped and left."

"You think I'm dumb, Dismas? I got it."

"I just couldn't handle caring anymore. That much."

"I said I got it. I had to."

He motioned with his head. "What's in there now?"

"It's my sewing room."

"You mind if I look at it?"

They got up. She opened the door and flicked on the light, watching

Dismas trying to imagine it as it had been. Now it was a different place —the alphabet wallpaper gone, no trinkets or kid stuff or upholstered edges. It was a working room, pleasant and dull.

Dismas, hands in pockets, just stood in the doorway, nodding. "I should've seen this about five years ago," he said. "I kept seeing it like it was."

"You thought nothing would change?"

"The old interior landscape," he said, "it never did."

She turned off the light, taking his hand. "So what happened?" she asked. "Now, I mean."

"I don't know," he said. "I really don't know."

"You're the same, but you're so different," Jane said.

"Who isn't?"

"I don't think I am."

"Which one, the same or different?"

"Different," she decided.

Dismas was sitting crosslegged on the bed. He drank some of his wine. "You must be different, too," he said, "or I don't think I could be here with you."

She reached over and touched his leg at the knee, where the jeans were worn nearly white. He was barefoot. His print shirt had a collar and needed ironing and the top two buttons were undone.

"Well, either way, I'm glad you are." She leaned over and kissed him.

"How am I different?" he asked. Then, as though to himself, "How am I the same, come to think of it?"

"Well, you're still intense."

"I am intense," he agreed.

"But it's like it's more controlled now. Like you think about things more before you do them."

He kept his eyes on her, gray sleepy eyes that didn't seem tired. She chuckled deep in her throat. "See, you're doing it now. Just looking, thinking about things."

"I do think about things," he said. "No, it's not that so much."

"It's not?"

"It's more the way I think. I guess I just don't jump into things anymore."

"But isn't this investigation . . . ? Didn't you just jump into that?"

"I make exceptions."

She touched his chest at the V of his shirt. "And Pico and his shark. And you definitely jumped all over me at Shroeder's."

"I did? I thought that was you."

"No, that was you." She kissed him again. "Mostly. Which makes three jumps in a week. There could be a pattern emerging there."

Dismas lay back on the bed, against the pillow, a hand back under his head. He held out his wineglass and Jane reached for the bottle on the floor and filled it.

"You know, it's funny," he said. "Running into those things again, that I jumped into. It's not like I see them and decide. It's almost automatic. Back then everything was passion. Being a cop, the law, you. I guess old Diz just lost himself with all that."

Jane put the bottle back on the floor and stretched herself out beside him. "Is that why you quit them all?"

"They filled me up. They were what I was." He closed his eyes and drank some wine. "Then when Michael died . . ."

"It's okay, Diz."

"I know, I know. But I realized all those . . . passions, they weren't me. I was just a guy who did things pretty well—played cops, argued, made love maybe . . ."

"Definitely," she said.

". . . but none of it mattered. Or maybe mattered too much. I guess losing the kid made me realize that. There wasn't any me—any Dismas—left there to handle it."

"So you dropped out?"

"I didn't look at it that way. I changed careers, that's all, killed off that romantic idiot. You can't have things be that important. You lose things. That's life. You gotta be able to deal with it."

She ran a hand over the stomach of the man who'd been her first husband. He was smiling at her, in spite of what he was saying. Still a wonderful smile. She kissed him on the cheek, the ear, the neck. His arms came around her.

"So have you been happy?" she asked.

"I haven't been unhappy. I haven't thought much about it."

"Except developed your theory of love the attitude, the love-without-pain theory."

He shrugged. "It's a good theory. Have you been happy? Who's happy, anyway? It's a dumb concept."

"I'm happy right now," she said. "I don't need to think about what it all might mean tomorrow."

"Another difference between us."

But really, saying it all as if it were suddenly a pose, his lips curving up a little, eyes twinkling. "But this isn't bad."

"Thank you so much."

The kiss now slow, deep, hands moving. Feeling his breath soft over her body. "This isn't bad either. Or this. Or . . ."

"Diz?"

"Huh?"

"Shhh."

It wasn't often Rose couldn't sleep.

The last time had been when they'd had the Paulist missionary for that week, and that had been in February, she thought, or March, she couldn't really remember. She did know that when the diocese sent around the missionaries, she was more nervous about her cooking, her housekeeping. It was, she felt, a reflection on the fathers, and she didn't want to do anything to embarrass them, so she tended to stay awake, going over things she might have forgotten or that she could do better.

But on the other, regular nights, like tonight was, normally she'd finish the dinner dishes for the fathers and whatever guests they might have had, then watch television doing her needlework in her room until nine or so, then turn out the light. The days started early at the rectory and she knew she wasn't a spring chicken anymore—she had to get her sleep.

But the thing with Father Cavanaugh just wouldn't get out of her mind. And it probably wasn't even important. She could bring it up to him in the morning, and that would be that. But her body just wouldn't listen to her, and she lay awake, waiting for him to get back from seeing how Steven was progressing over to the Cochrans'.

She looked at the clock glowing on her nightstand. It was after eleven. She'd be sore tired tomorrow. "Come on, you old woman," she said to herself, disgusted, "it'll keep."

But she kept returning to it, and it might really be something Father would have to act on right away. Even if they had a suspect already, it might make a difference. He'd want her to bring it to his attention, even if she turned out not to be right. If he'd told her once, he'd told her a thousand times, "Rose, nobody's infallible but the Pope."

So if he'd just made that little mistake—and she wasn't even sure it was a mistake (Lord knows, his memory was so much better than hers) —then she thought he'd want to know, especially since it concerned Eddie's death, to say nothing of the official police investigation.

And it had been gnawing at her ever since morning when Tibbs and Renko (that's what she called them—wouldn't that be a good show if they put those two together?) had had that discussion where she'd poured the coffee. She'd gone over it in her mind about fifty times since then, the question of whether it had been Sunday or Monday that Father had gone out with Eddie, and she was pretty sure it was Monday.

The only reason she was sure—or thought she was sure—was that Sunday, a week ago yesterday, they had had Bishop Wright over from Oakland and she'd made a prime rib for the dinner and everybody had commented on how good the Yorkshire pudding was, and the au jus sauce. They'd invited her to eat with them, even, which was special for when they had guests.

She thought she remembered Father Dietrick opening a second bottle of wine, and the three of them retiring into the library after dinner while she cleaned up. But, of course, she couldn't be a hundred percent sure, since she'd gone to her room after washing up and she hadn't seen either His Excellency or the fathers again that night.

And she knew it had been an early Sunday dinner—she had timed the roast to be done at 3:30, so she must have served at around 4:00— so it was possible that their "party" had broken up early and that Eddie had come by after that.

The thing was, she remembered somebody ringing the doorbell on Monday night after dinner, but again she hadn't seen whether or not it was Eddie. Father Cavanaugh had answered the door himself, sensitive to interrupting her, and that had been the last she'd seen of him. He hadn't come back until after she'd gone to bed, and unlike tonight, she had slept soundly.

But it was her memory of Sunday, of Bishop Wright being there, that made her believe it hadn't been Sunday that Eddie had come by. His Excellency had never gone home early before. Usually Father Cavanaugh and he would "burn the midnight oil" over some cognac (and nothing wrong with that—the men need to be allowed some release) while they discussed philosophy or theology or politics. She knew what they talked about because Father Cavanaugh would often share with her some of what they'd said the next morning.

She sighed, turning on her side. Eleven-twenty. Maybe she should just wake up Father Dietrick and ask him if he remembered what time their discussion had broken up that night. But no, he'd . . .

There it was! The back door opening and closing quietly. She swung her feet to the floor and grabbed her robe from where she'd hung it neatly on the chair next to her bed. She wanted to move quickly before Father had had a chance to get to bed—it wouldn't do to disturb him after that—but she wasn't about to go out with pins in her white, thin and brittle hair either, even in the middle of the night. She stopped by the bathroom and took them out. She stepped into her slippers.

Father stood in front of the open refrigerator, peering inside. Seeing him, bless him, she knocked softly on the wall by the kitchen door.

"Rose," he said, smiling. "Caught me, I'm afraid." She made some gesture. "What are you doing still awake?"

"I couldn't sleep." No point in rushing right into it now. It probably wasn't that important. She moved into the kitchen. "Can I make you something?"

He stepped back, acknowledging the kitchen as her domain. She knew what they had left over. He leaned over and pecked her on the cheek, which made her blush with pleasure. Father loved her, and it was a wonderful feeling, as comfortable as being married.

"I'll just sit at the table and you surprise me," he said. "But do you think a beer while I wait would be sinful?"

He opened a Mexican beer while she took out the plate with the chicken on it. (See! It paid to take the extra minutes to slice the meat from the carcass.) Then the Best Foods (nothing but) and Clausen's pickles. She saw the Swiss cheese. Swiss cheese? Why not. And the potato bread that came in such big slices.

"How is Steven?" she asked, assembling. Without turning around, she could see Father shaking his head. "That poor boy."

"Is he all right?"

"He's been through a lot, but he's all right. I'd say it'll be a couple of months before he's really over it." Now sipping his beer. It really was amazing, she thought, that she knew his rhythms so well. She didn't even have to be looking at him to know what he was doing. "Youth is really something, isn't it, Rose?"

"That it is, Father, though I'm not the expert on it I once was."

Father chuckled at her jokes, that was another thing. "None of us is, Rose, none of us is."

Lettuce? No, not with the pickles. One green was enough. "Frankly," Father said, "I'm almost more concerned about Erin and Big Ed."

Well, of course you are, she thought. But she kept it to herself. How he felt about Erin was a secret. At least he thought it was. But anyone who knew him like she did could tell without any effort.

She brought the sandwich over, along with another beer. It was a good big one, and she knew he'd finish the first beer right in the middle of it.

"Are they all right?" she asked.

He dug into the sandwich, chewed carefully, swallowed, then drank some beer. "Oh, Ed's a rock, you know. It's mostly Erin."

She nodded.

"She feels like she's neglected Steven, drove him to running away, so everything that happened because of that is her fault."

"How has she neglected Steven?"

"That's what I tried to tell her. It doesn't make sense. Maybe she had other things she was doing, but I really don't think it was at Steven's expense. Look at the other kids." He took another bite of the sandwich. "Besides, Erin's always been very active."

"Could it be Steven just needed more attention?"

"But how do you tell that, Rose? And how do you blame yourself for it?"

She nodded again. Nothing in the universe would convince Father that Erin Cochran had done something wrong. "Great sandwich, by the way."

She beamed.

"But you know what I think it is, really? I think—no, I'm sure—it's still Eddie. How do people bear with all that in one week?" He closed his fist on the table and pounded it. "Dear God, if I could just change one thing . . ."

She reached over and covered his hand. "Now, don't you go blaming yourself, Father. You've said it yourself—sometimes God takes the cream of the crop early, back to Himself. He took Eddie, and nothing you or anybody else does is going to change that. You've just to pick up and go on from there. Erin's strong, and Ed will help her."

"Go on from there?"

"That's all you can do, isn't it?"

His eyes softened. The pain visibly left his face. "Thank you, Rose. You're a gem."

She blushed again, looking down. "Finish your sandwich," she said. Now, she thought, would be a good time. "You know, Father, while we're talking about Eddie . . . What I mean is, the reason I couldn't sleep is I was wondering if you'd made a mistake."

Father swallowed and smiled. "No one's infallible but the Pope, Rose. What did I do this time?"

"Well, I don't know you did, but . . ." She outlined it all for him, everything she remembered or thought she did. It took only a couple of minutes, but sure enough, that must have been what had been keeping her up, because suddenly she was exhausted.

Father had left the second half of the sandwich (had she made it too big?), and didn't open the other beer. Maybe what she was telling him was important.

"You might be right, Rose," he said when she'd finished. His lips were tight, the wide forehead creased in concentration. "I'd better call the sergeant in the morning."

"I'm sorry, I just thought."

He patted her hand. "Nothing to be sorry about. You did the right thing. Exactly. I'm sorry I cost you some sleep."

She sat back in her chair, relieved, but only for a moment, then reached for the dish. Father held her hand again.

"I'll get the dishes, Rose. You get some sleep."

26 ❧

*I*NSPECTOR SERGEANT Glitsky answered the telephone on the first ring, his adrenaline pumping. Calls in the middle of the night meant one thing—one of his cases had come in.

He kissed Flo, who didn't even stir anymore when the phone rang after midnight, and looked in on the three kids, two in bunkbeds and one in a crib all in the same twelve-by-fourteen room (and they did have to get moving on a new house, even if they couldn't afford it, if he didn't make lieutenant). In the kitchen, sucking a quick microwaved cup of mud, he called Dismas Hardy as a courtesy. The phone rang four times and then the machine clicked on and Abe said, "Hardy, Glitsky. They got Alphonse." Then he hung up.

Now he was looking through the small hole in the door of the interrogation room at the Hall of Justice. It was, by his watch, exactly 3:11 A.M.

A familiar and therefore not ominous silence prevailed all around him. The silence was familiar, in this place normally strafed by obscenities and bedlam, because Glitsky had done this many times since becoming a homicide inspector—come down in the middle of the night to interrogate a suspect still without his lawyer and therefore perhaps likely to talk if, as was also likely, his IQ didn't hover much above room temperature.

If he waited until the morning, even a rookie court-appointed defense attorney would tell Alphonse to say nothing, and that would be that until the trial. This was the prosecution's one big chance to break something in any case, and if an inspector wasn't willing to forego a night's sleep for it, he was in the wrong job.

Alphonse slumped, maybe sleeping, at the small table. His hands were not visible—it was likely they were cuffed to the chair behind him.

A deputy, hands folded, also perhaps dozing, sat at one end of the table. Glitsky knocked.

"Alphonse, my man, how you doin'?"

Abe's voice boomed in the small room. Everybody was awake now. Alphonse even managed a more or less welcome look, possibly relieved that he was getting questioned by one of his brothers, a notion Glitsky was not above using but that, all in all, he found pretty funny.

"Hey, we got you, huh?"

Alphonse shrugged. He had abrasions on his forehead and cheek, a swollen mouth, a little clotted blood under his nose. "You get caught in a door or something?" Abe asked.

"Airport cops hurt me," he muttered. Glitsky glanced at the deputy, making a clucking sound. "We've got to do something about those airport cops. He been Mirandized?"

The deputy nodded. " 'Bout five times."

"Does he want to talk?"

"Ask him."

"Alphonse, you want to talk to me?"

"Yeah. You wanna do something about them beating me up?"

He flipped on the tape recorder, an old, squeaking reel-to-reel. Glitsky turned back to Alphonse. "Says in the report you resisted arrest and necessary force was used to restrain you."

Alphonse rolled his eyes. He had a way of saying "shit" that took about two seconds and didn't end in "t."

"Shi . . ."

"So why'd you run?"

"I knew you was after me."

"Saw your picture in the paper, huh? Hey, you got your hair cut. Looks bad, man."

Alphonse bobbed his head at the compliment.

"So why'd you have to kill her?"

"I didn't kill nobody."

Glitsky smiled, warm and inviting. "Oh, that's right. Somebody planted your knife there, smeared her blood on the pants we got out of the hamper in your mother's house." Glitsky raised his eyebrows.

Alphonse's brain squeaking made almost as much noise as the reel-to-reel. Finally he said, "What if I don't wanna talk to nobody? What if I wanna see my lawyer first?"

"Then absolutely it's what we're gonna do. We're gonna stop right now and get you a lawyer in here."

There was a long pause. Abe waited it out. Finally Alphonse said, "I got rights."

"No question."

"I don't like one lawyer, I can get another."

"Righteous. Right on!" Glitsky gave him a sarcastic black power fist, then folded his hands on the table and just sat there. After about thirty seconds Alphonse said, "What?"

"What do you mean, what?"

"What you just starin' at?"

"I'm just waiting. I thought you were thinking about it." Alphonse strained, stretching against the cuffs. Glitsky, Mr. Nice Guy, turned to the deputy. "Can't you undo those?"

Alphonse rubbed his hands together when the cuffs were off. He gingerly touched the bump on his forehead. "Thinking about what?" he asked.

Abe thought he ought to get his attention again. "You know Sam Polk's dead, too."

"Sam ain't dead."

"He ain't breathin'."

Abe grinned now, the tight-lipped grin that showed his scar. His eyes didn't grin. His hands were still folded, calm, in front of him. He twiddled his thumbs, slowly, finally resting his eyes on them, his thumbs.

"Hey, I didn't kill any Sam Polk. You not layin' that on me, too."

Glitsky shrugged. "I didn't say that."

"Who killed him?"

"I didn't say he was killed. What made you think he was killed?"

"You just said . . ."

Glitsky shook his head. "Uh-uh. I didn't say anything about him being killed. You did."

Glitsky had him on the ropes. It was almost depressing, how dumb these guys were. Alphonse didn't even know what was happening, but Glitsky knew that Alphonse understood one thing—he was in deep shit.

"Alphonse, talk to me, man. If you didn't kill him, I'm the only friend you got."

"Shi . . ."

"No shit, for real."

Alphonse put his hands back up to his face, rubbing his eyes, craning his neck. "I didn't kill no Sam Polk."

"Okay."

Abe sat there. Sometimes sitting was the best technique in the world. He looked somewhere midway between them with no expression at all on his face. He kept twiddling his thumbs. Alphonse fidgeted as though he had a hemorrhoid. "How we work something out?" he asked at last.

"We trade."

"Trade what?"

"You tell me what happened. You didn't kill him, I prove it and you don't go to the gas chamber. That sound fair?" Glitsky kept smiling. It was good, he knew, to drop the old gas chamber in there. Keep the intensity at the proper level. "You know we got a new court now, Alphonse. We got judges now believe in the death penalty."

Alphonse swallowed hard, touched his forehead again. He was beginning to sweat. Glitsky was, if anything, cool. The tape recorder spun around and around, squeaking, a little like the steady drip of Chinese water torture. It was the first time Abe remembered having a squeaky reel-to-reel in an interrogation, but he thought he might request one in the future. He wondered, waiting for Alphonse, whether there might be something like WD-40 in reverse—make things squeak. That made him smile again. He ran with it, the humor. "Alphonse, I got to draw you a picture or what?"

"What? What you want? I don't know nothin'."

Truer words, Abe thought, were never spoken. "See, the thing is, when we got multiple murders in the course of a crime, like we do here, it's the death penalty. Special circumstances, they call it, like if you kill a cop, that kind of thing." His eyes crinkled up. "You hear me? They find you guilty and you could fry. If you're lucky, you go to the joint and you never get out. They don't even talk about it."

It was shaking him, Glitsky could tell. Whatever passed for logic in the brain of this poor sorry son of a bitch was being whacked out of kilter. "But I tole you I didn't kill Sam Polk. An' what crime?"

"Hey, Alphonse," said Abe, his close personal friend. "You had a bag with like a hundred grand in it. You sell Girl Scout cookies for that? Sam give it to you?"

"Linda got it out."

Abe shook his head. "Nobody's gonna believe that. To a jury it's gonna look like you stole it. You killed Linda for it, then you slammed the safe."

"I didn't mean to kill Linda! I mean, that was an accident."

"You cut her throat by accident?"

Alphonse paused, maybe catching up to the fact that he'd just confessed to a killing. He shrugged as if to say "Hey, it happens."

"So the thing is," Abe continued, pressing his advantage, "that much money around, you're dealing, right? You know it, I know it, so why argue about it. You didn't kill Polk, maybe somebody else did, but it was about the dope. That's what we want to know."

What the hell, Abe thought, might as well go for it. They had him cold for Linda's murder. Might as well collect some bonus points for DEA if he could, then work it around to the Cochran thing. He looked at his watch, then at Alphonse. "And I don't got all night, okay?"

Alphonse was wrestling with the problem. The sweat was now pouring off him—Abe could smell it across the table—and his nose was running slightly. He sniffed and ran the back of his hand over his upper lip.

"I know what you're thinking, Alphonse," Abe said in his most gentle voice. "You're thinking you talk and your friends find out, they'll kill you, right?" The eyes across the table told him that's what he was thinking. "Okay, that might happen. It might, you understand. But you *don't* talk, and I guarantee—guar-an-tee—that you're going down. No maybe, no if. You go down. We don't get you for Sam Polk's death, we definitely hit you for Eddie Cochran's."

Alphonse's mouth just hung open.

"Now you're going to tell me you didn't kill Eddie. I know, Alphonse, you didn't mean to kill anybody. Save it, though, huh, I'm tired." Glitsky looked at his watch again. He wasn't particularly tired, but it was closing in on four A.M. and he had his confession. He ought to go home. He pushed his chair back from the table and stood up.

"Where you goin'?"

"I said I'm tired. If you're not gonna talk, I'm going home."

Alphonse reached his hand out across the table. "Hey, I mean it. I didn't kill Eddie. Sam mighta kilt him, but I didn't."

Abe pulled the chair around backward and straddled it. "We got your

hairs in his car, Alphonse, the same ones we found on Linda. So don't
give me any more of this shit."

"Hey, I swear to God."

How many times had he heard this? Everybody was innocent of
everything. Unknown was the man who said, "Yeah, I did that, and I
did it because . . ." No, it was always an accident, or a mistake, or
somebody else's fault. Often, the denial got so vehement that the perp
actually came to believe he hadn't done it. And since more than four
out of five were either drunk or on some controlled substance when the
crime occurred, it wasn't surprising that it might all seem like an hallu-
cination or dream, that it hadn't really happened.

"You swear to God," Abe replied wearily. "But you got a better
chance of talking yourself out of Sam Polk. We got you at the scene of
Eddie's murder." Almost, he added to himself.

"I wasn't there!" His eyes had widened. Abe found himself forced to
look closely at him. There was something about this denial that was
different. "Look, I rode in Eddie's car most days, maybe even that day,
I don't know. But you gotta believe me. I liked Eddie, I didn't kill
him."

Abe wasn't about to get suckered by sincerity. He shook his head,
made a production out of checking his watch. "You sure as fuck did."
Then he stood up, motioning to the deputy to turn off the recorder.
"Take him upstairs," he said.

He got his hand on the doorknob before Alphonse called out again.
"Hey!"

Slowly, acting frustrated and exhausted (though his adrenaline was
still pumping away—he wouldn't need any sleep the rest of the night),
Glitsky turned back.

"Look, I'll talk, okay, but I didn't kill nobody."

"You killed Linda."

He waved that off. "I just thought—I got people saw me that night
Eddie got killed. Like all night."

"Yeah? Who, your mother?"

"No, man. I play basketball, City League. That was a Monday,
right?"

Abe nodded.

Alphonse rolled his eyes up again, straining for the memory. "Finals
were that night. We played four games. Came in second."

"Good for you."

"Yeah, good for me. Who came in first?"

Abe glared at him, lips drawn tight.

Alphonse smiled. "Bunch of cops," he said, "whole team full of cops."

27 ❧

*T*HE MORNING sun cast long shadows over the Cruz parking lot. It was barely seven A.M., and Hardy had been there for over an hour, taking the chance that Cruz had told the truth about one thing—working bosses' hours.

He'd slept at Jane's, gotten up early and decided to find out about Arturo Cruz once and for all. He wrote Jane a note, then drove across the wakening city to China Basin, where the whole thing had begun.

And it was, he thought, a whole thing, a whole new thing. Jane was right. It could be a pattern emerging. Two weeks before, he was a bartender, he wasn't in love (either the feeling or the attitude), he hadn't talked to Abe Glitsky in almost a year, or walked sharks or cared about some stupid idea of Pico's to get them into the Steinhart.

He wasn't sure what was going on, exactly. But having an hour alone to think about it, on a morning they were probably shooting postcards all over the Bay, made it all very real and a little scary.

It was just a favor for Moses and Frannie, he had told himself at first, but that wasn't washing very well anymore. It had gotten inside him, this feeling that he might be doing something worthwhile. It reminded him of why he'd decided to join the police force and then go to law school what seemed about four lifetimes ago.

And it wasn't that he wasn't proud of tending bar. It took a certain kind of person to be good, he knew, and there was a simple and profound art to the pouring itself, especially of something like a draft Guinness. Also, there were principles, like you didn't put a call liquor with a sweet mix—a Jack Daniel's and Coke, a Tanqueray and tonic. No, you explained to your patron that the finest palate in the world could not tell the difference between a $2.50 call liquor and a ninety-cent well drink when it was mixed with some sugary bubbly stuff. Then you let them see for themselves. You even gave them that drink on the house. And then if they still wanted their Remy Martin VSOP Presbyterian, you directed them to another establishment. Hardy wouldn't pour that shit, and McGuire supported him. Hell, McGuire had trained him.

But—no doubt of it—something else had been going on since he had started digging into Eddie Cochran's death. As Jane had pointed out, he thought about the consequences of things, and he had a hard time just now envisioning going back behind the bar rail full-time. Or even part time. Maybe he was getting a little old to be a bartender. He didn't think he had wasted his life or anything like that, or wish he'd done things differently for the past few years—doing them had gotten him to here.

What really knocked him out—the surprise of it as much as anything —was that here, right now, felt so good. He wasn't worried about being hurt, or failing, or anything. He wasn't worried about his potential. He was having fun, getting to know who he was, not who he'd assumed he had become. It was interesting. In fact, he thought, it was a gas.

The Jaguar turned into Berry Street, and Hardy, parked opposite the Cruz building, not in its parking lot, got out of his car and started walking across the street. The Jag pulled into the empty lot, and by the time Arturo Cruz, alone, had opened the door and stepped out, Hardy was standing in front of him.

"Mr. Cruz," he said, "I've got a problem."

"Mr. Cruz, I've got a problem."

The questions weren't going to go away. He knew that now.

You couldn't build a whole fabric of lies, he thought, and have it all hang neatly together. And the weight of all of them was still affecting him and Jeffrey.

Especially after the story on Linda Polk had broken yesterday. Of course, they'd run it in *La Hora.* Thank God he'd been with Jeffrey the whole day Sunday, that the police had another suspect. Otherwise, Jeffrey might have thought he'd killed Linda too.

And now here was the man again. He might as well come clean right now, he thought, get it off his chest.

He couldn't see Hardy's face, though he had recognized him as he was driving up. He was forced, looking into the bright, low, morning sun, to squint, then try to shade his eyes. The man was a fighter plane coming out of the sun.

He turned back to the car. There, that was better. He could see fine. He reached inside for his briefcase, then straightened up. "Come inside," he said, and started walking toward the building. Hardy fell in beside him. "I was going to call you," he found himself saying. As he did every morning, he unlocked the huge glass double-doors.

"What about?"

Cruz pushed the door and held it open. "Linda Polk was killed Sunday?"

"Right."

"And Sam died when, yesterday? I heard about it yesterday, anyway."

"Sunday night, we think."

They were at the elevator, inside it. The doors closed shut quietly. The man, hands folded behind his back, didn't say another word. Was he humming? The doors opened on the secretary's station of the penthouse.

"Being in the news business, I tend to hear about things."

Why wasn't Hardy saying anything? Well, try again, at least now in his office, on his own turf. He sat behind his desk. "So what's your problem? You said you had a problem," Cruz said.

"Why were you going to call about Sam and Linda?"

"That's your problem?"

Hardy shook his head patiently. He was sitting, very relaxed, in one of the deep white leather half-banquettes in front of his desk. "No," he said, "you brought that up. I thought I'd pursue it a little."

"Well, I mean, since Linda and Sam and, uh, that other fellow, the one who died here . . ."

"Cochran. Ed Cochran."

"Yeah, since they all worked for the same company. That's a pretty large coincidence, wouldn't you say?"

"Absolutely."

"Well?"

"Well what?"

"Well, I mean . . ." What did he mean? He hadn't been planning to call Hardy. He didn't know why he'd said that—nerves, maybe. But Hardy—he could tell—wasn't going to let it go.

"What do you mean?" The persistent bastard.

"I mean there must be some connection, wouldn't you think? Between them."

I ought to shut up right now, he thought. Say good-bye to him and call my lawyer.

"It's funny you should mention that," Hardy said. "It kind of brings it back to my problem. See"—he crossed his legs elaborately, ankle on knee—"the only thing I can see that ties them all together is the Cruz Publishing Company, *La Hora*, you. And the other thing is, what brought me here in the first place after I thought about it enough, is you lied to me at least twice when we had our first interview." He paused, letting it sink in. "At least twice."

Cruz started to turn on The Glare, the one that worked with his employees, even sometimes with Jeffrey, but Hardy held up a hand, said, "No," meaning, that isn't going to work, and then folded up the hand, leaving one finger out. "One, you said you didn't know Ed. His wife says he saw you the week before he died, and had another appointment scheduled right around that night. Maybe exactly that night. The one he died, I mean."

Cruz was glad he was sitting down. He could feel a sponginess in his legs and knew they wouldn't have held him if he was standing. He would have had to slump against something.

"And two," Hardy continued, sticking up a second finger, "you described to me how bad it all looked, with the blood and all. Now my question, my problem" (the bastard was really enjoying himself) "is how you could know what it looked like if you went home at eight-thirty or nine when the lot was empty?"

He tried to swallow, then cleared his throat. No good. Wheeling around in his chair, moving slowly, carefully, he took one of the cut-crystal wineglasses from its tray on the bookshelf behind his desk and pushed the water button on his small refrigerator. God, the water was delicious. He spun back around. "I didn't kill him."

"There, now, that's direct."

Hardy stood up. Cruz didn't like looking up at him—it threw off any sense of balance between them—but he still felt too weak in the legs to risk rising himself. "You mind if I get a glass?"

Then Hardy had the water and was sitting back down on the edge of the chair, elbows on his knees, holding the glass in both of his hands in front of him.

"What about the black guy, the suspect? We ran his picture in *La Hora.*"

Hardy nodded. "He's a suspect."

"And so am I?"

"Let's just say my curiosity gets aroused when I get lied to." Eye to eye. In no hurry whatsoever. "Pretty natural reaction, don't you think?"

Cruz gulped down the last of his water. "Maybe I should call my lawyer."

Hardy sat back in the chair. "You're certainly welcome to. But I'm not here with a warrant. I came to talk."

"I really didn't kill him."

"But you saw him?"

He closed his eyelids, and the sight flashed up behind them again—turning into the dark lot, headlights finding the body. Keeping the beam on it as he drove up, he'd gotten out of the car and stood staring for who knew how long, not recognizing Ed Cochran—there wasn't much to recognize—but knowing who it had been in any case. "I should've called." He went to drink more water, raising the glass to his lips, but it was empty.

"When was that?"

"When I saw him."

"That night?"

He found himself sighing, feeling the release, wanting to keep talking now that it had started, with nothing to hide. "I had an appointment with him at nine-thirty. I stayed working until maybe eight, eight-thirty, got hungry and went out to dinner."

"Where?" Hardy asked.

He didn't have to think about it. Every minute of that night had been looping in his mind for over a week. "Place called The Rose up on Fourth."

Hardy nodded. "I know it. Anybody see you there? Could swear to it?"

Of course. Wendell could swear to it. They had flirted a little, discreetly. "I think the waiter I had might remember."

"What'd you have to eat?"

Again, no need to think. "Calves liver, pasta, some blush Zinfandel."

"Then what?"

"Then I came back here. There was a car—I assumed it was Ed's—in the middle of the lot."

"But you didn't have your meeting?"

"He was already dead."

"Just like the police found him?"

"Yes, I assume so."

Now that he'd said it, he started shaking again. He didn't trust his hands to reach for his water glass to refill it. He put them on his lap, out of sight under the desk. Hardy leaned back in his chair now, frowning.

"What was the meeting supposed to have been about?"

Did he really want to hear about it? All of it? Cruz realized it might not seem, on the surface, to have made a lot of sense, but if he could just make Hardy understand the issue with Jeffrey—how Jeffrey had started to take Ed's side—then it would be all right. Anything was better than trying to keep all those lies in his mind.

He hadn't realized at first how bad it would be, having Jeffrey not believe him, even think he was capable of murdering somebody. But now, once he came forward, the police would find no evidence. They could have an investigation and find him innocent, and that would end all this horrible distrust between himself and Jeffrey.

But when he had finished, Hardy was still frowning. "So how come you couldn't tell us this last week?"

He saw that his hands were back up on the desk, folded tightly together. He spread them, palms up. "I was afraid. I just . . . I know there's no excuse. I don't know." He tried to smile, man to man. "It was a lapse, that's all. I was nervous."

Hardy stretched, looked at his watch and slowly pushed himself up from the chair. "Can I use your phone?" he asked.

Though it was still probably too early for Abe to be in the office, Hardy felt he ought to get the police involved right now. This warranted bringing in the troops. They might or might not corroborate Cruz's story, but he had admitted being in the lot that night at the relevant time. That would be enough to get something official going. Then, whether he'd killed Ed would either come out or it wouldn't. Either way, it was now a police matter.

Hardy left a message for Abe and told Cruz that another officer would be coming by later in the day. He was, of course, welcome to have an attorney present at that time.

Though Hardy knew it was patently ridiculous—that no real cop would simply walk out on a murder suspect leaving the later interrogation to another officer—he couldn't think of a better way to continue with Cruz. He'd done what he'd set out to do, which was prove he'd lied. Finding out why was out of his province. If Cruz tried to run he'd only get in deeper, and the publisher was, after all, an established, wealthy and even well-known citizen. Hardy didn't think he would run.

At home, Hardy heard Abe's message of the night before about Alphonse and felt satisfaction. Between Alphonse and Cruz there seemed no doubt they had the man who'd killed Eddie. At the very least they would have enough, once and for all, to call it a homicide.

Of course, he'd wait for the official word before passing it along to Moses and Frannie or the Cochrans. And though it wasn't going to help anybody's immediate pain much to know that Eddie Cochran hadn't killed himself, it would eventually be a consolation. The rejection factor would be gone. His death—the death itself—was a tragedy, sure, but the wound could heal over now. The quarter of a million dollars for Frannie wouldn't hurt, either.

28 ❧

STEVEN KNEW his mom was trying. Maybe she just couldn't do it.

She changed the bandages religiously, brought his ice cream and sandwiches, opened and closed the window and turned on and off the television or radio and probably would try to build him an airplane and take him for a flight if he asked her.

It was all still Eddie.

He didn't blame her, couldn't blame her. He felt the same thing, or guessed he did. Maybe it was different losing a son than losing a brother. But either way, it was a bad loss.

All this reaction in him—probably even the running away—had to do with that, with losing Eddie. He'd had a couple of days to think about it and, bright kid that he was, had come up with this theory . . . there was this minimum amount of acceptance everybody needed to get along, no matter where they were. With Steven, it was this house. And up until last week it had been close but there was enough. He was at absolute zero—until you factored Eddie in. And even though he hadn't been living at home for a while, Eddie had always been there in a way. His presence, his attitude, was felt. And Frannie, too, though not so much. Still, though, he gave Frannie (in those hours while the drugs were wearing down and he hadn't yet called Mom) a plus three, more than anyone he lived with. And Eddie? Geez, Eddie was off the chart, maybe plus a hundred and six on a scale of one to ten. He couldn't exactly figure it out, but he knew that to Eddie he had been about the funniest, smartest, most fun little (but not so little) brother in history.

So with Eddie in the picture he belonged, weird though it sometimes felt here. He was accepted because Eddie dug him. Anyway, that's what it all felt like now, after he'd figured it out a little. So when Eddie had died, he'd been left with a vacuum, and he hadn't felt like he could continue to survive in that—not here at home. Not anymore.

Now, since he'd been hurt, he honestly thought something had changed. Of course, it didn't really count with everybody feeling sorry for him and trying to be nice. Most of all Mom. Mom, trying like hell.

It probably wasn't even conscious, but he knew he had become just a duty to her, like a paper drive or a cake sale, and Mom had always been somebody you could count on for that stuff.

Here she was now, Steven keeping his eyes closed, breathing regular, pretending to be asleep. Hand on the forehead to check for a fever, then tuck the blankets around. He opened his eyes a crack, groggy.

"How you feeling, honey?"

"Fine."

"Really? Anything I can get you?"

Slow shake of the head. She sits on the bed. He can feel her trying to say something else, but settles for reaching out a hand, rubbing it across his cheek. It feels oddly cold. He opens his eyes again.

"It's okay, Mom."

Her brave smile—still thinking of Eddie. It's so obvious. But he can't really worry about that. A little fake smile. "You just get better," she says. "Take it easy and get better."

She looks at her watch. Time for another dose? No, he doesn't hurt that bad. Close the eyes again. He feels her get up from the bed.

Alone again.

How about talking, Mom? How about suggesting I sit up and do something with you? Not just how I'm feeling. Well, it wasn't going to happen for a while. She wasn't ready for it. And it wasn't as though he thought he could take Eddie's place. Nobody could do that. But maybe if she'd just recognize him as something other than a duty they could start to get somewhere.

He didn't want much, he thought. If only he could do something to make Mom *see* him, maybe value him a little bit. That's all he needed, really. And it might fill in some of the hole left by Eddie. Probably not much, but maybe enough.

But Mom seemed below zero herself, and that made him real nervous, maybe more nervous than anything else.

Erin wore a green jogging suit and tennis shoes. The low white socks had a little pom-pom on the back just over each heel, and Hardy found himself staring at them as he followed her back into the house.

He tried to keep staring at the pom-pom, because seeing Erin Cochran in a jogging suit—even when she was still so obviously distraught—made him realize that another result of the sense of new life he was experiencing was a general increase in his libido.

"What's funny?" she said.

They had come out onto the deck into the bright sunlight and he'd been admiring something other than the pom-poms when she'd turned and caught him. He didn't think he ought to discuss it with her.

"The way my mind works," he said, striving to be suitably enigmatic. He pulled one of the multicolored canvas chairs out for her, catching a slight whiff of Ivory soap.

There was a wide red-and-green umbrella stuck through the center of the table. The sun was high, and he pulled his own chair in close to hers so they could share the shade.

"And how does your mind work?" She touched his arm lightly, reminding him of the way both she and Big Ed had used a hand on his arm to guide him on the day of the funeral. She looked directly into his eyes.

But no way was she flirting. She was one of those people to whom the world was a straightforward place. Obviously, she was happily married to Big Ed and, at the moment, grief-stricken. She couldn't be bothered with whether or not eye contact could be misinterpreted. The hand on the arm, though, the wide serious brown eyes—it was disconcerting.

"How does my mind work?" Hardy repeated. "Very slowly, I'm afraid."

"No, I don't think so." She poured coffee into two plain brown mugs and shifted the sugar-and-cream tray closer. "I don't think so."

"Rusty clock, guaranteed. Tick . . ." He paused, looked around, came back to her eyes. "Tick. Like that."

It was the first time Hardy had seen anything like humor in her eyes. She took her mug in both hands and leaned back in her chair.

"Jim—Father Cavanaugh—came by last night. Evidently there's a suspect?"

"You didn't see the paper?"

She shook her head. "With Steven, now . . ." she began, then stopped.

"How is he?"

She lifted her shoulders, noncommittal. "Anyway, the suspect is the reason I called."

"Well, I think we have two, actually."

He explained a little about Cruz, then went back and covered Alphonse. She listened, but her eyes were out of focus somewhere over the middle of her backyard. When Hardy finished she didn't react in any way.

"Mrs. Cochran?" he said.

She might have been talking to herself, trying to find reason in something absurd. "Two people," she said. "Two people might have killed Eddie, wanted to kill Eddie. How could two different people want to kill my Eddie." It wasn't a question. Hardy looked down into his mug. "I mean, it doesn't make sense."

"No, I guess it doesn't."

"But you think it happened?"

He shrugged. "It seems to be the only other option. You were certain he didn't kill himself."

"I don't know what's worse." She closed her eyes. "Now I don't know why I called you," she said, apologizing, trying and failing to smile. "I mean, I keep thinking something, like some . . ."—she paused—"some information is going to make a difference. I keep thinking we'll find out something and I won't feel this way anymore. It's stupid, really."

"No, it's not stupid. It's pretty natural."

She fixed him with a dark glare. "It's stupid! Nothing's going to bring Eddie back." Shocked at herself, she leaned forward in her chair, quickly, putting her hand on Hardy's arm again. "I'm sorry. I didn't mean to yell at you."

Hardy fought the urge to cover her hand with his own. She didn't need any kind of comfort right now. Or maybe she needed it, but it wouldn't take. Waste of time to try. Hardy was matter-of-fact. "It's natural to be curious about the truth. Once you know what happened, you can put it somewhere. It's not stupid."

She took a couple of deep breaths. "Jim said more or less the same thing."

"Jim's right."

She found a little nugget in that. "Of course," she said, her face softening. "Jim's always right." She continued the deep breathing. "So what does it mean, the suspects?"

"It means you might have a better idea of what really happened. With luck, you'll get some kind of a motive. Frannie stands to collect some insurance."

"That's good. I hadn't thought of that."

"It's the reason I took this job in the first place. But, as you say, none of it is going to bring Eddie back. Nobody's pretending it will. It's just a place to move on from, that's all."

"Where to?" she said all but to herself.

The coffee had gotten cold. The shade had moved enough so that Hardy's head was now in the sun. He shaded his eyes briefly with his left hand. "That's everybody's question."

She lowered her head. "I'm sorry," she said, "I'm still all inside myself."

As they took in the coffee stuff, she started talking about Steven. Though he remained on the pain drugs and was sleeping a lot, he'd sat up for the first time the previous night, talking to Jim and Big Ed. He acted sulky to her, or toward her, she couldn't tell which. "It's like the more I try to do for him, the more he withdraws," she said.

Dismas carried the mugs and rinsed them before putting them upside down on the drain.

She felt guilty, subjecting him and everybody else to this eating, horrible pain. It wasn't his business. She was becoming a talking junkie, where as long as someone was there to talk to, it kept it at a bearable distance. It shamed her, feeling that way, talking intimately to near-strangers, but she couldn't help herself.

She heard a faint "Mom" from the back of the house. "Would you like to see him?" she asked. "It's pretty lonely for him in there."

Steven had pushed himself up again, crookedly. She reached behind him to straighten the pillow.

"Come on, Mom."

It was hopeless. He nearly cringed at her touch. She turned with a half-broken smile. "Do you remember Mr. Hardy?"

He nodded. "You find the guy that killed Eddie?"

"We think so."

It was too dark in the room for such a beautiful day. Erin pulled up the shade. "Would you like the window open?"

"It doesn't matter." Then to Dismas: "Father Jim said you were sure."

Dismas came up and sat at the foot of the bed. "We ought to be sure by tonight." He reached into his back pocket and took out his wallet, then extracted a blue card and held it out to Steven. "Last one got pretty bent up," he said. "You want it?"

To her surprise, he took it.

"Thank you," he said. Just like that, formally. Not "Thanks" or "Sure," but "Thank you." Then: "What's keeping you from being sure?"

Dismas kind of laughed and shrugged at the same time.

"Can you tell me? I mean, all about it?"

Dismas looked at her, and she nodded. It was good he was starting to come out of the pain, show some interest in living.

But she wasn't sure whether she could handle hearing it all gone over again. "Are you hungry, Steven? Would you like some lunch?"

He paid no attention to her, all his concentration on Dismas.

"You're not too tired?" he asked Steven, catching her eye with a question. She nodded that it would be okay.

"No. I do nothing 'cept sleep anyway."

"Well, I'll go make a sandwich," she said. Dismas was already talking before she was out of the room.

Hardy sat at the Cliff House waiting for Pico to arrive for lunch. He was able to see clear to the Farallones. In front of him about a hundred sea lions cavorted on and around Seal Rock.

The place, jammed on weekends, was not too bad here on a Tuesday afternoon. He got a table by one of the floor-to-ceiling windows without any wait; his waitress was friendly but not too, and didn't even blink when he'd ordered his two Anchor Steams at once. He was halfway through the first.

His instinct had been to go back to the Shamrock, maybe take on his regular shift again or at least crow a little to Moses. But driving toward the place from the Cochrans', he decided not to jinx himself. One more day, or—more likely—a few hours, would be worth it to make sure the thing was nailed down.

He couldn't tell Moses he'd *almost* cracked the case, that *almost* surely Eddie had been murdered, that it was *likely* Fran would get some insurance, and oh, by the way, there was a *chance* that Moses owed him a quarter of the bar.

So he'd called Pico and turned west on Lincoln toward the Cliff House instead of east to the Shamrock. He'd told Pico he wanted to celebrate, but perhaps he'd been premature even in that. Everything with Jane seemed to be going so well, the case had just about concluded. So what was wrong with him that he couldn't be happy? Was he so much out of practice?

He sipped at his beer, watching the waves break against the rocks below him, and tried to figure it out. The feeling—the old gut "something is really wrong" feeling—started while he was talking to Steven. He'd started in with that just to loosen things up over there, because Steven so obviously needed to feel involved. He knew the kid couldn't really help him at this stage. There was nothing left to do.

Out on the ocean a couple of tugs were pulling a ship toward the Golden Gate. Hardy watched it for a while, then looked beyond it, up the Marin coast, seemingly all the way to Oregon. It was still a postcard day—a cloudless sky, the blue-green benign sea.

All right, so it seemed he'd finished the case, at least as far as he was concerned. He was spending all this time wondering why he wasn't happy, when really, why should he be happy? It wasn't like it had been a laugh riot. Maybe there would be some small sense of accomplishment down the line about the money he'd helped Frannie get or something like that, but he couldn't escape the basic ugliness he'd been mucking around in.

But it wasn't just that. Talking to Steven, trying to get it all straight for the boy, it had gone a little crooked on him. Almost every move he'd made had followed from a basic set of assumptions he had developed in the first day or two of looking at it. What if all those assumptions, or even one of them, had been wrong?

He shook his head. It was a police matter now. The proof would come out—possibly was coming out right now downtown—and then it would be over. It wasn't his problem anymore.

So what that someone had called in about the body from a phone booth three miles away from the Cruz lot? What did it matter if Alphonse killed Linda with a knife and Eddie was shot? And couldn't Cruz really have lied out of pure fear, not necessarily to cover up a murder?

Sure. Sure, and sure.

But there was one other thing. It had occurred to him—like a remembered taste—while he was talking to Steven, some vague feeling that he had said something that he had overlooked before about Eddie's murder, and didn't have shit-all to do with either Arturo Cruz or Alphonse Page.

He stared at the ship as it continued its slow progress toward the Bridge, sipping Anchor Steam, damned if he could put his finger on what the hell it was.

29 ❧

DICK WILLIS of the Drug Enforcement Agency was sure it was one of those situations where the guy's name had absolutely determined what he was going to be in life. Bargen had probably been called Plea since the first grade.

Willis, sitting across from him in his cubicle in the D.A.'s office, looked at the nameplate on his cluttered desk, the one that said "P. Bargen," and wondered if in fact that might be his real name. He didn't know him as anything else.

Plea leaned back, balancing his wooden chair on its hind legs. His feet were on the corner of his desk, crossed, and he appeared to be sleeping soundly, arms crossed behind his head. His tie was undone, his few hairs uncombed. Still, he wasn't a slob. His body was trim, his pants still had a crease in them and the shirt was ironed. He was paying attention.

They were listening to Abe Glitsky talk. Willis didn't intend to stay long. It was the end of the day, and he'd dropped by mostly as a courtesy. At the most, what they were talking about here with the Alphonse deal was about a hundred thousand dollars, and asking him, a major-league drug buster, to put out much effort on that kind of money was like asking a homicide cop to work a weekend to get a purse snatcher.

But he knew Abe and he knew Plea. They'd both delivered in the past, and they might stumble on something if they muddled around in it long enough, see if they could pull together anything that might lead to a bigger score. After all, small amounts of drugs tended to come from bigger shipments, and maybe they could work backward.

But Abe was talking all kinds of nonsense that Willis couldn't connect to a goddamn thing, and finally he had to hold up his hand and interrupt. "Maybe I came in the middle here, but aren't we talking about this Polk thing? Alphonse Page? We got a confession, right?"

Plea opened his eyes and came forward in one motion, very smooth. "That's covered, yeah," he said.

"So what's all this parking-lot bullshit?"

"Well, there was a guy killed there a week ago," Plea said, then added, with a look at Glitsky, "or killed himself."

"Uh-uh," Abe said, "nope."

Willis held up his hand again. "Guys, guys. We go back a ways, right? Right. So look, we're talking drugs or not? What's the connection here?"

"The connection is maybe the drop was going to be there."

Willis stared at Glitsky, wondering if he'd heard right. This was a veteran? He sucked at his front teeth. "Drop? Drop? Did you say drop?" He frowned at Plea. "He said drop, didn't he?"

Plea concurred.

Willis went back to Abe. "Abe, my man, there ain't no drop. This isn't like a shipment of brown coming in stuffed in Aztec jewelry. We're talking maybe a couple of bags, some condoms full. You forgetting what coke looks like, I got about fifteen tons down in evidence. For that, you need a drop. For this, you meet some guy on a streetcorner and if you're casing it and you blink, you miss it, it's over so fast."

Willis scratched his head, sucking at his teeth again. These guys were in the business, even. It killed him. "Drop. Jesus."

Plea rolled his eyes, tried to sound patient. "Dick, you dick . . ." Willis hated when he said that. "The dissertation was nice, but this guy Polk, it was his first buy. Maybe he was being careful, maybe he was nervous, you know."

Glitsky put in his two cents. "Alphonse said there was gonna be a *drop*. That's the word he used."

"Alphonse is never, ever gonna win the Nobel Prize. In anything."

"But he says Polk told him the stuff was out in the Bay. They were delivering it by boat. Polk never told Alphonse where, though now he figures they were coming up the canal and dropping it in Cruz's lot."

"What a wizard." This wasn't going anywhere, so Willis cooled himself down. "Look, spare me the lot noise. Do you guys want to plead down if he'll talk about his buyer? That's the extent of my interest."

The city employees had some other agenda going, but Willis wasn't going to get bogged down in it. "Unless you got something on Polk himself?"

Glitsky stood up, walked over to the doorsill and leaned against it looking out. Plea sighed. "Polk is a wash. Best we can tell, Polk died by accident in his hot tub." When Willis made a face, Plea shrugged. "M.E. down the Peninsula confirms it. So there you go. Anyway, nobody knew anything about his source. His wife—we saw her today—killer, by the way . . ." He stopped. "I mean it, Dick. Be worth your while to interview her."

Abe turned around, scowling. "Bargen," he said.

"Yeah, all right. Anyway, completely oblivious. Can't believe her husband had anything to do with drugs. He was a businessman, that's all. Straight as they come. Never did drugs himself."

"How old is she?" Willis asked.

"Christ!" Glitsky said. He walked a few steps out into the corridor. Plea again rolled his eyes, held his hands inverted out over his chest and blew out soundlessly. "Lungs to here, a face to die for." He raised his voice. "She wasn't what I call distraught, except maybe over the thought that she wouldn't get the money Alphonse stole."

"She won't if it's drug money."

"She will if it's stolen in this jurisdiction. It was Polk's, and Alphonse admitted taking it from the safe." Abe came back to the door, leaning against it. "She knew from nothing," he said.

"And Alphonse didn't know? About Polk's source, I mean?"

Plea and Abe looked at one another. "No chance."

Willis rubbed his palms against his pants and stood up. "So it's his buy or nothing?"

"Looks like," Plea said. "Maybe three, four hundred grand."

These guys couldn't see it. "Peanuts," Willis said, but added quickly, upbeat, "but it might lead someplace." No sense pissing them off. "Can I talk to him?"

"Sure."

"Well, set it up for tomorrow, and we'll see what we can do." Willis shook hands with both of them. "Thanks for the tip, guys. You never know." He was out the door about ten seconds when he poked his head back in. "The Polk woman? What was her first name?"

"Nika," Plea said. "I'll send you the report."

"Do it," Willis said.

At least he didn't wink.

"DEA," Abe said. "Don't Expect Anything."

Plea shrugged. "They got bigger fish to fry."

Abe plunked himself heavily on the corner of Plea's desk. "I don't care what perspective you have, half a million dollars isn't peanuts."

"Relativity, Abe. Relativity. It's the federal government, where a fucking hammer costs a hundred and forty dollars. You know their efficiency rate? They gotta cover for every G.S. One through Twelve lifer who wouldn't do more than an hour's work in a day for any reason on God's earth. So they gotta make maybe ten mil on a bust before they justify the overhead."

"Thank you, Mr. Bargen."

Plea noted the scar tightening through Abe's lips. "Come on, Abe, what's the problem? We got a righteous bust on the Linda Polk murder. We keep getting one a day, we end the year only about two hundred behind."

Glitsky twisted his face in what he thought was a smile. "What about Cruz? The Cochran thing?"

Plea shook his head. "That's a suicide/equivocal, not a homicide."

"The fuck it's not."

Plea held up a hand. "Hey. You prove it, I'll charge it, but I'd never even seen the file before twenty minutes ago. I don't make this stuff up. You guys tell me what to run with, remember?" He opened the file with a casual hand, perused it a second, closed it back up. "Nothing here gets me out of the blocks, Abe. If it's somewhere else, get it for me, would you? Otherwise . . ."

"Cruz was there. He admits it."

Plea nodded. "And because of that, because you're a good cop and you asked nice, we looked into it, didn't we? In spite of no official finding of homicide. Didn't we?"

Abe didn't answer.

Plea stared at the sergeant. Maybe he was working too hard. He felt sorry for him. "We got corroboration on the dinner from the waiter. Cruz himself passed a polygraph. His little boyfriend—I took the kid apart, Abe—and once he got over being scared, all he did was provide an even better alibi. He followed Cruz all night, for chrissakes. Thought the guy was running around on him. Couldn't have cared less about Cochran, just didn't want Cruz to get all mad at him because he'd been followed." Bargen paused, scratching his scalp. "Plus, there is no shred of physical evidence. No way we charge him."

"The perfect crime, huh?"

"Maybe, but I'd say he didn't do it."

"He had a motive. . . ."

"So did Alphonse, and he didn't do it either, unless you don't believe at least four of your fellow officers who were playing basketball with him, all of whom I'm sure want to protect a sweet and upstanding citizen like Alphonse." Plea sighed. "And while we're on it, the last guy with a motive didn't do it either."

Glitsky looked a question and Plea said, "Polk. His wife had a party that night. Twenty, thirty people. Polk was there the whole time."

"I hadn't even thought about him."

Plea nodded. "I know. You were too busy with ready-made suspects. Me, I took it fresh, and Polk popped up like a plum."

"But no, huh?"

"No."

Glitsky went and sat in Willis's chair. "What's your hard-on for this thing?" Plea asked.

"I don't know. Once in a while my sense of justice gets offended, I guess."

"You ought to have this job. There's no justice, there's just grinding 'em through. Plea 'em down and move 'em along."

"Yeah, I know."

"So why this one?"

He gave it a beat or two. "This one, Plea, is a murder. I'm a homicide cop."

"That simple, huh?"

Glitsky seemed to be asking himself the same question. His lips tightened again, loosened, tightened. "Yep," he said, standing up, "that simple."

The kids were asleep. He lay with his shoes off on the living-room couch, his head in his wife's lap as she massaged his temples. The television was on in the corner but was muted. It gave the only light in the room.

"I got my ass reamed. Frazelli, not so gently, suggested I just stay off it. It's Griffin's case."

"But I thought you'd—"

He shook his head. "Nope. Not anymore. That was when Frazelli thought there was new evidence."

"But why pull back now?"

"Because now, my love, I have suggested not one, not two, but three possible suspects to the same killing within a twelve-hour period. It doesn't do much for my credibility. Especially since two of them definitely didn't do it, and there's no evidence at all with the third."

"Are you sure it was a murder?" She moved from his temples to the forehead, smoothing the crinkled brow back with the palm of her hand.

"Feels so good," he said. He'd been awake since whatever time this morning. "I don't know, maybe it's Hardy."

"Is he sure?"

"He's dead positive now. I just got to wonder. Here's a guy was good, you know, good. Just a beat cop, but he had a feel for it. Hell, you knew him.

"Then he goes into law and suddenly burns out. Anyway, he lays low for maybe what, six eight years, and now he swings back in action. You got to ask yourself what for? He doesn't think he's jerking himself off, I'll tell you that."

"But maybe he's just wrong. Maybe he wants to believe it so bad, he's making it true for himself."

"Maybe," Abe said. "All I know is, I'm off it. I'm still interested, but I'm off it."

"And you told him that?"

He closed his eyes under her soothing hands. "Yeah. I told him he comes to me with a signed confession, I'll be delighted. Then I'll go shove it up—sorry, all worked up."

"Just forget Griffin tonight, forget all that stuff. They're not out to get you 'cause you're black."

"I'm only half black."

"Okay, they're still not out to get you."

He looked up into her face. "That's what you think. I'm not allowed the luxury of being wrong."

She leaned down and kissed his forehead. "Paranoid."

"Don't mean they're not after me."

She smiled and continued with the massage, her white hands seeming to shine in the dim room against the dark skin of her husband.

30 ❧

THE FIRST message on his machine said: "Dismas. Jim Cavanaugh. Just calling to find out how it all turned out, see if you'd like to have a drink. Give me a call when you can. 661-5081. Thank you."

The second was from Jane. "I'm just thinking about you. Maybe Thursday instead of Friday? Maybe tonight?"

The last was from Moses, who wanted to know how he was getting along and when and if he was coming back to work.

Hardy threw darts while he listened to the messages. His aim was off. Not that he ever missed the general pie he was half going for, but occasionally he'd miss his number two out of three. It didn't bother him. He was only throwing to be doing something. If he kept hard liquor in his house, he'd be drinking. Too wired to sleep, he threw darts.

After a while he went around to his desk, two of his three tungsten darts embedded in the *1* to the left of 20, the last one stuck in the 5 to its right. He'd missed 20 for two whole rounds, something he hadn't done in five years.

He rewound his machine. Since he didn't have hard liquor at home, he'd go and have some in a bar. It wasn't all that late, and Cavanaugh had offered. He didn't want to go to the Shamrock and have to answer questions from Moses about his progress. He got to the number, switched off the machine, wrote it down and dialed.

A woman's voice answered. "St. Elizabeth's."

"Hello, is Father Cavanaugh in?"

"Just a moment, I'll get him. Can I tell him who's calling?"

When Hardy told her, she paused, then said, "Did Father tell you? Oh, I'd better let him tell you."

Cavanaugh, now at the phone: "Dismas. Good of you to call."

"Okay, I'm curious. What were you going to tell me?"

"When?"

"Your housekeeper just now asked me if you'd told me something, then said you'd better tell me."

The priest paused, chuckled tolerantly. "I don't know, tell the truth. I'll have to ask her. How's your case coming?"

"That's kind of why I hoped you had something for me. There isn't any case anymore. It's gone south."

There was a longish pause. "What do you mean?"

"You mentioned a drink, and I could use one. Can I meet you somewhere? Tell you all about it then."

"You want to come over here?" Cavanaugh asked.

"Anywhere's fine."

"No, forget here. We might keep someone up."

"You name it."

Cavanaugh took a minute, then named a fern bar on Irving about midway between them. Hardy knew the place. He could get there in ten minutes.

These drugs were funny. One minute it'd be as though you were dead —no dreams, no memory of sleep even. And then, bingo, you were wide awake. Then you had somewhere between a half hour and an hour before the pain got you again.

The foot was the worst. It felt as though it was continually being crushed in a car door. Steven had done that the summer before with his thumb. He couldn't believe the next day how bad it had felt. It had affected his whole body, with a headache and throwing up and everything. He'd lost the nail.

But that was nothing next to now when the painkiller wore off. He had tried toughing it out this afternoon. He hadn't wanted to sleep anymore. There were too many things to think about—Eddie and the investigation.

But it hadn't worked. The foot had been the worst, but he was already beginning to feel his collarbone, and his head was throbbing. He hadn't been able to keep the tears back when Mom had come in. It was just from the pain, the water forming in his eyes and falling out over his cheeks.

The bad thing about the painkiller was you woke up so thirsty every time, which made you drink a lot of water, which then meant you had to pee like crazy, and since you couldn't move, that meant Mom had to come in with the bedpan.

You think crying's embarrassing, try a bedpan.

But this night it was Pop. He took care of it with a minimum of hassle, then poured a glass of water from the pitcher on the table by the bed and sat down right up next to him, hip to hip. He reached out his rough hand and touched Steven's forehead where it wasn't bandaged, very businesslike. He nodded to himself.

"So how's my boy?"

"Okay." That was always the answer. Now Pop would say "Good" and go out to the garage and do something.

But instead he said, "Really? Really okay?" Steven blinked a couple of times, and his dad continued, " 'Cause that'd make you the only one."

"Well, you know," Steven said.

"No, I don't. That's why I'm asking."

There was a small light on by the door and another out in the hallway, but Steven could tell it was pretty late. Everybody else was probably asleep. His dad loomed up in front of him, blocking out most of everything else. No wonder they called him Big Ed.

Steven had no idea how to answer. "I don't know. Not great, I guess."

"Me neither. Just general?"

Steven tried to shrug, but wound up making a face. Shrugging with a broken collarbone wasn't recommended. "You know. Eddie, I guess, mostly. Mom, a little."

Big Ed lifted a leg onto the bed and shifted to face him more. "You know," he said, "I can't say a damn thing." He put his hand out, resting it heavily on Steven's chest, and just sat there.

"What do you want to say?"

"I really don't even know that."

Well, that was okay, but it got uncomfortable. Steven, to say something, asked for another sip of water.

"How's the pain?" Big Ed asked. "You need some more pills?"

"No, okay?"

"You're the boss."

The room got blurred up slightly. He leaned his head back against the pillow. "What's in those things? The pills, I mean."

Ed picked up the little brown plastic bottle. He said: "It's called Percodan. 'Extremely addictive. Use only under the direction of a physician.' Well, we're doing that."

Steven said: "I don't think I'm addicted. I really don't want it, except for the pain. It makes me too tired."

Ed put the bottle back down. "Well, that's what it's for." He shifted again on the bed, as though he were thinking about getting up. But this was one of the longest conversations Steven had ever had with him, and he wanted to keep him there without being too nerdy about it.

"You know, drugs aren't that cool," he said, then blurted ahead. "I smoked some weed with the guys that beat me up."

His dad simply nodded, taking it in. "How'd you like it?"

"You're not mad?"

"I'll get mad later. Right now I'm still just glad you're alive. You mind if I have some of your water?" He poured half a glass and downed it in a gulp. "The pitcher's almost empty," he said.

He got up, blocking the light from the door as he passed through it, and left Steven alone. He heard a clock ticking somewhere, then some water running in the bathroom down the hall. He looked around the dark room at the rock-and-roll posters. Suddenly he didn't like them very much. They seemed kind of phony and stupid. They were one of the few things he and Eddie hadn't agreed on, but Steven had always felt that he had to have something that set him apart at home so they'd know he was alive.

His father returned with the pitcher filled up and sat back down where he'd been, on the side of the bed. Steven's foot was beginning to throb slightly.

"You want to do me a favor?" his dad asked.

"Sure."

"You want to try those things, try 'em at home."

"I don't think I—"

But Big Ed interrupted. "Look, there's going to be lots of things like marijuana. Beer, for example. Or maybe cigarettes or cigars or something, although God forbid you get into that. Sex . . ."

Steven almost jumped at the word.

"Sex, no, don't bring that home."

Was Pop, grinning at him like they were friends, saying this stuff out loud to him? It blew him away. "But the other stuff—you want to experiment, even with some other guys, you bring 'em around and go out to the garage and check it out. But do it here, okay? So we can be sure you're all right."

"You'd let me smoke weed?"

"I wouldn't be too thrilled about it. I wouldn't want it to become a habit, but it probably wouldn't kill you. It didn't last weekend, did it?"

"Almost."

Steven hung his chin down to the cast, but Big Ed lifted his head with a finger. "You're gonna do things we don't like. Hell, I'm sure we do things you hate. But we're living together here, and everybody cuts everybody else a little slack so we can get along. The main thing is we're a family, we stick together. Sound like a deal?" He punched him lightly under the chin.

That hurt a little, jerking the collarbone around, but obviously Big Ed hadn't meant it and Steven would take a lot more physical pain than that if his dad would talk to him like this once in a while.

"But what about Mom?" Steven asked.

"What about her?"

"What if she doesn't, uh, want to let me do stuff? Or even want me around?"

Ed slumped. His face clouded over. "Of course your mother wants you around."

Steven tried a response, but it didn't work. Big Ed sighed deeply. "Your mother is having a hard time, Steven. We're all having a hard time."

"You don't think I wish Eddie were still here?"

"No, I know you do. It's not that. It's just your mother . . . she's . . ."

"She wishes it would have been me instead of Eddie."

Ed shook his head. "No, she doesn't. Not on any level. She loves you, too, just like she loved Eddie."

There wasn't any use arguing over that one.

"She's just having a hard time accepting it. Her world's all turned around, and maybe she'd doesn't know where to put things so well for a while. Haven't you ever felt like that?"

He nodded.

"So, what I was saying about giving people some slack, maybe you've gotta be the first one. Try and understand what she's going through if you can."

"I know what she's going through. I miss Eddie too. So bad."

Big Ed took a deep breath. He swallowed, then jerked his head around toward the hallway. Still looking away, he spoke hoarsely. "We're all taking it differently, I suppose."

Steven's foot was really hurting now. He kept forgetting how bad it was, and hoping every time that it would let up the next time the pills wore off, but that wasn't happening yet.

He let a long time go by, or what seemed a long time, with his dad staring off somewhere breathing hard every couple of seconds. Then he said, "Pop."

Big Ed slowly came back around.

"I think I need one of those pills pretty soon. I'm sorry."

"Nothing to be sorry about."

"Yeah there is, Pop. There really is."

His dad reached for the medicine bottle, opened it and shook out two pills. "Well, let's start fresh, then. We've got a hell of a family left here, okay?"

He popped the pills and drank a little of the water.

"Maybe Frannie's kid will make up for Eddie a little. Mom might like that."

Big Ed jerked again as though he'd been stung. "Frannie's kid? What do you mean, Frannie's kid?"

It frightened him, Ed almost yelling like that. "You know, the kid Frannie's gonna have. Her and Eddie's kid."

"Frannie's pregnant?"

He strained to remember. Who had told him that? Damn. The pills were working gangbusters already. His eyelids were lead. Was it Jodie? He was sure it wasn't Mom. No, it wasn't her. Maybe Frannie while she'd been staying here?

He couldn't put his finger on the exact time he found out. "I don't know," he said lamely, "maybe I just dreamed it. I don't remember." But he knew he hadn't been dreaming at all. He couldn't recall even a scene from one dream.

Big Ed seemed to calm down. He put his palm flat against Steven's forehead again. "It's okay," he said. "It doesn't matter. We'll find out about that tomorrow."

He felt his dad's bulk get up from the bed. Big Ed's hand went through his hair, surprisingly gentle, and he felt a kiss on his forehead.

Maybe Pop did love him. And if he could only do something so Mom might think he was okay, they could all live together, maybe someday be happy again.

But it was getting harder, almost impossible, to keep thinking. He was sure Frannie was pregnant, but if Jodie and Mom and Frannie hadn't told him, who had? The only other people he'd talked to had been Father Jim last night and that guy Hardy today. And how would either of them know? Frannie would definitely have told Mom first, wouldn't she?

The light faded, then was out completely. He forced his lids apart, and there was Eddie standing in front of one of his posters, just looking down at him, smiling. He went to reach out to him, but then he was asleep.

Hardy, slouched over the table, was looking into the priest's face perhaps a foot from his. Something was there, still unsaid after a lot of talking, and the idea kept popping up between them like an insistent panhandler checking out the pickings at the late-night tables in near-empty bars.

Cavanaugh looked down through his Irish, Hardy thinking he might be trying to stare right through the table with his X-ray eyes. They'd been talking and drinking, starting with light stuff and getting heavier as things wore on, for the better part of three hours. Cavanaugh kept going in and out of focus.

"Maybe anybody can do anything," Hardy said, "you give 'em enough juice."

"Anybody—anything," Cavanaugh repeated.

"Not a priest, but—"

"Ha. The things I know priests have done, you wouldn't believe."

"I probably would. High school there were some guys like springs, they were so wound up. I'd hate to see what would happen if they let go."

Hardy and Cavanaugh, slowing down, just a couple of guys, finishing their drinks, closing a place. Half hearing each other, half listening to Billy Joel doing "Piano Man," that old bar-closer.

"You know what an incredible pain in the ass it is being a priest sometimes? That old turn the other cheek? Both my cheeks are callused turning them back and forth."

"Yeah, but you do it anyway. You keep doing it. What I'm talking about is guys who snap. Zinc buildup or whatever."

"Sex, you mean?"

Hardy nodded.

"Sex is easy. I mean, at least it's tangible, or understandable. You either get the physical release somehow or you, as we say, offer it up. But either way, it's out there and you can deal with it."

"You saying sex doesn't bother you guys?"

"What do you think? We cut our nuts off? I'm just saying that it's not always the hardest thing." He grabbed at his glass, swirled the ice and drained it.

As if by magic, Hardy thought, the waitress came around for last call. Cavanaugh ordered the round: "Give us a couple doubles."

Hardy didn't fight it. It was get-down time for him, too, that old "since we've already passed propriety time, let's hang it out and see where it goes."

"There's just no release ever," Cavanaugh was saying. "It's not a job where some guy goes to work and gets off at five and then gets drunk or fights somebody. It's like you can never ever"—he stabbed at the table —"ever do anything that really lets the valve loose. That's the hardest part."

"Hey, Jim, that's just adulthood. Who ever really gets to blow it out anymore? And you think you've got it tough, try being a cop."

Cavanaugh shook his head. The girl came back with the drinks. "Priests can make cops look like Boy Scouts."

Hardy paid for the round. "Cops can't let out a thing, Jim. They gotta keep it in control."

"Yeah, but they also let out a lot. You get the adrenaline pumped up pretty good and you're allowed—hell, you're *supposed*—to do something, direct it to something. Shoot a guy, make an arrest, get in somebody's way. I mean, there's something there. You don't go walking off —Mr. Mellow—and read your breviary."

Hardy took a good swig of his own Irish. "Cops don't let out near enough," Hardy said, defensive. "Why you think you got drinking cops? You got cops on drugs? You got just plain mean motherfuckers?"

"What I'm saying is just multiply that by about twenty for priests."

"That's bullshit."

"It isn't. Maybe that's where the sex comes in. Your cop at least has that option."

"So why do you do it? Why do you guys keep at it?"

Cavanaugh drank again. "I don't know. Sometimes I don't know at all. You believe in the theory, I guess. You believe that the suffering is worth it."

"You believe in God?"

"You had better do that. You sin and you sin and you sin again and you keep thinking maybe it's going to get easier someday and you won't have to feel like breaking out so often, that maybe God's gonna give you a break. Take a doctor with a headache, he knows fifty ways it can be terminal. You, it's a headache, it'll probably go away. A doctor knows it could be a tumor, cancer, the beginning of a stroke, or whatever. Same with priests. We can't even allow ourselves to think we're going to be okay. If we do, that's pride! The number-one sin. But if I think I'm a totally worthless piece of shit, then that's false modesty, another sin. Everything's a sin, Dismas. And if it's not, it's a near occasion. Being a little loaded right now—sure it's a release, but it's also one of the seven deadlies. Drunkenness. There's no escape ever," he concluded, reaching for his glass again, putting down half of what remained. "None. Ever."

Hardy sat back, shaking his head. "All this from the perfect priest."

"Who thinks that?"

"Erin Cochran."

Cavanaugh sucked in a breath. "What does she know?"

"One would think she knows you."

Cavanaugh sighed. "She's God's reminder to me that I'm not perfectible, much less perfect."

"What's that mean?"

"It means, you'd think after twenty, thirty years, the old spell she throws would wear out." He started to lift his glass, then put it back down carefully, as though afraid he might break it somehow, maybe squeezing it too hard. "Sometimes I still . . . I think I've been in love with her since the day I met her. And I wasn't close to being a priest back then."

Hardy wanted to ask, but Cavanaugh answered before he could get it out. "You don't think I haven't wanted to make love with her like any other man . . . ?"

Hardy lifted his own glass and took a drink. He thought about Jane, about getting back with her, their hurried and aching coupling after the years apart. He said, "That must be very tough."

The priest made some noise, like a laugh, but he wasn't laughing. "They say love and hate are so close. Sometimes, I don't know, I hate her, I hate 'em all. . . ."

And there he was, unbidden, that old panhandler again, reaching out his hand. Hardy looked at the hand a minute, then flipped a quarter that fell into the middle of his palm.

"Yeah, I've been tempted to wipe out all the happiness I see there. Why should they get it all? You think that seems fair?" He stared at Hardy, not seeing him, looking inside himself. "There was a moment, God help me, when I was almost happy about it, about Eddie being dead. Let them feel what it's like to have things go wrong, to have your love lost, the sum of your life reduced to zero. Erin thinks I'm perfect, huh?

"Not close, Dismas. Not even close. If I could feel like that, even for a second, when the boy was like my son, my only son . . ." He put a hand up to his face. "Going back to the Cochrans', burying Eddie"— he shook his head again—"after feeling that, as a penance. You believe in a good God, you believe you're doing something worthwhile, that being around someone you love, denying it, is strengthening you, making you a better priest, a better person. Your reward is in heaven, after all." He tipped up his glass. "You go back. You keep going back. It's like the old Augustine monks who slept in the same bed with their women every night to test their celibacy. The roots go way back. Deny, conquer, deny again, sin, conquer it again. That's the road to salvation, right? Ain't it a piece of cake?"

Hardy sat in the lengthening silence, sipping at his drink, shaken somewhere even through the booze. Cavanaugh was in such obvious pain he couldn't believe he'd been blind to it before.

"Hey," Hardy said. "Let's quit bullshitting around and talk about something we really care about."

Gradually, Cavanaugh's face softened. He laughed quietly. "You're okay, Dismas."

"You're not so bad yourself, Jim."

Another pause, then Cavanaugh saying, "So how 'bout them Giants, huh?"

"Humm baby," Hardy said.

Hardy switched on the light in his hallway, shivering slightly from driving home with the windows open in the light fog. He hadn't worn a jacket. On the way home, really cold with the Seppuku's top down, he'd bounced along singing a dirty country song about rodeos. A good song. Kept up his good mood.

Imagine feeling that a priest could be a regular friend of his, maybe even a close one. It was surprising, the charge Hardy got out of Cavanaugh's company. Jim's conversation was a soup, a stew, a goulash of politics, sports and what he called the "cheap m's" of popular culture —music and movies—all seasoned—peppered more like it—with roughly equal parts vulgarity and poetry. Like, who else but Cavanaugh would have known off the top of his head that Linda Polk wasn't, couldn't have been, descended from James K. Polk, eleventh President of the United States? Because Polk had been childless.

He was also fun to hang with because you met a lot of women. Though the guy had to be close to sixty, he had three times Hardy's hair, and all of it looked better. While they talked and drank (Cavanaugh in some baggy khakis and a loose blousy light-green thing with an open neck), three women had joked with them, butting in, leaving openings you could drive a truck through. But he'd closed the door on them all with a practiced grace that told Hardy this happened all the time.

Another reason they probably got along, he told himself, was that they still had Eddie Cochran in common. Except for Jane, it was pretty much the only thing on Hardy's mind, and once he'd started talking, Cavanaugh had seemed as obsessed with it as Hardy was himself. It didn't get boring—at least going over it with Jim, who still leaned toward the late Sam Polk as the murderer even after Hardy said that he'd been visible that whole night at a party his wife had thrown.

That was the bitch of the whole thing—none of the suspects could have done it unless one of them had at least one accomplice. And there was no indication of that at all.

Back in his office, undressed for bed, Hardy saw the three darts stuck on either side of the 20. About five drinks (and one double) unsteady (which he thought wasn't very), he pulled them from the board and went back to the line in front of his desk.

He took a deep breath and held it, then let it out slowly. He shook his head once quickly, then let fly the first dart, nodded as it plocked into the 20.

"Okay," he said.

One thing was certain—neither he nor Cavanaugh accepted Ed's death as a suicide, although Jim's feeling seemed to be more visceral than Hardy's. To Hardy, even forgetting the suspects and their alibis, the facts simply didn't support that finding. With Jim it was more an article of faith. Eddie Cochran wouldn't have done it—not that way, not any way.

Hardy's second dart hit the tiny slice of triple 20, a good shot by any standards. He put the last dart down on the desk. Tonight, for a change of pace, he'd quit winners.

The wooden chair was cold against the skin of his butt and back, but he forced himself down into it. There were scraps of paper on the desk —dribs and drabs of ideas he'd entertained over the last week or so, and he wanted to clear the decks for the morning. He was damned glad he hadn't seen Moses this afternoon. He probably wouldn't have been able to have stopped himself from bragging that the case was solved, which it pretty emphatically was not.

Suddenly the drink-and-talk-inspired euphoria faded. Hardy looked at the scraps of paper in his hand and wondered what the hell any of them meant. Fancy theories and clever words.

Absently, he reached over to his phone machine. He wanted to hear Jane's voice again, and he didn't think he'd erased the messages. The last thing had been Jim's phone number. There it was, in fact, on one of the pieces of paper.

He flicked the machine.

"Thank you," he heard. The end of Jim's earlier message.

Then Jane's voice again. "I'm just thinking about . . ."

But then he stopped listening. Something jangled deep in his brain, and the hairs on his arms and legs stood up over the chicken flesh. He switched the machine back to reverse.

". . . 5081. Thank you."

He closed his eyes, rewound again, listened. "Thank you." He played it over in his mind, hearing it fresh.

"Son of a bitch," he said.

He had put the police tape into the drawer down to his right. He held his breath, irrationally terrified that it wouldn't be there anymore, but it was. He spun around on the chair and carefully placed the tape into the machine. It was short enough. "There is a body in the parking lot of the Cruz Publishing Company." A tiny, strained pause, perhaps trying to think of something to add. Nope. Then just, "Thank you."

Back at his desk, he lifted the phone machine and brought it over next to the tape recorder. He played the two "Thank you's" one after the other, first one then the other, both ways.

Cavanaugh's message of earlier that night. The formal, cultured, unaccented voice without a personality, a smile, an attitude to color it.

Put it together, Diz, he said to himself. That's why the call had come from halfway across the city. Cavanaugh had been driving home. Or took a bus or a cab. Or got home and went out again, not wanting to call from the rectory, and maybe not knowing they had automatic tracing on 911 calls.

He played the police tape another time, hearing the voice he'd been listening to most of the night. The voice that had been telling him more than he'd been hearing. Jesus.

There was a safe in the room where he kept some papers and his guns. He opened it, took both tapes from their machines and put them inside, closing it then and spinning the combination.

Going back to his bedroom, he picked up the last dart. He put his weight on his left foot, feeling the tape with his toes. "Double bull's eye," he said out loud. He threw the dart.

Sure enough.

31 ❧

"*Dominus . . . ,*" he began, his arms spread wide. Immediately
he caught himself. "The Lord be with you."

Slipping back into Latin. His mind must really be miles away. Raising his eyes to the tiny congregation, he realized that no one, not even
the altar boys, had noticed the slip.

He had to concentrate. He was, after all, saying a Mass, and even a
sinful priest loses none of his powers. Believing otherwise was formal
heresy.

But it was difficult to pay attention. He had the altar boy pour quite a
lot of wine into the chalice hoping a little hair of the dog would help
the nagging headache. Still, he knew it wasn't his throbbing temples
that were distracting him.

He had so hoped it wouldn't come to this, but last night with Dismas
it was pretty clear that the police weren't going to be satisfied with their
suspects. And that meant the search was still on. If there was no new
evidence, though, they would be forced to leave it a suicide, or give up,
and his horrible . . . mistake would never be known.

And he couldn't let it be known, ever. It would do irreparable harm
to the Church, to say nothing of the further pain it would cause all
those close to him.

All right, he'd made his peace with God now. He'd confessed, and
that ought to be the end of it until he went before St. Peter.

Could God forgive him? He had to believe He could. Could he ever
forgive himself? No. He knew that now. Killing Eddie had been far, far
beyond the worst peccadilloes he'd indulged in over the years to ease
the terrible burden of living a holy life, the unending boredom of sin-
lessness. He thought he'd grown inured to the twinges of conscience
that the occasional sin, the moments of temporary weakness, had

driven him to. But killing Eddie had been, if there was such a thing, unforgivable.

When Eddie had come to the rectory that night—Erin's first son, the son *they* should have had together—with that special fire that only he possessed, and told him he and Frannie were going to have a baby, he finally could stand it no longer.

How did one boy deserve all he had been given? Surely he, Jim Cavanaugh, who had spent his whole life denying, denying, being denied, should have been given a chance, one brief moment, for this boy's happiness?

But that had never happened.

And now the son of the love of his life—God forgive him, but it was true—now Eddie would have it all. Everything he had ever really wanted, and now, clearly, would never have. It was too much to bear. He couldn't let him have it, couldn't let the privileged happiness go on for still another generation.

So that night, with Eddie's newfound strength and hope and confidence, he had suggested, since he was planning to meet Cruz anyway, that he go down with him, bring the whole weight of the moral argument to bear. Surely two such charming, persuasive, wonderful people could not help but succeed. In the heady flush of expectant fatherhood, Eddie had lapped up those oily words, believing as only he could that everything was possible.

And Jim Cavanaugh was convincing, wasn't he? Eddie could save Army, save Polk from himself, save the whole goddamn world. Why shouldn't he feel that? He was young, strong, his manhood verified! He, Eddie Cochran, could do it all!

Yes, it had just been too much to take. But now, now, living with it, Cavanaugh could see that the light, even the dim reflected light he'd lived for, had gone from Erin's eyes.

Still, he had to believe that God had forgiven him, though it was beyond his power to fathom such forgiveness. He would have to put his faith in the Lord. The greatest sin, after all, was despair—despair that God would abandon any, even the most unworthy, of his sheep. Despair was loss of hope, a graver sin even than murder. That was what he was fighting now, the temptation to despair.

Because he knew he had to kill again.

※

He was walking out to the garage with Dietrick, the sun bright in a deep-blue sky.

"Are you really worried about her?" the young priest asked.

Cavanaugh shook his head. "Ever since"—he stopped—"the Cochran boy—Eddie—died. You haven't noticed the change?"

Dietrick stopped halfway across the asphalt, trying to remember. "I guess I take Rose too much for granted. Another of my failings."

Cavanaugh laid a gentle arm on Dietrick's arm. "She confides in me. That's all. It's no reflection on you."

"Still . . ."

"I think"—Cavanaugh paused, wanting to phrase it right—"I think my reaction to Eddie's death, taking it so hard—" Dietrick started to interrupt, but Cavanaugh pressed on. "No, I know it's understandable, but maybe I should have hidden it from her a little better. It got Rose thinking about her . . . her own loneliness, I guess. Her husband. All that she's missed over the years."

They were walking again. "You think it's serious?" Dietrick asked.

"I think it's very serious," he answered quickly. But then he brought himself up short. "I don't mean to panic you. I don't know. She was up when I got in late a few times the past week, couldn't sleep. Sometimes that's an indication."

They got to the garage. Dietrick had parked his car beside it, not wanting to cram his new Honda into the smallish space next to Cavanaugh's. "Should we get her some help, do you think? Beyond ourselves, I mean."

"I think it's worth thinking about. She hides it well, but I believe she really has been very depressed."

Dietrick got in the car and rolled the window down, thinking about it. "I ought to pay more attention. It's good you noticed, Jim."

Cavanaugh waved it off. "I've got to be out all this morning, but maybe this afternoon when you get back . . . ?"

"Definitely, we'll get her straightened out."

Cavanaugh waited a minute, standing by the garage, watching the car disappear around the front of the rectory. All right, he thought. Dietrick was convinced, he was reasonably sure, that Rose has been badly depressed lately, would swear to it on a stack of Bibles.

❦

Bless Father, always thinking of others, Rose thought.

Father Dietrick had gone down to the airport to pick up one of the Maryknoll missionaries who would be spending the rest of the week at the rectory and preaching next Sunday. Father Cavanaugh, after saying early Mass and having breakfast, had of course offered to make the drive himself to the airport. He always offered, and he would have done it, too, but the younger priest thought it was his duty.

After they'd said good-bye to Father Dietrick, he'd given her his devil-may-care grin and said: "Well, Rose, m'dear, what are your plans on this fine day?"

Naturally, he knew that she'd have to get the rectory especially clean for their guest, so he was teasing and she told him so.

"Now, Rose, have you made the bed?"

"Of course, Father."

"And you've dusted and swept."

"Yes, but there's still the flowers and towels to lay out, and . . ."

He held up a hand. "Have you any idea what a treasure you are?" he asked. She felt herself flushing.

"Look at this day! God's glory shines down on us!"

"It is nice," she said, wishing she could string together a flowery phrase as he did so effortlessly and knowing she never could.

"It's more than nice," he said. "Here I've been drowning in depression, taking no advantage of these precious days of sunshine, when the Talmud tells us that man shall be called to account for every permitted pleasure he failed to enjoy. Do I want to be called to account for that?"

The Father was such a caution. He wouldn't be called to account for anything. She smiled at him. "No, Father, certainly not."

"Then how about if we go on a picnic together and celebrate this day? You've done enough for our guest's room. I'm sure he'll be very happy."

She tried to object, but he overrode her. "Rose, the man's been living in a hut with no floor in western Brazil for three years. I think our guest room will be fine."

"What about the fathers' lunches?" she asked, although a picnic sounded like her idea of heaven.

Father rolled his eyes as he sometimes did, too polite to laugh at her. "We'll write a note," he said. "They'll make do, I'm sure."

So now the sandwiches were made—mortadella and Swiss with the hot peppers Father liked on fresh sourdough rolls. She made two for him and one for herself, though she didn't think she could eat the whole thing. She put several dills in a big Zip-lock bag with some of the brine, and there was leftover potato salad in the fridge. They'd pick up some cold beer for Father on the way out to the park—that's where he thought they'd go, rowing out on Stow Lake—and a soft drink for herself.

Through the kitchen window, she saw Father coming from the garage, far out across the asphalt at the back edge of the wide parking lot. He still walked heavily, as though he carried the cares of the world with him on his shoulders. And in a sense, she thought, he probably did. The picnic would do him good, would get his mind off the Cochrans and the sadness of the past couple of weeks.

And she wouldn't be an old stick-in-the-mud, either. She could tease him along and get him laughing, and that's what he needed now—a dose of the carefree, a couple of beers, a day in the sunshine.

She turned back to pack the basket.

"So how're we coming?"

Lord, he had come in so quietly. It startled her.

"I'm sorry, Rose. Did I scare you?"

She was too jumpy, turning into an old woman. Well, today she wouldn't be—it wouldn't be fair to Father, and that was that.

"You never mind me," she said. "Can you think of anything else?"

He raised his eyebrows in anticipation, going over the items in the basket. Then, remembering something, he snapped his fingers. "The note."

Rose opened the drawer nearest the sink and got out her yellow pad, but Father shook his head. "Let's use some real paper." He winked at her. "Give our guest the right impression." With that he disappeared back into the house, reappearing a moment later rubbing his eyes.

"Rose, I've got something in my eye. Would you mind writing it? I'll dictate."

Rose sat at the table, taking the nice piece of white bond that Father offered. "Fathers," he said, and she began writing in her big round hand. "I'm sorry I'll miss you. Rose and I are going on a hot date—"

"Father," she said, clucking with pleasure.

"We'll be back in time for dinner," he continued, "but you'll have to

make do for lunch. Father Paul, welcome to San Francisco." He looked
over her shoulder. "Perfect, Rose. Now, just let me sign it."

He took the pen and quickly scribbled his name at the bottom.

It was an old two-car garage. In the seventies they'd put up drywall,
redone the old pockmarked benches and insulated the roof. Since kids
from the school had taken to using the garage as a place to sneak
cigarettes (and who knew what else), they had replaced the old side
door with a new, solid one that locked with a deadbolt. They had never
gone for the electric garage-door opener. Cavanaugh had joked that he
couldn't see Jesus using it.

But now the old garage door, while sealing completely enough when
it was closed, sagged badly when it was open and occasionally would
slam of its own accord after being opened because of its weakened
springs.

Father and Rose strolled out across the parking lot. On the other side
of the school building children were laughing. They could hear them in
their next to last day of school taking their morning recess, and Father
flashed Rose the slightly guilty smile of a kid playing hooky. He carried
the basket and opened the car door for Rose.

"Whew!" he said, fanning himself with his hand. "A little sticky,
isn't it?"

He crossed behind the car and got in the driver's seat. "Let's get
some air in here." He rolled down all the car's windows with the automatic button. "All right," he said, and smiled across at his housekeeper.
"Ready?"

He turned on the engine.

"Oh, look at that, would you?"

He wheeled halfway around in his seat.

"What's that, Father?"

"Look at the sag on that door."

"Oh, it's always that way."

"I know, but I'd just hate to have it come down on the car's roof
while we're pulling out."

He pulled the keys from the ignition, leaving the car running. "Let
me just make sure.

He went outside behind the car and pulled on the door, letting it
slam to the ground. The springs resonated inside. He lifted the door

slightly, slamming it down again, and again. As the springs rang out, he threw the bolt that locked the door, then pulled against it a couple of times for the effect.

"Rose!" he called out.

"Yes, Father."

"The door seems to be stuck. Are you all right?"

"Yes, I'm fine."

"All right. Now, just don't panic. I've got the keys to the deadbolt just back in the rectory, and I'll be right back."

He turned and began walking slowly across the parking lot. Recess had ended. The kids were back in class.

Father had said not to panic, and she'd resolved she was not going to be an old woman, not today when Father so badly needed some surcease from his cares.

Still, it was a little scary sitting here in the darkened garage, the car's motor running. But she would not panic. There was nothing to do anyway except wait, and Father would be back within a couple of minutes. She knew where the deadbolt key was, hanging by the back door of the rectory. It shouldn't take him long.

Well, it must seem like it's taking longer than it should, because I'm jumpy, she thought. She talked out loud to herself. "Just calm down, Rose. Father said not to panic. . . ."

She forced herself to take deep breaths. There, that was better. Big, deep breaths. She was getting so calm, it was almost silly. She supposed she should be worried a little. But there was no need to worry. Father would be back in just another second, and they'd go on their picnic. It would be a wonderful day, one they both needed.

She closed her eyes.

He really hadn't any choice. With the other suspects eliminated, he couldn't have taken the risk that she would have mentioned Monday night to anyone. She was the only one who could tie him in any way to Eddie's death, and now, or—he looked at his watch—certainly within another ten minutes . . .

In the kitchen he took the note she had written and carefully tore the paper so that it broke off after her name. He put a period after the word "sorry." The note now read: "Fathers. I'm sorry. I'm going to miss you. Rose."

It would do.

He walked back to the library and placed the note on Father Dietrick's chair. In the bathroom he touched a match to the rest of the note, held it for as long as he could while he watched the good bond curl into black ash. As the flame neared his fingers he let go of the corner he held and flushed the toilet. He waited. When the toilet had finished, he wiped down the bowl with toilet paper and flushed it again.

He'd had to think fast when Rose had pulled out the yellow pad. It wouldn't do to have secondary impressions of the note for someone to notice. The bond had been just the right answer.

There was a slight smell of smoke in the room, and he opened the bathroom window to get rid of it. He looked at his watch. It had only been twelve minutes. Rose was probably still alive.

It was important to establish his whereabouts and his calm. He did not feel like a man who was in the process of killing someone. He went out the side door of the rectory, crossed in front of the church and entered the school. In the office the principal's secretary, an Indian woman named Mrs. Ranji, stood up to greet him.

He told her his usual joke and said he had just come by to see if there were any last details about the upcoming graduation he needed to know, and if there were any, to have Sister give him a call. Sitting at Sister's desk, he proceeded to look over some correspondence, then asked Mrs. Ranji when the next period ended. She looked at the clock. Good. Fifteen minutes? No, that was too long to wait. He would check back with Sister later. He hummed loudly as he walked out.

Twenty-six minutes had passed. He went to the garage and opened the deadbolt, held his breath, and walked in. He flipped on the light at the switch by the door. Rose was still sitting up, propped by the door, looking like she was sleeping.

Moving quickly now, he took the picnic basket from behind the driver's seat. He was running out of breath.

Outside again, with the basket, he stopped by the door, relocked it and looked back toward the school, then at the rectory. No sign of anybody. He crossed the lot.

Three sandwiches. One for him, one for Dietrick, and one for Father Paul. He unwrapped them and put them on a plate in the refrigerator.

It was plausible, in character. Rose, planning to kill herself, might just have made sure she made lunch for the fathers first. He put the pickles back in the jar, washed out the Zip-lock bag and threw it in the garbage, scooped the potato salad back into the rest of it.

Breathing hard now, his nerves speaking, he once again began crossing the parking lot. About two-thirds of the way across, he called out Rose's name. He started running toward the garage, and in what would look like a panic threw back the bolt, the picture of a man making a horrifying discovery. "Rose!" he called again.

Don't forget to put the keys back in the ignition. He had to do that in any event to turn the car off, which is what he would do.

A final survey of the scene. He put his hand on Rose's still-warm forehead. She had died peacefully—he was glad of that. He made the sign of the cross over her, giving her his blessing, last rites of sorts. Then he started jogging back to the house. He was surprised to find he was crying. But he didn't try to stop himself. That was all right. Why shouldn't he cry?

And it would ring very true to the folks at 911.

32

STEVEN BELIEVED his mom was really trying.

After Dad and Jodie had left the house she came in and talked, or tried to talk, for a while. After she'd gone back out to her housework or whatever, he wondered what kind of teenager she'd been, if she had ever done anything like run away. It was the first time he'd thought of anything like that, and so it was a little hard to imagine—Mom screaming for Elvis Presley (as she said she'd done), or dating anybody but Pop.

Well, whatever she'd done, he was pretty sure it didn't prepare her for him. She didn't seem to be able to find a handle to grab on to, although Frannie's pregnancy was as close as she'd gotten in a long while.

She sat on the bed, much the way Pop had done last night. He felt a little stronger and had managed a decent breakfast. She ran her hand through his spiky hair and asked him how he knew about Frannie.

"It's true, isn't it?" he asked.

She shook her head. "I didn't want to call her yet. She'll tell us when she wants to."

"Why wouldn't she want to?"

His mom's face clouded, as though trying to decide whether to tell him one of the adult secrets. As usual, she came down saying no. "I don't know," she did say. "There are reasons. It might just be too soon. But how did you find out?"

He'd thought about it this morning after he woke up. It had been Hardy, yesterday. He was telling him about Father Jim and about his pride, how he had kind of blamed himself for Eddie's death because of talking Eddie into confronting his boss. Which was dumb. Eddie was going to do that anyway. He'd told Steven all about it the day before.

Anyway, once he got into it, Hardy was good at sounding like differ-
ent people, and he did Father Jim pretty well. Of course, he had an easy
voice—kind of regular, but the words he used in a certain way that
Hardy caught the rhythm exactly. He spent a lot of time talking about
Father Jim, even though he didn't really have any part of it. But Father
Jim was like that—he caught your attention.

Anyway, Hardy was "doing" Father and he said, "I sent Eddie off to
slay the dragon. Do I think about his pregnant wife, whether he's the
man for the job? No, not the smart Jim Cavanaugh." (That part
sounded perfect, and Steven had laughed.) "I only see what a wonderful notion it is." Then he goes: "My pride killed him."

But in there—that's where he'd heard about Frannie. It had been
like Hardy was telling him part of another story, not really telling him.
He tried to explain that to his mom, who wondered why Hardy hadn't
told her.

She put her hand up to her brow and said, "God." He could see that
she'd started thinking about Frannie now, or Eddie again. Her eyes
were gone, out to the backyard, staring at nothing.

"Mom?"

He was going to say something like "It's all right," or, "I'm going to
help," though he knew it wasn't and wasn't sure how he could. She
looked back to him, smiling with her mouth. So instead he asked if it
was too early to have another pill.

He'd just have to go ahead and do it, whatever it turned out to be.
Make his mom see he wasn't going to be any more trouble. He'd have
to do something that would help them all get over this, maybe forgive
him for running away and making them deal with him when Eddie—
naturally—was the hardest, most immediate thing.

He'd do something on his own. Something worthwhile, adult. Maybe
then his mom would appreciate him. Love him . . .

Next time she came in was only a couple of minutes later, but he was
sailing into oblivion pretty fast and almost couldn't answer when she
talked to him. Though she did come in and tell him about the call.

That's what he was starting to see. She was trying. "Steven."

Not faking at all, he had to use most of his strength to open an eye.

"That was Mr. Hardy on the phone."

He hadn't even heard it ring and it was right there, next to his bed. "He says yes, Frannie's pregnant."

"Maybe he'll look like Eddie."

He meant it as a good thought, but he saw when he said it that it kind of hurt her. She leaned against the doorsill, then walked the few steps over and plumped herself down on his bed again. "I hope so," she said. It was like she was forcing herself to talk. "He also"—she stopped and rubbed at her eyes—"he also said that neither one of the suspects killed Eddie."

He didn't think anything could pull him out of the haze the pills created, but that almost did. Suddenly he was nearly awake. "How could that be?"

She hunched down over her shoulders. "They were all someplace else, I guess." Then he heard her say . . . "I guess Eddie didn't love us that much. As much as we thought."

"What do you mean, Mom?"

"I mean, if he killed himself—"

"He *didn't* kill himself. I know he didn't."

She had that blank look again, that empty stare. She tousled his hair and kissed him on the forehead. "You try to get some sleep." She got up and turned to the door.

"Mom."

She stopped and faced him.

"He didn't."

"Okay," she said, nodding her head. "Okay."

It came to him. That's what he'd do. He'd find out who had killed Eddie. Never mind Hardy or the cops. They were obviously dildoes who didn't know Eddie the way he had known him. He'd find out the truth, all on his own, and then his mom at least would know Eddie hadn't deserted him. That might get her started back to being alive.

Hardy hung up and shook his head.

He hadn't called Erin to talk about Frannie's pregnancy, and he was mad at himself for having let that out to Steven. How had he been so careless and at the same time so obtuse? No wonder he'd blocked it out for so long.

Cavanaugh had referred to Frannie as pregnant, and even after mimicking his damned voice to Steven, Hardy hadn't put it together. The point was, how could Cavanaugh have known about the pregnancy if he hadn't seen Eddie after Frannie had told him, which was the night he'd been killed? Which meant he'd lied about seeing him Sunday. It had been Monday.

He closed his eyes, really pumping now. He'd only slept five hours, but it didn't matter. Things were falling into place.

The gun had bothered him a lot, and he'd stood in front of his desk from dawn until about an hour ago, drinking two full pots of espresso and throwing darts until it had come to him. The gun drive. Sixties liberal mania. Cavanaugh had collected some hundreds of unregistered guns. And what he'd done, of course, was to hold out on one or two of them. And the cops who were monitoring the thing—even the good ones like Abe—would never think that a priest would use a clean-the-streets gun drive to build his own arsenal. I mean, why would it occur to anyone to check that? But, Hardy was now certain, it was what Cavanaugh had done.

What he'd called Erin for was to ask her the exact date she and Ed had gotten married. That was a little bit of a wild hair, he knew, but it might tie in with something else that had occurred to him, something he needed to go back and check out before he went to see Glitsky.

If they'd already burned up three suspects, he'd better have the next one, the real one, trussed up and ready to carve. Glitsky might have been hot to get whoever'd done Eddie, but he would be a fool to risk his career on another hunch of a civilian. Now Hardy felt he owed him the collar for all the help he'd given him, but he knew he'd have to do it all, then call for the troops.

He had the two tapes in a heavy yellow envelope. He didn't know if he could get anybody to do voice-print comparisons on them, or what it would cost to do them himself, but he did know that if there was going to be a trial, they would be good evidence. In fact, they were the first pieces of hard evidence he had come upon.

But you never knew. He might get lucky with some technician, so he had decided to take them downtown. He'd stop by the Hall of Justice after his visit to the *Chronicle*. Glitsky himself might still be interested enough to do it on the sly.

He folded the piece of paper—the one with Ed's and Erin's wedding date—and put it in his wallet. He was tempted to call Cavanaugh, put the fear—if not of God—of man into him and see what he'd do.

But no. Build a case and blindside him. That was the way. Cavanaugh would have no idea that the noose was tightening. Especially after spending last night drinking with him (God, he was one confident man), he must think he was clear. He must also think his friend Hardy was a bit of a fool.

Well, he had always said he might be dumb but wasn't a fool. Cavanaugh playing him for one made him unhappy. He was out of his chair and heading for the door when he stopped. He had three guns in his safe. But what, after all, was he planning to do with a gun? He was off to do a little research. He wasn't planning to confront Cavanaugh. On the other hand . . .

He walked back toward the safe.

For a two-dollar fee anybody could go into the archives room of the San Francisco *Chronicle* and look up microfiche of newspapers from any date since the newspaper was founded in 1865.

Hardy was interested in the week of July 2, 1961. Driving downtown, his .38 Police Special now loaded and stowed in the glove box of his Seppuku, he spent a few minutes worrying about the what-ifs.

What if there was nothing in the newspaper? What if Glitsky wasn't in? What if nobody at the Hall was willing to let him look up the past Incident Reports?

He turned on the radio. It was still broken, which wasn't surprising since he'd done nothing to fix it. He wanted to listen to anything to get the other song out of his head. It was an old Conway Twitty tune called "This Time I Hurt Her More Than She Loves Me," and it had been number one on the Hardy brain parade for two days now. Well, he thought, the hell with the radio. He went back to the what-ifs.

What if I get in a car wreck? What if a meteor plunges from deep in outer space and punches me half a mile into the ground? He had to laugh at himself.

In the *Chronicle* archives room he put the what-ifs out of his mind and now was glad he'd wasted no more time on them. He wouldn't have to go see Glitsky about this, or wade through the hard copies of some faded and musty IRs. There it was, on page 8 of the first section for Monday, July 3, 1961.

It wasn't a big article. Most other big-city newspapers might not

even carry it, but it was one of the advantages of the *Chronicle*'s parochial view of what news was—they covered the city pretty well.

The article read:

CALL GIRL FOUND SLAIN
IN NOB HILL APARTMENT

The body of a call girl who had been strangled was discovered late
yesterday evening in her posh Taylor Street apartment after the
woman failed to report back to the escort service for which she
worked.

The victim, 22-year-old Traci Wagner, had been employed by the
BabyDolls dating service for approximately six months.

Police are seeking for questioning a white male in his early to mid-
twenties who picked up Miss Wagner in a dark, late-model car in the
midafternoon. The suspect gave his name as John Crane, but this
appears to have been fictitious. The investigation is continuing.

Hardy went to the desk with the spool of film and asked the clerk to
copy the page for him. That cost him another five dollars, but it would
be worth that to have for Glitsky.

John Crane, huh. Jim Cavanaugh. Funny about those initials, he
thought. Same as Jesus Christ.

"You got squat." Glitsky wasn't feeling patient. "And I simply cannot
take the risk."

"You can't listen to two tapes? Take you fifteen seconds."

Abe leaned his chair back and put his head against the wall of the
little cubicle. Hardy might be his friend, but he was getting on his
nerves.

"Nope. I got four—no, now five—live ones out there and,"—he
consulted his watch— "I got about ten minutes before I mosey out to
the Mo' and talk some jive."

Hardy sat down.

"Don't get comfortable. I mean it."

Hardy clucked at him. "Look, ten minutes you can hear this thing
thirty times. I take off a little for rewinding."

"It's gonna take me ten minutes to find two recorders."

Hardy looked outside of the cubicle into the main office, a wide-open expanse of green metal desks on linoleum. Guys were milling around, secretaries were talking on phones, occasionally typing. "I see at least four Walkmans from here," he said.

Griffin had seen Hardy wandering through the office, trying to borrow a Walkman from a secretary. After he scored it, Griffin followed him up to Glitsky's cubicle. "Still at it?" he asked Hardy. "Any luck?"

Glitsky knew that Carl was aware of the ninety-five or so suspects he'd suggested in the past day. He figured he'd imply some frustration with Diz, show that he was still a professional cop who realized the utter silliness of what his friend Hardy was doing. "Now it's the priest at St. Elizabeth's."

Griffin chuckled. "Well, you need any help, just call."

Smiling and helpful, he bowed out. Glitsky raised his blood red eyes at Hardy. "Prick," he said.

Abe was still trying to be reasonable. "This is just plain old dog doo, Diz. I mean it. Nothing."

Hardy shook his head. "He did it."

"Look, even if it is his voice—and I'm not saying it is—so what?"

"So what? It means he was there and didn't want us to know."

"I've heard that song before. Wasn't that why you thought Cruz killed him, when was it, yesterday?"

"He killed that hooker, too. He ran away from the seminary right after the Cochrans' wedding. Was missing for almost a week. I tell you it fits—"

"Oh, Jesus, Diz, spare me."

But Hardy pressed on. "We just saw the hooker's still an unsolved case—twenty years later!"

"We got a thousand unsolved cases."

"*Listen.* Cavanaugh got the gun from the gun drive. He knew about Frannie being pregnant, which means he saw Eddie after she told him, which was Monday, not Sunday. It all fits."

Glitsky wagged his head back and forth. He looked again at his watch. "Well, I listened to the tapes." He got up.

"You want to at least check the voice prints?"

Glitsky was putting on a jacket. "Nope," he said. Hardy followed him out. "Abe, come on."

Suddenly, his patience all gone, Glitsky wheeled around, his strained voice loud, very loud and pissed off, cutting through the office noise. "Where's your fucking *motive*?"

The room went silent.

"Hey, easy, Abe."

People were looking at them. Glitsky glared, first at Hardy, then back at the room in general.

Hardy, the voice of reason, said, "He's always wanted Erin Cochran."

Glitsky stared at his friend witheringly. "Do yourself a favor, Diz," he said, showing Hardy his back, "don't quit your day job."

33

*A*T FIRST it didn't seem all that hard to figure out, but the only thing Steven came up with that made any sense didn't make any sense. Father Jim had loved Eddie, probably more than anybody except maybe Mom. No *way* he could have killed him.

But how else did you figure it?

The day before, when Pop and Eddie had had that big fight about Hitler and doing the right thing, Steven remembered clearly enough— Eddie coming into his room afterward, really ticked off at Pop.

"He teaches you one thing, and then when it's time to do something about it he says forget it."

"So? What do you expect?" he'd said to Eddie.

And Eddie going, "I don't know. Something."

"What? From adults?"

"Hey, I'm an adult."

"You're a dork."

"You're the dork. What would you do?"

That was Eddie. Like his kid brother's advice really counted. But he hadn't had any advice to give. "I don't know."

"Maybe I'll ask Father Jim." Eddie seeing the face he made and saying, "What's the matter with *him* now? It's getting so you think something's wrong with everybody."

"He's okay."

"But you don't really think so?"

"I'm getting that way with everybody, 'cause everybody's that way."

"Not Father Jim, Steven."

"Doesn't he make you sort of nervous? A little, even? You know, when he flips out, like?"

Eddie had laughed. "That's not flipping out, it's just letting go a little. It's harmless. Even a priest can be too serious all the time."

"Sometimes it just makes me a little nervous, is all."

"That's 'cause you're not very mature." But teasing, kidding. Then saying, "I'm gonna call him."

So right there, in that bedroom, Eddie had called and talked to Father Jim, making an appointment to see him the next night. The night he'd been killed.

And Steven remembering that only now. And Eddie had kept the appointment—how else could Father know about Frannie being pregnant? Then Father went to where he kept the gun?

(He, Eddie and Father had gone shooting enough times below Candlestick. Like the switchblade, or the races down Highway 1 just flying along against the ocean, it was one of those secrets between Father Jim, Eddie and himself. Mick had never made the cut—he was too uptight. The secret things about Father Jim had been another of the bonds between Eddie and himself.)

It was still too far a stretch to imagine Father Jim thinking he was going to kill Eddie, or wanting to, but he could play with it for a minute, see where it led him. . . . Eddie had gone to visit Father, thinking about this problem he was having with a guy from work. (Steven wished he paid more attention about the details of that, but it had just been another thing Eddie was doing.) Then Father might have said that meeting a guy alone at night, trying to mess with his business, might be dangerous. He'd go along as moral support, and also, just to be safe, he'd bring the gun.

He wouldn't use it. They wouldn't plan on using it. But what if the other guy shows up and he's got a gun, too? Might as well be safe. It hurts nothing. Eddie might have thought the whole idea was dumb, but if Steven knew Father—and he thought he did—he'd make it seem like some kind of game and Eddie would go along with it.

Okay, so now he had Eddie and Father Jim together, with the gun, at the lot. And there it stopped for him. Maybe they'd been goofing around, shooting at things, and there'd been a mistake, an accident, and after that Father had gotten scared. Sure, that made sense. Father didn't plan to kill him. Steven could see how he'd feel, being like one of the family and all. And having to explain to Mom and Pop about the gun. They might see it as his—Father's—fault. And it wouldn't have been. It could easily have been an accident. . . .

And how about this? Father burying Eddie in the Catholic cemetery, absolutely—he used the world "morally"—certain that Eddie hadn't killed himself.

For all of his carrying on, Father was first and foremost a priest—he would never have buried Eddie in sacred ground unless he knew for a fact he hadn't committed suicide. And how could he know that if he hadn't been there?

Steven leaned his head back against the pillow. In the front of the house he heard his mother vacuuming.

Mom. That was the whole problem now. Her thinking that Eddie had somehow rejected them all, didn't love them enough. It was eating her up.

And suddenly there it was! The solution to everything. It was easy to explain, although it would be pretty hard to do. Except Father Jim and he were friends and maybe it was time to break out of the kid thing and take Eddie's place a little, be a little more adult. He wasn't as good at arguing as Eddie, but he was way better than Mick, and if he could only catch Father in the right mood, and alone, he might be able to get to him.

See? All Father had to do, he figured, was tell Mom. That's all. Not Pop. Not Hardy or anybody else. Mom was closer to Father, was more likely to forgive him. And that would be that. And *he*–Steven–would be the one who'd pulled it all together. For Mom. So she could start being okay again, and maybe find some room to fit him into her feelings.

Convincing Father to tell Mom, that would be the hard part. But really all he had to do was make Father realize how it had affected Mom, how she would certainly continue to waste away. Like him, like Eddie had been, Father couldn't stand it when Mom was unhappy. So all he had to do was make it clear to him that she was miserable, and why.

But first he had to make sure it had happened the way he'd figured it, and there was a way to do that. Just ask Father.

Hardy watched Glitsky disappear into the hallway. A guy sitting at a desk nearby, having heard Glitsky's heated exchange with Hardy, nodded after the sergeant and said he thought a blow job would be out of the question, and Hardy went back to Abe's cubicle to get his stuff and return the Walkman.

He still wanted verification on the voice prints. But, hey, he thought, I want to win the lottery, too. Still, the voice comparison looked doable.

The room had gone back to its business. There was somebody there, he was sure, that he could hit on and get the thing done as a favor. Everybody by now knew he was a friend of Abe's. Whether that was good or bad was a toss-up.

He stood, leaning against the particleboard that defined Abe's space. Lieutenant Joe Frazelli opened his door far to Hardy's right, scanned the room and called out a couple of names.

Two guys sitting at desks facing each other doing paperwork stopped and got up. "Yo," one of them said.

Hardy thought the woman he'd gotten the Walkman from was promising. She sat about midway between Glitsky's cubicle and the lieutenant's office, where the door had just opened, so Hardy found himself walking parallel to the two guys, back toward Frazelli. He was just about to open his mouth to the woman when he heard the lieutenant say: "We got an apparent suicide over at St. Elizabeth's Church. You know the place, out on Taraval? Carbon monoxide. You guys want to check it out? Get out of the office a while?"

Behind Hardy, another voice called out. "Hey, Joe, where was that?"

Frazelli looked right through Hardy at the voice behind him. "St. Elizabeth's."

Hardy saw Griffin saying something to another guy in his cubicle. When he turned back to Frazelli he saw Hardy standing there, staring at him. He spoke to the two officers who had been on their way to the lieutenant's office. "You guys mind if me and Vince take it? It might tie with something we're on."

"Sure, it's yours," one of them said.

Hardy spoke up. "I'm gonna tag along."

Griffin said, "It's a free country."

Steven woke up alert. The pills didn't seem to be knocking him out as bad as they had. Or maybe it was that there was so much for him to think about. Probably that was it.

The vacuuming had stopped. He heard his mother messing around in the kitchen, opening the refrigerator, emptying the dishwasher. It was something how quiet the house was with no TV or radio going, no records on, Mom not humming or singing while she worked. She'd stopped doing that, and she used to do it all the time.

In the quiet, the quiet deepened. Mom wasn't moving at all, maybe just leaning against the counter, or sitting at the table. The telephone rang and he heard her say: "Oh, hi, Jim." She paused. "What's the matter?"

Steven reached for the extension phone by his bed and picked up the receiver in time to hear Father Jim saying: ". . . can't believe this is happening again, right on top of . . ."

It sounded like he was crying.

"Mom," Steven said, "I'm on the extension."

"Hang up, Steven."

"I want to talk to Father Jim."

"He can't talk now."

Father said, "It's okay. Hi, Steven."

"What happened?" he asked.

"Steven, you hang up," his mom repeated. "You can talk when we're finished."

"Okay, don't forget," he said.

What was the boy saying?

Cavanaugh shook his head, trying to clear it. The first two black-and-white squad cars were out by the garage with a distraught Father Dietrick and a confused Father Paul. It had seemed to Cavanaugh to be an eminently logical thing to do—excuse himself to call Erin, his best friend and confidante. He'd establish, with Erin, how badly Rose's suicide had torn him up. Especially now, hard on the heels of Eddie. So that any suspicion that he might have killed Rose would have to get around Erin's testimony. He had figured that between Father Dietrick swearing Rose had been depressed and Erin describing how he, Cavanaugh, had been deeply hurt but not altogether surprised by the suicide, he would have covered all the bases.

So he had called Erin. But then her son wanted to talk.

And now Steven was saying to him that he knew all about it, describing it so closely it made him dizzy, as though he were about to topple from some great height. Steven sounding so much like Eddie. It was frightening, almost as though Eddie had come back to haunt him. And all of it whispered, not wanting Erin to hear.

He looked out at the garage again. Six men in uniform—four cops and two priests. A paramedic's van, or the coroner's, pulled into the driveway, went past the kitchen and continued out over the asphalt.

Steven was saying: "You know?"

He had to ask what. It was all about Steven understanding and having to tell Erin, all coming out jumbled, or sounding that way to him. Words in a torrent that was drowning him. Steven might even be making a point, but it was blunted by his own onset of panic.

All he knew was that once again, after having to do what he did to Rose . . .

He couldn't think about that. Even for a minute. This was Steven Cochran, Eddie's brother. He couldn't do that to Erin another time. No, he couldn't. If he did, that would really be the end of it.

But if he didn't, it would all come out, and he could never ever see Erin again.

He heard himself saying, after Steven had finished, "Can I talk to your mother again?"

"You're not going to tell her now, are you?"

"Steven, come on," he said, putting a light edge on it, "I promised."

Did he? It would have been seconds ago, but he didn't remember.

He stretched his neck to look out to the street. Dietrick had parked in front of the rectory, not in the back where all the commotion was. The spare keys to that car hung on the same peg by the kitchen door that the spare garage key had hung on.

Then Erin's voice: "Jim?"

He could easily explain when he got back that he'd just needed to clear his head, take a walk.

"Listen, I know this is an imposition but . . ." He struggled with the words. "But if you could come over here? I'm all . . . I don't know. It would help me a lot."

She didn't answer right away. He didn't wonder she thought about it —another suicide so close on the heels of her son. But when Erin was needed she came through. Except in one thing, for him. But he wasn't thinking about that now.

"I'm sorry," he said, "forget it. I don't know what I was thinking. It's not fair to you."

"No, it's not that," she said, covering, white-lying. "I was just thinking about Steven." He said nothing, letting her work on herself. "All right, Jim. I'll be over in a few minutes."

As soon as he hung up he took Dietrick's spare keys from the peg, walked through the rectory and out the front door. The car, a year-old Honda Accord, started right away. The drive to the Cochrans' took under three minutes. If he hurried and timed it right, he could take care of things and be back here in fifteen.

34

FATHER PAUL sat on the asphalt in the shade thrown by the garage, his back up against the building. Father Dietrick had propped himself up on the hood of one of the police cars and sat as though sleeping, his arms crossed over his cassock.

Once, in his second mission, Father Paul had come to his destination, a village of Tukuna Indians just outside of Tabatinga where Brazil met Peru (as though the national boundaries made any difference that far up the Amazon). He had arrived, alone, in time to witness the public execution of a thief, where in a carnival atmosphere most of the men of the tribe gathered around in a circle, keeping the condemned man inside their perimeter, closing in and beating him with heavy sticks, poking at his face, his eyes and throat, his groin. When the man finally went down, everybody, male and female—from the smallest child to the oldest grandmother—took a turn swatting at the prostrate figure until he wasn't much more than a smear on the dusty and rutted road.

Something about his timing, he thought. His bowels were hurting from the airplane food, and the culture shock here, with ubiquitous death here, too, in this civilized place, was almost harder to take than that execution had been. These trips home to ask for money—one every blessed two years—were supposed to recharge his batteries. Food, wine, conversation, a surcease from the endless monotony and misery of the bush.

But too much time in the bush, Father Paul was beginning to realize, and it got inside you. All these trappings of civilization—the asphalt, the beautiful church, the grass on the lawns, cars, clothes, everything— were just artifacts. Not necessarily phony but inessential to what was most human—the coping with mortality, the fear of being alone, the need to love.

He missed his woman, Sarita, badly.

But that was, in theory, why they sent you home—so that you didn't become one of the tribe. So you remembered what it was you were trying to do, which was bring the message of Jesus Christ to impoverished people and somehow convince them, since there was no hope in changing their situation, that there was at least nobility and holiness in it.

Father Paul sighed, sweating even in the shade. He feared he was losing his faith in God, that he might even already be a Marxist. Coming upon a death like this, in the first moments of what was supposed to be a vacation, had the strength of a message, and the message was: "Don't get too caught up in what looks like the security of the civilized world. The whole thing is pretty tenuous."

He got up. In the garage no one had moved the woman. Even though there were four policemen in uniform and three medical people of some kind, no one seemed inclined to do anything. The officials stood around in two groups, making chitchat.

He walked over to Father Dietrick, who still leaned against a car with his arms folded. On the way down from the airport they had passed the time pleasantly enough—Dietrick fascinated, as only someone who had never traveled could be, by Father Paul's account of his latest mission, the journey back. He was exactly what was expected—a likable young man (but they were about the same age!) with an anchorman's glib enthusiasm and sincerity whom Father Paul could tolerate because tolerance of the essentially benign was something he believed in.

"I would think they'd move her," Father Paul said. Dietrick opened his eyes, squinting in the sun. "This is a hell of a welcome, isn't it?"

Father Paul wondered at what point refusal to break out of social conventions stopped being benign and became a deliberate refusal to take responsibility. But he said: "Might they let us give her last rites?"

Dietrick said, "She's already dead."

He nodded. "Well, I'll ask anyway. Couldn't hurt."

At that moment, just as Father Paul was turning to speak to the policemen, two more cars pulled into sight by the rectory and began crossing the lot. The blue American car pulled up beside the van and stopped. Two men, casually dressed, got out. The other car, a jeeplike machine with a canvas top rolled back, drove almost into the garage. The driver of that car had an intensity that was totally different from the rest of the group. He fairly jumped from behind the wheel and walked quickly over to where he and Dietrick stood.

A flash of formal smile, gone immediately. "Where's Father Cavanaugh?"

Dietrick spoke up. "He went in to make a call."

"He's in the rectory?"

Father Dietrick, helpful, smiled. "Should be."

The man nodded. The two men from the American car had spoken to the uniformed police for a minute. Now they were walking into the garage. The man from the jeep followed them, and Father Paul trailed behind.

Rose lay as if sleeping, still sitting up, her head forward on her chest.

"Calm enough," one of the Americans said. "Just went to sleep," the other responded. "That's the way to go."

The jeep person said: "Why's she on that side of the car?"

"What?"

"Why isn't she behind the steering wheel?"

The two Americans looked at one another. Father Paul, suddenly, wondered about that himself. It was odd. There she had been for maybe a half hour and nobody had noticed that. Maybe they all saw what they expected to see.

For some reason the jeep guy didn't seem to see the same thing. "I don't want to tell you guys what to do," he said, "but I'd check the keys for her prints."

"Thanks, Hardy," one of the men said sarcastically. "Fingerprints, you mean?"

"Yeah," the man Hardy responded. "From her fingers, you know? Little whirly things." He turned away, nearly bumping into Father Paul. "I'd bet you won't find 'em." He said, 'Scuse me, Father," and went back out into the sunshine. "Who found her?" he asked Dietrick.

"I think Father Cavanaugh's already made a statement to the police."

Hardy was matter-of-fact. "I bet he has."

"What's the matter here?" Father Paul asked. "Didn't the woman kill herself?"

Hardy skewered him with a look. "Doubt it," he said. Then, to Dietrick, "The rectory, you said?"

Steven said, "I know how it happened. That's what I was talking to Father Jim about."

Erin, pouring a glass of water by Steven's bed, said, "How what happened?"

"You know, Mom. Eddie."

"Please, Steven."

"No, really. He didn't kill himself, Mom. He loved us. He *did*."

"Okay, Steven." She was having trouble with the top of the pill container. She grimaced, pushing down while trying to turn. "How's the foot?"

To be honest, the foot felt like it was being crushed in a vise, but he didn't want to bother her with that now. The pills would solve it quick enough. "You'll see. I can't tell you yet, but I know how it happened."

Okay, she'd listen. "Why can't you tell me?"

"There's one or two more things I want to get right."

She handed him the pills. He popped them and then took the glass. This having only one movable hand wasn't that much fun.

She took a breath and held it, then let it out slowly. Humoring him. "Well, when you get it right, I'll listen. How about that?"

She leaned over and kissed him, not really answering anything, just going through that motion, along with all the others.

He leaned his head back into the pillow. "Where are you going now?"

"Just over to the church a few minutes. I'll be back in time for lunch."

"Can Father Jim come back with you?"

She stopped by the door. "I don't know. I can ask. Why?"

"The thing about Eddie. I just want to ask him something."

She slumped a little. "I'll see what I can do," she said. "You get some rest, okay?"

Cavanaugh parked about six houses down the street, in the opposite direction of the way he knew Erin would drive. There was a three-quarter-ton Dodge pickup on blocks in one of the driveways between where he was parked and the Cochrans'. Erin wouldn't be able to see the Honda until she was in the street, and it would mean nothing to her if she did see it.

It had taken less than three minutes—two minutes, thirty-eight seconds—and he had stopped still at every one of the seven stop signs. It would be a poor time to get a ticket.

He waited.

After what seemed an hour he checked his watch and realized it had not yet been five minutes. He rolled down the car's window. The day was unnaturally still. He reached over and cracked the passenger window, hoping to get some cross-ventilation. It didn't do much good.

Could she have left in the time it took him to drive over? He thought about it. Unlikely. He had gotten out of the rectory within thirty seconds of hanging up with her. Unless she had been ready to walk out her own door when they were talking, she would have needed at least five minutes to say good-bye to Steven, comb her hair, get her purse.

Still, if she didn't come out within another couple of minutes, and only a couple, he would somehow have to check.

He took a handkerchief from his back pocket and ran it over his brow, around his neck. He felt clammy, and now a tiny breeze finally stirring in the car made him shiver. Was he getting sick? Even his hands felt sweaty, sticky.

Come on, Erin, he thought. Come on.

Ah, here she was.

She backed the Volvo wagon into the street. She didn't even glance behind her in his direction. His breathing started coming a little more easily. The Volvo stopped at the corner, let a UPS truck pass in front of her, then turned left out of sight.

Cavanaugh turned the key, pulled into the street and parked in the Cochrans' driveway. He walked across the familiar brick path to the front stoop, mounted the stairs and rang the doorbell.

"Steven," he called. "Erin!"

He rang the bell again.

"Who is it?" Steven's voice sounded thin and far away from back inside the house.

"Father Jim, Steven."

A pause, then another distant yell. "I can't get up, Father. Come on in."

❧

"What are you doing here?"

Hardy, seeing Erin crossing the little patch of lawn, opened the door and stood in the front doorway of the rectory.

Her face really was incredible, he thought. "I might ask you the same thing," she said. "Is Jim inside?"

"Jim isn't around."

She stopped, her expression flickering. "Well, of course he is. I just talked to him."

"You just talked to him?"

"He said he needed me over here."

"When?"

"I don't know. Maybe ten, fifteen minutes ago."

"Over here? At the rectory?"

"Yes, is something wrong?"

Still in the doorway, Hardy frowned. "I hope not."

They started back through the house. "Rose is dead, you know," Hardy said.

Erin touched Hardy's arm the way she did. They faced each other in the hallway. "Jim said she killed herself too."

"What do you mean, 'too'?"

Erin looked down. Hardy picked up her chin with his finger. "Eddie *didn't.*"

He could tell it was hard for her to hear it, but she had to know.

"Steven just said the same thing. He said he'd figured out how it happened. He was just talking to Jim about it."

Hardy felt the blood draining from his face.

"What's the matter?"

"When?"

"When what?"

"When was he talking to Jim about it?"

Erin had taken his hand, as though to steady him. "Just before I left, just before he asked me to come over, I think."

Hardy was frozen for a few seconds, letting the coins drop. "Jesus Christ!" He looked behind her. The front door was still closed. "Give me your keys."

"What?"

"Your keys. Give me your keys!"

Obediently, she opened her purse. Then he had the keys and was running for the door. "Come on, come on!" he said. "Your car. Let's go!"

35 ✿

*T*HE FRONT door was locked.

He was just about to call out for Steven again, then realized it would be better not to draw more attention to himself. He looked both ways down the street. It was a slow Tuesday, still before lunchtime. There was no one outside on the entire block. And Cavanaugh knew Steven couldn't get up—so what good would calling him do?

He tried the door again. No, it was locked. Probably deadbolted, too, if he knew Erin.

He went past the Honda again, along the side of the house on the driveway. All the windows were closed. In the backyard he went up onto the deck and tried the sliding glass doors. They, too, were locked, with a sawed-off broom handle wedged into the runner on the floor to make sure the door wouldn't open.

Cavanaugh looked at his watch, sweating now. Too much time was passing. He had to get inside, and it must not look like forced entry.

Walking off the deck, he rounded the corner and started up to the front again, along the other side of the house where there was just a strip of grass and a fence.

It was so vivid it could not have been a dream, but if it wasn't a dream, then where was Father Jim? Steven was sure he'd heard him call out from the front door. He'd even called back that he couldn't move, that he should just come in.

But had he heard him? He hadn't come.

His eyes were heavy, and he really couldn't remember if he'd dozed off or not before the bell rang. He knew he'd taken another dose of the pills before Mom had left. His foot didn't hurt, so they must have already kicked in.

He closed his eyes. Maybe it was like when he thought he'd seen Eddie here in his room the other night. That had seemed so real it wasn't until the next morning that he realized it couldn't have happened. Okay, the doorbell had seemed real, and Father Jim's voice. . . . But it had happened right after the pills, too.

Besides, it made no sense. Mom had just gone to see Father Jim. What would he be doing here?

He had begun to figure it out just as he saw the fingers come around the bottom of the windowsill, open about four inches to let in some air. The hand pushed at the window and it slid up until Father's arm had straightened—maybe another foot.

He heard his name again, quietly this time.

"Steven?"

Glitsky heard the followup call-in on his way to his appointment in the Projects. He was going to meet a steady source named Quicksand Barthelme that Dick Willis would love to get to know. But Glitsky didn't work for the DEA, and Quicksand was too valuable an ally in the Projects to worry about how he made his money. Quicksand could operate safely forever, as far as Glitsky was concerned. He was small time, was grateful for the umbrella of Glitsky's favor, and knew everybody. Willis no doubt had a few murderers among his sources, and it probably bothered him about as much as Quicksand's drug activities bothered Abe.

But today Quicksand didn't show. It happened. These guys, it wasn't like you made an appointment with their secretary and did a power lunch. Sometimes—hell, all the time—the street had its own rhythm and you had to go with it.

So Abe was half listening to the squawk box, still furious with himself and Hardy and pissed at Quicksand and the heat when he heard that there was a suicide at St. Elizabeth's. That decided what he was going to do with the rest of his morning.

One of the squad cars was pulling out as he turned into the driveway. He saw Hardy's car over by the garage as soon as he passed the rectory. The guy was persistent—he gave him that. He parked in the thinning strip of shade along the side of the garage.

Coming around the building, he saw two priests, neither of them Cavanaugh. One of them was leaning up against a workbench in the garage, silent. The other stood by the gurney, covered by a sheet, under which, presumably, was a body.

"Hi, guys," Abe said. Giometti and Griffin had drawn the call, he noticed, and somehow knew it wasn't a coincidence. "Fancy meeting you here."

They were dismissing the second squad car. The rest of the homicide team had arrived and there wasn't any use for beat cops at this stage. Abe walked into the relatively cooler shade of the garage and lifted the sheet, surprised to see Rose the housekeeper.

"Bored Abe?" Giometti asked, challenging, coming over.

"Yeah, yeah, I can't get enough." Then he explained, "I was here last week on something. You mind?"

Giometti shrugged. "Knock yourself out. No mysteries here, though."

"You don't think?"

"*Nada.*"

"You tow Hardy over here with you?"

Griffin heard this as he came up to them. "Here and gone."

"His car's still here."

Giometti smiled. "He's probably inside, interrogating a suspect."

Griffin added, "He thinks this was a murder too. Me, I'm leaning toward a gang hit." Said with a straight face.

Abe went back to the gurney. They had loaded it into the van. He picked up the sheet. "Any sign of struggle?"

Giometti joined him there. "The lady started the car and went to sleep, but as you can see we're running the usual."

The photographer had already finished his work, but the print guy was still kneeling in the front seat, brushing.

Giometti, shaking his head, said, "Waste of time. We got nothing."

Griffin kept playing. "Nothing? How could you forget? She sat on the passenger side?"

Glitsky said, "What?"

Giometti snorted. "Your friend Hardy noticed that she was sitting in the passenger's seat."

"Told us to make sure and dust the keys for her prints. Said we wouldn't find any," Griffin said.

"Very helpful guy," Giometti said. "We probably would have forgot, right, Carl?"

"Yeah, probably."

Glitsky, wondering where Hardy had gone and thinking it might in fact be a little unusual for someone who'd killed herself that way to be sitting in the passenger seat, walked back out into the sun.

He turned around and asked Giometti and Griffin would they mind if he checked out the house. He started across the asphalt.

Hardy could not believe he had forgotten his gun. Erin's car was closer, and so he'd run for that. It would have only taken him another minute to get to his own car with the .38 in the glove box. He might even have been able to talk one of the cops into going over with them. But he hadn't thought at all, he was in too much of a hurry, he might not have a minute.

And still it might be too late.

Erin had asked what they were doing as he pulled away from the curb in front of the rectory.

"What's the quickest way to your house?" And tried to figure out what he was going to do or say to Erin if they weren't in time.

And he could even be wrong. They could have called from the rectory and found out Steven was alone and all right. But he knew he wasn't wrong.

He kept his hand on the horn through the intersections, hardly slowing at all.

36

WHAT HE thought he would do was make a couple of jokes as he came through the window. Steven was used to that from him. When he got to the bed he would hold a pillow over his face until he was unconscious. He would have to be careful—he didn't want another investigation like Eddie's getting started, and there was no way Steven could suffocate himself.

When the boy was unconscious he would take the switchblade he had once given him and that Steven always kept hidden in the drawer next to his bed, and he would cut his wrists.

It would make sense. After all, the boy had just run away and been abused a few days before. He was deeply depressed over his brother's death. It would be compellingly believable. Steven had waited until he was alone—his mother had just gone out—then did what he had been building up to ever since his brother's death.

"Steven?" he said again, hoisting himself up into the window.

Steven willed every part of his body to move. Even with the pills, the pain was awesome. The bandages seemed to be ripping the skin off his whole side, and with the cast on his foot and his arm stuck out at this weird angle.

Still, he got himself sitting upright, though it had to be on the right side of the bed, facing away from the open window. He was trying to stand, twisting to look back, when Father Jim boosted himself onto the sill.

"Hey, why didn't you answer me?" he said, smiling.

Steven couldn't stop him from getting in. The only hope was if he could maybe get to the bathroom and lock the door. He stood, wobbly, not yet putting any weight on the bad foot.

"Steven, come on"—still smiling—"what are you doing up?" His upper body was through the window.

He had to move faster. He stepped onto the foot in the cast.

"Steven, what's the matter?"

It wouldn't hold him. The leg crumbled and he came down on top of it. He didn't mean to, but he cried out, a wordless scream of pain.

Father Jim in the room now, over him. Kneeling on one knee, still a gentle look on his face. His arms reached out as though to cradle him.

"Get away from me—"

"Steven . . ."

"You killed Eddie, you killed him. . . ."

Father pulled his arms back, no longer reaching for him. He sank back on his leg.

"What are you talking about? You can't believe that?" He was actually surprised.

"Now you're gonna kill me, aren't you? That's what you came here for?" Father Jim widened his benevolent smile. How can he be so relaxed if he's going to kill me . . . ?

"Steven, Steven, Steven," Father Jim said. "I came here to visit your mother."

"But she just went to see you."

"So that's why she's not home." He just kept smiling. "You'd think after all these years we'd communicate a little better. I thought we were meeting over here."

He reached down for Steven again. "I think those pills might make you hallucinate a little. Come on." He put one hand under his head. "Just lean into me. Let's get you back in bed."

It was hard to keep up this charade.

He lifted him first to a sitting position, then up onto the side of the bed. He had to be in the bed—that was essential. But this movement was so awkward, all plaster and bone. The joints didn't bend the way they should.

"I didn't mean it about Eddie," Steven said. "I don't know, I just thought . . ."

"It's okay, Steven."

"But the other thing, the accident . . ."

"I did want to talk to you about that." Put him at ease again. It was going to be all right. "Let me go get a beer," he said. "You get comfortable."

Out to the kitchen, seeing nothing, feeling nothing, like walking in a tunnel. He opened the refrigerator, took out a bottle, started twisting the neck going back to the bedroom.

Good, he was back lying down. Okay, now put the beer on the bed table. (And remember to take it when you go.)

"Here," he said, "let me get that pillow for you."

"Whose car is that?"

Erin didn't know, it wasn't Jim's car. But there was somebody there! In her house, with Steven. "Oh, God!"

Dismas pulled the Volvo up over the curb onto the lawn. She already had her door open, running.

Where's the knife?

Steven always kept the knife in the bottom of the drawer here—he'd seen him pull it out a dozen times.

Now he was beginning to moan again. He hadn't believed Steven had had that much strength.

Maybe in the second drawer. And if it wasn't there, he'd try to put him under again, but the timing of that was tough. He thought he'd held the pillow down too long last time when he'd pulled it up and the boy's lips were blue.

He opened the second drawer.

God! Dismas had the keys.

"The keys! The keys!" She pushed at the doorbell. "Steven! Steven!"

Dismas was up next to her, giving her the keys. Fumbling, seconds going by.

"Which one?"

Dismas taking the key, getting it in, turning it. Pushing it open, the door, pushing him aside, and running running into the hall, yelling her son's name.

Cavanaugh was standing by the bed when Steven opened his eyes. He was holding a pillow in front of him with both hands. And there was Mom in the door to the room.

"He's not dead? God say he's not dead!"

Then she was next to him, her arms around his neck. He couldn't move at all, or talk. Maybe he was dead.

And Mom saying, "You might as well kill me as kill my baby."

Her hand running down the side of his face, again and again, like a cool breeze.

Her baby. She thought of him as her baby. He might as well kill her as her baby.

"Erin . . ." Father began.

Hardy was standing in the doorway, and his mom started crying. "Oh, he's breathing, thank God!" She buried her face into the sheets up by his face.

He thought he heard Cavanaugh say his mom's name again, but she kept herself up near him, holding him, touching his face, his hair. "Oh, God, I love you," she said, still crying. "I love you, Steven, I love you. Please don't die. . . ."

Okay, he wouldn't, then. He wouldn't die.

"Leave 'em alone," Hardy said, motioning with his head, taking hold of Cavanaugh's arm and pulling him out to the living room. He still held the pillow.

Hardy sat on one of the stools near the bar. "Talk," he said.

Cavanaugh even now tried his smile, but it didn't work out just right. "I told you before, it wasn't fair," he said. "But you didn't understand. You can't know."

"I can't, huh?"

"You know what it's like to live right in the midst of everything you want—day in, day out—and never get to have it? To see the kids growing, perfect. Erin's kids, Ed's. We could've had that, Erin and me. And she so happy with that, that goddamned gardener. And then it starting to go on, another generation of it, of the perfect Cochrans and their perfect happiness."

"Well, you ended that," Hardy said.

"I couldn't accept it anymore. When Eddie told me they were pregnant. It was just for a moment. I didn't really plan it."

"You planned it enough. How'd you get him to fire the gun?"

Cavanaugh shrugged. "I just bet him he couldn't hit something out on the canal. It was easy. And he had to fire the gun, you see?"

"Sure."

"And then, once he had, there was nothing left to do."

"He just gave the gun back to you and you shot him."

He gripped at the pillow, raised it to his face, left it there, shutting out the world. Himself. Finally letting it down.

"It was too much. I broke—"

"Like you broke out of the seminary?"

Cavanaugh opened his eyes wide. "How did you . . . ?"

"When Erin got married, you couldn't handle that either, could you?"

"It isn't right. It wasn't the sex. Not having sex. Being celibate. It was Erin."

"Fuck you, Father," Hardy said. "Fuck yourself very hard."

Cavanaugh walked halfway across the room and looked out the sliding glass doors to the backyard. "So what do we do now?" he asked.

Hardy, breathing hard, waited a long time. Finally he said, "You know, you're the expert on suicide. I got a Suzuki parked out by where you killed Rose, looks like a Jeep. There's a loaded gun in the glove compartment." His face crinkled up. "You know how to use a gun, don't you?"

Cavanaugh let his hands all the way down in front of him. He dropped the pillow to the floor. Hardy found himself staring at the pillow, hearing the front door open and close as Cavanaugh went out.

Abe found the note in Father Dietrick's chair. It was a strange note. "I'm sorry. I'll miss you." Did people say they were going to miss people when they were going to kill themselves? Maybe. He didn't know what minds might do at that point.

He left the note where it was. He'd send one of the team back to pick it up, check it for handwriting, oils, all that. It seemed to close it up for him, though. Hardy was wrong on this one.

Speaking of which, where was Hardy? One of the priests from outside, the tan one, was walking toward him in the hallway. "I'm Father Paul," he said.

"You know anything about this?"

"No. I just got here. From Brazil."

"Is that right?"

He seemed to be waiting for Glitsky to say something else.

"So what can I do for you?"

"I thought I'd unpack," he said. "But the car seems to be gone."

"The car?"

"Father Dietrick's car. The one we came in."

"It's gone?"

He led him to the front door and opened it. "I'm sure we parked it right here, in front."

So what? Glitsky thought. "Look, Father, we're homicide. You got a stolen car, you should call the cops."

"But aren't you . . . ?" Then he pointed. "There it is. Who's that driving it?"

The car pulled into the driveway. "That's Father Cavanaugh," Abe said. "I want to talk to him."

The hawk-faced black policeman jogged across the blacktop and got to the Honda as Father Cavanaugh was getting out. They shook hands, and while Father Paul was still crossing the lot, fighting the glare from the van and the other automobiles, he heard a funny, high-pitched laugh. It must have been Father Cavanaugh, as though he'd just heard a good joke, though it seemed poor taste to be laughing right then in the presence of mortal-sin death.

The two other policemen came out from inside the garage. Father Cavanaugh, the hawk-faced policeman and the other two all stood in a knot out in the sun. Father Dietrick had become a statue. Maybe he was in shock. Father Paul should go over to him, try to help him. That would be the Christian thing to do.

But he was more interested in what Father Cavanaugh was saying to the policemen. He hurried his pace a little, getting there in time to hear Father Cavanaugh saying, "I'm not lying."

And the hawk-faced policeman saying, "I don't think you're lying."

Father Cavanaugh wiped the sweat from his forehead. "You mind if I sit down a minute?" His face had a sick look, shiny white as though he might faint. "I'd like a minute alone." Telling a joke, like. "I think it's my last chance to be alone for a while."

They watched him walk the ten yards or so over to the Jeep and get in the front seat. All three policemen were quiet, watching him. He sat there, seeming to be catching his breath, taking out his handkerchief and wiping his forehead.

"Father, you all right?" the shorter white man asked. Father Cavanaugh nodded. The other men closed in on one another, and Father Paul stepped up to hear them. Father Paul glanced over to the Jeep one time. Father Cavanaugh was doing something, like fussing with the radio knobs.

He heard the taller man say, "Well, that was easy," and the hawk-faced one started to say something when suddenly Father Dietrick yelled "Father!" but it was drowned out almost immediately by a tremendous explosion.

Father Cavanaugh had come halfway out of the Jeep. His upper body lay out on the ground, one leg caught at a funny angle as though it had stuck up under the front seat.

37

*T*HOUGH HE generally preferred to stand in his doorway and bellow, this time Lieutenant Joe Frazelli elected to use his intercom. He pushed the button, got an answer, and said, "Frank, come in here you get a sec."

Maybe a minute later there was a knock on his door and he was looking up at the tall frame of Frank Batiste.

"Close the door," he said. Then, "What kind a cake you like, Frank?"

Batiste stayed standing. He was a quiet, thorough officer who was especially good when paired with less experienced men. Of everyone in homicide, he had perhaps the least pugnacious character. Not that he couldn't mix it up when he had to, but he preferred to leave alone the office posing and pecking. Well, Frazelli thought, somebody's got to be that way. It sets him off a little, and that's to the good.

"Cake?" Batiste asked. "I don't know. I guess they're pretty much the same. I'm not much of a cake eater, Joe."

Perfect. Frazelli loved it. "Goddammit, Frank, I don't give a shit about what you like. I got Marylouise out there humping her telephone to make a call down to the bakery and get a cake, and if she don't hear from me in about another minute then the whole goddamn office is gonna know before I want 'em to."

Batiste, not born yesterday, nodded and broke a smile. "Plain chocolate, sir. Chocolate icing. Chocolate on the inside. Boy, makes my mouth water."

Frazelli punched the intercom again and whispered to Marylouise that Frank liked chocolate cake. He asked her how long it would take, and she said usually about twenty-five minutes.

"Sit down, Frank, you make me nervous hovering like that. But before you do . . ." Frazelli stood up behind his desk and extended a hand. "Congratulations, Lieutenant," he said.

"You mind if I call my wife?" Batiste asked.

Frazelli shook his head. "Wait 'til after the cake, would you? The whole timing of this office is centered around Marylouise and her fucking cakes. We can't get new cops, but we got petty cash for cakes up the wazoo. Well," he said, grinning, "it ain't my problem anymore. You'll get used to it."

Batiste scanned the office. "How long you been here, sir, as lieutenant?"

Frazelli twisted his wedding ring. "Fourteen years," he said with a little laugh. "My stepping stone to Chief." He sighed. "You want a little peace-of-mind advice? This isn't a step to anything. Just treat it like its own job. God knows it'll keep you busy. On the other hand, Rigby"—the current Chief—"had the job before I did."

"I'll do what I do," Frank said. "See where I wind up." But a cloud crossed his face. "You don't mind my asking, who's going down? The new guys, I mean."

"Giometti's staying, let's put it positive. I decided not to make him pay for getting in the middle of a pissing contest. Being around it he probably learned more than a year here would teach him in the normal course of events anyway."

"Abe and Carl?"

Frazelli nodded. "That's the trouble with pissing contests. You wind up all covered with piss."

They both laughed.

"I really thought one of them had it, the promotion."

"No, you three were up all along. You, though, had the good sense to not let a murder suspect kill himself in your armed and august presence." Frazelli got a little worked up. "And thank God it was only himself and not everybody else in the whole fucking parking lot."

"I can't believe . . . I couldn't believe it when I heard that happened."

"I still can't believe it."

"What were they thinking about?"

"Probably what kind of cake they were gonna order when I called them in here." Frazelli sat back. "Fuck it, though, they're both good cops. They just timed this one bad. So they'll get a nod next time—they're both due."

"I wouldn't want 'em off the squad."

Frazelli said, "Nah, you won't lose 'em, Frank. They're here 'cause it's what they do." He punched his intercom again. "Marylouise, how many people we got out there?"

"Everybody," she said. "I haven't let anybody out."

"All right, don't." He stabbed the button again. "She hasn't let anybody out. Jesus! You know who runs this department? Fucking Marylouise Bezdikian!" He stopped spewing. "You think we ought to get Abe and Carl in, let 'em know before the others?"

Batiste shrugged. "Tough call, Joe. Up to you."

Frazelli worried it a minute, twisting his ring. "Fuck it," he said. "Who needs it? It's their problem."

In Frazelli's office, in the outer office, everything went suddenly silent, then picked up again.

"Angels passing," Batiste said.

"What's that?"

"Like that, when it's all of a sudden quiet. My wife says it's angels passing."

"Passing gas, more likely," said Frazelli, poetic as a cement truck. He went back to twisting his ring.

"You know," Batiste said, "I got one other question you don't mind?"

"Shoot."

"Well, you know, you hear things . . ."

Frazelli listened, knowing what was coming.

"Well, point is, I don't want to come in some morning and find a Triple-A bumper sticker on the door, you know?"

Frazelli knew. Triple-A was department slang for Affirmative Action Asshole. The wedding ring suddenly was getting a real workout. Realizing what he was doing, the lieutenant stopped himself, put his hands behind his head and leaned back in his chair, feet on his desk.

Frank had plenty of time to find out how things worked. Why ruin the moment for him now? "You know, Frank," Frazelli said, "you hear that shit all the time. But you got the gig 'cause you earned it, pure and simple. Anybody thinks otherwise, you send 'em to me, even after I'm retired and out on the Bay fishin'."

The intercom buzzed. Marylouise said, "The cake's here."

Frazelli stood up. "You ready?" he asked. "Let's go have some cake."

Jane was with him, her hand resting easily on the inside of his thigh. She sat close up next to him at the end of the bar by the large windows, drinking a negroni. She'd throw her head back and laugh her deep laugh. She glowed in the Friday dusk.

Hardy had opened up a little after one, working a short shift. McGuire preferred to work Friday night because of the good tips, where Hardy liked to come in and set up, then have Friday night to himself. Jane and he used to call it date night. Maybe it would be again.

He'd gone back to work on Wednesday, using his time behind the bar, he realized—the way he always had—to keep the pretense of being a social animal without really having to interact. It suited him now, the disengagement, so long as he knew why he was doing it. He had felt dazed, somehow, wanting to be alone.

Yesterday, he'd gone downtown and worked out his statement. Glitsky hadn't been around. The new lieutenant told him that with Glitsky, Griffin and the two priests corroborating their story, they'd declared Eddie's death a homicide.

Moses's reaction had been mixed. At first he was all hyped up, happy to have Frannie covered. But then a distance, a sullen melancholy politeness crept in that Hardy had only now just figured out.

He understood it, but it didn't seem right to him. Moses, after all, had hired him to do a job and offered him something as payment. It had been a contract, as binding as anything written up, signed and notarized.

And Hardy wasn't worried about Moses reneging on their deal—he wouldn't do that. What bothered him was Moses's reaction to it. How could they work as partners, after being friends for so long, with that friction between them? And it was obvious that Moses, having thought about the reality of it and not the grand romance of the gesture, was resenting it—losing a quarter of the bar he'd owned for most of a decade.

When he'd come in tonight, with a scowl and a manila folder, Hardy guessed he'd brought some papers to sign. Even Jane, who hadn't laid eyes on the man in some years, had said, "This isn't the McGuire I knew."

The crowd wouldn't really get going for another half hour. Hardy pushed himself up off his stool. He kissed Jane casually, saying he'd be right back, then walked the length of the bar to where Moses was watching a game of liar's dice as though it were the World Series. In other words, pointedly ignoring Hardy.

"Hey, Mose."

He looked up.

"I quit," Hardy said.

Moses squinted, moved over and forward a step, and leaned over the bar. "What?"

"I quit. I'm not bartending anymore, starting now."

He flashed him a broad and phony grin and went back to join Jane.

"What do you mean, you quit?" Moses was in front of him again.

"Just send me my profit checks," Hardy said. "I couldn't live around you feeling guilty all the time. Let's go, Jane."

"You've still got this pan?" Jane said. "It looks brand new."

Hardy nodded over his eggs. "Treat things right, they last," he said.

They'd gone to dinner, then back to Hardy's, then to bed too early to sleep, so now, sometime after midnight, they were eating before going back in and devouring each other some more.

The doorbell rang.

"Reasonable hour," Hardy said. He yelled down the hallway. "Go away."

The bell rang again. Hardy swore, went into his room and put on a pair of jogging shorts.

"Who is it?" he asked at the door.

It was McGuire. He held the folder in one hand. "I'm a horse's ass," he said.

"Yep, you are."

"You want this stuff?"

Hardy shifted on his bare feet. "You want to give it to me?"

"You earned it."

"That's not what I asked."

McGuire gave it a last thought. "Yeah." He nodded. "You want to sign these papers?"

"No. Tomorrow will be fine. I've got some company now."

"But you could just . . ."

"Tomorrow, Mose, when I come in to open, okay?"

He closed the door on his friend and, turning, saw Jane standing waiting for him at the end of the long hall.